The Napoleonic Novels
Volume 2

The Napoleonic Novels Volume 2

The Blockade of Phalsburg

The Invasion of France in 1814

Erckmann-Chatrian

LEONAUR

The Napoleonic Novels
Volume 2
by Erckmann-Chatrian

First published under the titles
The Blockade of Phalsburg
and
The Invasion of France in 1814

Leonaur is an imprint
of Oakpast Ltd

ISBN: 978-1-84677-706-6 (hardcover)
ISBN: 978-1-84677-705-9 (softcover)

http://www.leonaur.com

Publisher's Notes

In the interests of authenticity, the spellings, grammar and place names used have been retained from the original editions.

The opinions of the authors represent a view of events in which he was a participant related from his own perspective, as such the text is relevant as an historical document.

The views expressed in this book are not necessarily those of the publisher.

Contents

The Blockade of Phalsburg

ALL WERE DEAD, AS IT WERE ONE LONG CEMETRY

Contents

Introductory Note

The Blockade of Phalsburg contains one of the happiest portraits in the Erckmann-Chatrian gallery that of the Jew Moses who tells the story and who is always in character, however great the patriotic or romantic temptation to idealize him, and whose character is nevertheless portrayed with an almost affectionate appreciation of the sterling qualities underlying its somewhat usurious exterior.

The time is 1814, during the invasion of France by the allies after the disastrous battle of Leipsic and the campaign described in *The Conscript.* The dwellers in Phalsburg a little walled town of two or three thousand inhabitants in Lorraine defend themselves with great intrepidity and determination during the siege which lasts until the capitulation of Paris. The daily life of the citizens and garrison, the various incidents of the blockade, the bombardment by night, the scarcity of food, the occasional sortie for foraging, all pass before the reader depicted with the authors' customary fidelity and life-likeness, and form as perfect a picture of a siege as *The Conscript* does of a campaign.

CHAPTER 1

Father Moses and His Family

Since you wish to know about the blockade of Phalsburg in 1814, I will tell you all about it, said Father Moses of the Jews' street.

I lived then in the little house on the corner, at the right of the market. My business was selling iron by the pound, under the arch below, and I lived above with my wife Sorlé (Sarah) and my little Sâfel, the child of my old age.

My two other boys, Itzig and Frômel, had gone to America, and my daughter Zeffen was married to Baruch, the leather-dealer, at Saverne.

Besides my iron business, I traded in old shoes, old linen, and all the articles of old clothing which conscripts sell on reaching the depot, where they receive their military outfit. Travelling pedlers bought the old linen of me for paper-rags, and the other things I sold to the country people.

This was a profitable business, because thousands of conscripts passed through Phalsburg from week to week, and from month to month. They were measured at once at the mayoralty, clothed, and filed off to Mayence, Strasburg, or wherever it might be.

This lasted a long time; but at length people were tired of war, especially after the Russian campaign and the great recruiting of 1813.

You may well suppose, Fritz, that I did not wait till this time before sending my two boys beyond the reach of the recruiting officers' clutches. They were boys who did not lack sense. At twelve years old their heads were clear enough, and rather than go and fight for the King of Prussia, they would see themselves safe at the ends of the earth.

At evening, when we sat at supper around the lamp with its seven burners, their mother would sometimes cover her face and say:

"My poor children! My poor children! When I think that the time is near when you will go in the midst of musket and bayonet fire—in the midst of thunder and lightning!—oh, how dreadful!"

And I saw them turn pale. I smiled at myself and thought: "You are no fools. You will hold on to your life. That is right!"

If I had had children capable of becoming soldiers, I should have died of grief. I should have said, "These are not of my race!"

But the boys grew stronger and handsomer. When Itzig was fifteen he was doing a good business. He bought cattle in the villages on his own account, and sold them at a profit to butcher Borich at Mittelbronn; and Frômel was not behind him, for he made the best bargains of the old merchandise, which we had heaped in three barracks under the market.

I should have liked well to keep the boys with me. It was my delight to see them with my little Sâfel—the curly head and eyes bright as a squirrel's yes, it was my joy! Often I clasped them in my arms without a word, and even they wondered at it; I frightened them; but dreadful thoughts passed through my mind after 1812. I knew that whenever the Emperor had returned to Paris, he had demanded four hundred millions of *francs* and two or three hundred thousand men, and I said to myself:

"This time, everybody must go, even children of seventeen and eighteen!"

As the tidings grew worse and worse, I said to them one evening:

"Listen! You both understand trading, and what you do not yet know you can learn. Now, if you wait a few months, you will be on the conscription list, and be like all the rest; they will take you to the square and show you how to load a gun, and then you will go away, and I never shall hear of you again!"

Sorlé sighed, and we all sighed together. Then, after a moment, I continued:

"But if you set out at once for America, by the way of Havre, you will reach it safe and sound; you will do business there as well as here; you will make money, you will marry, you will increase according to the Lord's promise, and you will send me back money, according to God's commandment, *Honour thy father and thy mother.* I will bless you as Isaac blessed Jacob, and you will have a long life. Choose!"

They at once chose to go to America, and I went with them myself as far as Sorreburg. Each of them had made twenty *louis* in his own business, so that I needed to give them nothing but my blessing.

And what I said to them has come to pass; they are both living, they have numerous children, who are my descendants, and when I want anything they send it to me.

Itzig and Frômel being gone, I had only Sâfel left, my Benjamin, dearer even, if possible, than the others. And then, too, I had my daughter Zeffen, married at Saverne to a good respectable man, Baruch; she was the oldest, and had already given me a grandson named David, according to the Lord's will that the dead should be replaced in his own family, and David was the name of Baruch's grandfather. The one expected was to be called after my father, Esdras.

You see, Fritz, how I was situated before the blockade of Phalsburg, in 1814. Everything had gone well up to that time, but for six weeks everything had gone wrong in town and country. We had the typhus; thousands of wounded soldiers surrounded the houses; the ground had lacked labourers for the last two years, and everything was dear—bread, meat, and drink. The people of Alsace and Lorraine did not come to market; our stores of merchandise did not sell; and when merchandise does not sell, it might as well be sand or stones; we are poor in the midst of abundance. Famine comes from every quarter.

Ah, well! In spite of it all, the Lord had a great blessing in store for me, for just at this time, early in November, came the news that a second son was born to Zeffen, and that he was in fine health. I was so glad that I set out at once for Saverne.

You must know, Fritz, that if I was very glad, it was not only on account of the birth of a grandson, but also because my son-in-law would not be obliged to leave home, if the child lived. Baruch had always been fortunate; at the moment when the Emperor had made the Senate vote that unmarried men must go, he had just married Zeffen; and when the Senate voted that married men without children must go, he had his first child. Now, after the bad news, it was voted that married men with only one child should go, all the same, and Baruch had two.

At that time it was a fortunate thing to have quantities of children, to keep you from being massacred; no greater blessing could be desired! This is why I took my cane at once, to go and find out whether the child were sound and healthy, and whether it would save its father.

But for long years to come, if God spares my life, I shall remember that day, and what I met upon my way.

Imagine the roadside blocked, as it were, with carts filled with the sick and wounded, forming a line all the way from Quatre-Vents to Saverne.

The peasants who, in Alsace, were required to transport these poor creatures, had unharnessed their horses and escaped in the night, abandoning their carts; the hoar-frost had passed over them there was not motion or sign of life—all dead, as it were one long cemetery! Thousands of ravens covered the sky like a cloud; there was nothing to be seen but wings moving in the air, nothing to be heard but one murmur of innumerable cries. I would not have believed that heaven and earth could produce so many ravens. They flew down to the very carts; but the moment a living man approached, all these creatures rose and flew away to the forest of La Bonne-Fontaine, or the ruins o the old convent of Dann.

As for myself, I lengthened my steps, feeling that I must not stop, that the typhus was marching at my heels.

Happily the winter sets in early at Phalsburg. A cold wind blew from the Schneeberg, and these strong draughts of mountain air disperse all maladies, even, it is said, the Black Plague itself.

What I have now told you is about the retreat from Leipsic, in the beginning of November.

When I reached Saverne, the city was crowded with troops, artillery, infantry, and cavalry, pell-mell.

I remember that, in the principal street, the windows of an inn were open, and a long table with its white cloth was seen, all laid, within. All the guard of honour stopped there. These were young men of rich families, who had money in spite of their tattered uniforms. The moment they saw this table in passing, they leaped from their horses and rushed into the hall. But the innkeeper, Hannès, made them pay five *francs* in advance, and just as the poor things began to eat, a servant ran in, crying out, "The Prussians! the Prussians!" They sprang up at once and mounted their horses like madmen, without once looking back, and in this way Hannès sold his dinner more than twenty times.

I have often thought since that such scoundrels deserve hanging; yes, this way of making money is not lawful business. It disgusted me.

But if I should describe the rest—the faces of the sick, the way in which they lay, the groans they uttered, and, above all, the tears of those who tried in vain to go on—if I should tell you this, it would be still worse, it would be too much. I saw, on the slope of the old tan-house bridge, a little guardsman of seventeen or eighteen years, stretched out, with his face flat upon the stones. I have never forgotten that boy; he raised himself from time to time, and showed his hand as black as soot: he had a ball in the back, and his hand was half gone. The poor fellow had doubtless fallen from a cart. Nobody dared to help him because they heard it said, "He has the typhus! he has the typhus." Oh, what misery! It is too dreadful to think of!

Now, Fritz, I must tell you another thing about that day, and

17

that is how I saw Marshal Victor.

It was late when I started from Phalsburg, and it was dark when, on going up the principal street of Saverne, I saw all the windows of the Hotel du Soleil illuminated from top to bottom. Two sentinels walked to and fro under the arch, officers in full uniform went in and out, magnificent horses were fastened to rings all along the walls; and, within the court, the lamps of a calash shone like two stars.

The sentinels kept the street clear, but I must pass, because Baruch dwelt farther on. I was going through the crowd, in front of the hotel, and the first sentinel was calling out to me, "Back! back!"when an officer of hussars, a short, stout man, with great red whiskers, came out of the arch, and as he met me, exclaimed, "Ah! is it you, Moses! I am glad to see you!"

He shook hands with me.

I opened my eyes with amazement, as was natural: a superior officer shaking hands with a plain citizen is not an everyday occurrence. I looked at him in astonishment, and recognized Commandant Zimmer.

Thirty years before we had been at Father Genaudet's school, and we had scoured the city, the moats, and the glacis together, as children. But since then Zimmer had been a good many times in Phalsburg, without remembering his old comrade, Samuel Moses.

"Ho!"said he, smiling, and taking me by the arm, "come, I must present you to the marshal."

And, in spite of myself, before I had said a word, I went in under the arch, into a large room where two long tables, loaded with lights and bottles, were laid for the staff-officers.

A number of superior officers, generals, colonels, command-ers of hussars, of dragoons and of *chasseurs*, in plumed hats, in helmets, in red shakos, their chins in their huge cravats, their swords dragging, were walking silently back and forth, or talking with each other, while they waited to be called to table.

It was difficult to pass through the crowd, but Zimmer kept hold of my arm, and led me to the end of the room, to a little lighted door.

We entered a high room, with two windows opening upon the gardens.

The marshal was there, standing, his head uncovered; his back was toward us, and he was dictating orders which two staff-officers were writing.

This was all which I noticed at the moment, in my confusion.

Just after we entered, the marshal turned; I saw that he had the good face of an old Lorraine peasant. He was a tall, powerful man, with a grayish head; he was about fifty years old, and very heavy for his age.

"Marshal, here's our man!"said Zimmer. "He is one of my old schoolmates, Samuel Moses, a first-rate fellow, who has been traversing the country these thirty years, and knows every village in Alsace and Lorraine."

The marshal looked at me a few steps off. I held my hat in my hand in great fear. After looking at me a couple of seconds, he took the paper which one of the secretaries handed him, read and signed it, then turned back to me:

"Well, my good man," said he, "what do they say about the last campaign? What do the people in your village think about it?"

On hearing him call me "my good man," I took courage, and answered "that the typhus had made bad work, but the people were not disheartened, because they knew that the Emperor with his army was at hand."

And when he said abruptly: "Yes! But will they defend themselves?" I answered: "The Alsatians and the Lorraines are people who will defend themselves till death, because they love their Emperor, and they would all be willing to die for him!"

I said that by way of prudence; but he could plainly see in my face that I was no fighting man, for he smiled good-humouredly, and said: "That will do, commandant, that is enough!"

The secretaries had kept on writing. Zimmer made a sign to me and we went out together. When we were outside he called out:

"Goodbye, Moses, goodbye!"

The sentinels let me pass, and still trembling, I continued my journey.

I was soon knocking at the little door of Baruch's house at the end of the lane where the cardinal's old stables were.

It was pitch dark.

What a joy it was, Fritz, after having seen all these terrible things, to come to the place where those I loved were resting! How softly my heart beat, and how I pitied all that power and glory which made so many people miserable!

After a moment I heard my son-in-law enter the passage and open the door. Baruch and Zeffen had long since ceased expecting me.

"Is it you, my father?" asked Baruch.

"Yes, my son, it is I. I am late. I have been hindered."

"Come!" said he.

And we entered the little passage, and then into the chamber where Zeffen, my daughter, lay pale and happy, upon her bed.

She had recognized my voice. As for me, my heart beat with joy; I could not speak; and I embraced my daughter, while I looked around to find the little one. Zeffen held it in her arms under the coverlet.

"There he is!" she said.

Then she showed him to me in his swaddling-clothes. I saw at once that he was plump and healthy, with his little hands closed tight, and I exclaimed:

"Baruch, this is Esdras, my father! Let him be welcome!"

I wanted to see him without his clothes, so I undressed him. It was warm in the little room from the lamp with seven burners. Tremblingly I undressed him; he did not cry, and my daughter's white hands assisted me:

"Wait, my father, wait!" said she.

My son-in-law looked on behind me. We all had tears in our eyes.

At last I had him all undressed; he was rosy, and his large head tossed about, sleeping the sleep of centuries. Then I lifted him above my head; I looked at his round thighs all in creases, at his little drawn-up feet, his broad chest and plump back, and I wanted to dance like David before the ark; I wanted to chant:

Praise the Lord! Praise him ye servants of the Lord! Praise the name of the Lord! Blessed be the name of the Lord from this time forth and forever more! From the rising of the sun, unto the going down of the same, the Lord's name is to be praised! The Lord is high above all nations, and his glory above the heavens! Who is like unto the Lord our God, who raiseth up the poor out of the dust, who maketh the barren woman to keep house, and to be a joyful mother of children? Praise ye the Lord!

Yes, I felt like chanting this, but all that I could say was: "He is a fine, perfect child! He is going to live! He will be the blessing of our race and the joy of our old age!"

And I blessed them all.

Then giving him back to his mother to be covered, I went to embrace the other who was sound asleep in his cradle.

We remained there together a long time, to see each other, in this joy. Without, horses were passing, soldiers shouting, carriages rolling by. Here all was quiet: the mother nursed her infant.

Ah! Fritz, I am an old man now, and these far-off things are always before me, as at the first; my heart always beats in recalling them, and I thank God for His great goodness,—I thank Him. He has loaded me with years, He has permitted me to see the third generation, and I am not weary of life; I should like to live on and see the fourth and the fifth—His will be done!

I should have liked to tell them of what had just happened to me at the Hotel du Soleil, but everything was insignificant in comparison with my joy; only after I had left the chamber, while I was taking a mouthful of bread and drinking a glass of wine in the side hall so as to let Zeffen sleep, I related the adventure to Baruch, who was greatly surprised.

"Listen, my son," said I, "this man asked me if we want to defend ourselves. That shows that the allies are following our armies, that they are marching by hundreds of thousands, and that they cannot be hindered from entering France. So you see that, in the midst of our joy, there is danger of terrible evils; you see that all the harm which we have been doing to others for these last ten years may return upon us. I fear so. God grant that I may be mistaken!"

After this we went to bed. It was eleven o'clock, and the tumult without still continued.

CHAPTER 2

Father Moses's Speculation

Early the next morning, after breakfast, I took my cane to return to Phalsburg. Zeffen and Baruch wanted to keep me longer, but I said:

"You do not think of your mother, who is expecting me. She does not keep still a minute; she keeps going upstairs and down, and looking out of the window. No, I must go. Sorlé must not be uneasy while we are comfortable."

Zeffen said no more, and filled my pockets with apples and nuts for her brother Sâfel. I embraced them again, the little ones and the big; then Baruch led me far back of the gardens, to the place where the roads to Schlittenbach and Lutzelburg divide.

The troops had all left, only stragglers and the sick remaining. But we could still see the line of carts in the distance, on the hill, and bands of day-labourers who had been set to work digging graves back of the road.

The very thought of passing that way disturbed me. I shook hands with Baruch at this fork of the road, promising to come again with grandmother to the circumcision, and then took the valley road, which follows the Zorn through the woods.

This path was full of dead leaves, and for two hours I walked on thinking at times of the Hotel du Soleil, of Zimmer, of Marshal Victor, whom I seemed to see again, with his tall figure, his square shoulders, his gray head, and coat covered with embroidery. Sometimes I pictured to myself Zeffen's chamber, the little babe and its mother; then, the war which threatened us—that mass of enemies advancing from every side!

Several times I stopped in the midst of these valleys sloping into each other as far as the eye can reach, all covered with firs, oaks and beeches, and I said to myself:

"Who knows? Perhaps the Prussians, Austrians and Russians will soon pass along here!"

But there was comfort in this thought; "Moses, your two boys, Itzig and Frômel, are in America far from the reach of cannon; they are there with their packs on their shoulders, going from village to village without danger. And your daughter Zeffen, too, may sleep in quiet; Baruch has two fine children, and will have another every year while the war lasts. He will sell leather to make bags and shoes for those who have to go, but, for his part, he will. stay at home."

I smiled as I thought that I was too old to be conscripted, that I was a gray-head, and the conscriptors could have none of us. Yes; I smiled as I saw that I had acted very wisely in everything, and that the Lord had, as it were, cleared my path.

It is a great satisfaction, Fritz, to see that everything is working to our advantage.

In the midst of these thoughts I came quietly to Lutzelburg, and I went to Brestel's at the Swan Hotel to take a cup of coffee.

There I found Bernard, the soap merchant, whom you do not know—a little man, bald to the very nape of the neck, with great wens on his head—and Donadieu, the Harberg forest-keeper. One had laid his dosser and the other his gun against the wall, and they were emptying a bottle of wine between them. Brestel was helping.

"Ha! it is Moses," exclaimed Bernard. "Where the devil dost thou come from, so early in the morning?"

Christians in those days were in the habit of *thouing* the Jews—even the old men. I answered that I had come from Saverne, by the valley.

"Ah! thou hast seen the wounded," said the keeper. "What thinkest thou of that, Moses?"

"I have seen them," I replied sadly, "I saw them last evening. It is dreadful!"

"Yes, it is; everybody has gone up there today, because old Grédal of Quatre-Vents found her nephew under a cart Joseph Bertha, the little lame watchmaker who worked last year with Father Goulden; so the people from Dagsberg, Houpe, and Garburg, expect to find their brothers, or sons, or cousins in the heap."

He shrugged his shoulders compassionately.

"These things are dreadful," said Brestel, "but they must come. There has been no business these two years; I have back here, in my court, three thousand pounds' worth of planks and timber. That would formerly have lasted me for six weeks or two months; but now it is all rotting on the spot; nobody wants it on the Sarre, nobody wants it in Alsace, nobody orders anything or buys anything. It is just so with the hotel. Nobody has a *sous*; everybody stays at home, thankful if they have potatoes to eat and cold water to drink. Meanwhile my wine and beer turn sour in the cellar, and are covered with mildew. And all that does not keep off the duties; you must pay, or the officer will be upon you."

"Yes," cried Bernard, "it is the same thing everywhere. But what is it to the Emperor whether planks and soap sell or not, provided the contributions come in and the conscripts arrive?"

Donadieu perceived that his comrade had taken a glass too much; he rose, put back his gun into his shoulder-belt, and went out, calling to us.

"Goodbye to you all, goodbye! We will talk about this another time."

A few minutes afterward, I paid for my cup of coffee, and followed his example.

I had the same thoughts as Brestel and Bernard; I saw that my trade in iron and old clothes was at an end; and as I went up the Barracks' hill I thought, "Try to find something else, Moses. Everything is at a standstill. But one cannot use up his money to the last farthing. I must turn to something else—I must find an article which is always saleable. But what is always saleable? Every trade has its day, and then it comes to an end."

While thus meditating, I passed the Barracks of the Bois-de-Chênes. I was on the plateau from which I could see the glacis, the line of ramparts, and the bastions, when the firing of a cannon gave notice that the marshal was leaving the place. At the same time I saw at the left, in the direction of Mittelbronn, the line of sabres flashing like lighting in the distance among the poplars of the highway. The trees were leafless, and I could see, too, the carriage and postilions passing like the wind through the plumes and caps.

The cannon pealed, second after second; the mountains gave back peal after peal, from the very depths of their valleys; and as for myself, I was quite carried away by the thought of having seen this man the day before; it seemed like a dream.

Then, about ten o'clock, I passed the bridge of the French gate. The last cannon sounded upon the bastion of the powder-house; the crowd of men, women and children descended the ramparts, as if it were a festival; they knew nothing, thought of nothing, while cries of "*Vive l'Empereur!*"rose in every street.

I passed through the crowd, well pleased at bringing good news to my wife; and I was saying to myself beforehand, "The little one is doing well, Sorlé!"when, at the corner of the market, I saw her at our door. I raised my cane at once, and smiled, as much as to say "Baruch is safe—we may laugh!"

She understood me, and went in at once; but I overtook her on the stairs, and embraced her, saying:

"It is a good, hearty little fellow—there! Such a baby—so round and rosy! And Zeffen is doing well. Baruch wished me to embrace you for him. But where is Sâfel?"

"Under the market, selling."

"Ah, good!"

We went into our room. I sat down and began to praise Zeffen's baby. Sorlé listened with delight, looking at me with her great black eyes, and wiping my forehead, for I had walked fast, and could hardly breathe.

And then, all of a sudden, our Sâfel came in. I had not time to turn my head before he was on my knees, with his hands in my pockets. The child knew that his sister Zeffen never forgot him; and Sorlé, too, liked to bite an apple.

You see, Fritz, when I think of these things, everything comes back to me; I could talk to you about it forever.

It was Friday, the day before the Sabbath; the *schabbésgoïé*[1] was to come in the afternoon. While we were still alone at dinner, and I related for the fifth and sixth time how Zimmer had recognized me, how he had taken me into the presence of the Duke of Bellune, my wife told me that the marshal had made the tour of our ramparts on horseback, with his staff-officers; that he had examined the advanced works, the bastions, the glacis, and that he had said, as he went down the college street, that the place would hold out for eighteen days, and that it must be fortified immediately.

I remembered at once that he had asked me if we wished to defend ourselves, and I exclaimed: "He is sure that the enemy is coming; since he is going to put cannon upon the ramparts, it is because there will be need of them. It is not natural to make preparations which are not to be used. And, if the allies come, the gates will be shut. What will become of us without our business? The country people can neither go in nor out, and what will become of us?"

Then Sorlé showed her good sense, for she said:

"I have already thought about this, Moses; it is only the peasants who buy iron, old shoes, and our other things. We must undertake a city business for all classes—a business which will oblige citizens, soldiers and workmen to buy of us. That is what we must do."

I looked at her in surprise. Sâfel, with his elbow on the table, was also listening.

"It is all very well, Sorlé," I replied, "but what business is there which will oblige citizens, soldiers, everybody to buy of us-

---

1. Woman, not Israelite, who on Saturday performs in a Jewish household the labours forbidden by the law of Moses.

what business is there?"

"Listen," said she; "if the gates are shut and the country people cannot enter, there will be no eggs, butter, fish, or anything in the market. People will have to live on salt meats and dried vegetables, flour, and all kinds of preserved articles. Those who have bought up these can sell them at their own price; they will grow rich."

As I listened I was struck with astonishment.

"Ah, Sorlé! Sorlé!" I exclaimed, "for thirty years you have been my comfort. Yes, you have crowned me with all sorts of blessings, and I have said a hundred times, ' A good wife is a diamond of pure water, and without flaw. A good wife is a rich treasure for her husband.' I have repeated it a hundred times. But now I know still better what you are worth, and esteem you still more highly."

The more I thought of it, the more I perceived the wisdom of this advice. At length I said:

"Sorlé, meat and flour, and everything which can be kept, are already in the storehouses, and the soldiers will not need such things for a long time, because their officers will have provided them. But what will be wanted is brandy, which men must have to massacre and exterminate each other in war, and brandy we will buy! We will have plenty of it in our cellar, we will sell it, and nobody else will have it. That is my idea!"

"It is a good idea, Moses!" said she; "your reasons are good; I approve of them."

"Then I will write," said I, "and we will invest everything in spirits of wine. We will add water ourselves, in proportion as people wish to pay for it. In this way the freight will be less than if it were brandy, for we shall not have to pay for the transportation of the water, which we have here."

"That is well, Moses," she said.

And so we agreed.

Then I said to Sâfel:

"You must not speak of this to anyone."

She answered for him:

"There's no need of telling him that, Moses. Sâfel knows very well that this is between ourselves, and that our well-being depends upon it."

The child for a long time resented my words: "You must not speak of this to anyone." He was already full of good sense, and said to himself:

"So my father thinks I am an idiot."

This thought humiliated him. Some years afterward he told me of it, and I perceived that I had been wrong.

Everybody has his notions. Children should not be humiliated in theirs, but rather upheld by their parents.

CHAPTER 3

A Circumcision Feast

So I wrote to Pézenas. This is a southern city, rich in wools, wines, and brandies. The price of brandies at Pézenas controls that of all Europe. A trading man ought to know that, and I knew it, because I had always liked to read the list of prices in the newspapers. I sent to M. Quataya, at Pézenas, for a dozen pipes of spirits of wine. I calculated that, after paying the freight, a pipe would cost me a thousand *francs*, delivered in my cellar.

As I had sold no iron for a year, I disposed of my merchandise without asking anything for it; the payment of the twelve thousand *francs* did not trouble me. Only, Fritz, those twelve thousand *francs* were half my fortune, and you may suppose that it required some courage to risk in one venture the gains of fifteen years.

As soon as my letter was gone, I wished I could bring it back, but it was too late. I kept a good face before my wife, and said, "It will all do well! We shall gain double, triple, etc."

She, too, kept a good face, but we both had misgivings; and during the six weeks necessary for the receipt of the acknowledgment and acceptance of my order, and the arrival of the spirits of wine, every night I lay awake, thinking, "Moses, you have lost everything! You are ruined from top to toe!"

The cold sweat would cover my body. Still, if anyone had come to me and said, "Be easy, Moses, I will relieve you of this business," I should have refused, because my hope of gain was as great as my fear of loss. And by this you may know who are the true merchants, the true generals, and all who accomplish anything. Others are but machines for selling tobacco, or filling glasses, or firing guns.

It all comes to the same thing. One man's glory is as great as another's. This is why, when we speak of Austerlitz, Jena or Wagram, it is not a question of Jean Claude or Jean Nicholas, but of Napoleon alone; he alone risked everything, the others risked only being killed.

I do not say this to compare myself with Napoleon, but the buying of these twelve pipes of spirits of wine was my battle of Austerlitz.

And when I think that, on reaching Paris, Napoleon had demanded four hundred and forty millions of money, and six hundred thousand men! and that then everybody, understanding that we were threatened with an invasion, undertook to sell and to make money at any cost, while I bought, unhampered by the example of others—when I think of this, I am proud of it still and congratulate myself.

It was in the midst of these disquietudes that the day for the circumcision of little Esdras arrived. My daughter Zeffen had recovered, and Baruch had written to us not to trouble ourselves, for they would come to Phalsburg.

My wife then hastened to prepare the meats and cakes for the festival: the *bie-kougel*, the *haman*, and the *schlachmoness*, which are great delicacies.

On my part, I had tested my best wine on the old Rabbi Heymann, and I had invited my friends, Leiser of Mittelbronn and his wife Boûné, Senterlé Hirsch, and Professor Burguet. Burguet was not a Jew, but he was worthy of being one on account of his genius and extraordinary talents.

When a speech was wanted in the Emperor's progress, Burguet made it; when songs were needed for a national festival, Burguet composed them between two sips of beer; when a young candidate for law or medicine was perplexed in writing his thesis, he went to Burguet, who wrote it for him, whether in French or in Latin; when fathers and mothers were to be moved to tears at the distribution of school prizes, Burguet was the man to do it; he would take a blank sheet of paper, and read them a discourse on the spot, such as nobody else could have written in ten years; when a petition was to be made to the Emperor or prefect, Burguet was the first man thought of; and when Burguet took the trouble to defend a deserter before the court-martial at the mayoralty, the deserter, instead of being shot on the bastion of the barracks, was pardoned.

After all this, Burguet would return and take his part in piquet with the little Jew, Solomon, at which he always lost; and people troubled themselves no more about him.

I have often thought that Burguet must have greatly despised those to whom he took off his hat. Yes, to see the fellows putting on important airs because they were rural guard or secretary of the mayoralty, must have made a man like him laugh in his sleeve. But he never told me so; he knew the ways of the world too well.

He was an old constitutional priest, a tall man, with a noble figure and very fine voice; the very tones of it would move you in spite of yourself. Unfortunately, he did not take care of his own interests; he was at the mercy of the first comer. How many times I have said to him:

"Burguet, in heaven's name, don't get mixed up with thieves! Burguet, don't let yourself be robbed by simpletons! Trust me about your college expenses. When anybody comes to impose upon you I will be on the spot; I will pay the bills and hand you the account."

But he did not think of the future, and lived very carelessly.

I had thus invited all my old friends for the morning of the twenty-fourth of November, and they all came to the festival.

The father and mother, with the little infant, and its godfather and godmother, came early, in a large carriage. By eleven the ceremony had taken place in our synagogue, and we all, in great joy and satisfaction, for the child had not uttered a cry, returned together to my house, which had been made ready beforehand—the large table on the first floor, the meats in their pewter dishes, the fruits in their baskets—and we had begun in great glee to celebrate the happy day.

The old Rabbi Heymann, Leiser, and Burguet sat at my right, my little Sâfel, Hirsch, and Baruch at my left, and the women Sorlé, Zeffen, Jételé, and Boûné, facing us on the other side, according to the command of the Lord, that men and women should be separate at festivities.

Burguet, with his white cravat, his handsome maroon coat and his ruffled shirt, did me honour. He made a speech, raising his voice and making fine gestures like a great orator—telling of the ancient customs of our nation, of our religious ceremonies, of *Paeçach* (the feast of Passover), of *Roschhaschannah* (the New Year), of *Kippour* (the day of expiation), like a true *Ied* (Jew), thinking our religion very beautiful and glorifying the genius of Moses.

He knew the *Lochene Koïdech* (Chaldaic) as well as a *bal-kebolé* (cabalistic doctor).

The Saverne people turned to their neighbours and asked in a whisper:

"Pray, who is this man who speaks with authority, and says such fine things? Is he a rabbi? Is he a *schamess* (Jewish beadle)? or is he the *parness* (civil head) of your community?"

And when they learned he was not one of us, they were astonished. The old Rabbi Heymann alone was able to answer him, and they agreed on all points, like learned men talking on familiar subjects and conscious of their own learning.

Behind us, on its grandmother's bed, inside of the curtains, slept our little Esdras, with his sweet face and little clinched hands—slept so soundly, that neither our shouts of laughter, nor the talking, nor the sound of the glasses could wake him. Sometimes one, sometimes another, went to look at him, and everybody said:

"What a beautiful child! He looks like his grandfather Moses!"

That pleased me, of course; and I would go and look at him, bending over him for a long while, and finding a still stronger resemblance to my father.

At three o'clock, the meats having been removed and the delicacies spread upon the table, as we came to the dessert, I went down to find a bottle of better wine, an old bottle of Rousillon which I dug out from under the others, all covered with dust and cobwebs. I took it up carefully and placed it among the flowers on the table, saying:

"You thought the other wine very good; what will you say to this?"

Then Burguet smiled, for old wine was his special delight; he stretched up his hand and exclaimed:

"Oh! noble wine, the consoler, the restorer and benefactor of poor men in this vale of misery! Oh, venerable bottle, thou bearest all the signs of old nobility!"

He said this with his mouth full, and everybody laughed.

I asked Sorlé to bring the corkscrew.

As she was rising, suddenly trumpets sounded without, and we all listened and asked, "What is that?"

At the same time the sound of many horses' steps came up the street, and the earth and the houses trembled under an enormous weight.

Everybody sprang up, throwing down their napkins and rushing to the windows.

And from the French gate to the little square we saw trains of artillerymen advancing, with their great shakos covered with oil-cloth, and their saddles in sheepskins and driving caissons full of round shot, shells and intrenching tools.

Imagine, Fritz, my thoughts at that moment!

"This is war, my friends!" said Burguet. "This is war! It is coming! Our turn has come, at the end of twenty years!"

I stood leaning down with my hand on the stone, and thought:

"Now the enemy cannot delay coming. These are sent to fortify the place. And what if the allies surround us before I have received my spirits of wine? What if the Austrians or Russians should stop the wagons and seize them? I should have to pay for it all the same, and I should not have a farthing left!"

I turned pale at the thought. Sorlé looked at me, undoubtedly having the same fears, but she said nothing.

We stood there till they all passed by. The street was full. Some old soldiers, Desmarets the Egyptian, Paradis the gunner, Rolfo, Faisard the sapper, of the Beresina, as he was called, and some others, cried "*Vive l'Empereur!*"

Children ran behind the wagons, repeating the cry, "*Vive l'Empereur!*" But the greater number, with closed lips and serious faces, looked on in silence.

When the last carriage had turned the Fouquet corner, all the crowd returned with bowed heads; and we in the room looked at each other, with no wish to continue the feast.

"You are not well, Moses," said Burguet. "What is the matter?"

"I am thinking of all the evils which are coming to the city."

"Bah! don't be afraid," he replied. "We shall be strongly defended! And then, God help us! what can't be cured must be endured! Come! cheer up; this old wine will keep up our spirits."

We resumed our places. I opened the bottle, and it was as Burguet said. The old Rousillon did us good, and we began to laugh.

Burguet called out:

"To the health of the little Esdras! May the Lord cover him with his right hand!"

And the glasses clinked. Someone exclaimed: "May he long rejoice the hearts of his grandfather Moses and his grandmother Sorlé! To their health!"

We ended by looking at everything in rose-colour, and glorifying the Emperor, who was hastening to defend us, and was soon going to crush all the beggars beyond the Rhine.

But it is equally true that, when we separated about five o'clock, everybody had become serious, and Burguet himself, when he shook hands with me at the foot of the stairs, looked anxious.

"We shall have to send home our pupils," said he, "and we must sit with our arms folded."

The Saverne people, with Zeffen, Baruch, and the children, got into their carriage, and started silently for home.

CHAPTER 4

Father Moses Compelled
to Bear Arms

All this, Fritz, was but the beginning of troubles.

You should have seen the city the next morning, at about eleven o'clock, when the engineering officers had finished inspecting the ramparts, and the tidings suddenly spread that there were needed seventy-two platforms inside the bastions, three bomb-proof block-houses, for thirty men each, at the right and left of the German gate, ten *palankas* with battlements forming stronghold intrenchments for forty men, and four blindages upon the great square of the mayoralty to shelter each a hundred and ten men; and when it was known that the citizens would be obliged to work at all these, to provide themselves with shovels, pickaxes, and wheelbarrows, and the peasants to bring trees with their own horses!

As for Sorlé, Sâfel, and myself, we did not even know what blindages and *palankas* were; we asked our neighbour Bailly, an old armourer, what they were for, and he answered with a smile:

"You will find out, neighbour, when you hear the balls roar and the shells hiss. It would take too long to explain. You will see, by and by; never too late to learn."

Imagine how the people looked! I remember that everybody ran to the square, where our mayor, Baron Parmentier, made a speech. We ran there with all the rest.

Sorlé held me by the arm, and Sâfel by the skirt of my coat.

There, in front of the mayoralty, the whole city, men, women, and children, formed in a semicircle, and listened in the deepest silence, now and then crying all together, "*Vive l'Empereur!*"

Parmentier, a tall, thin man, in a sky-blue dress- coat, a white cravat, and the tri-coloured sash around his waist, stood on the top of the steps of the guard-house, with the members of the municipal council behind him, under the arch, and shouted out:

"Phalsburgians! The time has come in which to show your devotion to the Empire. A year ago all Europe was with us, now all Europe is against us. We should have everything to fear without the energy and power of the people. He who will not do his duty now will be a traitor to his country! Inhabitants of Phalsburg, show what you are! Remember that your children have perished through the treachery of the allies. Avenge them! Let everyone be obedient to the military authority, for the sake of the safety of France," etc.

Only to hear him made one's flesh creep, and I said to myself:

"Now there will not be time for the spirits of wine to get here—that is plain! The allies are on their way!"

Elias the butcher, and Kalmes Levy the ribbon-merchant, were standing near us. Instead of crying "*Vive l'Empereur!*"with the rest, they said to each other:

"Good! we are not barons, you and I! Barons, counts, and dukes have but to defend themselves. Are we to think only of their interests?"

But all the old soldiers, and especially those of the Republic, old Goulden, the clockmaker, Desmarels, the Egyptian—creatures with not a hair left on their heads, nor as much as four teeth to hold their pipes—these creatures fell in with the mayor, and cried out:

"*Vive la France!* We must defend ourselves to the death!"

I saw several looking askance at Kalmes Levy, and I whispered to him:

"Keep still, Kalmes! For heaven's sake, keep still! They will tear you in pieces!"

It was true. The old men gave him terrible looks; they grew pale, and their cheeks shook.

Then Kalmes stopped talking, and even left the crowd to return home. But Elias stayed till the end of the speech, and, as the whole mass of people were going down the main street, shouting "*Vive l'Empereur!*"he could not help saying to the old clockmaker:

"What! you, Mr. Goulden, a reasonable man, who have never wanted anything of the Emperor, you are now going to take his part, and cry out that we must defend ourselves till death! Is it our business to be soldiers? Have not we furnished enough soldiers to the Empire these last ten years? Have not enough men been killed? Must we give, besides, our own blood to support barons, counts, and dukes?"

But old Goulden did not let him finish, and replied, as if indignant: "Listen, Elias! try to keep still! The thing now to be done is not to know what is right or wrong—it is to save France. I warn you, that if you try to discourage others, it will be bad for you. Believe me—go!"

Already a number of superannuated soldiers were gathered round us, and Elias had only time to retreat by the opposite lane.

From this time public notices, requisitions, forced labours, domiciliary visits for tools and wheelbarrows, came one after another, incessantly. A man was nothing in his own house; the officers of the place assumed authority over everything: only to be sure, they gave receipts.

All the tools from my storehouse of iron were in use on the ramparts. Fortunately I had sold a good many beforehand, for these tickets in place of my wares would have ruined me.

From time to time the mayor made a speech, and the governor, a fat man, covered with pimples, expressed his satisfaction to the citizens; that made up for their money!

When my time came to take the pickaxe and draw the wheelbarrow, I arranged with Carabin, the wood-sawyer, to take my place for thirty *sous*. Ah, what misery! Such a time will never come again.

While the governor commanded us within the city, the soldiers were always outside to superintend the peasants. The road to Lutzelburg was but one line of carts, laden with old oaks for building block-houses. These are large sentry-boxes, or turrets, built up of solid trunks of trees, laid crosswise one upon another, and then covered with earth. These are more solid than an arch. Shells and bombs might rain upon them without disturbing anything within, as I found afterward.

These trees were also used to make lines of enormous palisades, pointed and pierced with holes for firing; these are what they call *palankas*.

I seem still to hear the shouts of the peasants, the neighing of the horses, the strokes of the whips, and all the other noises, which never stopped, day or night.

My only consolation was in thinking, "If the spirits of wine comes now, it will be well defended; the Austrians, Prussians, and Russians will not drink it here!"

Every morning Sorlé expected to receive the invoice.

One Sabbath day we had the curiosity to go and see the works of the bastions. Everybody was talking about it, and Sâfel kept coming to me, saying: "The work is going on; they are filling the shells in front of the arsenal; they are taking out the cannon; they are mounting them on the ramparts!"

We could not keep the child away. He had nothing to sell now under the market, and it would be too tedious for him to stay at home. He scoured the city, and brought us back the news.

On this day, then, having heard that forty-two pieces were ranged in battery, and that they were continuing the work upon the bastion of the infantry-barracks, I told Sorlé to bring her shawl, and we would go and see.

We first went down to the French gate. Hundreds of wheelbarrows were going up the ramparts of the bastion, from which could be seen the road to Metz on the right and the road to Paris on the left.

There, above, crowds of labourers, soldiers and citizens, were heaping up a mass of earth in the form of a triangle, at least twenty-five feet in height, and two hundred in length and breadth.

An engineering officer had discovered with his spy-glass that this bastion was commanded by the hill opposite, and so everybody was set to work to place two pieces on a level with the hill.

It was the same everywhere else. The interiors of these bastions, with their platforms, were shut in all around, for seven feet from the ground, like rooms. Nothing could fall into them except from the sky. In the turf, however, were dug narrow openings, larger without, like funnels; the mouths of the cannon, which were raised upon immense carriages, were drawn out through these apertures; they could be pushed forward and backward, and turned in all directions, by means of great levers passed in rings over the hind wheels of the carriages.

I had not yet heard the sound of these forty-eight pounders. But the mere sight of them on their platforms gave me a terrible idea of their power. Even Sorlé said: "It is fine, Moses; it is well done!"

She was right, for within the bastions all was in complete order; not a weed remained, and upon the sides were piled great bags filled with earth to protect the artillerymen.

But what lost labour! and to think that every firing of these large guns costs at least a *louis*—money spent to kill our fellow-men!

In fine the people worked at these things with more enthusiasm than if they were gathering in their own harvests. I have often thought that if the French bestowed as much pains, good sense, and courage upon matters of peace, they would be the richest and happiest people in the world. Yes, they would long ago have surpassed the English and Americans. But when they have toiled and economized, when they have opened roads everywhere, built magnificent bridges, dug out harbours and canals, and riches come to them from all quarters, suddenly the fury of war possesses them, and in three or four years they ruin themselves with grand armies, with cannon, with powder, with bullets, with men, and become poorer than before. A few soldiers are their masters, and look down upon them. This is all it profits them!

In the midst of all this, news from Mayence, from Strasburg, from Paris, came by the dozens; we could not go into the street without seeing a courier pass. They all stopped before the Bockhold house, near the German gate, where the governor lived. A circle formed around the house, the courier mounted, then the news spread through the city that the allies were concentrated at Frankfort, that our troops guarded the islands of the Rhine; that the conscripts from 1803 to 1814 were recalled; that those of 1815 would form the reserve corps at Metz, at Bordeaux, at Turin; that the deputies were going to assemble; then, that the gates had been shut upon them, etc., etc.

There came also smugglers of all sorts from Graufthal, Pirmasens, and Kaiserslautern, with Franz Sépel, the one-armed man, at their head, and others from the villages around, who secretly scattered the proclamations of Alexander, Francis Joseph and Frederic William, saying "that they did not make war upon France, but upon the Emperor alone to prevent his further desolation of Europe."

They spoke of the abolition of duties, and of taxes of all sorts. The people at night did not know what to think.

But one fine morning it was all explained. It was the eighth or ninth of December. I had just risen, and was putting on my clothes, when I heard the rolling of a drum at the corner of the main street.

It was cold, but nevertheless I opened the window and leaned out to hear the announcements. Parmentier opened his paper, young Engelheider kept up his drum-beating, and the people assembled.

Then Parmentier read that the governor of the place ordered all citizens to present themselves at the mayoralty between eight in the morning and six in the evening, without fail, to receive their muskets and cartridge-boxes, and that those who did not come, would be court-martialed.

There was the end at last! Everyone who was able to march was on his way, and the old men were to defend the fortifications; sober-minded men—citizens—men accustomed to living quietly at home, and attending to their own affairs! now they must mount the ramparts and every day run the risk of losing their lives!

Sorlé looked at me without a word, and indignation made me also speechless. Not till after a quarter of an hour, when I was dressed, did I say:

"Make the soup ready. I am going to the mayoralty to get my musket and cartridge-box."

Then she exclaimed: "Moses, who would have believed that you would have to go and fight at your age? Oh! what misery!"

And I answered: "It is the Lord's will."

Then I started with a sad heart. Little Sâfel followed me.

As I arrived at the corner of the market, Burguet was coming down the mayoralty steps, which swarmed with men; he had his musket on his shoulder, and said with a smile:

"Ah, well, Moses! We are going to turn Maccabees in our old age?"

His cheerfulness encouraged me, and I replied:

"Burguet, how is it they can take rational men, heads of families, and make them destroy themselves? I cannot comprehend it; no, there is no sense in it!"

"Ah," said he, "what would you have? If they can't get thrushes, they must take blackbirds."

I could not smile at his pleasantries, and he said:

"Come, Moses, don't be so disconsolate; this is only a formality. We have troops enough for active service; we shall have only to mount guard.

If sorties are to be made, or attacks repulsed, they will not take you; you are not of an age to run, or to give a bayonet stroke! You are gray and bald. Don't be troubled!"

"Yes," I said, "that is very true, Burguet, I am broken down-more so, perhaps, than you think,"

"That is well," said he, "but go and take your musket and cartridge-box."

"And are we not going to stay in the barracks?"

"No, no!"he cried, laughing aloud,"we are going to live quietly at home."

He shook hands with me, and I went under the arch of the mayoralty. The stairway was crowded with people, and we heard names called out.

And there, Fritz, you should have seen the looks of the Robinots, the Gourdiers, the Mariners, that mass of tilers, knife-grinders, house-painters, people who, every day, in ordinary times, would take off their caps to you to get a little work you should have seen them straighten themselves up, look at you pityingly over the shoulder, blow in their cheeks, and call out:

"Ah, Moses, is it thou? Thou wilt make a comical soldier. He! he! he! They will cut thy moustaches according to regulation!"

And such-like nonsense.

Yes, everything was changed; these former bullies had been named in advance sergeants, sergeant-majors, corporals, and the rest of us were nothing at all. War upsets everything; the first become last, and the last first. It is not good sense but discipline which carries the day. The man who scrubbed your floor yesterday, because he was too stupid to gain a living any other way, becomes your sergeant, and if he tells you that white is black, you must let it be so.

At last, after waiting an hour, someone called out, "Moses!"and I went up.

The great hall above was full of people. They all exclaimed:

"Moses! Wilt thou come, Moses? Ah, see him! He is the old guard! Look now, how he is built! Thou shalt be ensign, Moses! Thou shalt lead us on to victory!"

And the fools laughed, nudging each others' elbows. I passed on, without answering or even looking at them.

In the room at the farther end, where the names were drawn at conscriptions, Governor Moulin, Commandant Petitgenet, the mayor, Frichard, secretary of the mayoralty, Rollin, captain of apparel, and six or seven other superannuated men, crippled with rheumatism, brought from all parts of the world, were met in council, some sitting, the rest standing.

These old ones began to laugh as they saw me come in. I heard them say to one another: "He is strong yet! Yes, he is all right."

So they talked, one after another. I thought to myself: "Say what you like, you will not make me think that you are twenty years old, or that you are handsome."

But I kept silence.

Suddenly the governor, who was talking with the mayor in a corner, turned around, with his great *chapeau* awry, and looking at me, said:

"What do you intend to do with such a patriarch? You see very well that he can hardly stand."

I was pleased, in spite of it all, and began to cough.

"Good, good!" said he, "you may go home; take care of your cold!"

I had taken four steps toward the door, when Frichard, the secretary of the mayoralty, called out:

"It is Moses! The Jew Moses, colonel, who has sent his two boys off to America! The oldest should be in the service."

This wretch of a Frichard had a grudge against me, because we had the same business of selling old clothes under the market, and the country people almost always preferred buying of me; he had a mortal grudge against me, and that is why he began to inform against me.

The governor exclaimed at once: "Stop a minute! Ah ha, old fox! You send your boys to America to escape conscription! Very well! Give him his musket, cartridge-box, and sabre."

Indignation against Frichard choked me. I would have spoken, but the wretch laughed and kept on writing at the desk; so I followed the *gendarme* Werner to a side room, which was filled with muskets, sabres, and cartridge-boxes.

Werner himself hung a cartridge-box crosswise on my back, and gave me a musket, saying:

"Go, Moses, and try always to answer to the call."

I went down through the crowd so indignant that I heard no longer the shouts of laughter from the rabble.

On reaching home I told Sorlé what had happened. She was very pale as she listened. After a moment, she said: "This Frichard is the enemy of our race; he is an enemy of Israel. I know it; he detests us! But just now, Moses, do not say a word; do not let him see that you are angry; it would please him too much. By and by you can have your revenge! You will have a chance. And if not yourself, your children, your grandchildren; they shall all know what this wretch has done to their grandfather—they shall know it!"

She clinched her hand, and little Sâfel listened.

This was all the comfort she could give me. I thought as she did, but I was so angry that I would have given half my fortune to ruin the wretch. All that day, and in the night, too, I exclaimed more than twenty times:

"Ah, the scoundrel!—I was going—they had said to me, 'You may go!'—He is the cause of all my misery!"

You cannot imagine, Fritz, how I have always hated that man. Never have my wife and I forgotten the harm he did us—never shall my children forget it.

CHAPTER 5

Father Moses Receives
Welcome News

The next day we must answer to the call before the mayor-alty. All the children in town surrounded us and whistled. Fortunately, the blindages of the Place d'Armes were not finished, so that we went to learn our exercises in the large court of the college, near the *chemin de ronde* at the corner of the powder-house. As the pupils had been dismissed for some time, the place was at liberty.

Imagine to yourself this large court filled with citizens in bonnets, coats, cloaks, vests, and breeches, obliged to obey the orders of their former tinkers, chimney-sweeps, stable-boys, now turned into corporals, sergeants, and sergeant-majors. Imagine these peaceable men, in fours, in sixes, in tens, stretching out their legs in concert, and marching to the step, "One—two! One—two! Halt! Steady!"while others, marching backward, frowning, called out insolently: "Moses, dress thy shoulders!"

"Moses, bring thy nose into line!"

"Attention, Moses! Carry arms! Ah, old shoe, thou'lt never be good for anything! Can anyone be so stupid at his age? Look just look! Thunder! Canst thou not do that? One—two! What an old blockhead! Come, begin again! Carry arms!"

This is the way my own cobbler, Monborne, ordered me about. I believe he would have beaten me if it had not been for Captain Vigneron.

All the rest treated their old patrons in the same way. You would have said that it had always been so—that they had always been sergeants and we had always been soldiers. I heaped up gall enough against this rabble to last fifty years.

They in fine were the masters! And the only time that I remember ever to have struck my own son, Sâfel, this Monborne was the cause of it. All the children climbed upon the wall of the *chemin de ronde* to look at us and laugh at us. On looking up, I saw Sâfel among them, and made a sign of displeasure with my finger. He went down at once; but at the close of the exercise, when we were ordered to break ranks before the town-house, I was seized with anger as I saw him coming toward me, and I gave him two good boxes on the ear, and said: "Go hiss—and mock at your father, like Shem, instead of bringing a garment to cover his nakedness—go!"

He wept bitterly, and in this state I went home. Sorlé seeing me come in looking very pale, and the little one following me at a distance, sobbing, came down at once to the door, and asked what was the matter. I told her how angry I was, and went upstairs.

Sorlé reproved Sâfel still more severely, and he came and begged my pardon. I granted it with all my heart, as you may suppose. But when I thought that the exercises were to be repeated every day, I would gladly have abandoned everything if I could possibly have taken with me my house and wares.

Yes, the worst thing I know of is to be ordered about by bullies who cannot restrain themselves when chance sets them up for a moment, and who are not capable of receiving the idea that in this life everybody has his turn.

I should say too much if I continued on this head. I would rather go on.

The Lord granted me a great consolation. I had scarcely laid aside my cartridge-box and musket, so as to sit at the table, when Sorlé smilingly handed me a letter.

"Read that, Moses," said she, "and you will feel better."

I opened and read it. It was the notice from Pézenas that my dozen pipes of spirits were on their way. I drew a long breath.

"Ah! that is good, now!" I exclaimed; "the spirits are coming by the ordinary conveyance; they will be here in three weeks. We hear nothing from the direction of Strasburg and Sarrebruck; the allies are collecting still, but they do not move; my spirits of wine are safe! They will sell well! It is a grand thing!"

I smiled, and was quite myself again, when Sorlé pushed the armchair toward me, saying: "And what do you think of that, Moses?"

She gave me, as she spoke, a second letter, covered with large stamps, and at the first glance I recognized the handwriting of my two sons, Frômel and Itzig.

It was a letter from America! My heart swelled with joy, and I silently thanked the Lord, deeply moved by this great blessing. I said: "The Lord is good. His understanding is infinite. He delighteth not in the strength of a horse; he taketh not pleasure in the legs of a man. He taketh pleasure in those that hope in his mercy."

Thus I spoke to myself while I read the letter, in which my sons praised America, the true land of commerce, the land of enterprising men, where everything is free, where there are no taxes or impositions, because people are not brought up for war, but for peace; the land, Fritz, where every man becomes, through his own labour, his intelligence, his economy, and his good intentions, what he deserves to be, and everyone takes his proper place, because no important matter is decided without the consent of all;—a just and sensible thing, for where all contribute, all should give their opinions.

This was one of their first letters. Frômel and Itzig wrote me that they had made so much money in a year, that they need no longer carry their own packs, but had three fine mules, and that they had just opened at Catskill, near Albany, in the State of New York, an establishment for the exchange of European fabrics with cow-hides, which were very abundant in that region.

Their business was prospering, and they were respected in the town and its vicinity. While Frômel was travelling on the road with their three mules, Itzig stayed at home, and when Itzig went in his turn his brother had charge of the shop.

They already knew of our misfortunes, and thanked the Lord for having given them such parents, to save them from destruction. They would have liked to have us with them, and after what had just happened, in being maltreated by a Monborne, you can believe that I should have been very glad to be there. But it was enough to receive such good news, and in spite of all our misfortunes, I said to myself, as I thought of Frichard: "But it is only to me that you can be an ass! You may harm me here, but you can't hurt my boys. You are nothing but a miserable secretary of mayoralty, while I am going to sell my spirits of wine. I shall gain double and treble. I will put my little Sâfel at your side, under the market, and he will beckon to everybody that is going into your shop; and he will sell to them at cost price rather than lose their custom, and he will make you die of anger."

The tears came into my eyes as I thought of it, and I ended by embracing Sorlé, who smiled, full of satisfaction.

We pardoned Sâfel over again, and he promised to go no more with the cursed race. Then, after dinner, I went down to my cellar, one of the finest in the city, twelve feet high and thirty-five feet long, all built of hewn stone, under the main street. It was as dry as an oven, and even improved wine in the long run.

As my spirits of wine might arrive before the end of the month, I arranged four large beams to hold the pipes, and saw that the well, cut in the rock, had enough water for mixing it.

On going up about four o'clock, I perceived the old architect, Krômer, who was walking across the market, his measuring-stick under his arm.

"Ah!" said I, "come down a minute into my cellar; do you think it will be safe against the bombs?"

We went down together. He examined it, measured the stones and the thickness of the arch with his stick, and said: "You have six feet of earth over the key-stone. "When the bombs enter here, Moses, it will be all over with all of us. You may sleep with both ears shut."

We took a good drink of wine from the spout, and went up in good spirits.

Just as we set foot on the pavement, a door in the main street opened with a crash, and there was a sound of glass broken. Krômer raised his nose, and said: "Look yonder, Moses, at Camus's steps! Something is going on."

We stopped and saw at the top of the railed staircase a sergeant of veterans, in a gray coat, with his musket dangling, dragging Father Camus by the collar. The poor old man clung to the door with both hands to keep himself from falling; he succeeded at last in getting loose, by tearing the collar from his coat, and the door shut with a noise like thunder.

"If war begins now between citizens and soldiers," said Krômer, "the Germans and Russians will have fine sport."

The sergeant, seeing the door shut and bolted within, tried to force it open with blows from the butt-end of his musket, which caused a great uproar; the neighbours came out, and the dogs barked. We were watching it all, when we saw Burguet come along the passage in front, and begin to talk vehemently with the sergeant.

At first the man did not seem to hear him, but after a moment he raised his musket to his shoulder with a rough movement, and went down to the street, with his shoulders up and his face dark and furious. He passed by us like a wild boar. He was a veteran with three chevrons, sunburnt, with a gray moustache, large straight wrinkles the whole length of his cheeks, and a square chin. He muttered as he passed us, and went into the little inn of the Three Pigeons.

Burguet followed at a distance, with his broad hat down to his eyebrows, wrapped in his beaver-cloth great-coat, his head thrown back, and his hands in his pockets. He smiled.

"Well," said I, "what has been going on at Camus's?"

"Oh!" said he, "it is Sergeant Trubert, of the Fifth Company of veterans, who had just been playing his tricks. The old fellow wants everything to go by rule and measure. In the last fortnight he has had five different lodgings, and cannot get along with anybody. Everybody complains of him, but he always makes excuses which the governor and commandant think excellent."

"And at Camus's house?"

"Camus has not too much room for his own family. He wished to send the sergeant to the inn; but the sergeant had already chosen Camus's bed to sleep in, had spread his cloak upon it, and said, 'My billet is for this place. I am very comfortable here, and do not wish to change.' Old Camus was vexed, and finally, as you have just seen, the sergeant tried to pull him out, and beat him."

Burguet smiled, but Krômer said: "Yes, all that is laughable. And yet when we think of what such people must have done on the other side of the Rhine!"

"Ah!"exclaimed Burguet, "it was not very pleasant for the Germans, I am sure. But it is time to go and read the newspaper. God grant that the time for paying our old debts may not have come! Good-evening, gentlemen."

He continued his walk on the side of the square. Krômer went toward his own house, while I shut the two doors of my cellar; after which I went home.

This was the tenth of December. It was already very cold. Every night, after five or six o'clock, the roofs and pavements were covered with frost. There was no more noise without, because people kept at home, around their stoves.

I found Sorlé in the kitchen, preparing our supper. The red flame flickered upon the hearth around the saucepan. These things are now before my eyes, Fritz—the mother, washing the plates at the stone sink, near the gray window; little Sâfel blowing in his big iron pipe, his cheeks round as an apple, his long curly hair all disordered, and myself sitting on the stool, holding a coal to light my pipe.Yes, it all seems here present!

We said nothing.We were happy in thinking of the spirits of wine that were coming, of the boys who were doing so well, of the good supper that was cooking. And who would ever have thought, then, that twenty-five days afterward the city would be surrounded by enemies, and shells hissing in the air?

CHAPTER 6

A Disagreeable Guest

Now, Fritz, I am going to tell you something which has often made me think that the Lord takes an interest in our affairs, and that He orders everything for the best. At first it seems dreadful, and we exclaim, "Lord have mercy on us!" and afterward we are surprised to find that it has all been for our good.

You know that Frichard, the secretary of the mayoralty, disliked me. He was a little, yellow, dried-up old man, with a red wig, flat ears, and hollow cheeks. This rascal was bent on doing me an injury, and he soon found an opportunity.

As the time of the blockade drew nearer, people were more and more anxious to sell, and the day after I received the good news from America—it was Friday, a market-day—so many of the Alsatian and Lorraine people came with their great dossers and panniers of fruit, eggs, butter, cheese, poultry, etc., that the marketplace was crowded with them.

Everybody wanted money, to hide it in his cellar, or under a tree in the neighbouring wood. You know that large sums were lost at that time; treasures which are now discovered from year to year, at the foot of oaks and beeches, hidden because it was feared that the Germans and Russians would pillage and destroy everything, as we had done to them. The men died, or perhaps could not find the place where they had hidden their money, and so it remained buried in the ground.

This day, the eleventh of December, it was very cold; the frost penetrated to the very marrow of your bones, but it had not yet begun to snow. Very early in the morning, I went down, shivering, with my woollen waistcoat buttoned up to my throat, and my seal-skin cap drawn down over my ears.

Both the little and the great squares were already swarming with people, shouting and disputing about prices. I had only time to open my shop, and to hang up my large scales in the arch, before a crowd of country people stood about the door, some asking for nails, others iron for forging; and some bringing their own old iron with the hope of selling it.

They knew that if the enemy came there would be no way of entering the city, and that was what brought the crowd, some to sell and others to buy.

I opened shop and began to weigh. We heard the patrols passing without; the guard was everywhere doubled, the drawbridges in good condition, and the outside barriers fortified anew. We were not yet declared to be in a state of siege, but we were like the bird on the branch; the last news from Mayence, Sarrebruck, and Strasburg announced the arrival of the allies on the other bank of the Rhine.

As for me, I thought of nothing but my spirits of wine, and all the time I was selling, weighing, and handling money, it was never out of my mind. It had, as it were, taken root in my brain.

This had lasted about an hour, when suddenly Burguet appeared at my door, under the little arch, behind the crowd of country people, and said to me:

"Moses, come here a minute, I have something to say to you."

I went out.

"Let us go into your passage," said he.

I was much surprised, for he looked very grave. The peasants behind called out:

"We have no time to lose. Make haste, Moses!"

But I paid no attention. In the passage Burguet said to me:

"I have just come from the mayoralty, where they are busy in making out a report to the prefect in regard to the state of feeling among our population, and I accidentally heard that they are

"Be so good as to come in Mr. Sergeant"

going to send Sergeant Trubert to your house."

This was indeed a blow for me. I exclaimed:

"I don't want him! I don't want him! I have lodged six men in the last fortnight, and it isn't my turn."

He answered:

"Be quiet, and don't talk so loud. You will only make the matter worse."

I repeated:

"Never, never shall this sergeant enter my house! It is abominable! A quiet man like myself, who has never harmed any one, and who asks nothing but peace!"

While I was speaking, Sorlé, on her way to market, with her basket on her arm, came down, and asked what was the matter.

"Listen, Madame Sorlé," said Burguet to her; "be more reasonable than your husband! I can understand his indignation, and yet for all that, when a thing is inevitable we must submit to it. Frichard dislikes you; he is secretary of the mayoralty; he distributes the billets for quartering soldiers according to a list. Very well; he sends you Sergeant Trubert, a violent, bad man, I allow, but he needs lodging as well as the others. To everything which I have said in your favour, Frichard has always replied: 'Moses is rich. He has sent away his boys to escape conscription. He ought to pay for them.' The mayor, the governor, everybody thinks he is right. So, you see, I tell you as a friend, the more resistance you make, so much the more the sergeant will affront you, and Frichard laugh at you, and there will be no help for it. Be reasonable!"

I was still more angry on finding that I owed these misfortunes to Frichard. I would have exclaimed, but my wife laid her hand on my arm, and said:

"Let me speak, Moses. Monsieur Burguet is right, and I am much obliged to him for telling us beforehand. Frichard has a spite against us. Very well; he must pay for it all, and we will settle with him by and by. Now, when is the sergeant coming?"

"At noon," replied Burguet.

"Very well," said my wife; "he has a right to lodging, fire, and candles. We can't dispute that; but Frichard shall pay for it all."

She was pale, and I listened, for I saw that she was right.

"Be quiet, Moses," she said to me afterward, "and don't say a word; let me manage it."

"This is what I had to say to you," said Burguet, "it is an abominable trick of Frichard's. I will see, by and by, if it is possible to rid you of the sergeant. Now I must go back to my post."

Sorlé had just started for the market. Burguet pressed my hand, and as the peasants grew more impatient in their cries, I had to go back to my scales.

I was full of rage. I sold that day more than two hundred *francs'* worth of iron, but my indignation against Frichard, and my fear of the sergeant, took away all pleasure in anything. I might have sold ten times more without feeling any better.

"Ah! the rascal!" I said to myself; "he gives me no rest. I shall have no peace in this city."

As the clock struck twelve the market closed, and people went away by the French gate. I shut up my shop and went home, thinking to myself:

"Now I shall be nothing in my own house; this Trubert is going to rule everything. He will look down upon us as if we were Germans or Spaniards."

I was in despair. But in the midst of my despair on the staircase, I suddenly perceived an odour of good things from the kitchen, and I went up in surprise, for I smelt fish and roast, as if it were a feast day.

I was going into the kitchen, when Sorlé appeared and said:

"Go into your chamber, shave yourself, and put on a clean shirt."

I saw, at the same time, that she was dressed in her Sabbath clothes, with her ear-rings, her green skirt, and her red silk neckerchief.

"But why must I shave, Sorlé?" I exclaimed.

"Go quick; you have no time to lose!" replied she.

This woman had so much good sense, she had so many

times set things right by her ready wit, that I said nothing more, and went into my bedroom to shave myself and put on a clean shirt.

As I was putting on my shirt I heard little Sâfel cry out:

"Here he is, mamma! here he is!"

Then steps were heard on the stairs, and a rough voice called:

"*Holla*! you folks. *Ho*!"

I thought to myself: "It is the sergeant," and I listened.

"Ah! here is our sergeant!" cried Sâfel, triumphantly.

"Oh! that is good," replied my wife, in a cheerful tone. "Come in, Mr. Sergeant, come in! We were expecting you. I knew that we were to have the honour of having a sergeant; we were glad to hear it, because we have had only common soldiers before. Be so good as to come in, Mr. Sergeant."

She spoke in this way as if she were really pleased, and I thought to myself:

"O Sorlé, Sorlé! You shrewd woman! You sensible woman! I see through it now. I see your cunning. You are going to mollify this rascal! Ah, Moses! what a wife you have! Congratulate yourself! Congratulate yourself!"

I hastened to dress myself, laughing all the while; and I heard this brute of a sergeant say:

"Yes, yes! It is all very well. But that isn't the point! Show me my room, my bed. You can't pay me with fine speeches; people know Sergeant Trubert too well for that."

"Certainly, Mr. Sergeant, certainly," replied my wife, "here is your room and your bed. See, it is the best we have."

Then they went into the passage, and I heard Sorlé open the door of the handsome room which Baruch and Zeffen occupied when they came to Phalsburg.

I followed them softly. The sergeant thrust his fist into the bed to feel if it was soft. Sorlé and Sâfel looked on smilingly behind him. He examined every corner with a scowl. You never saw such a face, Fritz; a gray bristling moustache, a long thin nose, hooked over the mouth; a yellow skin, full of wrinkles: he

58

dragged the butt-end of his gun on the floor, without seeming to notice anything, and muttered ill-naturedly:

"Hem! hem! What is that down there?"

"It is the wash-basin, Mr. Sergeant."

"And these chairs, are they strong? Will they bear anything?"

He knocked them rudely down. It was evident he wanted to find fault with something.

On turning round he saw me, and looking at me sideways, asked:

"Are you the citizen?"

"Yes, sergeant; I am."

"Ah!"

He put his gun in a corner, threw his knapsack on the table, and said:

"That will do! You may go."

Sâfel had opened the kitchen door, and the good smell of the roast came into the room.

"Mr. Sergeant," said Sorlé very pleasantly, "allow me to ask a favour of you."

"You!" said he, looking at her over his shoulder, "ask a favour of me!"

"Yes. It is that since you now lodge with us, and will be in some respects one of the family, you will give us the pleasure of dining with us, at least for once."

"All, ah!" said he, turning his nose toward the kitchen, "that is another thing!"

He seemed to be considering whether to grant us this favour or not. We waited for him to answer, when he gave another sniff and threw his cartridge-box on the bed, saying:

"Well, so be it! We will go and see!"

"Wretch!" thought I, "if I could make you eat potatoes!"

But Sorlé seemed satisfied, and said:

"This way, Mr. Sergeant; this way, if you please."

When we went into the dining-room I saw that everything was prepared as if for a prince; the floor swept, the table carefully laid, a white table-cloth, and our silver knives and forks.

Sorlé placed the sergeant in my armchair at the head of the table, which seemed to him the most natural thing in the world.

Our servant brought in the large tureen and took off the cover; the odour of a good cream soup filled the room, and we began our dinner.

Fritz, I could tell you everything we had for dinner; but believe me, neither you nor I ever had a better. We had a roasted goose, a magnificent pike, sauerkraut, everything, in fact, which could be desired for a grand dinner, and all served by Sorlé in the most perfect manner. We had, too, four bottles of Beaujolais warmed in napkins, as was the custom in winter, and an abundant dessert.

Well! do you believe that the rascal once had the grace to seem pleased with all this? Do you believe that all through this dinner, which lasted nearly two hours, he once thought of saying, "This pike is excellent!"or, "This fat goose is well cooked!"or, "You have very good wine!"or any of the other things which we know are pleasant for a host to hear, and which repay a good cook for his trouble? No, Fritz, not once! You would have supposed that he had such dinners every day. The more even that my wife flattered him, and the more kindly she spoke to him, the more he rebuffed her, the more he scowled, the more defiantly he looked at us, as if we wanted to poison him.

From time to time I looked indignantly at Sorlé, but she kept on smiling; she kept on giving the nicest bits to the sergeant; she kept on filling his glass.

Two or three times I wanted to say, "Ah, Sorlé, what a good cook you are! How nice this force-meat is!"But suddenly the sergeant would look down upon me as if to say, "What does that signify? Perhaps you want to give me lessons? Don't I know better than you do whether a thing is good of bad?"

So I kept silence. I could have wished him—well, in worse company; I grew more and more indignant at every morsel which he swallowed in silence. Nevertheless Sorlé's example encouraged me to put a good face on the matter, and toward the end I thought, "Now, since the dinner is eaten, since it is almost over, we will go on, with God's help. Sorlé was mistaken, but it is all the same; her idea was a good one, except for such a rascal!"

And I myself ordered coffee; I went to the closet, too, to get some cherry-brandy and old rum.

"What is that?" asked the sergeant.

"Rum and cherry-brandy; old cherry-brandy from the 'Black Forest'," I replied.

"Ah," said he, winking, "everybody says, 'I have got some cherry-brandy from the Black Forest!' It is very easy to say; but they can't cheat Sergeant Trubert; we will see about this!"

In taking his coffee he twice filled his glass with cherry-brandy, and both times said, "He! he! We will see whether it is genuine."

I could have thrown the bottle at his head.

As Sorlé went to him to pour a third glassful, he rose and said, "That is enough; thank you! The posts are doubled. This evening I shall be on guard at the French gate. The dinner, to be sure, was not a bad one. If you give me such now and then, we can get along with each other."

He did not smile, and, indeed, seemed to be ridiculing us.

"We will do our best, Mr. Sergeant," replied Sorlé, while he went into his room and took his great-coat to go out.

"We will see," said he as he went downstairs, "we will see!"

Till now I had said nothing, but when he was down I exclaimed, "Sorlé, never, no never, was there such a rascal! We shall never get along with this man. He will drive us all from the house."

"Bah! bah! Moses," she replied, laughing, "I do not think as thou dost! I have quite the contrary idea; we will be good friends, thou'lt see, thou'lt see!"

"God grant it!" I said; "but I have not much hope of it."

She smiled as she took off the tablecloth, and gave me too a little confidence, for this woman had a good deal of shrewdness, and I acknowledged her sound judgment.

CHAPTER 7

Sergeant Trubert in a New Light

You see, Fritz, what the common people had to endure in those days. Ah, well! just as we were performing extra service, while Monborne was commanding me at the drilling, while Sergeant Trubert was down upon me, while we were hearing of domiciliary visits of inspection to ascertain what provisions the citizens had—in the midst of all this, my dozen pipes of spirits of wine were being slowly wheeled over the road.

How I repented of having ordered them! How often I could have torn my hair as I thought that half my thirty years' gains were at the mercy of circumstances! How I prayed for the Emperor! How I ran every morning to the coffee-houses and ale-houses to learn the news, and how I trembled as I read!

Nobody knew what I suffered, not even Sorlé, for I kept it all from her. She was too keen-sighted not to perceive my anxiety, and sometimes she would say, "Come, Moses, have courage! All will come right—patience a little longer!"

But the rumours which came from Alsace, and German Lorraine, and Hundsruck, quite upset me: "They are coming! They will not dare to come! We are ready for them! They will take us by surprise! Peace is going to be made! They will pass by tomorrow! We shall have no fighting this winter! They can wait no longer! The Emperor is still in Paris! Marshal Victor is at Huninguen! They are impressing the custom-house officers, the forest-keepers, and the *gendarmerie!* Some Spanish dragoons went down by Saverne yesterday! The mountaineers are to defend the Vosges! There will be fighting in Alsace!"etc., etc. Your head would have been turned, Fritz. In the morning the wind would blow one way and put you in good spirits; at night it would blow another way and you would be miserable.

And my spirits of wine were coming nearer and nearer, and at last arrived, in the midst of this conflict of news, which might any day turn into a conflict of bullets and shells. If it had not been for my other troubles I should have been beside myself. Fortunately, my indignation against Monborne and the other villains diverted my mind.

We heard nothing more of Sergeant Trubert after the great dinner for the remainder of that day, and the night following, as he was on guard; but the next morning, as I was getting up, behold, he came up the stairs, with his musket on his shoulder; he opened the door and began to laugh, with his moustaches all white with frost. I had just put on my pantaloons, and looked at him in astonishment. My wife was still in her room.

"He! he! Father Moses," said he, in a good-natured voice, "it has been a dreadful cold night." He did not look or speak like the same person.

"Yes, sergeant," I replied, "it is December, and that is what we must expect."

"What we must expect," he repeated;—"all the more reason for taking a drop. Let us see, is there any more of that old cherry-brandy?"

He looked, as he spoke, as if he could see through me. I got up at once from my armchair, and ran to fetch the bottle: "Yes, yes, sergeant," I exclaimed, "there is more, drink and enjoy it."

As I said this, his face, still a little hard, seemed to smile all over. He placed his gun in a corner, and, standing up, handed me the glass, saying, "Pour out, Father Moses, pour out!"

I filled it brimful. As I did so, he laughed quietly. His yellow face puckered up in hundreds of wrinkles at the corners of his eyes, and around his cheeks and moustaches and chin. He did not laugh so as to be heard, but his eyes showed his good-humour.

"Famous cherry-brandy this, in truth, Father Moses!"he said as he drank it. "A body knows who has drank it in the Black Forest, where it cost nothing! Aren't you going to drink with me?"

"With pleasure," I answered. And we drank together. He looked at me all the time. Suddenly he said, with a mischievous look, "Hey, Father Moses, say, you were afraid of me yesterday?" He smiled as he spoke.

"Oh—Sergeant—"

"Come, come," said he, laying his hand upon my shoulder-"confess that I frightened you."

He smiled so pleasantly that I could not help saying: "Well, yes, a little!"

"He! he! he! I knew it very well," said he. "You had heard them say, 'Sergeant Trubert is a tough one!' You were afraid, and you gave me a dinner fit for a prince to coax me!"

He laughed aloud, and I ended by laughing too. Sorlé had heard all, in the next room, and now came to the door and said, "Good-morning, Mr. Sergeant."

He exclaimed, "Father Moses, here is what may be called a woman! You can boast of having a spirited woman, a sly woman, slyer than you are, Father Moses; he, he, he! That is as it should be—that is as it should be!"

Sorlé was delighted.

"Oh! Mr. Sergeant," said she, "can you really think so?"

"Bah! bah!"he exclaimed. "You are a first-rate woman! I saw you when I first came, and said to myself, 'Take heed, Trubert! They make a fair pretence; it is a stratagem to send you to the hotel to sleep. We will let the enemy unmask his batteries!"

"Ha! ha! ha! You are nice folks. You gave me a dinner fit for a Marshal of the Empire. Now, Father Moses, I invite myself to take a small glass of cherry-brandy with you now and then. Put the bottle aside, by itself, it is excellent! And as for the rest, the room which you have given me is too handsome; I don't like such gewgaws; this fine furniture and these soft beds are good for women. What I want is a small room, like that at the side, two good chairs, a pine table, a plain bed with a mattress, *paillasse*, and coverings, and five or six nails in the wall for hanging my things. You just give me that!"

"Since you wish it, Mr. Sergeant."

"Yes, I wish it; the handsome room will be for state occasions."

"You will breakfast with us?" asked my wife, well pleased.

"I breakfast and dine at the cantine," replied the sergeant. "I do very well there; and I don't want to have good people go to any expense for me. When people respect an old soldier as he ought to be respected, when they treat him kindly, when they are like you,—Trubert, too, is what he ought to be."

"But, Mr. Sergeant!"said Sorlé.

"Call me sergeant," said he, "I know you now. You are not like all the rabble of the city; rascals who have been growing rich while we have been off fighting; wretches who do nothing but heap up money and grow big at the expense of the army, who live on us, who are indebted to us for everything, and who send us to sleep in nests of vermin. Ah! a thousand million thunders!"

His face resumed its bad look; his moustaches shook with his anger, and I thought to myself, "What a good idea it was to treat him well! Sorlé's ideas are always good!"

But in a moment he relaxed, and laying his hand on my arm, he exclaimed:

"To think that you are Jews! a kind of abominable race; everything that is dirty and vile and niggardly! To think that you are Jews! It is true, is it not, that you are Jews?"

"Yes, sir," replied Sorlé.

"Well, upon my word, I am surprised to hear it," said he; "I have seen so many Jews, in Poland and Germany, that I thought to myself 'They are sending me to some Jews; they had better look out or I'll smash everything.'"

We kept silent in our mortification, and he added, "Come, we will say no more about that. You are good, honest people; I should be sorry to trouble you. Your hand, Father Moses!"

I gave him my hand.

"I like you," said he. "Now, Madame Moses, the side room!"

We showed him the small room that he asked for, and he went at once to fetch his knapsack from the other, saying as he went:

"Now I am among honest people! We shall have no difficulty in getting along together. You do not trouble me, I do not trouble you; I come in and go out, by day or night; it is Sergeant Trubert, that is enough. And now and then, in the morning, we will take our little glass; it is agreed, is it not, Father Moses?"

"Yes, sergeant."

"And here is the key of the house." said Sorlé.

"Very well; everything is arranged; now I am going to take a nap; goodbye, my friends."

"I hope you will sleep well, sergeant." "We went out at once, and heard him lie down.

"You see, Moses, you see," whispered my wife, in the alley, "it has all come right."

"Yes," I replied, "all right, excellent; your plan was a good one; and now, if the spirits of wine only come, we shall be happy."

CHAPTER 8

Father Moses's First Encouter

From that time the sergeant lived with us without troubling anybody. Every morning, before he went to his duties, he came and sat a few minutes in my room, and talked with me while he took his glass. He liked to laugh with Sâfel, and we called him "our sergeant," as if he were one of the family. He seemed to like to be with us; he was a careful man; he would not allow our *schabisboïé* to black his shoes; he cleaned his own buff-skins, and would not let any one touch his arms.

One morning, when I was going to answer to the call, he met me in the alley, and, seeing a little rust on my musket, he began to swear like the devil.

"Ah! Father Moses, if I had you in my company, it would go hard with you!"

"Yes," thought I; "but, thank God. I'm not."

Sorlé, leaning over the balustrades above, laughed heartily.

From that time the sergeant regularly inspected my equipments; I must clean my gun over and over, take it to pieces, clean the barrel and furbish the bayonet, as if I expected to go and fight. And even when he knew how Monborne treated me, he also wanted to teach me the exercises. All my remonstrances were of no avail, he would frown, and say:

"Father Moses, I can't stand it, that an honest man like you should know less than the rabble. Go along!"

And then we would up to the loft. It was very cold, but the sergeant was so provoked at my want of briskness in performing the movements, that he always put me in a great perspiration before we finished.

"Attention to the word of command, and no laziness!"he would exclaim.

I used to hear Sorlé, Sâfel, and the servant laughing in the stairway, as they peeped through the laths, and I did not dare to turn my head. In fine, it was entirely owing to this good Trubert that I learned to charge well, and became one of the best vaulters in the company.

Ah! Fritz, it would all have been very well if the spirits of wine had come; but instead of my dozen pipes, there came half a company of marine artillery, and four hundred recruits for the Sixth Light Infantry.

About this time the governor ordered that a space six hundred metres wide should be cleared all round the city.

You should have seen the havoc that was made in the place; the fences, palisades, and trees hewn down, the houses demolished, from which everybody carried away a beam or some timbers. You should have looked down from the ramparts and seen the little gardens, the line of poplars, the old trees in the orchards felled to the ground and dragged away by swarms of workmen. You should have seen all this to know what war is!

Father Frise, the two Camus boys, the Sades, the Bosserts, and all the families of the gardeners and small farmers who lived at Phalsburg, suffered the most. I can almost hear old Fritz exclaim:

"Ah! my poor appletrees! Ah! my poor peartrees; I planted you myself, forty years ago. How beautiful you were, always covered with fine fruit! Oh, misery! misery!"

And the soldiers still chopped away. Toward the end, old Fritz went away, his cap drawn over his eyes, and weeping bitterly.

The rumour spread also that they were going to burn the Maisons Rouges at the foot of the Mitteibronn Hill, the tile-kiln at Pernette, and the little inns of *l'Arbre Vert* and *Panier Fleuri*, but it seemed that the governor found it was not necessary as these houses were out of range; or rather, that they would reserve that till later; and, that the allies were coming sooner than they were expected.

Of what happened before the blockade, I remember, too, that on the twenty-second of December, about eleven o'clock in the morning, the call was beat. Everybody supposed that it was for the drill, and I set out quietly, with my musket on my shoulder, as usual; but, as I reached the corner of the mayoralty, I saw the troops of the garrison formed under the trees of the square.

They placed us with them in two ranks; and then Governor Moulin, Commandants Thomas and Pettigenet, and the mayor, with his tri-coloured sash, arrived.

They beat the march, and then the drum-major raised his baton, and the drums stopped. The governor began to speak, everybody listened, and the words heard from a distance were repeated from one to another.

"Officers, non-commissioned, National Guards, and Soldiers!

"The enemy is concentrated upon the Rhine, only three days' march from us. The city is declared to be in a state of siege; the civil authorities give place to martial law. A permanent court-martial replaces ordinary tribunals.

"Inhabitants of Phalsburg! we expect from you courage, devotion, obedience! *Vive l'Empereur!*"

And a thousand cries of "*Vive l'Empereur!*" filled the air.

I trembled to the ends of my hair; my spirits of wine were still on the road; I considered myself a ruined man.

The immediate distribution of cartridges, and the order to the battalion to go and forage for provisions, and bring in cattle from the surrounding villages for the supply of the city, prevented me from thinking of my misfortune.

I had also to think of my own life, for, in receiving such an order, we supposed of course that the peasants would resist, and it is abominable to have to fight the people you are robbing.

I was very pale as I thought of all this.

But when Commandant Thomas cried out, "Charge!" and I tore off my first cartridge, and put it in the barrel, and, instead of

hearing the ramrod I felt a ball at the bottom!—when they ordered us:"By file—left! left! forward! quick step! march!"and we
set out for the barracks of the Bois-de-Chênes, while the first
battalion went on to Quatre-Vents and Bichelberg, the second
to Wechern and Melting; when I thought that we were going
to seize and carry away everything, and that the court-martial
was at the mayoralty to pass sentence upon those who did not
do their duty;—all these new and terrible things completely
upset me. I was troubled as I saw the village in the distance,
and pictured to myself beforehand the cries of the women and
children.

You see, Fritz, to take from the poor peasant all his living at
the beginning of winter; to take from him his cow, his goats, his
pigs, everything in short, it is dreadful! and my own misfortune
made me feel more for that of others.

And then, as we marched, I thought of my daughter Zeffen,
and Baruch, and their children, and I exclaimed to myself:

"Mercy on us! if the enemy comes, what will they do in an
exposed town like Saverne? They will lose everything. We may
be beggared any day."

These thoughts took away my breath, and in the midst of them
I saw some peasants, who, from their little windows, watched
our approach over the fields and along their street, without stirring. They did not know what we were coming for.

Six mounted soldiers preceded us; Commandant Thomas ordered them to pass to the right and left of the barracks, to prevent the peasants from driving their cattle into the woods, when
they had found out that we had come to rob them.

They set off on a gallop.

We came to the first house, where there is the stone crucifix.
We heard the order:

"Halt!"

Then thirty men were detached to act as sentinels in the little
streets, and I was among the number, which I liked, for I preferred being on duty to going into their stables and barns.

As we filed through the principal street the peasants asked

us:

"What is going on? Have they been cutting wood? Have they been making arrests?" and such like questions. But we did not answer them, and hastened on.

Monborne placed me in the third street to the right, near the large house of Father Franz, who raised bees on the slope of the valley behind his house. We heard the sheep bleating and the cattle lowing; that wretch of a Monborne said, winking at me:

"It will be jolly! We will make the Baraquois open their eyes."

He had no mercy in him. He said to me:

"Moses, thou must stay there. If anyone tries to pass, cross your bayonet. If anyone resists, prick him well and then fire. The law must be supported by force."

I don't know where the cobbler picked up that expression; but he left me in the street, between two fences white with frost, and went on his way with the rest of the guard.

I waited there nearly twenty minutes, considering what I should do if the peasants tried to save their property, and thinking it would be much better to fire upon the cattle than upon their owners.

I was much perplexed and was very cold, when I heard a great shouting; at the same time the drum began to beat. Some men went into the stables and drove the cattle. The Baraquins swore and wept; some tried to defend themselves. Commandant Thomas cried out:

"To the square! Drive them to the square!"

Some cows escaped through the fences, and you can't imagine what a tumult there was. I congratulated myself that I was not in the midst of this pillage. But this did not last long, for suddenly a herd of goats, driven by two old women, filed down the street on their way to the valley.

Then I had to stop them with my bayonet and call out:

"Halt!"

One of the women, Mother Migneron, knew me; she had a pitchfork, and was very pale.

71

"Let me pass, Moses," said she.

I saw that she was coming slowly toward me, meaning to throw me down with her pitchfork. The other tried to drive the goats into a little garden at the side, but the slats were too near together, and the fence too high.

I should have liked to let them go by, and deny having seen anything; but, unfortunately, Lieutenant Rollet came up and called out:

"Attention!"

And two men of the company followed: Mâcry and Schweyer, the brewer.

Old Migneron, seeing me cross the bayonet, began to grind her teeth, saying:

"Ah! wretch of a Jew, thou'lt pay for this!"

She was so angry that she had no fear of my musket, and three times she tried to thrust her pitchfork into me; then I found the benefit of my drilling, for I parried all her attacks.

Two goats escaped between my legs; the rest were taken. The soldiers pushed back the old women, broke their pitchforks, and finally regained the chief street, which was full of cattle, lowing and kicking.

Old Migneron sat down on the fence and tore her hair.

Just then two cows came along, their tails in the air, leaping over the fences and upsetting everything, the baskets of bees and their old keeper. Fortunately, as it was winter, the bees remained as if dead in their baskets, or else I believe they would have routed our whole battalion.

The horn of the *hardier*[1] sounded in the village. He had been summoned in the name of the law. This old *hardier*, Nickel, passed along the street, and the animals became quiet, and could be put in some order. I saw the procession go along the street; the oxen and cows in front, then the goats, and the pigs behind.

The Baraquins followed, flinging stones and throwing sticks. I saw that, if I should be forgotten, these wretches would fall upon me, and I should be murdered; but Sergeant Monborne,

---

1. Herdsman.

with, other comrades, came and relieved me. They all laughed and said:

"We have shaved them well! There is not a goat left at the Barracks; we have taken everything at one haul."

We hastened to rejoin the column, which marched in two lines at the right and left of the road, the cattle in the middle, our company behind, and Nickel, with Commandant Thomas, in front. This formed a file of at least three hundred paces. On every animal a bundle of hay had been tied for fodder.

In this way we passed slowly into the cemetery lane.

Upon the glacis we halted, and tied up the animals, and the order came to take them down into the fosses behind the arsenal.

We were the first that returned; we had seized thirty oxen, forty-five cows, a quantity of goats and pigs, and some sheep.

All day long the companies were coming back with their booty, so that the fosses were filled with cattle, which remained in the open air. Then the governor said that the garrison had provisions for six months, and every inhabitant must prove that he had enough to last as long, and that domiciliary visits were to begin.

We broke ranks before the city hall. I was going up the main street, my gun on my shoulder, when someone called me:

"Hey! Father Moses!"

I turned and saw our sergeant.

"Well," said he, laughing, "you have made your first attack; you have brought us back some provisions. Well and good!"

"Yes, sergeant, but it is very sad!"

"What, sad? Thirty oxen, forty-five cows, some pigs and goats—it is magnificent!"

"To be sure, but if you had heard the cries of these poor people, if you had seen them!"

"Bah! bah!" said he. "*Primo*, Father Moses, soldiers must live; men must have their rations if they are going to fight. I have often seen these things done in Germany and Spain and Italy! Peasants are selfish; they want to keep their own; they do not regard the honour of the flag; that is trash! In some respects they would be worse than townspeople, if we were foolish enough to listen to them; we must be strict."

"We have been, sergeant," I replied; "but if I had been master, we should not have robbed these poor wretches; they are in a pitiable condition enough already."

"You are too compassionate, Father Moses, and you think that others are like yourself. But we must remember that peasants, citizens, civilians, live only by the soldiers, and have all the profit without wanting to pay any of the cost. If we followed your advice we should die of hunger in this little town; our peasants would support the Russians, the Austrians, and Bavarians at our expense. This pack of scoundrels would be having a good time from morning to night, and the rest of us would be as poor as church-mice. That would not do—there is no sense in it!"

He laughed aloud. We had now come into our passage, and I went upstairs.

"Is it thou, Moses?" asked Sorlé in the darkness, for it was nightfall.

"Yes, the sergeant and I."

"Ah, good!" said she; "I was expecting you."

"Madame Moses," exclaimed the sergeant, "your husband can boast now of being a real soldier; he has not yet seen fire, but he has charged with his bayonet."

"Ah!" said Sorlé, "I am very glad to see him back."

In the room, through the little white door-curtains, we saw the lamp burning, and smelt the soup. The sergeant went to his room, as usual, and we into ours. Sorlé looked at me with her great black eyes, she saw how pale I was, and knew what I was thinking about. She took from me my cartridge-box, and placed my musket in the closet.

"Where is Sâfel?" I asked.

"He must be in the square. I sent him to see if you had come back. Hark! There he is coming up!"

Then I heard the child come up the stairs; he opened the

door at once and ran joyfully to embrace me.

We sat down to dinner, and, in spite of my trouble, I ate with a good appetite, having taken nothing since morning.

Suddenly Sorlé said: "If the invoice does not come before the city gates are closed we shall not have to pay anything, for goods are at the risk of the merchant until they are delivered. And we have not received the inventory."

"Yes," I replied, "you are right; M. Quataya, instead of sending us the spirits of wine at once, waited a week before answering us. If he had sent the twelve pipes that day or the day after, they would be here by this time. The delay is not our fault."

You see, Fritz, how anxious we were; but, as the sergeant came to smoke his pipe at the corner of the stove, as usual, we said no more about it.

I spoke only of my fears in regard to Zeffen, Baruch, and their children, in an exposed town like Saverne. The sergeant tried to put my mind at ease, and said that in such places they made, to be sure, all sorts of requisitions in wines, brandies, provisions, carriages, carts, and horses, but, except in case of resistance, the people were let alone, and the soldiers even tried to keep on good terms with them.

We kept on talking till nearly ten o'clock; then the sergeant, who had to keep guard at the German gate, went away, and we went to bed.

This was the night of the twenty-second and twenty-third of December, a very cold night.

CHAPTER 9

Approach of the Enemy

The next morning, when I threw back the shutters of our room, everything was white with snow; the old elms of the square, the street, the roofs of the mayoralty and market and church. Some of our neighbours, Recco the tinman, Spick the baker, and old Durand the mattress-maker, opened their doors and looked as if dazzled, while they exclaimed:

"He! Winter has come!"

Although we see it every year yet it is like a new existence. We breathe better out of doors, and within it is a pleasure to sit in the corner of the fireplace and smoke our pipes, while we watch the crackling of the red fire. Yes, I have always felt so for seventy-five years, and I feel so still!

I had scarcely opened the shutters when Sâfel sprang from his bed like a squirrel, and came and flattened his nose against a pane of glass, his long hair dishevelled and his legs bare.

"Oh! snow! snow!" he exclaimed. "Now we can have some slides!"

Sorlé, in the next room, made haste to dress herself and run in. We all looked out for some minutes; then I went to make the fire, Sorlé went to the kitchen, Sâfel dressed himself hastily, and everything fell back into the ordinary channel.

Notwithstanding the falling snow, it was very cold. You need only to see the fire kindle at once, and hear it roar in the stove, to know that it was freezing hard.

As we were eating our soup, I said to Sorlé, "The poor sergeant must have passed a dreadful night. His little glass of cherry-brandy will taste good."

"Yes," she said, "it is well you thought of it."

She went to the closet, and filled my little pocket-flask from the bottle of cherry-brandy.

You know, Fritz, that we do not like to go into public houses when we are on our way to our own business. Each of us carries his own little bottle and crust of bread; it is the best way and most conformed to the law of the Lord.

Sorlé then filled my flask, and I put it in my pocket, under my great-coat, to go to the guard-house. Sâfel wanted to follow me, but his mother told him to stay, and I went down alone, well pleased at being able to do the sergeant a kindness.

It was about seven o'clock, The snow falling from the roofs at every gust of wind was enough to blind you. But going along the walls, with my nose in my great-coat, which was well drawn up on the shoulders, I reached the German gate, and was about going down the three steps of the guard-house, under the arch at the left, when the sergeant himself opened the heavy door and exclaimed:

"Is it you, Father Moses! What the devil has brought you here in this cold?"

The guard-house was full of mist; we could hardly see some men stretched on camp-beds at the farther end, and five or six veterans near the red-hot stove.

I stood and looked.

"Here," I said to the sergeant as I handed him my little bottle, "I have brought you your drop of cherry-brandy; it was such a cold night, you must need it."

"And you have thought of me, Father Moses!" he exclaimed, taking me by the arm, and looking at me with emotion.

"Yes, sergeant."

"Well, I am glad of it."

He raised the flask to his mouth and took a good drink. At that moment there was a distant cry "Who goes there?" and the guard of the outpost ran to open the gate.

"That is good!" said the sergeant, tapping on the cork, and giving me the bottle; "take it back, Father Moses, and thank you!"

Then he turned toward the half-moon and asked, "News! What is it?"

We both looked and saw a hussar quartermaster, a withered, gray old man, with quantities of chevrons on his arm, arrive in great haste.

All my life I shall have that man before my eyes; his smoking horse, his flying sabretash, his sword clinking against his boots; his cap and jacket covered with frost; his long, bony, wrinkled face, his pointed nose, long chin, and yellow eyes. I shall always see him riding like the wind, then stopping his rearing horse under the arch in front of us, and calling out to us with a voice like a trumpet: "Where is the governor's house, sergeant?"

"The first house at the right, quartermaster. What is the news?"

"The enemy is in Alsace!"

Those who have never seen such men—men accustomed to long warfare, and hard as iron—can have no idea of them. And then if you had heard the exclamation, "The enemy is in Alsace!" it would have made you tremble.

The veterans had gone away; the sergeant, as he saw the hussar fasten his horse at the governor's door, said to me: "Ah, well, Father Moses, now we shall see the whites of their eyes!"

He laughed, and the others seemed pleased.

As for myself, I set forth quickly, with my head bent, and in my terror repeating to myself the words of the prophet:

One post shall run to meet another, and one messenger to meet another, to show the king that his passages are stopped, and the reeds they have burned with fire, and the men of war are affrighted.

The mighty men have forborne to fight, they have remained in their holds, their might hath failed, and the bars are broken.

Set ye up a standard in the land, blow the trumpet among the nations, prepare the nations against her, call together against her

the kingdoms, appoint a captain against her.
And the land shall tremble and sorrow; for every purpose of the
Lord shall be performed, to make the land a desolation without
an inhabitant!

I saw my ruin at hand—the destruction of my hopes.

"Mercy, Moses!"exclaimed my wife, as she saw me come back, "what is the matter? Your face is all drawn up. Something dreadful has happened."

"Yes, Sorlé," I said, as I sat down; "the time of trouble has come of which the prophet spoke:"

The king of the south shall push at him, and the king of the
north shall come against him like a whirlwind; and he shall enter
into the countries and shall overflow and pass over.

This I said with my hands raised toward heaven. Little Sâfel squeezed himself between my knees, while Sorlé looked on, not knowing what to say; and I told them that the Austrians were in Alsace; that the Bavarians, Swedes, Prussians, and Russians were coming by hundreds of thousands; that a hussar had come to announce all these calamities; that our spirits of wine were lost, and ruin was threatening us.

I shed a few tears, and neither Sorlé nor Sâfel would comfort me.

It was eight o'clock. There was a great commotion in the city. We heard the drum beat, and proclamations read; it seemed as if the enemy were already there.

One thing which I remember especially, for we had opened a window to hear, was that the governor ordered the inhabitants to empty immediately their barns and granaries; and that, while we were listening, a large Alsatian wagon with two horses, with Baruch sitting on the pole, and Zeffen behind on some straw—her infant in her arms, and her other child at her side—turned suddenly into the street.

They were coming to us for safety!

The sight of them upset me, and raising my hands, I exclaimed:

"Lord, take from me all weakness! Thou seest that I need to live for the sake of these little ones. Therefore be thou my strength, and let me not be cast down!"

And I went down at once to receive them, Sorlé and Sâfel following me. I took my daughter in my arms, and helped her to the ground, while Sorlé took the children, and Baruch exclaimed:

"We came at the last minute! The gate was closed as soon as we had come in. There were many others from Quatre-Vents and Saverne who had to stay outside."

"God be praised, Baruch!" I replied. "You are all welcome, my dear children! I have not much, I am not rich; but what I have, you have—it is all yours. Come in!"

And we went upstairs; Zeffen, Sorlé, and I carrying the children, while Baruch stayed to take their things out of the wagon, and then he came up.

The street was now full of straw and hay, thrown out from the lofts; there was no wind, and the snow had stopped falling. In a little while the shouts and proclamations ceased.

Sorlé hastened to serve up the remains of our breakfast, with a bottle of wine; and Baruch, while he was eating, told us that there was a panic in Alsace, that the Austrians had turned Basle, and were advancing by forced marches upon Schlestadt, Neuf Brisach, and Strasburg, after having surrounded Huninguen.

"Everybody is escaping," said he. "They are fleeing to the mountain, taking their valuables on their carts, and driving their cattle into the woods. There is a rumour already that bands of Cossacks have been seen at Mutzig, but that is hardly possible, as the army of Marshal Victor is on the Upper Rhine, and dragoons are passing every day to join him. How could they pass his lines without giving battle?"

We were listening very attentively to these things when the sergeant came in. He was just off duty, and stood outside of the door, looking at us with astonishment.

I took Zeffen by the hand, and said: "Sergeant, this is my daughter, this is my son-in-law, and these are my grandchildren, about whom I have told you. They know you, for I have told them in my letter? how much we think of you."

The sergeant looked at Zeffen. "Father Moses," said he, "you have a handsome daughter, and your son-in-law looks like a worthy man."

Then he took little Esdras from Zeffen's arms, and lifted him up, and made a face at him, at which the child laughed, and everybody was pleased. The other little one opened his eyes wide and looked on.

"My children have come to stay with me," I said to the sergeant; "you will excuse them if they make a little noise in the house?"

"How! Father Moses," he exclaimed. "I will excuse everything! Do not be concerned; are we not old friends?"

And at once, in spite of all we could say, he chose another room looking upon the court.

"All the nestful ought to be together," said he. "I am the friend of the family, the old sergeant, who will not trouble anybody, provided they are willing to see him here."

I was so much moved that I gave him both my hands.

"It was a happy day when you entered my house," said I. "The Lord be thanked for it!"

He laughed, and said: "Come now, Father Moses; come! Have I done anything more than was natural? Why do you wonder at it?"

He went at once to get his things and carry them to his new room; and then went away, so as not to disturb us.

How we are mistaken! This sergeant, whom Frichard had sent to plague us, at the end of a fortnight was one of our family; he consulted our comfort in everything—and, notwithstanding all the years that have passed since then, I cannot think of that good man without emotion.

When we were alone, Baruch told us that he could not stay at Phalsburg; that he had come to bring his family, with everything that he could provide for them in the first hurried moments; but that, in the midst of such dangers, when the enemy could not long delay coming, his duty was to guard his house, and prevent, as much as possible, the pillage of his goods.

This seemed right, though it made us none the less grieved to have him go. We thought of the pain of living apart from each other; of hearing no tidings; of being all the time uncertain about the fate of our beloved ones! Meanwhile we were all busy. Sorlé and Zeffen prepared the children's bed; Baruch took out the provisions which he had brought; Sâfel played with the two little ones, and I went and came, thinking about our troubles.

At last, when the best room was ready for Zeffen and the children, as the German gate was already shut, and the French gate would be open only until two o'clock at the latest, for strangers to leave the city, Baruch exclaimed: "Zeffen, the moment has come!"

He had scarcely said the words when the great agony began cries, embraces, and tears!

Ah! it is a great joy to be loved, the only true joy of life. But what sorrow to be separated! And how our family loved each other! How Zeffen and Baruch embraced one another! How they leaned over their little ones, how they looked at them, and began to sob again!

What can be said at such a moment? I sat by the window, with my hands before my face, without strength to speak. I thought to myself: "My God, must it be that a single man shall hold in his hands the fate of us all! Must it be that, for his pleasure, for the gratification of his pride, everything shall be confounded, overturned, torn asunder! My God, shall these troubles never end? Hast thou no pity on thy poor creatures?"

I did not raise my eyes, but I heard the lamentations which rent my heart, and which lasted till the moment when Baruch, perceiving that Zeffen was quite exhausted, ran out, exclaiming: "It must be! It must be! *Adieu*, Zeffen! *Adieu*, my children! *Adieu*, all!"

No one followed him.

We heard the carriage roll away, and then was the great sorrow—that sorrow of which it is written:

*By the rivers of Babylon, there we sat down; yea, we wept when
we remembered Zion.*

We hanged our harps upon the willows.

*For there they that carried us away captive, required of us a song,
saying: 'Sing us one of the songs of Zion!'*

How shall we sing the Lord's song in a strange land?

CHAPTER 10

An Engagement with the Cossacks

But that day I was to have the greatest fright of all. You remember, Fritz, that Sorlé had told me at supper the night before, that if we did not receive the invoice, our spirits of wine would be at the risk of M. Quataya of Pézenas, and that we need feel no anxiety about it.

I thought so, too, for it seemed to me right; and as the French and German gates were closed at three o'clock, and nothing more could enter the city, I supposed that that was the end of the matter, and felt quite relieved.

"It is a pity, Moses!" I said to myself, as I walked up and down the room; "yes, for if these spirits had been sent a week sooner, we should have made a great profit; but now, at least, thou art relieved of great anxiety. Be content with thine old trade. Let alone for the future such harassing undertakings. Don't stake thine all again on one throw, and let this be a lesson to thee!"

Such thoughts were in my mind, when, about four o'clock, I heard someone coming up our stairs. It was a heavy step, as of a man trying to find his way in the dark.

Zeffen and Sorlé were in the kitchen, preparing supper. Women always have something to talk about by themselves, for nobody else to hear. So I listened, and then opened the door.

"Who is there?" I asked.

"Does not Mr. Moses, the wine-merchant, live here?" asked the man in a blouse and broad-brimmed felt hat, with his whip on his shoulder—a wagoner's figure, in short. I turned pale as I heard him, and replied: "Yes, my name is Moses. What do you want?"

He came in, and took out a large leather portfolio from under his blouse. I trembled as I looked on.

"There!" said he, giving me two papers, "my invoice and my bill of lading! Are not the twelve pipes of three-six from Pézenas for you?"

"Yes, where are they?"

"On the Mittelbronn hill, twenty minutes from here," he quietly answered. "Some Cossacks stopped my wagons, and I had to take off the horses. I hurried into the city by a postern under the bridge."

My legs failed me as he spoke. I sank into my armchair, unable to speak a word.

"You will pay me the portage," said the man, "and give me a receipt for the delivery."

"Sorlé! Sorlé!" I cried in a despairing voice. And she and Zeffen ran to me. The wagoner explained it all to them. As for me, I heard nothing. I had strength only to exclaim: "Now all is lost! Now I must pay without receiving the goods."

"We are willing to pay, sir," said my wife, "but the letter states that the twelve pipes shall be delivered in the city."

The wagoner said: "I have just come from the justice of the peace, as I wanted to find out before coming to you what I had a right to claim; he told me that you ought to pay for everything, even my horses and carriages, do you understand? I unharnessed my horses, and escaped, myself, which is so much the less on your account. Will you settle? Yes or no?"

We were almost dead with fright when the sergeant, came in. He had heard loud words, and asked: "What is it, Father Moses? What is it about? What does this man want?"

Sorlé, who never lost her presence of mind, told him the whole story, shortly and clearly; he comprehended it at once.

"Twelve pipes of three-six, that makes twenty-four pipes of cognac. What luck for the garrison! what luck!"

"Yes," said I, "but it cannot come in; the city gates are shut,

85

and the wagons are surrounded by Cossacks."

"Cannot come in!"cried the sergeant, raising his shoulders. "Go along! Do you take the governor for a fool? Is he going to refuse twenty-four pipes of good brandy, when the garrison needs it? Is he going to leave this windfall to the Cossacks? Madame Sorlé, pay the portage at once; and you, Father Moses, put on your cap and follow me to the governor's, with the letter in your pocket. Come along! Don't lose a minute! If the Cossacks have time to put their noses in your casks, you will find a famous deficit, I warrant you!"

When I heard that I exclaimed:"Sergeant, you have saved my life!"And I hastened to get my cap.

"Shall I pay the portage?" asked Sorlé.

"Yes! pay!"I answered as I went down, for it was plain that the wagoner could compel us. I went down with an anxious heart.

All that I remember after this is that the sergeant walked before me in the snow, that he said a few words to the sapper on orderly duty at the governor's house, and that we went up the grand stairway with the marble balustrade.

Upstairs, in the gallery with the balustrade around it, he said to me:"Be easy, Father Moses! Take out your letter, and let me do the talking."

He knocked softly at a door as he spoke:

Somebody said:"Come in!"

We went in.

Colonel Moulin, a fat man in a dressing-gown and little silk cap, was smoking his pipe in front of a good fire. He was very red, and had a carafe of rum and a glass at its side on the marble mantelpiece, where were also a clock and vases of flowers.

"What is it?" he asked, turning round.

"Colonel, this is what is the matter," replied the sergeant: "twelve pipes of spirits of wine have been stopped on the Mittelbronn hill, and are surrounded by Cossacks."

"Cossacks!"exclaimed the governor. "Have they broken through our lines already?"

"Yes," said the sergeant, "a sudden attack of Cossacks! They have possession of the twelve pipes of three-six which this patriot brought from Pézenas to sustain the garrison."

"Some bandits," said the governor—"thieves!"

"Here is the letter," said the sergeant, taking it from my hand.

The colonel cast his eyes over it, and said hastily:

"Sergeant, go and take twenty-five men of your company. Go on the run, free the wagons, and put in requisition horses from the village to bring them into the city."

And, as we were going: "Wait!"said he; and he went to his bureau and wrote four words; "here is the order."

When we were once on the stairway, the sergeant said: "Father Moses, run to the cooper's; we may perhaps need him and his boys. I know the Cossacks; their first thought will be to unload the casks so as to be more sure of keeping them. Have them bring ropes and ladders; and I will go to the Barracks and get my men together."

Then I ran home like a hart, for I was enraged at the Cossacks. I went in to get my musket and cartridge-box. I could have fought an army: I could not see straight.

"What is it? Where are you going?" asked Sorlé and Zeffen.

"You will know by and by," I replied.

I went to Schweyer's. He had two large saddle- pistols, which he put quickly into his apron-belt with the axe; his two boys, Nickel and Frantz, took the ladder and ropes, and we ran to the French gate.

The sergeant was not yet there; but two minutes after he came running down the street by the rampart with thirty veterans in file, their muskets on their shoulders.

The officer guarding the postern had only to see the order to let us go out, and a few minutes after we were in the trenches behind the hospital, where the sergeant ranged his men.

"It is cognac!" he told them; "twenty-four pipes of cognac! So, comrades, attention! The garrison is without brandy; those who do not like brandy have only to fall to the rear."

But they all wanted to be in front, and laughed in anticipation.

We went up the stairway, and were ranged in order in the covered ways. It might have been five o'clock. Looking from the top of the glacis we could see the broad meadow of Eichmatt, and above it the hills of Mittelbronn covered with snow. The sky was full of clouds, and night was coming on. It was very cold.

"Forward!" said the sergeant.

And we gained the highway. The, veterans ran, in two files, at the right and left, their backs rounded, and their muskets in their shoulder-belts; the snow was up to their knees.

Schweyer, his two boys, and I walked behind.

At the end of a quarter of an hour, the veterans, who ran all the way, had left us far behind; we heard for some time their cartridge-boxes rattling, but soon this sound was lost in the distance, and then we heard the dog of the Trois-Maisons barking in his chain.

The deep silence of the night gave me a chance to think. If it had not been for the thought of my spirits of wine, I would have gone straight back to Phalsburg, but fortunately that thought prevailed, and I said:

"Make haste, Schweyer, make haste!"

"Make haste!" he exclaimed angrily, "you can make haste to get back your spirits of wine, but what do we care for it? Is the highway the place for us? Are we bandits that we should risk our lives?"

I understood at once that he wanted to escape, and was enraged.

"Take care, Schweyer," said I, "take care! If you and your boys go back, people will say that you have been a traitor to the city brandy, and that is worse than being a traitor to the flag, especially in a cooper."

"The devil take thee!" said he, "we ought never to have come."

However, he kept on ascending the hill with me. Nickel and Frantz followed us without hurrying.

When we reached the plateau we saw lights in the village. All was still and seemed quiet, although there was a great crowd around the two first houses.

The door of the Bunch of Grapes was wide open, and its kitchen fire shone through the passage to the street where my two wagons stood.

This crowd came from the Cossacks who were carousing at Heitz's house, after tying their horses under the shed. They had made Mother Heitz cook them a good hot soup, and we saw them plainly, two or three hundred paces distant, go up and down the outside steps, with jugs and bottles which they passed from one to another. The thought came to me that they were drinking my spirits of wine, for a lantern hung behind the first wagon, and the rascals were all going from it with their elbows raised. I was so furious that, regardless of danger, I began to run to put a stop to the pillage.

Fortunately the veterans were in advance of me, or I should have been murdered by the Cossacks; I had not gone half way when our whole troop sprang from the fences of the highway, and ran like a pack of wolves, crying out, "To the bayonet!"

You never saw such confusion, Fritz. In a second the Cossacks were on their horses, and the veterans in the midst of them; the front of the inn with its trellis, its pigeon-house, and its little fenced garden, was lighted up by the firing of muskets and pistols. Heitz's two daughters stood at the windows, with their arms lifted and screamed so that they could be heard all over Mittelbronn.

Every minute, in the midst of the confusion, something fell upon the road, and then the horses started and ran through the fields like deer, with their heads run out, and their manes and tails flying. The villagers ran; Father Heitz slipped into the barn, and climbed up the ladder, and I came up breathless, as if out of my senses.

I had not gone more than fifteen steps when a Cossack, who was running away at full speed, turned about furiously close to me, with his lance in the air, and called out, "Hurra!"

I had only time to stoop, and I felt the wind from the lance as it passed along my body.

I never felt so in my life, Fritz; I felt the chill of death, that trembling of the flesh, of which the prophet spoke: "Fear came upon me and trembling; the hair of my flesh stood up."

But what shows the spirit of wisdom and prudence which the Lord puts into his creatures, when he means to spare them for a good old age, is that immediately afterward, in spite of my trembling knees, I went and sat under the first wagon, where the blows of the lances could not reach me; and there I saw the veterans finish the extermination of the rascals, who had retreated into the court, and not one of whom escaped.

Five or six were in a heap before the door, and three others were stretched upon the highway.

This did not take more than ten minutes; then all was dark again, and I heard the sergeant call: "Cease firing!"

Heitz, who had come down from his hayloft, had just lighted a lantern; the sergeant seeing me under the wagon, called out: "Are you wounded, Father Moses?"

"No," I replied, "but a Cossack tried to thrust his lance into me, and I got into a safe place."

He laughed aloud, and gave me his hand to help me to rise.

"Father Moses," said he, "I was frightened about you. Wipe your back; people might think you were not brave."

I laughed too, and thought: "People may think what they please! The great thing is to live in good health as long as possible."

We had only one wounded, Corporal Duhem, an old man, who bandaged his own leg, and tried to walk. He had had a blow from a lance in the right calf. He was placed on the first wagon, and Lehnel, Heitz's granddaughter, came and gave him a drop of cherry-brandy, which at once restored his strength and even his good spirits.

"It is the fifteenth," he exclaimed. "I am in for a week at the hospital; but leave me the bottle for the compresses."

I was delighted to see my twelve pipes on the wagons, for

I SHUDDERED IN MY VERY SOUL AND MY HAIR BRISTLED

Schweyer and his two boys had run away, and without their help we could hardly have reloaded.

I tapped at once at the bung-hole of the hindmost cask to find out how much was missing. These scamps of Cossacks had already drunk nearly half a measure of spirits; Father Heitz told me that some of them scarcely added a drop of water. Such creatures must have throats of tin; the oldest topers among us could not bear a glass of three-six without being upset.

At last all was ready and we had only to return to the city. When I think of it, it all seems before me now: Heitz's large dapple-gray horses going out of the stable one by one; the sergeant standing by the dark door with his lantern in his hand, and calling out, "Come, hurry up! The rascals may come back!" On the road in front of the inn, the veterans surrounded the wagons; farther on the right some peasants, who had hastened to the scene with pitchforks and mattocks, were looking at the dead Cossacks, and myself, standing on the stairs above, singing praises to God in my heart as I thought how glad Sorlé and Zeffen and little Sâfel would be to see me come back with our goods.

And then when all is ready, when the little bells jingle, when the whip snaps, and we start on the way—what delight!

Ah Fritz! everything looks bright after thirty years; we forget fears, anxieties, and fatigues; but the memory of good men and happy hours remains with us forever!

The veterans, on both sides of the wagons, with their muskets under their arms, escorted my twelve pipes as if they were the tabernacle; Heitz led the horses, and the sergeant and I walked behind.

"Well, Father Moses!" said he laughing, "it has all gone off well; are you satisfied?"

"More than I can possibly tell, sergeant! What would have been my ruin will make the fortune of my family, and we owe it all to you."

"Go along," said he, "you are joking."

He laughed, but I felt deeply; to have been in danger of losing everything, and then to regain it all and make profit out of it—it makes one feel deeply.

I exclaimed inwardly: "I will praise thee, O Lord, among the people; and I will sing praises unto thee among the nations.

"For thy mercy is great above the heavens, and thy truth reacheth unto the clouds."

CHAPTER 9

Father Moses Returns in Triumph

Now I must tell you about our return to Phalsburg.

You may suppose that my wife and children, after seeing me take my gun and go away, were in a state of great anxiety. About five o'clock Sorlé went out with Zeffen to try to learn what was going on, and only then they heard that I had started for Mittelbronn with a detachment of veterans.

Imagine their terror!

The rumour of these extraordinary proceedings had spread through the city, and quantities of people were on the bastion of the artillery barracks, looking on from the distance. Burguet was there, with the mayor, and other persons of distinction, and a number of women and children, all trying to see through the darkness. Some insisted that Moses marched with the detachment, but nobody would believe it, and Burguet exclaimed: "It is not possible that a sensible man like Moses would go and risk his life in fighting Cossacks—no, it is not possible!"

If I had been in his place I should have said the same of him. But what can you do, Fritz? The most prudent of men become blind when their property is at stake; blind, I say, and terrible, for they lose sight of danger.

This crowd was waiting, as I said, and soon Zeffen and Sorlé came, as pale as death, with their large shawls over their heads. They went up the rampart and stood there, with their feet in the snow, too much frightened to speak.

I learned these things afterward.

When Zeffen and her mother went up on the bastion, it was, perhaps, half -past five; there was not a star to be seen. Just at that time, Schweyer and his boys ran away, and five minutes later the skirmish began.

Burguet told me afterward that, notwithstanding the darkness and the distance, they saw the flash of the muskets around the inn as plainly as if they were a hundred paces off, and everybody was still and listened to hear the shots, which were repeated by the echoes of the Bois-de-Chênes and Lutzelburg.

When they ceased Sorlé descended from the slope leaning on Zeffen's arm, for she could not support herself. Burguet helped them to reach the street, and took them into old Prise's house on the corner, where they found him warming himself gloomily by his hearth.

"My last day has come!" said Sorlé. Zeffen wept bitterly.

I have often reproached myself for having caused this sorrow, but who can answer for his own wisdom? Has not the wise man himself said: "I turned myself to behold wisdom, and madness, and folly; and I saw that wisdom excelleth folly; and I myself perceived that one event happeneth to the wise man and the fool. Wherefore, I said in my heart, that wisdom also is vanity."

Burguet was going out from Father Prise's when Schweyer and his sons came up the postern stairs, crying out that we were surrounded by Cossacks and lost. Fortunately my wife and daughter could not hear them, and the mayor soon came along and ordered them to stop talking and go home quickly, if they did not want to be sent to prison.

They obeyed, but that did not prevent people from believing what they said, especially as it was all dark again in the direction of Mittelbronn.

The crowd came down from the ramparts and filled the street; many of them went to their homes thinking they should never see us again, when, just as the clock struck seven, the sentinel of the outworks called out, "Who goes there?"

We had reached the gate.

The crowd was soon on the ramparts again. The squad in

front of the sergeant on duty flew to arms; they had just recognized us.

We heard the murmur, without knowing what it was. So, when, after a reconnaissance, the gates were slowly opened to us, and the two bridges lowered for us to pass, what was our surprise at hearing the shouts: "Hurrah for Father Moses! Hurrah for the spirits of wine!"

The tears came to my eyes. And my wagons rolling heavily under the gates, the soldiers presented arms to us, the great crowd surrounding us, shouting: "Moses! Hey, Moses! are you all right? you have not been killed?" the shouts of laughter, the people seizing my arm to hear me tell about the fight,—all these things were very pleasant.

Everybody wanted to talk with me, even the mayor, and I had not time to answer them.

But all this was nothing compared with the joy I felt at seeing Sorlé, Zeffen, and little Sâfel run from Father Frise's and throw themselves all at once into my arms, exclaiming: "He is safe! he is safe!"

Ah, Fritz! what are honours by the side of such love? What is all the glory of the world compared with the joy of seeing our beloved ones? The others might have cried out, "Hurrah for Moses!" a hundred years, and I would not even have turned my head; but I was terribly moved by the sight of my family.

I gave Sâfel my gun, and while the wagons, escorted by the veterans, went on toward the little market, I led Zeffen and Sorlé through the crowd to old Frise's, and there, when we were alone, we began to hug each other again.

Without, the shouts of joy were redoubled; you would have thought that the spirits of wine belonged to the whole city. But within the room, my wife and daughter burst into tears, and I confessed my imprudence.

So, instead of telling them of the dangers I had experienced, I told them that the Cossacks ran away as soon as they saw us, and that we had only to put horses to the wagons before starting.

A quarter of an hour afterward, when the cries and tumult

had ceased, I went out, with Zeffen and Sorlé on my arms, and little Sâfel in front, with my gun on his shoulder, and in this way we went home, to see to the unloading of the brandy.

I wanted to put everything in order before morning, so as to begin to sell at double price as soon as possible.

When a man runs such risks he ought to make something by it; for if he should sell at cost price, as some persons wish, nobody would be willing to run any risk for the sake of others; and if it should come to pass that a man should sacrifice himself for other people, he would be thought a blockhead; we have seen it a hundred times, and it will always be so.

Thank God! such ideas never entered into my head! I have always thought that the true idea of trade was to make as much profit as we can, honestly and lawfully.

That is according to justice and good sense.

As we turned at the corner of the market, our two wagons were already unharnessed before our house. Heitz was running back with his horses, so as to take advantage of the open gates, and the veterans, with their arms at will, were going up the street toward the infantry quarters.

It might have been eight o'clock. Zeffen and Sorlé went to bed, and I sent Sâfel for Gros the cooper, to come and unload the casks. Quantities of people came and offered to help us. Gros came Boon with his boys, and the work began.

It is very pleasant, Fritz, to see great tuns going into your cellar, and to say to yourself, "These splendid tuns are mine: it is spirits which cost me twenty *sous* the quart, and which I am going to sell for three *francs*!" This shows the beauty of trade; but everybody can imagine the pleasure for himself—there is no use in speaking of it.

About midnight my twelve pipes were down on the stands, and there was nothing left to do but to broach them.

While the crowd was dispersing, I engaged Gros to come in the morning to help me mix the spirits with water, and we went up, well pleased with our day's work. We closed the double oak door, and I fastened the padlock and went to bed.

What a pleasure it is to own something and feel that it is all safe!

This is how my twelve pipes were saved.

You see now, Fritz, what anxieties and fears we had at that time. Nobody war sure of anything; for you must not suppose that I was the only one living like a bird on the branch; there were hundreds of others who were not able to close their eyes. You should have seen how the citizens looked every morning, when they heard that the Austrians and Russians occupied Alsace, that the Prussians were marching upon Sarrebruck, or when an order was published for domiciliary visits, or for days' labour to wall up the posterns and orillons of the place, or to form companies of firemen to remove at once all inflammable matter, or to report to the governor the situation of the city treasury, and the list of the principal persons subject to taxes for the supply of shoes, caps, bed-linen, and so forth.

You should have seen how people looked at each other.

In war times civil life is nothing, and they will take from you your last shirt, giving you the governor's receipt for it. The first men of the land are zeros when the governor has spoken. This is why I have often thought that everybody who wishes for war, or at least wants to be a soldier, is either demented or half ruined, and hopes to better himself by the ruin of everybody else. It must be so.

But notwithstanding all these troubles, I could not lose time, and I spent all the next day in mixing my spirits. I took off my cloak, and drew out with great gusto. Gros and his boys brought jugs, and emptied them in the casks which I had bought beforehand, so that by evening these casks were brimful of good white brandy, eighteen degrees.

I had caramel prepared, also, to give the brandy a good colour of old cognac, and when I turned the faucet, and raised the glass before the candle, and saw that it was exactly the right tint, I was in ecstasies, and exclaimed: "Give strong drink unto him that is ready to perish, and wine unto those that be of heavy hearts! Let him drink and remember his misery no more."

Father Gros, standing at my side on his great flat feet, smiled quietly, and his boys looked well pleased.

I filled the glass for them; they passed it to each other and were delighted with it.

About five o'clock we went upstairs. Sâfel, on the same day, had brought three workmen, and had them remove our old iron into the court under the shed. The old rickety storehouse was cleaned. Desmarets, the joiner, put up some shelves behind the door in the arch, for holding bottles, and glasses,, and tin measures, when the time for selling should come, and his son put together the planks of the counter. This was all done at once, as at a time o great pressure, when people like to make a good sun& of money quickly.

I looked at it all with a good deal of satisfactions Zeffen, with her baby in her arms, and Sorlé, had also come down. I showed my wife the place behind the counter, and said, "That is the place where you are to sit, with your feet in loose slippers, and a warm tippet on your shoulders, and sell our brandy."

She smiled as she thought of it

Our neighbours, Bailly the armourer, Koffel the little weaver, and several others, came and looked on without speaking; they were astonished to see what quick work we were making.

At six o'clock, just as Desmarets laid aside his hammer, the sergeant arrived in great glee, on his return from the cantine.

"Well, Father Moses!" he exclaimed, "the work goes on! But there is still something wanting."

"What is that, sergeant?"

"Hi! It is all right, only you must put a screen up above, or look out for the shells!"

I saw that he was right, and we were all well frightened, except the neighbours, who laughed to see our surprise.

"Yes," said the sergeant, "we must have it."

This took away all my pleasure; I saw that our troubles were not yet at an end.

Sorlé, Zeffen, and I went up, while Desmarets closed the door. Supper was ready; we sat down thoughtfully, and little

Sâfel brought the keys.

The noise had ceased without; now and then a citizen on patrol passed by.

The sergeant came to smoke his pipe as usual. He explained how the screens were made, by crossing beams in the form of a sentry-box, the two sides supported against the gables, but while he maintained that it would hold like an arch, I did not think it strong enough, and I saw by Sorlé's face that she thought as I did.

We sat there talking till ten o'clock, and then all went to bed.

Chapter 12

The Enemy Repulsed

About one o'clock in the morning of the sixth of January, the day of the feast of the Kings, the enemy arrived on the hill of Saverne.

It was terribly cold, our windows under the persiennes were white with frost. I woke as the clock .struck one; they were beating the call at the infantry barracks.

You can have no idea how it sounded in the silence of the night.

"Dost thou hear, Moses?" whispered Sorlé.

"Yes, I hear," said I, almost without breathing.

After a minute some windows were opened in our street, and we knew that others too were listening; then we heard running, and suddenly the cry, "To arms! to arms!"

It made one's hair stand on end.

I had just risen, and was lighting a lamp, when we heard two knocks at our door.

"Come in!" said Sorlé, trembling.

The sergeant opened the door. He was in marching equipments, with his gaiters on his legs,, his large gray cap turned up at the sides, his musket on his shoulder, and his sabre and cartridge-box on his back.

"Father Moses," said he, "go back to bed and be quiet: it is the battalion call at the barracks, and has nothing to do with you."

And we saw at once that he was right, for the drums did not come up the street two by two, as when the National Guard was called in.

"Thank you, sergeant," I said.

"Go to sleep!"said he, and he went down the stairs.

The door of the alley below slammed to. Then the children, who had waked up, began to cry. Zeffen came in, very pale, with her baby in her arms, exclaiming, "Mercy! What is the matter?"

"It is nothing, Zeffen," said Sorlé. "It is nothing, my child: they are beating the call for the soldiers."

At the same moment the battalion came down the main street. "We heard them march as far as to the Place d'Armes, and beyond it toward the German gate.

We shut the windows, Zeffen went back to her room, and I lay down again.

But how could I sleep after such a start? My head was full of a thousand thoughts: I fancied the arrival of the Russians on the hill this cold night, and our soldiers marching to meet them, or manning the ramparts. I thought of all the blindages and block-houses, and batteries inside the bastions, and that all these great works had been made to guard against bombs and shells, and I exclaimed inwardly: "Before the enemy has demolished all these works, our houses will be crushed, and we shall be exterminated to the last man."

I took on in this way for about half an hour, thinking of all the calamities which threatened us, when I heard outside the city, toward Quatre-Vents, a kind of heavy rolling, rising and falling like the murmur of running water. This was repeated every second. I raised myself on my elbow to listen, and I knew that it was a fight far more terrible than that at Mittelbronn, for the rolling did not stop, but seemed rather to increase.

"How they are fighting, Sorlé, how they are fighting!" I exclaimed, as I pictured to myself the fury of those men murdering each other at the dead of night, not knowing what they were doing. "Listen! Sorlé, listen! If that does not make one shudder!"

"Yes," said she. "I hope our sergeant will not be wounded; I hope he will come back safe!"

"May the Lord watch over him!"I replied, jumping from my bed, and lighting a candle.

I could not control myself. I dressed myself as quickly as if I were going to run away; and afterward I listened to that terrible rolling, which came nearer or died away with every gust of wind.

When once dressed, I opened a window, to try to see something. The street was still black; but toward the ramparts, above the dark line of the arsenal bastions, was stretched a line of red.

The smoke of powder is red on account of the musket shots which light it up. It looked like a great fire. All the windows in the street were open: nothing could be seen, but I heard our neighbour the armourer say to his wife, "It is growing warm down there! It is the beginning of the dance, Annette; but they have not got the big drum yet; that will come, by and by!"

The woman did not answer, and I thought, "Is it possible to jest about such things! It is against nature."

The cold was so severe that after five or six minutes I shut the window. Sorlé got up and made a fire in the stove.

The whole city was in commotion; men were shouting and dogs barking. Sâfel, who had been wakened by all these noises, went to dress himself in the warm room. I looked very tenderly on this poor little one, his eyes still heavy with sleep; and as I thought that we were to be fired upon, that we must hide ourselves in cellars, and all of us be in danger of being killed for matters which did not concern us, and about which nobody had asked our opinion, I was full of indignation. But what distressed me most was to hear Zeffen sob and say that it would have been better for her and her children to stay with Baruch at Saverne and all die together.

Then the words of the prophet came to me:

Is not this thy fear, thy confidence, thy hope, and the uprightness of thy ways?
Remember, I pray thee, who ever perished being innocent, or where were the righteous cut off.
No, they that plough iniquity and sow wickedness, reap the

same.

*By the blast of God they perish, and by the breath of his nostrils
are they consumed.*

But thee, his servant, he shall redeem from death.

*Thou shalt come to thy grave in a full age, like as a shock of corn
cometh in his season.*

In this way I strengthened my heart, while I heard the great
tumult of the panic-stricken crowd, running and trying to save
their property.

About seven o'clock it was announced that the casemates
were open, and that everybody might take their mattresses there,
and that there must be tubs full of water in every house, and the
wells left open in case of fire.

Think, Fritz, what ideas these orders suggested.

Some of our neighbours, Lisbeth Dubourg, Bével Ruppert,
Camus's daughters, and some others, came up to us exclaiming,
"We are all lost!"

Their husbands had gone out, right and left, to see what they
could see, and these women hung on Zeffen and Sorlé's necks,
repeating again and again, "Oh, dear! oh, dear! what misery!"

I could have wished them all to the devil, for intead of com-
forting us they only increased our fears; but at such times wom-
en will get together and cry out all at once; you can't talk reason
to them; they like these loud cryings and groanings.

Just as the clock struck eight, Bailly the armourer came to
find his wife: he had come from the ramparts. "The Russians,"
he said, "have come down in a mass from Quatre-Vents to the
very gate, filling the whole plain—Cossacks, Baskirs, and rabble!
Why don't they fire down upon them from the ramparts? The
governor is betraying us."

"Where are our soldiers?" I asked.

"Retreating!"exclaimed he. "The wounded came back two
hours ago, and our men stay yonder, with folded arms."

His bony face shook with rage. He led away his wife; then
others came crying out, "The enemy has advanced to the lower
part of the gardens, upon the glacis." I was astonished at these

things.

The women had gone away to cry somewhere else, and just then a great noise of wheels was heard from the direction of the rampart. I looked out of the window, and saw a wagon from the arsenal, some citizen gunners; old Goulden, Holender, Jacob Cloutier, and Barrier galloped at its sides; Captain Jovis ran in front. They stopped at our door.

"Call the iron-merchant!" cried the captain. "Tell him to come down."

Baker Chanoine, the brigadier of the second battery, came up. I opened the door.

"What do you want of me?" I asked in the stairway.

"Come down, Moses," said Chanoine. And I went down.

Captain Jovis, a tall old man, with his face covered with sweat, in spite of the cold, said to me, "You are Moses, the iron-merchant?"

"Yes, sir."

"Open your storehouse. Your iron is required for the defence of the city."

So I had to lead all these people into my court, under the shed. The captain on looking round, saw some cast-iron bars, which were used at that time for closing up the backs of fireplaces. They weighed from thirty to forty pounds each, and I sold a good many in the vicinity of the city. There was no lack of old nails, rusty bolts, and old iron of all sorts.

"This is what we want," said he. "Break up these bars, and take away the old iron, quick!"

The others, with the help of our two axes, began at once to break up everything. Some of them filled a basket with the pieces of cast-iron, and ran with it to the wagon.

The captain looked at his watch, and said, "Make haste! We have just ten minutes!"

I thought to myself, "They have no need of credit; they take what they please; it is more convenient."

All my bars and old iron were broken in pieces—more than fifteen hundred pounds of iron.

As they were starting to run to the ramparts, Chanoine laughed, and said to me, "Capital grapeshot, Moses! Thou canst get ready thy pennies. "We'll come and take them tomorrow."

The wagon started through the crowd which ran behind it, and I followed too.

As we came nearer the ramparts the firing became more and more frequent. As we turned from the curate's house two sentinels stopped everybody, but they let me pass on account of my iron, which they were going to fire.

You can never imagine that mass of people, the noise around the bastion, the smoke which covered it, the orders of the infantry officers whom we heard going up the glacis, the gunners, the lighted match, caissons with the piles of bullets behind! No, in all these thirty years I have not forgotten those men with their levers, running back the cannon to load them to their mouths; those firings in file, at the bottom of the ramparts; those volleys of balls hissing in the air; the orders of the gun-captains, "Load! Ram! Prime!"

What crowds upon those gun-carriages, seven feet high, where the gunners were obliged to stand and stretch their arms to fire the cannon! And what a frightful smoke!

Men invent such machines to destroy each other, and they would think that they did a great deal if they sacrificed a quarter as much to assist their fellow-men, to instruct them in infancy, and to give them a little bread in their old age.

Ah! those who make an outcry against war, and demand a different state of things, are not in the wrong.

I was in the corner, at the left of the bastion, where the stairs go down to the postern behind the college, among three or four willow baskets as high as chimneys, and filled with clay. I ought to have stayed there quietly, and made use of the right moment to get away, but the thought seized me that I would go and see what was going on below the ramparts, and while they were loading the cannon, I climbed to the level of the glacis, and lay down flat between two enormous baskets, where there was scarcely a chance that balls could reach me.

If hundreds of others who were killed in the bastions had done as I did, how many of them might be still living, respectable fathers of families in their villages!

Lying in this place, and raising my nose, I could see over the whole plain. I saw the cordon of the rampart below, and the line of our skirmishers behind the *palankas*, on the other side of the moat; they did nothing but tear off their cartridges, prime, charge, and fire. There one could appreciate the beauty of drilling; there were only two companies of them, and their firing by file kept up an incessant roll.

Farther on, directly to the right, stretched the road to Quatre-Vents. The Ozillo farm, the cemetery, the horse-post-station, and George Mouton's farm at the right; the inn of La Roulette and the great poplar-walk at the left, all were full of Cossacks, and such-like rascals, who were galloping into the very gardens, to reconnoitre the environs of the place. This is what I suppose, for it is against nature to run without an object, and to risk being struck by a ball.

These people, mounted on small horses, with large gray cloaks, soft boots, fox-skin caps, like those of the Baden peasants, long beards, lances in rest, great pistols in their belts, came whirling on like birds.

They had not been fired upon as yet, because they kept themselves scattered, so that bullets would have no effect; but their trumpets sounded the rally from La Roulette, and they began to collect behind the buildings of the inn.

About thirty of our veterans, who had been kept back in the cemetery lane, were making a slow retreat; they made a few paces, at the same time hastily reloading, then turned, shouldered, fired, and began marching again among the hedges and bushes, which there had not been time to cut down in this locality.

Our sergeant was one of these; I recognized him at once, and trembled for him.

Every time these veterans gave fire, five or six Cossacks came on like the wind, with their lances lowered; but it did not frighten them: they leaned against a tree and levelled their bayonets.

Other veterans came up, and then some loaded, while others parried the blows. Scarcely had they torn open their cartridges when the Cossacks fled right and left, their lances in the air. Some of them turned for a moment and fired their large pistols behind like regular bandits. At length our men began to march toward the city.

Those old soldiers, with their great shakos set square on their heads, their large capes hanging to the back of their calves, their sabres and cartridge-boxes on their backs, calm in the midst of these savages, reloading, trimming, and parrying as quietly as if they were smoking their pipes in the guard-house, were something to be admired. At last, after seeing them come out of the whirlwind two or three times, it seemed almost an easy thing to do.

Our sergeant commanded them. I understood then why he was such a favourite with the officers, and why they always took his part against the citizens: there were not many such. I wanted to call out, "Make haste, sergeant; let us make haste!"but neither he nor his men hurried in the least.

As they reached the foot of the glacis, suddenly a huge mass of Cossacks, seeing that they were escaping, galloped up in two files, to cut off their retreat. It was a dangerous moment, and they formed in a square instantly.

I felt my back turn cold, as if I had been one of them.

Our sharpshooters behind the ammunition wagons did not fire, doubtless for fear of hitting their comrades; our gunners on the bastion leaned down to see, and the file of Cossacks stretched to the corner near the drawbridge.

There were seven or eight hundred of them. We heard them cry, "Hurra! hurra! hurra!"like crows. Several officers in green cloaks and small caps galloped at the sides of their lines, with raised sabres. I thought our poor sergeant and his thirty men were lost; I thought already, "How sorry little Sâfel and Sorlé will be!"

But then, as the Cossacks formed in a half-circle at the left of the outworks, I heard our gun-captain call out, "Fire!"

I turned my head; old Goulden struck the match, the fusee glittered, and at the same instant the bastion with its great baskets of clay shook to the very rocks of the rampart.

I looked toward the road; nothing was to be seen but men and horses on the ground.

Just then came a second shot, and I can truly say that I saw the grapeshot pass like the stroke of a scythe into that mass of cavalry; it all tumbled and fell; those who a second before were living beings were now nothing. We saw some try to raise themselves, the rest made their escape.

The firing by file began again, and our gunners, without waiting for the smoke to clear away, reloaded so quickly that the two discharges seemed to come at once.

This mass of old nails, bolts, broken bits of cast iron, flying three hundred metres, almost to the little bridge, made such slaughter that, some days after, the Russians asked for an armistice in order to bury their dead.

Four hundred were found scattered in the ditches of the road.

This I saw myself.

And if you want to see the place where those savages were buried, you have only to go up the cemetery lane.

On the other side, at the right, in M. Adam Ottendorf's orchard, you will see a stone cross in the middle of the fence; they were all buried there, with their horses, in one great trench.

You can imagine the delight of our gunners at seeing this massacre. They lifted up their sponges and shouted, "*Vive l'Empereur!*"

The soldiers shouted back from the covered ways, and the air was filled with their cries.

Our sergeant, with his thirty men, their guns on their shoulders, quietly reached the glacis. The barrier was quickly opened for them, but the two companies descended together to the moat and came up again by the postern.

I was waiting for them above.

When our sergeant came up I took him by the arm, "Ah,

sergeant!"said I, "how glad I am to see you out of danger!"

I wanted to embrace him. He laughed and squeezed my hand.

"Then you saw the engagement, Father Moses!"said he, with a mischievous wink. "We have shown them what stuff the Fifth is made of!"

"Oh, yes! yes! you have made me tremble."

"Bah!"said he, "you will see a good deal more of it; it is a small affair."

The two companies re-formed against the wall of the *chemin de ronde*, and the whole city shouted, "*Vive l'Empereur!*"

They went down the rampart street in the midst of the crowd. I kept near our sergeant.

As the detachment was turning our corner, Sorlé, Zeffen, and Sâfel called out from the windows, "Hurrah for the veterans! Hurrah for the Fifth!"

The sergeant saw them and made a little sign to them with his head. As I was going in I said to him, "Sergeant, don't forget your glass of cherry-brandy."

"Don't worry, Father Moses," said he.

The detachment went on to break ranks at the Place d'Armes as usual, and I went up home at a quarter to four. I was scarcely in the room before Zeffen, Sorlé, and Sâfel threw their arms round me as if I had come back from the war; little Dayid clung to my knee, and they all wanted to know the news.

I had to tell them about the attack, the grapeshot, the routing of the Cossacks. But the table was ready. I had not had my breakfast, and I said, "Let us sit down. You shall hear the rest by and by. Let me take breath."

Just then the sergeant entered in fine spirits, and set the butt-end of his musket on the floor. We were going to meet him when we saw a tuft of red hair on the point of his bayonet, that made us tremble.

"Mercy, what is that?" said Zeffen, covering her face.

He knew nothing about it, and looked to see, much surprised.

"That?" said he, "oh! it is the beard of a Cossack that I touched as I passed him—it is not much of anything."

He took the musket at once to his own room; but we were all horror-struck, and Zeffen could not recover herself. When the sergeant came back she was still sitting in the armchair, with both hands before her face.

"Ah, Madame Zeffen," said he sadly, "now you are going to detest me!"

I thought, too, that Zeffen would be afraid of him, but women always like these men who risk their lives at random. I have seen it a hundred times. And Zeffen smiled as she answered: "No, sergeant, no; these Cossacks ought to stay at home and not come and trouble us! You protect us—we love you very much!"

I persuaded him to breakfast with us, and it ended by his opening a window, and calling out to some soldiers passing by to give notice at the cantine that Sergeant Trubert was not coming to breakfast.

So we were all calmed down, and seated ourselves at the table. Sorlé went down to get a bottle of good wine, and we began to eat our breakfast.

We had coffee, too, and Zeffen wanted to pour it out herself for the sergeant. He was delighted.

"Madame Zeffen," said he, "you load me with kindness!"

She laughed. We had never been happier.

While he was taking his cherry-brandy, the sergeant told us all about the attack in the night; the way in which the Wurtemberg troops had stationed themselves at La Roulette, how it had been necessary to dislodge them as they were forcing open the two large gates, the arrival of the Cossacks at daybreak, and the sending out two companies to fire at them.

He told all this so well that we could almost think we saw it. But about eleven o'clock, as I took up the bottle to pour out another glassful, he wiped his moustache, and said, as he rose: "No, Father Moses, we have something to do besides taking our ease and enjoying ourselves; tomorrow, or next day, the shells will be coming; it is time to go and screen the garret."

We all became sober at these words.

"Let us see!"said he; "I have seen in your court some long logs of wood which have not been sawed, and there are three or four large beams against the wall. Are we two strong enough to carry them up? Let us try!"

He was going to take off his cape at once; but, as the beams were very heavy, I told him to wait and I would run for the two Carabins, Nicolas, who was called the Greyhound, and Mathis, the wood- sawyer. They came at once, and, being used to heavy work, they carried up the timber. They had brought their saws and axes with them; the sergeant made them saw the beams, so as to cross them above in the form of a sentry-box. He worked himself like a regular carpenter, and Sorlé, Zeffen, and I looked on. As it took some time, my wife and daughter went down to prepare supper, and I went down with them, to get a lantern for the workmen.

I was going up again very quietly, never thinking of danger, when, suddenly, a frightful noise, a kind of terrible rumbling, passed along the roof, and almost made me drop my lantern.

The two Carabins turned pale and looked at each other.

"It is a ball!"said the sergeant.

At the same time a loud sound of cannon in the distance was heard in the darkness.

I had a terrible feeling in my stomach, and I thought to my- self, "Since one ball has passed, there may be two, three, four!"

My strength was all gone. The two Carabins doubtless thought the same, for they took down at once their waistcoats, which were hanging on the gable, to go away.

"Wait!" said the sergeant. "It is nothing. Let us keep at our work—it is going on well. It will be done in an hour more."

But the elder Carabin called out, "You may do as you please! I am not going to stay here—I have a family!"

And while he was speaking, a second ball, more frightful than the first, began to rumble upon the roof, and five or six seconds after we heard the explosion.

It was astonishing! The Russians were firing from the edge of the Bois-de-Chênes, more than a half -hour distant, and yet we saw the red flash pass before our two windows, and even under the tiles.

The sergeant tried to keep us still at work.

"Two bullets never pass in the same place," said he. "We are in a safe spot, since that has grazed the roof. Come, let us go to work!"

It was too much for us. I placed the lantern on. the floor and went down, feeling as if my thighs were broken. I wanted to sit down at every step.

Out of doors they were shouting as if it were morning, and in a more frightful way. Chimneys were falling, and women running to the windows; but I paid no attention to it, I was so frightened myself.

The two Carabins had gone away paler than death.

All that night I was ill. Sorlé and Zeffen were no more at ease than myself. The sergeant kept on alone, placing the logs and making them fast. About midnight he came down.

"Father Moses," said he, "the roof is screened, but your two men are cowards; they left me alone."

I thanked him, and told him that we were all sick, and as for myself I had never felt anything like it. He laughed.

"I know what that is," said he. "Conscripts always feel so when they hear the first ball; but that is soon over—they only need to get a little used to it."

Then he went to bed, and everybody in the house, except myself, went to sleep.

The Russians did not fire after ten o'clock that night; they had only tried one or two field-pieces, to warn us of what they had in store.

All this, Fritz, was but the beginning of the blockade; you are going to hear now of the miseries we endured for three months.

CHAPTER 13

A Deserter Captured

The city was joyful the next day, notwithstanding the firing in the night. A number of men who came from the ramparts about seven o'clock, came down our street shouting: "They are gone! There is not a single Cossack to be seen in the direction of Quatre-Vents, nor behind the barracks of the Bois-de-Chênes! *Vive l'Empereur!*"

Everybody ran to the bastions.

I had opened one of our windows, and leaned out in my nightcap. It was thawing, the snow was sliding from the roofs, and that in the streets was melting in the mud. Sorlé, who was turning up our bed, called to me: "Do shut the window, Moses! We shall catch cold from the draught!"

But I did not listen. I laughed as I thought: "The rascals have had enough of my old bars and rusty nails; they have found out that they fly a good way: experience is a good thing!"

I could have stayed there till night to hear the neighbours talk about the clearing away of the Russians, and those who came from the ramparts declaring that there was not one to be seen in the whole region. Some said that they might come back, but that seemed to me contrary to reason. It was clear that the villains would not quit the country at once, that they would still for a long time pillage the villages, and live on the peasants; but to believe that the officers would excite their men to take our city, or that the soldiers would be foolish enough to obey them, never entered my head.

At last Zeffen came into our room to dress the children, and I shut the window. A good fire roared in the stove. Sorlé made ready our breakfast, while Zeffen washed her little Esdras in a basin of warm water.

"Ah, now, if I could only hear from Baruch, it would all be well," said she.

Little David played on the floor with Sâfel, and I thanked the Lord for having delivered us from the scoundrels.

While we were at breakfast, I said to my wife:"It has all gone well! We shall be shut up for a while until the Emperor has carried the day, but they will not fire upon us, they will be satisfied with blockading us; and bread, wine, meats, and brandies, will grow dearer. It is the right time for us to sell, or else we might fare like the people of Samaria when Ben-Hadad besieged their city.

There was a great famine, so that the head of an ass sold for four-score pieces of silver, and the fourth part of a *cab* of dove's-dung for five pieces. It was a good price; but still the merchants were holding back, when a noise of chariots and horses and of a great host came from heaven, and made the Syrians escape with Ben-Hadad, and after the people had pillaged their camp, a measure of fine flour sold for only a *shekel*, and two measures of barley for a *shekel*. So let us try to sell while things are at a reasonable price; we must begin in good season."

Sorlé assented, and after breakfast I went down to the cellar to go on with the mixing.

Many of the mechanics had gone back to their work. Klipfel's hammer sounded on his anvil. Chanoine put back his rolls into his windows, and Tribolin, the druggist, his bottles of red and blue water behind his panes.

Confidence was restored everywhere. The citizen-gunners had taken off their uniforms, and the joiners had come back to finish our counter; the noise of the saw and plane filled the house.

Everybody was glad to return to his own business, for war brings nothing but harm; the sooner it is over the better.

As I carried my jugs from one tun to another, in the cellar, I saw the passers-by stop before our old shop, and heard them say to each other, "Moses is going to make his fortune with the brandy; these rascals of Jews always have good scent; while we have been selling this month past, he has been buying. Now that we are shut up he can sell at any price he pleases."

You can judge whether that was not pleasant to hear! A man's greatest happiness is to succeed in his business; everybody is obliged to say: "This man has neither army, nor generals, nor cannon, he has nothing but his own wit, like everybody else; when he succeeds he owes it to himself, and not to the courage of others. And then he ruins no one; he does not rob, or steal, or kill; while, in war, the strongest crushes the weakest and often the best."

So I worked on with great zeal, and would have kept on till night if little Sâfel had not come to call me to dinner. I was hungry, and was going upstairs, glad in the thought of sitting down in the midst of my children, when the call-beat began on the Place d'Armes, before the town-house. During a blockade a court-martial sits continually at the mayoralty to try those who do not answer to the call. Some of my neighbours were already leaving their houses with their muskets on their shoulders.

I had to go up very hastily, and swallow a little soup, a morsel of meat, and a glass of wine.

I was very pale. Sorlé, Zeffen, and the children said not a word. The drum corps continued the call to arms; it came down the main street and stopped at last before our house, on the little square. Then I ran for my cartridge-box and musket.

"Ah!" said Sorlé, "we thought we were going to have a quiet time, and now it is all beginning again."

Zeffen did not speak, but burst into tears.

At that moment the old Rabbi Heymann came in, with his old martin-skin cap drawn down to the nape of his neck.

"For heaven's sake let the women and children hurry to the casemates! An envoy has come threatening to burn the whole city if the gates are not opened. Fly, Sorlé! Zeffen, fly!"

Imagine the cries of the women on hearing this; as for myself, my hair stood on end.

"The rascals have no shame in them!"I exclaimed. "They have no pity on women or children! May the curse of heaven fall on them!"

Zeffen threw herself into my arms. I did not know what to do.

But the old rabbi said:"They are doing to us what our people have done to them! So the words of the Lord are fulfilled: *As thou hast done unto thy brother so shall it be done unto thee!*—But, you must fly quickly."

Below, the call-beat had ceased; my knees trembled. Sorlé, who never lost courage, said to me: "Moses, run to the square, make haste, or they will send you to prison!"

Her judgment was always right; she pushed me by the shoulders, and in spite of Zeffen's tears I went down, calling out: "Rabbi, I trust in you—save them!"

I could not see clearly; I went through the snow, miserable man that I was, running to the town-house where the National Guard was already assembled. I came just in time to answer the call, and you can imagine my trouble, for Zeffen, Sorlé, Sâfel, and the little ones were abandoned before my eyes. What was Phalsburg to me? I would have opened the gates in a minute to have had peace.

The others did not look any better pleased than myself; they were all thinking of their families.

Our governor, Moulin, Lieutenant-Colonel Brancion, and Captains Renvoyé,Vigneron, Grébillet, with their great military caps put on crosswise, these alone felt no anxiety. They would have murdered and burnt everything for the Emperor.The governor even laughed, and said that he would surrender the city when the shells set his pocket-handkerchief on fire. Judge from this, how much sense such a being had!

While they were reviewing us, groups of the aged and infirm, of women and children, passed across the square on their way to the casemates.

I saw our little wagon go by with the roll of coverings and mattresses on it. The old rabbi was between the shafts—Sâfel pushed behind. Sorlé carried David, and Zeffen Esdras. They were walking in the mud, with their hair loose as if they were escaping from a fire; but they did not speak, and went on silently in the midst of that great trouble.

I would have given my life to go and help them I must stay in the ranks. Ah, the old men of my time have seen terrible things! How often have they thought:—"Happy is he who lives alone in the world; he suffers only for himself, he does not see those whom he loves weeping and groaning, without the power to help them."

Immediately after the review, detachments of citizen-gunners were sent to the armouries to man the pieces, the firemen were sent to the old market to get out the pumps, and the rest of us, with half a battalion of the Sixth Light Infantry, were sent to the guard-house on the square, to relieve the guards and supply patrols.

The two other battalions had already gone to the advance-posts of Trois-Maisons, of La Fontaine-du-Château,—to the block-houses, the half moons, the Ozillo farm, and the Maisons-Rouges, outside of the city.

Our post at the mayoralty consisted of thirty-two men; sixteen soldiers of the line below, commanded by Lieutenant Schnindret, and sixteen of the National Guard above, commanded by Desplaces Jacob. We used Burrhus's lodging for our guard-house. It was a large hall with six-inch planks, and beams such as you do not find nowadays in our forests. A large, round, cast-iron stove, standing on a slab four feet square, was in the left-hand corner, near the door; the zigzag pipes went into the chimney at the right, and piles of wood covered the floor.

It seems as if I were now in that hall. The melted snow which we shook off on entering ran along the floor. I have never seen a sadder day than that; not only because the bombshells and balls might rain upon us at any moment, and set everything on fire, but because of the melting snow, and the mud, and the dampness which reached your very bones, and the orders of the sergeant, who did nothing but call out: "Such and such an one, march! Such an one forward, it is your turn!"etc.

And then the jests and jokes of this mass of tilers, and cobblers, and plasterers, with their patched blouses, shoes run down at the heel, and caps without visors, seated in a circle around the stove, with their rags sticking to their backs, thouing you like all the rest of their beggarly race: "Moses, pass along the pitcher! Moses, give me some fire!—Ah, rascals of Jews, when a body risks his life to save property, how proud it makes them! Ah, the villains!"

And they winked at each other, and pushed each other's elbows, and made up faces askance. Some of them wanted me to go and get some tobacco for them, and pay for it myself! In fine, all sorts of insults, which a respectable man could endure from the rabble! Yes, it disgusts me whenever I think of it.

In this guard-house, where we burned whole logs of wood as if they were straw, the steaming old rags which came in soaking wet did not smell very pleasantly. I had to go out every minute to the little platform behind the hall, in order to breathe, and the cold water which the wind blew from the spout sent me in again at once.

Afterward, in thinking it over, it has seemed as if, without these troubles, my heart would have broken at the thought of Sorlé, Zeffen, and the children shut up in a cellar, and that these very annoyances preserved my reason.

This lasted till evening. We did nothing but go in and out, sit down, smoke our pipes, and then begin again to walk the pavement in the rain, or remain on duty for hours together at the entrance of the posterns.

Toward nine o'clock, when all was dark without, and nothing was to be heard but the pacing of the patrols, the shouts of the sentries on the ramparts: "Sentries, attention!"and the steps of our men on their rounds up and down the great wooden stairway of the admiralty, the thought suddenly came to me that the Russians had only tried to frighten us, that it meant nothing;

and that there would be no shells that night.

In order to be on good terms with the men, I had asked Monborne's permission to go and get a jug full of brandy, which he at once granted. I took advantage of the opportunity to bite a crust and drink a glass of wine at home. Then I went back, and all the men at the station were very friendly; they passed the jug from one to another, and said that my brandy was very good, and that the sergeant would give me leave to go and fill it as often as I pleased.

"Yes, since it is Moses," replied Monborne, "he may have leave, but nobody else."

We were all on excellent terms with each other and nobody thought of bombardment, when a red flash passed along the high windows of the room. We all turned round, and in a few seconds the shell rumbled on the Bichelberg Hill. At the same time a second, then a third flash passed, one after the other, through the large dark room, showing us the houses opposite.

You can never have an idea, Fritz, of those first lights at night! Corporal Winter, an old soldier, who grated tobacco for Tribou, stooped down quietly and lighted his pipe, and said: "Well, the dance is beginning!"

Almost instantly we heard a shell burst at the right in the infantry quarters, another at the left in the Piplinger house on the square, and another quite near us in the Hemmerlé house.

I can't help trembling as I think of it now after thirty years.

All the women were in the casemates, except some old servants who did not want to leave their kitchens; they screamed out: "Help! Fire!"

We were all sure that we were lost; only the old soldiers, crooked on their bench by the stove, with their pipes in their mouths, seemed very calm, as people might who have nothing to lose.

What was worst of all, at the moment when our cannon at the arsenal and powder-house began to answer the Russians', and made every pane of glass in the old building rattle, Sergeant Monborne called out: "Somme, Chevreux, Moses, Dubourg:

Forward!"

To send fathers of families roaming about through the mud, in danger, at every step, of being struck by bursting shells, tiles, and whole chimneys falling on their backs, is something against nature; the very mention of it makes me perfectly furious.

Somme and the big innkeeper Chevreux turned round, full of indignation also; they wanted to exclaim: "It is abominable!"

But that rascal of a Monborne was sergeant, and nobody dared speak a word or even give a side-look; and as Winter, the corporal of the round, had taken down his musket, and made a signal for us to go on, we all took our arms and followed him.

As we went down the stairway, you should have seen the red light, flash after flash, lighting up every nook and corner under the stairs and the worm-eaten rafters; you should have heard our twenty-four pounders thunder; the old rat-hole shook to its foundations, and seemed as if it was all falling to pieces. And under the arch below, toward the Place d'Armes, this light shone from the snow banks to the tops of the roofs, showing the glittering pavements, the puddles of water, the chimneys, and dormer-windows, and, at the very end of the street, the cavalry barracks, even the sentry in his box near the large gate:—what a sight!

"It is all over! We are all lost!" I thought.

Two shells passed at this moment over the city: they were the first that I had seen; they moved so slowly that I could follow them through the dark sky; both fell in the trenches, behind the hospital. The charge was too heavy, luckily for us.

I did not speak, nor did the others—we kept our thoughts to ourselves. We heard the calls "Sentries, attention!" answered from one bastion to another all around the place, warning us of the terrible danger we were in.

Corporal Winter, with his old faded blouse, coarse cotton cap, stooping shoulders, musket in shoulder-belt, pipe-end between his teeth, and lantern full of tallow swinging at arm's length, walked before us, calling out: "Look out for the shells! Lie flat! Do you hear?"

I have always thought that veterans of this sort despise citizens, and that he said this to frighten us still more.

A little farther on, at the entrance of the *cul-de-sac* where Cloutier lived, he halted.

"Come on!"he called, for we marched in file without seeing each other. When we had come up to him he said, "There, now, you men, try to keep together! Our patrol is to prevent fire from breaking out anywhere; as soon as we see a shell pass, Moses will run up and snatch the fuse."

He burst into a laugh as he spoke, so that my anger was roused.

"I have not come here to be laughed at," said I; "if you take me for a fool, I will throw down my musket and cartridge-box, and go to the casemates."

He laughed harder than ever. "Moses, respect thy superiors, or beware of the court-martial!"said he.

The others would have laughed too, but the shell flashes began again; they went down the rampart street, driving the air before them like gusts of wind; the cannon of the arsenal bastion had just fired. At the same time a shell burst in the street of the Capuchins; Spick's chimney and half his roof fell to the ground with a frightful noise.

"Forward! March!"called Winter.

They had now all become sober. We followed the lantern to the French gate. Behind us, in the street of the Capuchins, a dog howled incessantly. Now and then Winter stopped, and we all listened; nothing was stirring, and nothing was to be heard but the dog and the cries: "Sentries, attention!"The city was as still as death.

We ought to have gone into the guard-house, for there was nothing to be seen; but the lantern went on toward the gate, swinging above the gutter. That Winter had taken too much brandy!

"We are of no use in this street," said Chevreux; "we can't keep the balls from passing."

But Winter kept calling out:"Are you coming?"And we had to obey.

In front of Genodet's stables, where the old barns of the *gendarmerie* begin, a lane turned to the left toward the hospital. This was full of manure and heaps of dirt—a drain in fact. Well, this rascal of a Winter turned into it, and as we could not see our feet without the lantern, we had to follow him. We went groping, under the roofs of the sheds, along the crazy old walls. It seemed as if we should never get out of this gutter; but at last we came out near the hospital in the midst of the great piles of manure, which were heaped against the grating of the sewer.

It seemed a little lighter, and we saw the roof of the French gate, and the line of fortifications black against the sky; and almost immediately I perceived the figure of a man gliding among the trees at the top of the rampart. It was a soldier stooping so, that his hands almost touched the ground. They did not fire on this side; the distant flashes passed over the roofs, and did not lighten the streets below.

I caught Winter's arm, and pointed out to him this man; he instantly hid his lantern under his blouse. The soldier whose back was toward us, stood up, and looked round, apparently listening. This lasted for two or three minutes; then he passed over the rampart at the corner of the bastion, and we heard something scrape the wall of the rampart.

Winter immediately began to run, crying out: "A deserter! To the postern!"

"We had heard before this of deserters slipping down into the trenches by means of their bayonets. We all ran. The sentry called out: "Who goes there?"

"The citizen patrol," replied Winter.

He advanced, gave the order, and we went down the postern steps like wild beasts.

Below, at the foot of the large bastions built on the rock, we saw nothing but snow, large black stones, and bushes covered with frost. The deserter needed only to keep still under the bushes; our lantern, which shone only for fifteen or twenty feet, might have wandered about till morning without discovering him: and we should ourselves have supposed that he had escaped. But unfortunately for him, fear urged him on, and we saw him in the distance running to the stairs which lead up to the covered ways. He went like the wind.

"Halt! or I fire!" cried Winter; but he did not stop, and we all ran together on his track, calling out "Halt! Halt!"

Winter had given me the lantern so as to run faster; I followed at a distance, thinking to myself: "Moses, if this man is taken, thou will be the cause of his death." I wanted to put out the lantern, but if Winter had seen me he would have been capable of knocking me down with the butt-end of his musket. He had for a long time been hoping for the cross, and was all the time expecting it and the pension with it.

The deserter ran, as I said, to the stairs. Suddenly he perceived that the ladder, which takes the place of the eight lower steps, was taken away, and he stopped, stupefied! We came nearer—he heard us and began to run faster, to the right toward the half-moon. The poor devil rolled over the snow-banks. Winter aimed at him, and called out: "Halt! Surrender!"

But he got up and began to run again.

Behind the outworks, under the drawbridge, we thought we had lost him: the corporal called to me, "Come along! A thousand thunders!" and at that moment we saw him leaning against the wall, as pale as death. Winter took him by the collar and said: "I have got you!"

Then he tore an epaulette from his shoulder: "You are not worthy to wear that!" said he; "come along!"

He dragged him out of his corner, and held the lantern before his face. We saw a handsome boy of eighteen or nineteen, tall and slender, with small, light moustaches, and blue eyes.

Seeing him there so pale, with Winter's fist at his throat, I thought of the poor boy's father and mother; my heart smote me, and I could not help saying: "Come, Winter, he is a child, a mere child! He will not do it again!"

But Winter, who thought that now surely his cross was won, turned upon me furiously:

"I tell thee what, Jew, stop, or I will run my bayonet through

WINTER TOOK HIM BY THE COLLAR, AND SAID: "I HAVE YOU NOW."

thy body!"

"Wretch!" thought I, "what will not a man do to make sure of his glass of wine for the rest of his days?"

I had a sort of horror of that man; there are wild beasts in the human race!

Chevreux, Somme, and Dubourg did not speak.

Winter began to walk toward the postern, with his hand on the deserter's collar.

"If he stops," said he, "strike him on the back with your muskets! Ah, scoundrel, you desert in the face of the enemy! Your case is clear: next Sunday you will sleep under the turf of the half-moon! Will you come on? Strike him with the butt-end, you cowards!"

What pained me most was to hear the poor fellow's heavy sighs; he breathed so hard, from his fright at being taken, and knowing that he would be shot, that we could hear him fifteen paces off; the sweat ran down my forehead. And now and then he turned to me and gave me such a look as I shall never forget, as if to say: "Save me!"

If I had been alone with Dubourg and Chevreux, we would have let him go; but Winter would sooner have murdered him.

We came in this way to the foot of the postern. They made the deserter pass first. When we reached the top, a sergeant, with four men from the next station, was already there, waiting for us.

"What is it?" asked the sergeant.

"A deserter," said Winter.

The sergeant—an old man—looked at him, and said: "Take him to the station."

"No," said Winter, "he will go with us to the station on the square."

"I will reinforce you with two men," said the sergeant.

"We do not need them," replied Winter roughly. "We took him ourselves, and we are enough to guard him."

The sergeant saw that we ought to have all the glory of it, and he said no more.

We started off again, shouldering our arms; the prisoner, all in tatters and without his shako, walked in the midst.

We soon came to the little square; we had only to cross the old market before reaching the guard-house. The cannon of the arsenal were firing all the time; as we were starting to leave the market, one of the flashes lighted up the arch in front of us; the prisoner saw the door of the jail at the left, with its great locks, and the sight gave him terrible strength; he tore off his collar, and threw himself from us with both arms stretched out behind.

Winter had been almost thrown down, but he threw himself at once upon the deserter, exclaiming, "Ah, scoundrel, you want to run away!"

We saw no more, for the lantern fell to the ground.

"Guard! guard!" cried Chevreux.

All this took but a moment, and half of the infantry post were already there under arms. Then we saw the prisoner again; he was sitting on the edge of the stairway among the pillars; blood was running from his mouth; not more than half his waistcoat was left, and he was bent forward, trembling from head to foot.

Winter held him by the nape of the neck, and said to Lieutenant Schnindret, who was looking on: "A deserter, lieutenant! He has tried to escape twice, but Winter was on hand."

"That is right," said the lieutenant. "Let them find the jailer."

Two soldiers went away. A number of our comrades of the National Guard had come down, but nobody spoke. However hard men may be, when they see a wretch in such a condition, and think, "the day after tomorrow he will be shot!" everybody is silent, and a good many would even release him if they could.

After some minutes Harmantier arrived with his woollen jacket and his bunch of keys.

The lieutenant said to him, "Lock up this man!"

"Come, get up and walk!" he said to the deserter, who rose and followed Harmantier, while everybody crowded round.

The jailer opened the two massive doors of the prison; the prisoner entered without resistance, and then the large locks and bolts fastened him in.

"Every man return to his post!" said the lieutenant to us. And we went up the steps of the mayoralty.

All this had so upset me that I had not thought of my wife and children. But when once above, in the large warm room, full of smoke, with all that set who were laughing and boasting at having taken a poor, unresisting deserter, the thought that I was the cause of this misery filled my soul with anguish; I stretched myself on the camp-bed, and thought of all the trouble that is in the world, of Zeffen, of Sâfel, of my children, who might, perhaps, some day be arrested for not liking war. And the words of the Lord came to my mind, which He spake to Samuel, when the people desired a king:

Hearken unto the voice of the people in all that they say unto thee; for they have not rejected thee, but they have rejected me, that I should not reign over them. Howbeit yet protest solemnly unto them, and show them the manner of the king that shall reign over them. He will take your sons and appoint them for himself; and some shall run before his chariots. He will set them to make his instruments of war. And he will take your daughters to be cooks and bakers. And he will take your fields and your vineyards, and your olive-yards, even the best of them, and give them to his servants. He will take your men-servants, and your maid-servants, and your goodliest young men. He will take the tenth of your sheep; and ye shall be his servants. And ye shall cry out in that day, and the Lord will not hear you.

These thoughts made me very wretched; my only consolation was in knowing that my sons Frômel and Itzig were in America. I resolved to send Sâfel, David, and Esdras there also, when the time should come.

These reveries lasted till daylight. I heard no longer the shouts of laughter or the jokes of the ragamuffins. Now and then they would come and shake me, and say, "Go, Moses, and fill your brandy jug! The sergeant gives you leave."

But I did not wish to hear them.

About four o'clock in the morning, our arsenal cannon having dismounted the Russian howitzers on the Quatre-Vents hill, the patrols ceased.

Exactly at seven we were relieved. We went down, one by one, our muskets on our shoulders. We were ranged before the mayoralty, and Captain Vigneron gave the orders: "Carry arms! Present arms! Shoulder arms! Break ranks!"

We all dispersed, very glad to get rid of glory.

I was going to run at once to the casemates when I had laid aside my musket, to find Sorlé, Zeffen, and the children; but what was my joy at seeing little Sâfel already at our door! As soon as he saw me turn the corner, he ran to me, exclaiming: "We have all come back! We are waiting for you!"

I stooped to embrace him. At that moment Zeffen opened the window above, and showed me her little Esdras, and Sorlé stood laughing behind them. I went up quickly, blessing the Lord for having delivered us from all our troubles, and exclaiming inwardly:

The Lord is merciful and gracious, slow to anger and plenteous in mercy. Let the glory of the Lord endure forever! Let the Lord rejoice in his works!

Chapter 14

Burguet's Visit to the Deserter

I still think it one of the happiest moments of my life, Fritz. Scarcely had I come up the stairs when Zeifen and Sorlé were in my arms; the little ones clung to my shoulders, and I felt their lovely full lips on my cheeks; Sâfel held my hand, and I could not speak a word, but my eyes filled with tears.

Ah! if we had had Baruch with us, how happy we should have been!

At length I went to lay aside my musket, and hang my cartridge-box in the alcove. The children were laughing, and joy was in the house once more. And when I came back in my old beaver cap, and my large, warm woollen stockings, and sat down in the old arm-chair, in front of the little table set with porringers, in which Zeffen was pouring the soup; when I was again in the midst of all these happy faces, bright eyes, and outstretched hands, I could have sung like an old lark on his branch, over the nest where his little ones were opening their beaks and flapping their wings.

I blessed them in my heart a hundred times over. Sorlé, who saw in my eyes what I was thinking, said: "They are all together, Moses, just as they were yesterday; the Lord has preserved them."

"Yes, blessed be the name of the Lord, forever and ever!" I replied.

While we were at breakfast, Zeffen told me about their going to the large casemate at the barracks, how it was full of people stretched on their mattresses in every direction the cries of some, the fright of others, the torment from the vermin, the water dropping from the arch, the crowds of children who could not sleep, and did nothing but cry, the lamentations of five or six old men who kept calling out, "Ah! our last hour has come! Ah! how cold it is! Ah! we shall never go home—it is all over!"

Then suddenly the deep silence of all, when they heard the cannon about ten o'clock—the reports, coming slowly at first, then like the roar of a tempest—the flashes, which could be seen even through the blindages of the gate, and old Christine Evig telling her beads as loud as if she were in a procession, and the other women responding together.

As she told me this, Zeffen clasped her little Esdras tightly, while I held David on my knees, embracing him as I thought to myself, "Yes, my poor children, you have been through a great deal!"

Notwithstanding the joy of seeing that we were all safe, the thought of the deserter in his dungeon at the town-house would come to me; he too had parents! And when you think of all the trouble which a father and mother have in bringing up a child, of the nights spent in soothing his cries, of their cares when he is sick, of their hopes in seeing him growing up; and then imagine to yourself some old soldiers sitting around a table to try him, and coolly send him to be shot behind the bastion, it makes you shudder, especially when you say to yourself: "But for me, this boy would have been at liberty; he would be on the road to his village; tomorrow perhaps he would have reached the poor old people's door, and have called out to them, 'Open! it is I!'"

Such thoughts are enough to make one wild.

I did not dare to speak to my wife and children of the poor fellow's arrest; I kept my thoughts to myself.

Without, the detachments from La Roulette, Trois-Maisons, and La Fontaine-du-Château, passed through the street, keeping step; groups of children ran about the city to find the pieces of shells; neighbours collected to talk about the events of the night—the roofs torn off, chimneys thrown down, the frights they had had. We heard their voices rising and falling, and their shouts of laughter. And I have since seen that it is always the same thing after a bombardment; the shower is forgotten as soon as it is over, and they exclaim: "Huzza! the enemy is routed!"

While we were there meditating, someone came up the stairs. We listened, and our sergeant, with his musket on his shoulder, and his cape and gaiters covered with mud, opened the door, exclaiming: "Good for you, Father Moses! Good for you!—You distinguished yourself last night!"

"Ha! what is it, sergeant?" asked my wife in astonishment.

"What! has he not told you of the famous thing he did, Madame Sorlé? Has he not told you that the national guard Moses, on patrol about nine o'clock at the Hospital bastion, discovered and then arrested a deserter in the very act! It is on Lieutenant Schnindret's affidavit!"

"But I was not alone," I exclaimed in despair; "there were four of us."

"Bah! You discovered the track, you went down into the trenches, you carried the lantern! Father Moses, you must not try to make your good deed seem less; you are wrong. You are going to be named for corporal. The court-martial will sit to-morrow at nine. Be easy, they will take care of your man!"

Imagine, Fritz, how I looked; Sorlé, Zeffen, and the children looked at me, and I did not know what to say.

"Now I must go and change my clothes," said the sergeant, shaking my hand. "We will talk about it again, Father Moses. I always said that you would turn out well in the end."

He gave a low laugh as was his custom, winking his eyes, and then went across the passage into his room.

My wife was very pale.

"Is it true, Moses?" she asked after a minute.

"He! I did not know that he wanted to desert, Sorlé," I replied. "And then the boy ought to have looked round on all sides; he ought to have gone down on the Hospital square, gone round the dunghills, and even into the lane to see if anyone was coming; he brought it on himself; I did not know anything, I —"

But Sorlé did not let me finish.

"Run quickly, Moses, to Burguet's!"she exclaimed; "if this man is shot, his blood will be upon our children. Make haste, do not lose a minute."

She raised her hands, and I went out, much troubled.

My only fear was that I should not find Burguet at home; fortunately, on opening his door, on the first floor of the old Cauchois house, I saw the tall barber Vésenaire shaving him, in the midst of the old books and papers which filled the room.

Burguet was sitting with the towel at his chin.

"Ah! It is you, Moses!"he exclaimed, in a glad tone. "What gives me the pleasure of a visit from you?"

"I come to ask a favour of you, Burguet."

"If it is for money," said he, "we shall have difficulty."

He laughed, and his servant-woman, Marie Loriot, who heard us from the kitchen, opened the door, and thrust her red head-gear into the room, as she called out, "I think that we shall have difficulty! We owe Vésenaire for three months' shaving; do not we, Vésenaire?"

She said this very seriously, and Burguet, instead of being angry, began to laugh. I have always fancied that a man of his talents had a sort of need of such an incarnation of human stupidity to laugh at, and help his digestion. He never was willing to dismiss this Marie Loriot.

In short, while Vésenaire kept on shaving him, I gave him an account of our patrol and the arrest of the deserter; and begged him to defend the poor fellow. I told him that he alone was able to save him, and restore peace, not only to my own mind, but to Sorlé, Zeffen, and the whole family, for we were all in great distress, and we depended entirely upon him to help us.

"Ah! you take me at my weak point, Moses! If it is possible for me to save this man, I must try. But it will not be an easy matter. During the last fortnight, desertions have begun—the court-martial wishes to make an example. It is a bad business. You have money, Moses; give Vésenaire four *sous* to go and take a drop."

I gave four *sous* to Vésenaire, who made a grand bow and went out. Burguet finished dressing himself.

"Let us go and see!"said he, taking me by the arm.

And we went down together on our way to the mayoralty.

Many years have passed since that day. Ah, well! it seems now as if we were going under the arch, and I heard Burguet saying: "Hey, sergeant! Tell the turnkey that the prisoner's advocate is here."

Harmantier came, bowed, and opened the door.

We went down into the dungeon full of stench, and saw in the right-hand corner a figure gathered in a heap on the straw.

"Get up!"said Harmantier, "here is your advocate."

The poor wretch moved and raised himself in the darkness. Burguet leaned toward him and said: "Come! Take courage! I have come to talk with you about your defence."

And the other began to sob.

When a man has been knocked down, torn to tatters, beaten till he cannot stand, when he knows that the law is against him, that he must die without seeing those whom he loves, he becomes as weak as a baby. Those who maltreat their prisoners are great villains.

"Let us see!"said Burguet. "Sit down on the side of your camp-bed. What is your name? Where did you come from? Harmantier, give this man a little water to drink and wash himself!"

"He has some, M. Burguet; he has some in the corner."

"Ah, well!"

"Compose yourself, my boy!"

The more gently he spoke, the more did the poor fellow weep. At last, however, he said that his family lived near Gérarmer, in the Vosges; that his father's name was Mathieu Belin, and that he was a fisherman at Retournemer.

Burguet drew every word out of his mouth; he wanted to know every particular about his father and mother, his brothers and sisters.

I remember that his father had served under the Republic,

and had even been wounded at Fleurus; that his oldest brother had died in Russia; that he himself was the second son taken from home by the conscription, and that there was still at home three sisters younger than himself.

This came from him slowly; he was so prostrated by Winter's blows, that he moved and sank down like a soulless body.

There was still another thing, Fritz, as you may think the boy was young! and that brought to my mind the days when I used to go in two hours from Phalsburg to Marmoutier, to see Sorlé—Ah, poor wretch! As he told all this, sobbing, with his face in his hands, my heart melted within me.

Burguet was quite overcome. When we were leaving, at the end of an hour, he said, "Come, let us be hopeful!—You will be tried tomorrow. Don't despair! Harmantier, we must give this man a cloak; it is dreadfully cold, especially at night. It is a bad business, my boy, but it is not hopeless. Try to appear as well as you can before the audience; the court-martial always thinks better of a man who is well dressed."

When we were out, he said to me: "Moses, you send the man a clean shirt. His waistcoat is torn; don't forget to have him decently dressed every way; soldiers always judge of a man by his appearance."

"Be easy about that," said I.

The prison doors were closed, and we went across the market.

"Now," said Burguet, "I must go in. I must think it over. It is well that the brother was left in Russia, and that the father has been in the service—it is something to make a point of."

We had reached the corner of the rampart street; he kept on, and I went home more miserable than before.

You cannot imagine, Fritz, how troubled I was; when a man has always had a quiet conscience it is terrible to reproach one's self, and think: "If this man is shot, if his father, and mother, and sisters, and that other one, who is expecting him, are made miserable, thou, Moses, wilt be the cause of it all!"

Fortunately there was no lack of work to be done at home;

Sorlé had just opened the old shop to begin to sell our brandies, and it was full of people. For a week the keepers of coffee-houses and inns had had nothing wherewith to fill their casks; they were on the point of shutting up shop. Imagine the crowd! They came in a row, with their jugs and little casks and pitchers. The old topers came too, sticking out their elbows; Sorlé, Zeffen, and Sâfel had not time to serve them.

The sergeant said that we must put a policeman at our door to prevent quarrels, for some of them said that they lost their turn, and that their money was as good as anybody's.

It will be a good many years before such a crowd will be seen again in front of a Phalsburg shop.

I had only time to tell my wife that Burguet would defend the deserter, and then went down into the cellar to fill the two tuns at the counter, which were already empty.

A fortnight after, Sorlé doubled the price; our first two pipes were sold, and this extra price did not lessen the demand.

Men always find money for brandy and tobacco, even when they have none left for bread. This is why governments impose their heaviest taxes upon these two articles; they might be heavier still without diminishing their use—only, children would starve to death.

I have seen this—I have seen this great folly in men, and I am astonished whenever I think of it. That day we kept on selling until seven o'clock in the evening, when the tattoo was sounded.

My pleasure in making money had made me for- get the deserter; I did not think of him again till after supper, when night set in; but I did not say a word about him; we were all so tired and so delighted with the day's profits that we did not want to be troubled with thinking of such things. But after Zeffen and the children had retired, I told Sorlé of our visit to the prisoner. I told her, too, that Burguet had hopes, which made her very happy.

About nine o'clock, by God's blessing, we were all asleep.

CHAPTER 15

Trial of the Deserter

You can believe, Fritz, that I did not sleep much that night, notwithstanding my fatigue. The thought of the deserter tormented me. I knew that if he should be shot, Zeffen and Sorlé would be inconsolable; and I knew, too, that after three or four years the vile race would say: "Look at this Moses, with his large brown cloak, his cape turned down over the back of his neck, and his respectable look—well, during the blockade he caused the arrest of a poor deserter, who was shot: so much you can trust a Jew's appearance!"

They would have said this, undoubtedly; for the only consolation of villains is to make people think that everybody is like themselves.

And then how often should I reproach myself for this man's death, in times of misfortune or in my old age, when I should not have a minute's peace! How often should I have said that it was a judgment of the Lord, that it was on account of this deserter.

So I wanted to do immediately all that I could, and by six o'clock in the morning I was in my old shop in the market with my lantern, selecting epaulettes and my best clothes. I put them in a napkin and took them to Harmantier at daybreak.

The special council of war, which was called I do not know why—the Ventose council, was to meet at nine o'clock. It was composed of a major, president, four captains, and two lieutenants. Monbrun, the captain of the foreign legion, was judge-advocate, and Brigadier Duphot recorder.

It was astonishing how the whole city knew about it before-hand, and that by seven o'clock the Nicaises, and Pigots, and Vi-natiers, etc., had left their rickety quarters, and had already filled the whole mayoralty, the arch, the stairway, and the large room above, laughing, whistling, stamping, as if it were a bear-fight at Klein's inn, the "Ox."

You do not see things like that nowadays, thank God! men have become more gentle and humane. But after all these wars, a deserter met with less pity than a fox caught in a trap, or a wolf led by the muzzle.

As I saw all this, my courage failed; all my admiration for Burguet's talents could not keep me from thinking:

The man is lost! Who can save him, when this crowd has come on purpose to see him condemned to death, and led to the Glacière bastion?

I was overwhelmed by the thought.

I went trembling into Harmantier's little room, and said to him: "This is for the deserter; take it to him from me."

"All right!" said he.

I asked him if he had confidence in Burguet. He shrugged his shoulders, and said: "We must have examples."

The stamping outside continued, and when I went out there was a great whistling in the balcony, the arch, and everywhere, and shouts of "Moses! hey, Moses! this way!"

But I did not turn my head, and went home very sad.

Sorlé handed me a summons to appear as a witness before the court-martial, which a *gendarme* had just brought; and till nine o'clock I sat meditating behind the stove, trying to think of some way of escape for the prisoner.

Sâfel was playing with the children; Zeffen and Sorlé had gone down to continue our sales.

A few minutes before nine I started for the town-house, which was already so crowded that, had it not been for the guard at the door, and the *gendarmes* scattered within the building, the witnesses could hardly have got in.

Just as I got there, Captain Monbrun was beginning to read his report. Burguet sat opposite, with his head leaning on his hand.

They showed me into a little room, where were Winter, Chevreux, Dubourg, and the *gendarme* Fiegel; so that we didn't hear anything before being called.

On the wall at the right it was written in large letters that any witness who did not tell the truth, should be delivered to the council, and suffer the same penalty as the accused. This made one consider, and I resolved at once to conceal nothing, as was right and sensible. The *gendarme* also informed us that we were forbidden to speak to each other.

After a quarter of an hour Winter was summoned, and then, at intervals of ten minutes, Chevreux, Dubourg, and myself.

When I went into the court-room, the judges were all in their places; the major had laid his hat on the desk before him; the recorder was mending his pen. Burguet looked at me calmly. Without they were stamping, and the major said to the brigadier:

"Inform the public that if this noise continues, I shall have the mayoralty cleared."

The brigadier went out at once, and the major said to me:

"National guard Moses, make your deposition, What do you know?"

I told it all simply. The deserter at the left, between two *gendarmes*, seemed more dead than alive. I would gladly have acquitted him of everything; but when a man fears for himself, when old officers in full dress are scowling at you as if they could see through you, the simplest and best way is not to lie. A father's first thought should be for his children! In short, I told everything that I had seen, nothing more or less, and at last the major said to me:

"That is enough; you may go."

But seeing that the others, Winter, Chevreux, Dubourg, remained sitting on a bench at the left, I did the same.

Almost immediately five or six good-for-nothings began to

stamp and murmur, "Shoot him! shoot him!" The president ordered the brigadier to arrest them, and in spite of their resistance they were all led to prison. Silence was then established in the court-room, but the stampings without continued.

"Judge-advocate, it is your turn to speak," said the major.

This judge-advocate, who seems now before my eyes, and whom I can almost hear speak, was a man of fifty, short and thick, with a short neck, long, thick, straight nose, very wide forehead, shining black hair, thin moustaches, and bright eyes. While he was listening, his head turned right and left as if on a pivot; you could see his long nose and the corner of his eye, but his elbows did not stir from the table. He looked like one of those large crows which seem to be sleeping in the fields at the close of autumn, and yet see everything that is going on around them.

Now and then he raised his arm as if to draw back his sleeve, as advocates have a way of doing. He was in full dress, and spoke terribly well, in a clear and strong voice, stopping and looking at the people to see if they agreed with him; and if he saw even a slight grimace, he began again at once in some other way, and, as it were, obliged you to understand in spite of yourself.

As he went on very slowly, without hurrying or forgetting anything, to show that the deserter was on the road when we arrested him, that he not only had the intention of escaping, but was already outside of the city, quite as guilty as if he had been found in the ranks of the enemy—as he clearly showed all this, I was angry because he was right, and I thought to myself, "Now, what was there to be said in reply."

And then, when he said that the greatest of crimes was to abandon one's flag, because one betrays at once his country, his family, all that has a right to his life, and makes himself unworthy to live; when he said that the court would follow the conscience of all who had a heart, of all who held to the honour of France; that he would give a new example of his zeal for the safety of the country and the glory of the Emperor; that he would show the new recruits that they could only succeed by doing their duty and by obeying orders; when he said all this with terrible power and clearness, and I heard from time to time, a murmur of assent and admiration, then, Fritz, I thought that the Lord alone was able to save that man!

The deserter sat motionless, his arms folded on the dock, and his face upon them. He felt, doubtless, as I did, and everyone in the room, and the court itself. Those old men seemed pleased as they heard the judge-advocate express so well what had all along been their own opinion. Their faces showed their satisfaction.

This lasted for more than an hour. The captain sometimes stopped a moment to give his audience time to reflect on what he had said. I have always thought that he must have been attorney-general, or something more dangerous still to deserters.

I remember that he said, in closing, "You will make an example! You will be of one mind. You will not forget that, at this time, firmness in the court is more necessary than ever to the safety of the country."

When he sat down, such a murmur of approbation arose in the room that it reached the stairway at once, and we heard the shouts outside, "*Vive l'Empereur!*"

The major and the other members of the council looked smilingly at each other, as if to say, "It is all settled. What remains is a mere formality!"

The shouts without increased. This lasted more than ten minutes. At last the major said:

"Brigadier, if the tumult continues, clear the town-house! Begin with the courtroom!"

There was silence at once, for everyone was curious to know what Burguet would say in reply. I would not have given two farthings for the life of the deserter.

"Counsel for the prisoner, you have the floor!" said the major, and Burguet rose.

Now, Fritz, if I had an idea that I could repeat to you what Burguet said, for a whole hour, to save the life of a poor conscript; if I should try to depict his face, the sweetness of his voice, and then his heart-rending cries, and then his silent pauses and his appeals—if I had such an idea, I should consider myself a being full of pride and vanity!

No; nothing finer was ever heard. It was not a man speaking; it was a mother, trying to snatch her babe from death! Ah! what a great thing it is to have this power of moving to tears those who hear us! But we ought not to call it talent, it is heart.

"Who is there without faults? Who does not need pity?"

This is what he said, as he asked the council if they could find a perfectly blameless man; if evil thoughts never came to the bravest; if they had never, for even a day or a moment, had the thought of running away to their native village, when they were young, when they were eighteen, when father and mother and the friends of their childhood were living, and they had not another in the world. A poor child without instruction, without knowledge of the world, brought up at hap-hazard, thrown into the army—what could you expect of him? What fault of his could not be pardoned? What does he know of country, the honour of his flag, the glory of his Majesty? Is it not later in life that these great ideas come to him?

And then he asked those old men if they had not a son, if they were sure that, even at that moment, that son were not committing an offence which was liable to the punishment of death. He said to them:

"Plead for him! What would you say? You would say, 'I am an old soldier. For thirty years I have shed my blood for France. I have grown gray upon the battle-fields, I am riddled with wounds, I have gained every rank at the point of the sword. Ah, well! take my epaulettes, take my decorations, take everything; but save my child! Let my blood be the ransom for his offence! He does not know the greatness of his crime; he is too young; he is a conscript; he loved us; he longed to embrace us, and then go back again he loved a maiden. Ah! you, too, have been young! Pardon him. Do not disgrace an old soldier in his son.'

"Perhaps you could say, too, 'I had other sons. They died for their country. Let their blood answer for his, and give me back this one the last that I have left!'

"This is what you would say, and far better than I, because you would be the father, the old soldier speaking of his own services! Well, the father of this youth could speak like you! He is an old soldier of the Republic! He went with you, perhaps, when the Prussians entered Champagne! He was wounded at Fleurus! He is an old comrade in arms! His oldest son was left behind in Russia!"

And Burguet turned pale as he spoke. It seemed as if grief had robbed him of his strength, and he were about to fall. The silence was so great that we heard the breathing throughout the courtroom. The deserter sobbed. Everybody thought, "It is done! Burguet need say no more! It must be that he has gained his cause!"

But all at once he began again in another and more tender manner. Speaking slowly, he described the life of a poor peasant and his wife, who had but one comfort, one solitary hope on earth their child! As we listened we saw these poor people, we heard them talk together, we saw over the door the old *chapeau* of the time of the Republic. And when we were thinking only of this, suddenly Burguet showed us the old man and his wife learning that their son had been killed, not by Russians or Germans, but by Frenchmen. We heard the old man's cry!

But it was terrible, Fritz! I wanted to run away. The officers of the council, several of whom were married men, looked before them with fixed eyes, and clinched hands; their gray moustaches shook. The major had raised his hand two or three times, as if to signify that it was enough, but Burguet had always something still more powerful, more just, more grand to add. His plea lasted till nearly eleven, when he sat down. There was not a murmur to be heard in the three rooms nor outside.

And the judge-advocate on the other side began again, saying that all that signified nothing, that it was unfortunate for the father that his son was unworthy, that every man clung to his children, that soldiers must be taught not to desert in face of the enemy; that, if the court yielded to such arguments, nobody would ever be shot, discipline would be utterly destroyed, the army could not exist, and that the army was the strength and glory of the country.

Burguet replied almost immediately. I cannot recall what he said; my head could not hold so many things at once: but I shall never forget this, that about one o'clock, the council having sent us away that they might deliberate the prisoner meanwhile having been taken back to his cell after a few minutes we were allowed to return, and the major, standing on the platform where conscriptions were drawn, declared that the accused Jean Balin was acquitted, and gave the order for his immediate release.

It was the first acquittal since the departure of the Spanish prisoners before the blockade; the rowdies, who had come in crowds to see a man condemned and shot, could not believe it; several of them exclaimed: "We are cheated!"

But the major ordered Brigadier Descarmes to take the names of these brawlers, so that they should be seen to; then the whole mass trampled down the stairs in five minutes, and we, in our turn, were able to descend.

I had taken Burguet by the arm, my eyes full of tears.

"Are you satisfied, Moses?" said he, already quite his own joyous self again.

"Burguet!" said I, "Aaron himself, the own brother of Moses, and the greatest orator of Israel, could not have spoken better than you did; it was admirable! I owe my peace of mind to you! Whatever you may ask for so great a service I am ready to give to the extent of my means."

We went down the stairs; the members of the council following us thoughtfully, one by one. Burguet smiled.

"Do you mean it, Moses?" said he, stopping under the arch.

"Yes, here is my hand."

"Very well!" said he, "I ask you to give me a good dinner at the *Ville-de-Metz*."

"With all my heart !"

Several citizens, Father Parmentier, Cochois the tax-gatherer, and Adjutant Muller, were waiting for Burguet at the foot of the mayoralty steps, to congratulate him. As they were surrounding and shaking hands with him, Sâfel came and rushed into my arms; Zeffen had sent him to learn the news. I embraced him, and said joyously: "Go, tell your mother that we have won! Take your dinner. I am going to dine at the *Ville-de-Metz* with Burguet. Make haste, my child!"

He started running.

"You dine with me, Burguet," said Father Parmentier.

"Thank you, Mr. Mayor, I am engaged to dine with Moses; I will go at another time."

And, with our arms around each other, we entered Mother Barrière's large corridor, where there was still the odour of good roasts, in spite of the blockade.

"Listen, Burguet," said I; "we are going to dine alone, and you shall choose whatever wines and dishes you like best; you know them better than I do."

I saw his eyes sparkle.

"Good! good!" said he, "it is understood."

In the large dining-hall the war-commissioner and two officers were dining together; they turned round, and we saluted them.

I sent for Mother Barrière, who came at once, her apron on her arm, as smiling and chubby as usual. Burguet whispered a couple of words in her ear, and she instantly opened the door at the right, and said:

"Walk in, gentlemen, walk in! You will not have to wait long."

We went into the square room at the corner of the square, a small, high room, with two large windows covered with muslin curtains, and the porcelain stove well heated, as it should be in winter.

A servant came to lay the table, while we warmed our hands upon the marble.

"I have a good appetite, Moses; my pleading is going to cost you dear," said Burguet, laughing.

"So much the better; it cannot be too dear for the gratitude I owe you."

"Come," said he, putting his hand on my shoulder, "I won't ruin you, but we must have a good dinner."

When the table was ready, we sat down, opposite each other, in soft, comfortable armchairs; and Burguet, fastening his napkin in his button-hole, as was his custom, took up the bill of fare. He pondered over it a long time; for you know, Fritz, that though nightingales are good singers, they have the sharpest beaks in the world. Burguet was like them, and I was delighted at seeing him thus meditating.

At last he said to the servant, slowly and solemnly:

"This and that, Madeleine, cooked so and so. And such a wine to begin with, and such another at the end."

"Very well, M. Burguet," replied Madeleine, as she went out.

Two minutes afterward she brought us a good toast soup. During a blockade this was something greatly to be desired; three weeks later we should have been very fortunate to have got one.

Then she brought us some Bordeaux wine, warmed in a napkin. But you do not suppose, Fritz, that I am going to tell you all the details of this dinner? although I remember it all, with great pleasure, to this day. Believe me, there was nothing wanting, meats nor fresh vegetables, nor the large well-smoked ham, nor any of the things which are dreadfully scarce in a shut-up city. We had even salad! Madame Barrière had kept it in the cellar, in earth, and Burguet wished to dress it himself with olive oil. We had, too, the last juicy pears which were seen in Phalsburg, during that winter of 1814.

Burguet seemed happy, especially when the bottle of old Lironcourt was brought, and we drank together.

"Moses," said he with softened eyes, "if all my pleas had as good pay as you give, I would resign my place in college; but this is the first fee I have received."

"And if I were in your place, Burguet," I exclaimed, "instead of staying in Phalsburg, I would go to a large city. You would have plenty of good dinners, good hotels, and the rest would soon follow."

"Ah! twenty years ago this might have been good advice," said he, rising, "but it is too late now. Let us go and take our coffee, Moses."

Thus it is that men of great talents often bury themselves in small places, where nobody values them at their true worth; they fall gradually into their own ruts, and disappear without notice.

Burguet never forgot to go to the coffee-house at about five o'clock, to play a game of cards with the old Jew Solomon, whose trade it was. Burguet and five or six citizens fully supported this man, who took his beer and coffee twice a day at their expense, to say nothing of the crowns he pocketed for the support of his family.

So far as the others were concerned, I was not surprised at this, for they were fools! but for a man like Burguet I was always astonished at it; for, out of twenty deals, Solomon did not let them win more than one or two, with the risk before his eyes of losing his best practice, by discouraging them altogether.

I had explained this fifty times to Burguet; he assented, and kept on all the same.

When we reached the coffee-house, Solomon was already there, in the corner of a window at the left his little dirty cap on his nose, and his old greasy frock hanging at the foot of the stool. He was shuffling the cards all by himself. He looked at Burguet out of the corner of his eye, as a bird-catcher looks at larks, as if to say:

"Come! I am here! I am expecting you!"

But Burguet, when with me, dared not obey the old man; he was ashamed of his weakness, and merely made a little motion of his head while he seated himself at the opposite table, where coffee was served to us.

The comrades came soon, and Solomon began to fleece them. Burguet turned his back to them; I tried to divert his attention, but his heart was with them; he listened to all the throws, and yawned in his hand.

About seven o'clock, when the room was full of smoke, and the balls were rolling on the billiard tables, suddenly a young man, a soldier, entered, looking round in all directions.

It was the deserter.

He saw us at last, and approached us with his foraging cap in his hand. Burguet looked up and recognized him; I saw him turn red; the deserter, on the contrary, was very pale; he tried to speak, but could not say a word.

"Ah! my friend!"said Burguet, "here you are, safe!"

"Yes, sir," replied the conscript, "and I have come to thank you for myself, for my father, and for my mother!"

"Ah!"said Burguet, coughing, "it is all right! it is all right!"

He looked tenderly at the young man, and asked him softly, "You are glad to live?"

"Oh! yes, sir," replied the conscript, "very glad."

"Yes," said Burguet, in a low voice, looking at the clock; "it would have been all over now! Poor child!"

And suddenly beginning to use the thou he said, "Thou hast had nothing with which to drink my health, and I have not another *sou*. Moses, give him a hundred *sous*."

I gave him ten *francs*. The deserter tried to thank me.

"That is good!"said Burguet, rising. "Go and take a drink with thy comrades. Be happy, and do not desert again."

He made as if he would follow Solomon's playing; but when the deserter said, "I thank you, too, for her who is expecting me!" he looked at me sideways, not knowing what to answer, so much was he moved.

Then I said to the conscript, "We are very glad that we have been of assistance to you; go and drink the health of your advocate, and behave yourself well."

He looked at us for a moment longer, as if he were unable to move; we saw his thanks in his face, a thousand times better than he had been able to utter them. At length he slowly went out, saluting us, and Burguet finished his cup of coffee.

We meditated for some minutes upon what had passed. But soon the thought of seeing my family seized me.

Burguet was like a soul in purgatory. Every minute he got up to look on, as one or another played, with his hands crossed behind his back; then he sat down with a melancholy look. I should have been very sorry to plague him longer, and, as the clock struck eight, I bade him good-evening, which evidently pleased him.

"Good-night, Moses," said he, leading me to the door. "My compliments to Madame Sorlé, and Madame Zeffen."

"Thank you! I shall not forget it." I went, very glad to return home, where I arrived in a few minutes. Sorlé saw at once that I was in good spirits, for, meeting her at the door of our little kitchen, I embraced her joyfully.

"It is all right, Sorlé," said I, "all just right!"

"Yes," said she, "I see that it is all right!" She laughed, and we went into the room where Zeffen was undressing David. The poor little fellow, in his shirt, came and offered me his cheek to kiss. Whenever I dined in the city, I used to bring him some of the dessert, and, in spite of his sleepy eyes, he soon found his way to my pockets.

You see, Fritz, what makes grandfathers happy is to find out how bright and sensible their grandchildren are.

Even little Esdras, whom Sorlé was rocking, understood at once that something unusual was going on; he stretched out his little hands to me, as if to say, "I like cake too!"

We were all of us very happy. At length, having sat down, I gave them an account of the day, setting forth the eloquence of Burguet, and the poor deserter's happiness. They all listened attentively. Sâfel, seated on my knees, whispered to me, "We have sold three hundred *francs'* worth of brandy!"

This news pleased me greatly: when one makes an outlay, he ought to profit by it.

About ten o'clock, after Zeffen had wished us goodnight, I went down and shut the door, and put the key underneath for the sergeant, if he should come in late.

While we were going to bed, Sorlé repeated what Sâfel had said, adding that we should be in easy circumstances when the blockade was over, and that the Lord had helped us in the midst of great calamities. We were happy and without fear of the future.

CHAPTER 16

A Sortie of the Garrison

Nothing extraordinary occurred for several days. The governor had the plants and bushes growing in the crevices of the ramparts torn away, to make desertion less easy, and he forbade the officers being too rough with the men, which had a good effect.

At this time, hundreds of thousands of Austrians, Russians, Bavarians, and Wurtemburgers, by squadrons and regiments, passed around the city beyond range of our cannon, and marched upon Paris.

Then there were terrible battles in Champagne, but we knew nothing of them.

The uniforms changed every day outside the city; our old soldiers on top of the ramparts recognized all the different nations they had been fighting for twenty years.

Our sergeant came regularly after the call, to take me upon the arsenal bastion; citizens were there all the time, talking about the invasion, which, did not come to an end.

It was wonderful! In the direction of St. Jean, on the edge of the forest of La Bonne-Fontaine, we saw, for hours at a time, cavalry and infantry defiling, and then convoys of powder and balls, and then cannon, and then files of bayonets, helmets, red and green and blue coats, lances, peasants' wagons covered with cloth—all these passed, passed like a river.

On this broad white plateau, surrounded by forests, we could see everything.

Now and then some Cossacks or dragoons would leave the main body, and push on galloping to the very foot of the glacis, in the lane *des Dames*, or near the little chapel. Instantly one of our old marine artillerymen would stretch out his gray moustaches upon a rampart gun, and slowly take aim; the bystanders would all gather round him, even the children, who would creep between your legs, fearless of balls or shells—and the heavy rifle-gun would go off!

Many a time I have seen the Cossack or Uhlan fall from his saddle, and the horse rush back to the squadron with his bridle on his neck. The people would shout with joy; they would climb up on the ramparts and look down, and the gunner would rub his hands and say, "One more out of the way!"

At other times these old men, with their ragged cloaks full of holes, would bet a couple of *sous* as to who should bring down this sentinel or that *vidette*, on the Mittelbronn or Bichelberg Hill.

It was so far that they needed good eyes to see the one they designated; but these men, accustomed to the sea, can discern everything as far as the eye can reach.

"Come, Paradis, there he is!" one would say.

"Yes, there he is! Lay down your two *sous*; there are mine!"

And they would fire. They would go on as if it were a game of ninepins. God knows how many men they killed for the sake of their two *sous*. Every morning about nine o'clock I found these marines in my shop, drinking "to the Cossack," as they said. The last drop they poured into their hands, to strengthen their nerves, and started off with rounded backs, calling out:

"Hey! good-day, Father Moses! The *kaiserlich* is very well!"

I do not think that I ever saw so many people in my life as in those months of January and February, 1814; they were like the locusts of Egypt! How the earth could produce so many people I could not comprehend.

I was naturally greatly troubled on account of it, and the other citizens also, as I need not say; but our sergeant laughed and winked.

"Look, Father Moses!"said he, pointing from Quatre- Vents to Bichelberg—"all these that are passing by, all that have passed, and all that are going to pass, are to enrich the soil of Champagne and Lorraine! The Emperor is down there, waiting for them in a good place—he will fall upon them! The thunderbolt of Austerlitz, of Jena, of Wagram, is all ready—it can wait no longer! Then they will file back in retreat; but our armies will follow them, with our bayonets in their backs, and we shall go out from here, and flank them off. Not one shall escape. Their account is settled. And then will be the time for you to have old clothes and other things to sell, Father Moses! He! he! he! How fat you will grow!"

He was merry at the thought of it; but you may suppose, Fritz, that I did not count much upon those uniforms that were running across the fields; I would much rather they had been a thousand leagues away.

Such are men—some are glad and others miserable from the same cause. The sergeant was so confident that sometimes he persuaded me, and I thought as he did.

We would go down the rampart street together, he would go to the cantine where they had begun to distribute siege-rations, or perhaps he would go home with me, take his little glass of cherry-brandy, and explain to me the Emperor's grand strokes since '96 in Italy. I did not understand anything about it, but I made believe that I understood, which answered all the purpose.

There came envoys, too, sometimes on the road from Nancy, sometimes from Saverne or Metz. They raised, at a distance, the little white flag; one of their trumpeters sounded and then withdrew; the officer of the guard received the envoy and bandaged his eyes, then he went under escort through the city to the governor's house. But what these envoys told or demanded never transpired in the city; the council of defence alone were informed of it.

We lived confined within our walls as if we were in the middle of the sea, and you cannot believe how that weighs upon one after a while, how depressing and overpowering it is not to be able to go out even upon the glacis. Old men who had been nailed for ten years to their armchairs, and who never thought of moving, were oppressed by grief at knowing that the gates remained shut. And then everyone wants to know what is going on, to see strangers and talk of the affairs of the country—no one knows how necessary these things are until he has had experience like ours. The meanest peasant, the lowest man in Dagsburg who might have chanced to come into the city, would have been received like a god; everybody would have run to see him and ask for the news from France.

Ah! those are right who hold that liberty is the greatest of blessings, for it is insupportable being shut up in a prison—let it be as large as France. Men are made to come and go, to talk and write, and live together, to carry on trade, to tell the news; and if you take these from them, you leave nothing desirable.

Governments do not understand this simple matter; they think that they are stronger when they prevent men from living at their ease, and at last everybody is tired of them. The true power of a sovereign is always in proportion to the liberty he can give, and not to that which he is obliged to take away. The allies had learned this for Napoleon, and thence came their confidence.

The saddest thing of all was that, toward the end of January, the citizens began to be in want. I cannot say that money was scarce, because a centime never went out of the city, but everything was dear; what three weeks before was worth two *sous* now cost twenty! This has often led me to think that scarcity of money is one of the fooleries invented by scoundrels to deceive the weak-minded. What else can make money scarce? You are not poor with two *sous*, if they are enough to buy your bread, wine, meat, clothes, etc.; but if you need twenty times more to buy these things, then not only are you poor, but the whole country is poor. There is no want of money when everything is cheap; it is always scarce when the necessaries of life are dear.

So, when people are shut up as we were, it is very fortunate to be able to sell more than you buy. My brandy sold for three *francs* the quart, but at the same time we needed bread, oil, potatoes, and their prices were all proportionately high.

One morning old Mother Quéru came to my shop weeping; she had eaten nothing for two days! and yet that was the least thing, said she; she missed nothing but her glass of wine, which I gave her gratis. She gave me a hundred blessings and went away happy. A good many others would have liked their glass of wine! I have seen old men in despair because they had nothing to snuff; they even went so far as to snuff ashes; some at this time smoked the leaves of the large walnut-tree by the arsenal, and liked it well.

Unfortunately, all this was but the beginning of want: later we learned to fast for the glory of His Majesty.

Toward the end of February, it became cold again. Every evening they fired a hundred shells upon us, but we became accustomed to all that, till it seemed quite a thing of course. As soon as the shell burst everybody ran to put out the fire, which was an easy matter, since there were tubs full of water ready in every house.

Our guns replied to the enemy; but as after ten o'clock the Russians fired only with field-pieces, our men could aim only at their fire, which was changing continually, and it was not easy to reach them.

Sometimes the enemy fired incendiary balls; these are balls pierced with three nails in a triangle, and filled with such inflammable matter that it could be extinguished only by throwing the ball under water, which was done.

We had as yet had no fires; but our outposts had fallen back, and the allies drew closer and closer around the city. They occupied the Ozillo farm, Pernette's tile-kiln, and the Maisons-Rouges, which had been abandoned by our troops. Here they intended to pass the winter pleasantly. These were Wurtemburg, Bavarian, and Baden troops, and other *landwehr*, who replaced in Alsace the regular troops that had left for the interior.

We could plainly see their sentinels in long, grayish-blue coats, flat helmets, and muskets on their shoulders, walking slowly in the poplar alley which leads to the tile-kiln.

From thence these troops could any moment, on a dark night, enter the trenches, and even attempt to force a postern.

They were in large numbers and denied themselves nothing, having three or four villages around them to furnish their provisions, and the great fires of the tile-kiln to keep them warm.

Sometimes a Russian battalion relieved them, but only for a day or two, being obliged to continue its route. These Russians bathed in the little pond behind the building, in spite of the ice and snow which filled it.

All of them, Russians, Wurtemburgers, and Baden men, fired upon our sentinels, and we wondered that our governor had not stopped them with our balls. But one day the sergeant came in joyfully, and whispered to me, winking:

"Get up early tomorrow morning, Father Moses; don't say a word to anyone, and follow me. You will see something that will make you laugh."

"All right, sergeant!" said I.

He went to bed at once, and long before day, about five o'clock, I heard him jump out of bed, which astonished me the more, as I had not heard the call.

I rose softly. Sorlé sleepily asked me: "What is it, Moses?"

"Go to sleep again, Sorlé," I replied; "the sergeant told me that he wanted to show me something."

She said no more, and I finished dressing myself.

Just then the sergeant knocked at the door; I blew out the candle, and we went down. It was very dark.

We heard a faint noise in the direction of the barracks; the sergeant went toward it, saying: "Go up on the bastion; we are going to attack the tile-kiln."

I ran up the street at once. As I came upon the ramparts I saw in the shadow of the bastion on the right our gunners at their pieces. They did not stir, and all around was still; matches lighted and set in the ground gave the only light, and shone like stars in the darkness.

Five or six citizens, in the secret, like myself, stood motionless at the entrance of the postern. The usual cries, "Sentries, attention!" were answered around the city; and without, from the part of the enemy, we heard the cries "*Verdâ!*" and "*Souïda!*"[1]

It was very cold, a dry cold, notwithstanding the fog.

Soon, from the direction of the square in the interior of the city, a number of men went up the street; if they had kept step the enemy would have heard them from the distance upon the glacis; but they came pell-mell, and turned near us into the postern stairway. It took full ten minutes for them to pass. You can imagine whether I watched them, and yet I could not recognize our sergeant in the darkness.

The two companies formed again in the trenches after their defiling, and all was still.

My feet were perfectly numb, it was so cold; but curiosity kept me there.

At last, after about half an hour, a pale line stretched behind the bottom-land of Fiquet, around the woods of La Bonne-Fontaine. Captain Rolfo, the other citizens, and myself, leaned against the rampart, and looked at the snow-covered plain, where some German patrols were wandering in the fog, and nearer to us, at the foot of the glacis, the Wurtemburg sentinel stood motionless in the poplar alley which leads to the large shed of the tile-kiln.

Everything was still gray and indistinct; though the winter sun, as white as snow, rose above the dark line of firs. Our soldiers stood motionless, with grounded arms, in the covered ways. The "*Verdâs!*" and "*Souïdas!*" went their rounds. It grew lighter every moment.

No one would have believed that a fight was preparing, when six o'clock sounded from the mayoralty, and suddenly our two companies, without command, started, shouldering their arms, from the covered ways, and silently descended the glacis.

In less than a minute, they reached the road which stretches along the gardens, and defiled to the left, following the hedges.

---

1. Who goes there?

You cannot imagine my fright when I found that the fight was about to begin. It was not yet clear daylight, but still the enemy's sentinel saw the line of bayonets filing behind the hedges, and called out in a terrible way: "*Verdâ!*"

"Forward!" replied Captain Vigneron, in a voice like thunder, and the heavy soles of our soldiers sounded on the hard ground like an avalanche.

The sentinel fired, and then ran up the alley, shouting I know not what. Fifteen of the *landwehr*, who formed the outpost under the old shed used for drying bricks, started at once; they did not have time for repentance, but were all massacred without mercy.

"We could not see very well at that distance, through the hedges and poplars, but after the post was carried, the firing of the musketry and the horrible cries were heard even in the city.

All the unfortunate *landwehr* who were quartered in the Pernette farmhouse—a large number of whom were undressed, like respectable men at home, so as to sleep more comfortably-jumped from the windows in their pantaloons, in their drawers, in their shirts, with their cartridge-boxes on their backs, and ranged themselves behind the tile-kiln, in the large Seltier meadow. Their officers urged them on, and gave their orders in the midst of the tumult.

There must have been six or seven hundred of them there, almost naked in the snow, and, notwithstanding their being thus surprised, they opened a running fire which was well sustained, when our two pieces on the bastion began to take part in the contest.

Oh! what carnage!

Looking down upon them, you should have seen the bullets hit, and the shirts fly in the air! And, what was worst for these poor wretches, they had to close ranks, because, after destroying everything in the tile-kiln, our soldiers went out to make an attack with their bayonets!

What a situation!—just imagine it, Fritz, for respectable citizens, merchants, bankers, brewers, innkeepers—peaceable men who wanted nothing but peace and quietness.

I have always thought, since then, that the *landwehr* system is a very bad one, and that it is much better to pay a good army of volunteers, who are attached to the country, and know that their pay, pensions, and decorations come from the nation and not from the government; young men devoted to their country like those of '92, and full of enthusiasm, because they are respected and honoured in proportion to their sacrifices. Yes, this is what they ought to be—and not men who are thinking of their wives and children.

Our balls struck down these poor fathers and husbands by the dozen. To add to all these abominations, two other companies, sent out with the greatest secrecy by the council of defence from the posterns of the guard and of the German gate, and which came up, one by the Saverne road, and the other by the road of Petit-Saint-Jean, now began to outflank them, and forming behind them, fired upon them in the rear.

It must be confessed that these old soldiers of the Empire had a diabolical talent for stratagem! Who would ever have imagined such a stroke!

On seeing this, the remnant of the *landwehr* disbanded on the great white plain like a whirlwind of sparrows. Those who had not had time to put on their shoes did not mind the stones or briers or thorns of the Fiquet bottom; they ran like stags, the stoutest as fast as the rest.

Our soldiers followed them as skirmishers, stopping not a second except to make ready and fire. All the ground in front, up to the old beech in the middle of the meadow of Quatre-Vents, was covered with their bodies.

Their colonel, a burgomaster doubtless, galloped before them on horseback, his shirt flying out behind him.

If the Baden soldiers, quartered in the village, had not come to their assistance, they would all have been exterminated. But two battalions of Baden men being deployed at the right of Quatre-Vents, our trumpets sounded the recall, and the four

THE SORTIE FROM THE LIME-KILN

companies formed in the alley *des Dames* to await them.

The Baden soldiers then halted, and the last of the Wurtemburgers passed behind them, glad to escape from such a terrible destruction. They could well say: "I know what war is I have seen it at the worst!"

It was now seven o'clock the whole city was on the ramparts. Soon a thick smoke rose above the tile-kiln and the surrounding buildings; some sappers had gone out with fagots and set it on fire. It was all burned to cinders; nothing remained but a great black space, and some rubbish behind the poplars.

Our four companies, seeing that the Baden soldiers did not mean to attack them, returned quietly, the trumpeter leading.

Long before this, I had gone down to the square, near the German gate, to meet our troops as they came back. It was one of the sights which I shall never forget; the post under arms, the veterans hanging by the chains of the lowered drawbridge; the men, women, and children pushing in the street; and outside, on the ramparts, the trumpets sounding, and answered from the distance by the echoes of the bastions and half-moon; the wounded, who, pale, tattered, covered with blood, came in first, supported on the shoulders of their comrades; Lieutenant Schnindret, in one of the tile-kiln armchairs, his face covered with sweat, with a bullet in his abdomen, shouting with thick voice and extended hand, "*Vive l'Empereur!*" the soldiers who threw the Wurtemburg commander from his litter to put one of our own in it; the drums under the gate beating the march, while the troops, with arms at will, and bread and all kinds of provisions stuck on their bayonets, entered proudly in the midst of the shouts: "Hurra for the Sixth Light Infantry!" These are things which only old people can boast of having seen!

Ah, Fritz, men are not what they once were! In my time, foreigners paid the cost of war. The Emperor Napoleon had that virtue; he ruined not France, but his enemies. Nowadays we pay for our own glory.

And, in those times, the soldiers brought back booty, sacks, epaulettes, cloaks, officers' sashes, watches, etc., etc.! They remembered that General Bonaparte had said to them in 1796: "You need clothes and shoes; the Republic owes you much, she can give you nothing. I am going to lead you into the richest country in the world; there you will find honours, glory, riches!" In fine, I saw at once that we were going to sell glasses of wine at a great rate.

As the sergeant passed I called to him from the distance, "Sergeant!"

He saw me in the crowd, and we shook hands joyfully. "All right, Father Moses! All right!" he said.

Everybody laughed.

Then, without waiting for the end of the procession, I ran to the market to open my shop.

Little Sâfel had also understood that we were going to have a profitable day, for, in the midst of the crowd, he had come and pulled my coat-tails, and said, "I have the key of the market; I have it; let us make haste! Let us try to get there before Frichard!"

Whatever natural wit a child may have, it shows itself at once; it is truly a gift of God.

So we ran to the shop. I opened my windows, and Sâfel remained while I went home to eat a morsel, and get a good quantity of *sous* and small change.

Sorlé and Zeffen were at their counter selling small glassfuls. Everything went well as usual. But a quarter of an hour later, when the soldiers had broken ranks and put back their muskets in their places at the barracks, the crowd at my shop in the market, of people wishing to sell me coats, sacks, watches, pistols, cloaks, epaulettes, etc., was so great that without Sâfel's help I never could have got out of it.

I got all these things for almost nothing. Men of this sort never trouble themselves about tomorrow; their only thought was to live well from one day to another, to have tobacco, brandy, and the other good things which are never wanting in a garrisoned town.

That day, in six hours' time, I refurnished my shop with coats, cloaks, pantaloons, and thick boots of genuine German leather, of the first quality, and I bought things of all sorts—nearly fifteen hundred pounds' worth—which I afterward sold for six or seven times more than they cost me. All those *landwehr* were well-to-do, and even rich citizens, with good, substantial clothes.

The soldiers, too, sold me a good many watches, which Goulden the old watchmaker did not want, because they were taken from the dead.

But what gave me more pleasure than all the rest, was that Frichard, who was sick for three or four days, could not come and open his shop. It makes me laugh now to think of it. It gave the rascal that green jaundice which never left him as long as he lived.

At noon Sâfel went to fetch our dinner in a basket; we ate under the shed so as not to lose custom, and could not leave for a minute till night. Scarcely had one set gone, before two and often three others came at once.

I was sinking with fatigue, and so was Sâfel; nothing but our love of trade sustained us.

Another pleasant thing which I recall is that, on going home a few minutes before seven, we saw at a distance that our other shop was full. My wife and daughter had not been able to close it; they had raised the price, and the soldiers did not even notice it,—it seemed all right to them; so that not only the French money which I had just given them, but also Wurtemburg florins came to my pocket.

Two trades which help each other along are an excellent thing, Fritz: remember that! Without my brandies I should not have had the money to buy so many goods, and without the market where I gave ready money for the booty, the soldiers would not have had wherewith to buy my brandy. This shows us plainly that the Lord favours orderly and peaceable men, provided they know how to make the best use of their opportunities.

At length, as we could not do more, we were obliged to close the shop, in spite of the protestations of the soldiers, and defer business till tomorrow.

About nine o'clock, after supper, we all sat down together around the large lamp, to count our gains. I made rolls of three *francs* each, and on the chair next me the pile reached almost to the top of the table. Little Sâfel put the white pieces in a wooden bowl. It was a pleasant sight to us all, and Sorlé said: "We have sold twice as much as usual. The. more we raise the price the better it sells."

I was going to reply that still we must use moderation in all things—for these women, even the best of them, do not know that—when the sergeant came in to take his little glass. He wore his foraging coat, and carried hung across his cape a kind of bag of red leather.

"He, he, he!"said he, as he saw the rolls. "The devil! the devil! You ought to be satisfied with this day's work, Father Moses?"

"Yes, not bad, sergeant," I joyfully replied.

"I think," said he, as he sat down and tasted the little glass of cherry-brandy, which Zeffen had just poured out for him, "I think that after one or two sorties more, you will do for colonel of the shop- keepers' regiment. So much the better; I am very glad of it!"

Then, laughing heartily, he said,

"He, Father Moses! see what I have here; these rascals of *kai-serlichs* deny themselves nothing."

At the same time he opened his bag, and began to draw out a pair of mittens lined with fox-skin, then some good woollen stockings, and a large knife with a horn handle and blades of very fine steel. He opened the blades:

"There is everything here," said he, "a pruning-knife, a saw, small knives and large ones, even to a file for nails."

"For finger-nails, sergeant!"said I.

"Ah! very likely!" said he. This big *landwehr* was as nice as a new crown-piece. He would be likely to file his finger-nails. But wait!"

My wife and children, leaning over us, looked on with eager eyes. Thrusting his hand into a sort of portfolio in the side of the bag, he drew out a handsome miniature, surrounded with a circle of gold in the shape of a watch, but larger.

"See! What ought this to be worth?"

I looked, then Sorlé, then Zeffen, and Sâfel. "We were all surprised at seeing a work of such beauty, and even touched, for the miniature represented a fair young woman and two lovely children, as fresh as rose-buds.

"Well, what do you think of that?" asked the sergeant.

"It is very beautiful," said Sorlé.

"Yes, but what is it worth?"

I took the miniature and examined it.

"To anyone else, sergeant," said I, "I should say that it was worth fifty *francs*; but the gold alone is worth more, and I should estimate it at a hundred *francs*; we can weigh it."

"And the portrait, Father Moses?"

"The portrait is worth nothing to me, and I will give it back to you. Such things do not sell in this country; they are of no value except to the family."

"Very well," said he, "we will talk about that by and by."

He put back the miniature into the bag.

"Do you read German?" he asked.

"Very well."

"Ah, good! I am curious to hear what this *kaiserlich* had to write. See, it is a letter! He was keeping it doubtless for the baggage-master to send it to Germany. But we came too soon! What does it say?"

He handed me a letter addressed to Madame Roedig, Stuttgart, No. 6 Bergstrasse. That letter, Fritz, here it is. Sorlé has kept it; it will tell you more about the *landwehr* than I can.

Bichelberg, Feb. 95, 1814.

Dear Aurelia: Thy good letter of January 29th reached Coblentz too late; the regiment was on its way to Alsace. We have had a great many discomforts, from rain and snow. The regiment came first to Bitche, one of the most terrible forts possible, built upon rocks up in the sky. We were to take part in blockading it, but a new order sent us on farther to the fort of Lutzelstein, on the mountain, where we remained two days at the village of Pétersbach, to summon that little place to surrender. The veterans who held it having replied by cannon, our colonel did not judge it necessary to storm it, and, thank God! we received orders to go and blockade another fortress surrounded by good villages which furnish us provisions in abundance; this is Phalsburg, a couple of leagues from Saverne. We relieve, here, the Austrian regiment of Vogelgesang, which has left for Lorraine.

Thy good letter has followed me everywhere, and it fills me now with joy. Embrace little Sabrina and our dear little Henry for me a hundred times, and receive my embraces yourself, too, thou dear, adored wife!

Ah! when shall we be together again in our little pharmacy? When shall I see again my vials nicely labelled upon their shelves, with the heads of Æsculapius and Hippocrates above the door? When shall I take my pestle, and mix my drugs again after the prescribed formulas? When shall I have the joy of sitting again in my comfortable armchair, in front of a good fire, in our back shop, and hear Henry's little wooden horse roll upon the floor—Henry whom I so long for? And thou, dear, adored wife, when wilt thou exclaim: 'It is my Henry!' as thou seest me return crowned with palms of victory.

"These Germans," interrupted the sergeant, "are blockheads as well as asses! They are to have 'palms of victory!' What a silly letter!"

But Sorlé and Zeffen listened as I read, with tears in their eyes. They held our little ones in their arms, and I, too, thinking that Baruch might have been in the same condition as this poor man, was greatly moved.

Now, Fritz, hear the end:

We are here in an old tile-kiln, within range of the cannon of the fort. A few shells are fired upon the city every evening, by order of the Russian general, Berdiaiw, with the hope of making the inhabitants decide to open the gates. That must be before long; they are short of provisions! Then we shall be comfortably lodged in the citizens' houses, till the end of this glorious campaign; and that will be soon, for the regular armies have all passed without resistance, and we hear daily of great victories in Champagne. Bonaparte is in full retreat; field-marshals Blücher and Schwartzenberg have united their forces, and are only five or six days' march from Paris—"

"What? What? What is that? What does he say?" stammered out the sergeant, leaning over toward the letter. "Read that again!"

I looked at him; he was very pale, and his cheeks shook with anger.

"He says that generals Blücher and Schwartzenberg are near Paris."

"Near Paris! They! The rascals !" he faltered out.

Suddenly, with a bad look on his face, he gave a low laugh and said:

"Ah! thou meanest to take Phalsburg, dost thou? Thou meanest to return to thy land of *sauerkraut* with palms of victory? He! he! he! I have given thee thy palms of victory!"

He made the motions of pricking with his bayonet as he spoke, "One—two—hop!"

It made us all tremble only to look at him.

"Yes, Father Moses, so it is," said he, emptying his glass by little sips. "I have nailed this sort of an apothecary to the door of the tile-kiln. He made up a funny face—his eyes starting from his head. His Aurelia will have to expect him a good while! But never mind! Only, Madame Sorlé, I assure you that it is a lie. You must not believe a word he says. The Emperor will give it to them! Don't be troubled."

I did not wish to go on. I felt myself grow cold, and I finished the letter quickly, passing over three-quarters of it which contained no information, only compliments for friends and acquaintances.

The sergeant himself had had enough of it, and went out soon afterward, saying, "Goodnight! Throw that in the fire!"

Then I put the letter aside, and we all sat looking at each other for some minutes. I opened the door. The sergeant was in his room at the end of the passage, and I said, in a low voice:

"What a horrible thing! Not only to kill the father of a family like a fly, but to laugh about it afterward!"

"Yes," replied Sorlé. "And the worst of it is that he is not a bad man. He loves the Emperor too well, that is all!"

The information contained in the letter caused us much serious reflection, and that night, notwithstanding our stroke of good fortune in our sales, I woke more than once, and thought of this terrible war, and wondered what would become of the country if Napoleon were no longer its master. But these questions were above my comprehension, and I did not know how to answer them.

CHAPTER 17

Famine and Fever

After this story of the *landwehr*, we were afraid of the sergeant, though he did not know it, and came regularly to take his glass of cherry-brandy. Sometimes in the evening he would hold the bottle before our lamp, and exclaim:

"It is getting low, Father Moses, it is getting low! We shall soon be put upon half-rations, and then quarter, and so on. It is all the same; if a drop is left, anything more than the smell, in six months, Trubert will be very glad."

He laughed, and I thought with indignation:

"You will be satisfied with a drop! What are you in want of? The city storehouses are bombproof, the fires at the guard-house are burning every day, the market furnishes every soldier with his ration of fresh meat, while respectable citizens are glad if they can get potatoes and salt meat!"

This is the way I felt in my ill-humour, while I treated him pleasantly, all the same, on account of his terrible wickedness.

And it was the truth, Fritz, even our children had nothing more nourishing to eat than soup made of potatoes and salt beef, which cause many dangerous maladies.

The garrison had no lack of anything; but, notwithstanding, the governor was all the time proclaiming that the visits were to be recommenced, and that those who should be found delinquent should be punished with the rigor of military law. Those people wanted to have everything for themselves; but nobody minded them, everybody hid what he could.

Fortunate in those times was he who kept a cow in his cellar, with some hay and straw for fodder: milk and butter were beyond all price. Fortunate was he who owned a few hens; a fresh egg, at the end of February, was valued at fifteen *sous*, and they were not to be had even at that price. The price of fresh meat went up, so to speak, from hour to hour, and we did not ask if it was beef or horseflesh.

The council of defence had sent away the paupers of the city before the blockade, but a large number of poor people remained. A good many slipped out at night into the trenches by one of the posterns; they would go and dig up roots from under the snow, and cut the nettles in the bastions to boil for spinach. The sentries fired from above, but what will not a man risk for food? It is better to feel a ball than to suffer with hunger.

We needed only to meet these emaciated creatures, these women dragging themselves along the walls, these pitiful children, to feel that famine had come, and we often said to ourselves:

"If the Emperor does not come and help us, in a month we shall be like these wretched creatures! What good will our money do us, when a radish will cost a hundred *francs*?"

Then, Fritz, we smiled no more as we saw the little ones eating around the table; we looked at each other, and this glance was enough to make us understand each other.

The good sense and good feeling of a brave woman are seen at times like this. Sorlé had never spoken to me about our provisions; I knew how prudent she was, and supposed that we must have provisions hidden somewhere, without being entirely sure of it. So, at evening, as we sat at our meagre supper, the fear that our children might want the necessary food sometimes led me to say:

"Eat! feast away! I am not hungry. I want an omelette or a chicken. Potatoes do not agree with me."

I would laugh, but Sorlé knew very well what I was thinking.

"Come, Moses," she said to me one day; "we are not as badly

off as you think; and if we should come to it, ah, well! do not be troubled, we shall find some way of getting along! So long as others have something to live upon, we shall not perish, more than they."

She gave me courage, and I ate cheerfully, I had so much confidence in her.

That same evening, after Zeffen and the children had gone to bed, Sorlé took the lamp, and led me to her hiding-place.

Under the house we had three cellars, very small and very low, separated by lattices. Against the last of these lattices, Sorlé had thrown bundles of straw up to the very top; but after removing the straw, we went in, and I saw at the farther end, two bags of potatoes, a bag of flour, and on the little oil-cask a large piece of salt beef.

We stayed there more than an hour, to look, and calculate, and think. These provisions might serve us for a month, and those in the large cellar under the street, which we had declared to the commissary of provisions, a fortnight. So that Sorlé said to me as we went up:

"You see that, with economy, we have what will do for six weeks. A time of great want is now beginning, and if the Emperor does not come before the end of six weeks, the city will surrender. Meanwhile, we must get along with potatoes and salt meat."

She was right, but every day I saw how the children were suffering from this diet. We could see that they grew thin, especially little David; his large bright eyes, his hollow cheeks, his increasing dejected look, made my heart ache.

I held him, I caressed him; I whispered to him that, when the winter was over, we would go to Saverne, and his father would take him to drive in his carriage. He would look at me dreamily, and then lay his head upon my shoulder, with his arm around my neck, without answering. At last he refused to eat.

Zeffen, too, became disheartened; she would often sob, and take her babe from me, and say that she wanted to go, that she wanted to see Baruch! You do not know what these troubles are,

Fritz; a father's troubles for his children; they are the cruellest of all! No child can imagine how his parents love him, and what they suffer when he is unhappy.

But what was to be done in the midst of such calamities? Many other families in France were still more to be pitied than we.

During all this time, you must remember that we had the patrols, the shells in the evening, requisition and notices, the call to arms at the two barracks and in front of the mayoralty, the cries of "Fire!" in the night, the noise of the fire-engines, the arrival of the envoys, the rumours spread through the city that our armies were retreating, and that the city was to be burned to the ground!

The less people know the more they invent.

It is best to tell the simple truth. Then everyone would take courage, for, during all such times, I have always seen that the truth, even in the greatest calamities, is never so terrible as these inventions. The republicans defended themselves so well, because they knew everything, nothing was concealed from them, and every one considered the affairs of his nation as his own.

But when men's own affairs are hidden from them, how can they have confidence? An honest man has nothing to conceal, and I say it is the same with an honest government.

In short, bad weather, cold, want, rumours of all kinds, increased our miseries. Men like Burguet, whom we had always seen firm, became sad; all that they could say to us was:

"We shall see!—we must wait!" The soldiers again began to desert, and were shot!

Our brandy-selling always kept on: I had already emptied seven pipes of spirit, all my debts were paid,, my storehouse at the market was full of goods, and I had eighteen thousand *francs* in the cellar; but what is money, when we are trembling for the life of those we love?

On the sixth of March, about nine o'clock in the evening, we had just finished supper as usual, and the sergeant was smoking his pipe, with his legs crossed, near the window, and looking at us without speaking.

It was the hour when the bombarding began; we heard the first cannon-shots, behind the Fiquet bottom-land; a cannon-shot from the outposts had answered them; that had somewhat roused us, for we were all thoughtful.

"Father Moses," said the sergeant, "the children are pale!"

"I know it very well," I replied, sorrowfully.

He said no more, and as Zeffen had just gone out to weep, he took little David on his knee, and looked at him for a long time. Sorlé held little Esdras asleep in her arms. Sâfel took off the tablecloth and rolled up the napkins, to put them back in the closet.

"Yes," said the sergeant. "We must take care, Father Moses; we will talk about it another time."

I looked at him with surprise; he emptied his pipe at the edge of the stove, and went out, making a sign for me to follow him. Zeffen came in, and I took a candle from her hand. The sergeant led me to his little room at the end of the passage, shut the door, sat down on the foot of the bed, and said:

"Father Moses, do not be frightened—but the typhus has just broken out again in the city; five soldiers were taken to the hospital this morning; the commandant of the place, Moulin, is taken. I hear, too, of a woman and three children!" He looked at me, and I felt cold all over.

"Yes," said he, "I have known this disease for a long time; we had it in Poland, in Russia, after the retreat, and in Germany. It always comes from poor nourishment."

Then I could not help sobbing and exclaiming:

"Ah, tell me! What can I do? If I could give my life for my children, it would all be well! But what can I do?"

"Tomorrow, Father Moses, I will bring you my portion of meat, and you shall have soup made of it for your children. Madame Sorlé may take the piece at the market, or, if you prefer, I will bring it myself. You shall have all my portions of fresh meat till the blockade is over, Father Moses."

I was so moved by this, that I went to him and took his hand, saying:

"Sergeant, you are a noble man! Forgive me, I have thought evil of you."

"What about?" said he, scowling.

"About the *landwehr* at the tile-kiln!"

"Ah, good! That is a different thing! I do not care about that," said he. "If you knew all the *kaiserlichs* that I have despatched these ten years, you would have thought more evil of me. But that is not what we are talking about; you accept, Father Moses?"

"And you, sergeant," said I, "what will you have to eat?"

"Do not be troubled about that; Sergeant Trubert has never been in want!"

I wanted to thank him. "Good!" said he, "that is all understood. I cannot give you a pike, or a fat goose, but a good soup in blockade times is worth something, too."

He laughed and shook hands with me. As for myself I was quite overcome, and my eyes were full of tears.

"Let us go; goodnight!" said he, as he led me to the door. "It will all come out right! Tell Madame Sorlé that it will all come out right!"

I blessed that man as I went out, and I told it all to Sorlé, who was still more affected by it than myself. We could not refuse; it was for the children! and during the last week there had been nothing but horsemeat in the market.

So the next morning we had fresh meat to make soup for those poor little ones. But the dreadful malady was already upon us, Fritz! Now, when I think of it, after all these years, I am quite overcome. However, I cannot complain; before going to take the bit of meat, I had consulted our old rabbi about the quality of this meat according to the law, and he had replied:

"The first law is to save Israel; but how can Israel be saved if the children perish?"

But after a while I remembered that other law:

The life of the flesh is in the blood, therefore I said unto the children of Israel: Ye shall eat the blood of no manner of flesh, for the life of all flesh is the blood thereof; whosoever eateth it shall be cut off; and whosoever eateth of any sick beast shall be unclean."

In my great misery the words of the Lord came to me, and I wept.

All these animals had been sick for six weeks; they lived in the mire, exposed to the snow and wind, between the arsenal and guard bastions.

The soldiers, almost all of whom were sons of peasants, ought to have known that they could not live in the open air, in such cold weather; a shelter could easily have been made. But when officers take the whole charge, nobody else thinks of anything; they even forget their own village trades. And if, unfortunately, their commanders do not give the order, nothing is done.

This is the reason that the animals had neither flesh nor fat; this is the reason that they were nothing but miserable, trembling carcasses, and their suffering, unhealthy flesh had become unclean, according to the law of God.

Many of the soldiers died. The wind brought to the city the bad air from the bodies, scattered by hundreds around the tile-kiln, the Ozillo farm, and in the gardens, and this also caused much sickness.

The justice of the Lord is shown in all things; when the living neglect their duties toward the dead, they perish.

I have often remembered these things when it was too late, so that I think of them only with grief.

CHAPTER 18

Death of Little David

The most painful of all my recollections, Fritz, is the way in which that terrible disease came to our family.

On the twelfth of March we heard of a large number of men, women, and children who were dying. "We dared not listen; we said:

"No one in our house is sick, the Lord watches over us!"

After David had come, after supper, to cuddle in my arms, with his little hand on my shoulder, I looked at him; he seemed very drowsy, but children are always sleepy at night. Esdras was already asleep, and Sâfel had just bidden us good-night.

At last Zeffen took the child, and we all went to bed.

That night the Russians did not fire; perhaps the typhus was among them, too. I do not know.

About midnight, when by God's goodness we were asleep, I heard a terrible cry.

I listened, and Sorlé said to me:

"It is Zeffen!"

I rose at once, and tried to light the lamp; but I was so much agitated that I could not find anything.

Sorlé struck a light, I drew on my pantaloons and ran to the door. But I was hardly in the passageway when Zeffen came out of her room like an insane person, with her long black hair all loose.

"The child!" she screamed.

Sorlé followed me. We went in, we leaned over the cradle.

The two children seemed to be sleeping; Esdras all rosy, David as white as snow.

At first I saw nothing, I was so frightened, but at last I took up David to waken him; I shook him, and called, "David!"

And then we first saw that his eyes were open and fixed.

"Wake him! wake him!" cried Zeffen.

Sorlé took my hands and said:

"Quick! make a fire! heat some water!"

And we laid him across the bed, shaking him and calling him by name. Little Esdras began to cry.

"Light a fire!" said Sorlé again to me. "And, Zeffen, be quiet! It does no good to cry so! Quick, quick, a fire!"

But Zeffen cried out incessantly, "My poor child!"

"He will soon be warm again," said Sorlé; "only, Moses, make haste and dress yourself, and run for Doctor Steinbrenner."

She was pale and more alarmed than we, but this brave woman never lost her presence of mind or her courage. She had made a fire, and the fagots were crackling in the chimney.

I ran to get my cloak, and went down, thinking to myself:

"The Lord have mercy upon us! If the child dies I shall not survive him! No, he is the one that I love best, I could not survive him!"

For you know, Fritz, that the child who is most unhappy, or in the greatest danger, is always the one that we love best; he needs us the most; we forget the others. The Lord has ordered it so, doubtless for the greatest good.

I was already running in the street.

A darker night was never known. The wind blew from the Rhine, the snow blew about like dust; here and there the lighted windows showed where people were watching the sick.

My head was uncovered, yet I did not feel the cold. I cried within myself:

"The last day had come! That day of which the Lord has said:

*Afore the harvest, when the bud is perfect, and the sour grape
is ripening in the flower, he shall both cut off the sprigs with*

pruning-hooks, and take away and cut down the branches.

Full of these fearful thoughts, I went across the large market-place, where the wind was tossing the old elms, full of frost.

As the clock struck one, I pushed open Doctor Steinbrenner's door; its large pulley rattled in the vestibule. As I was groping about, trying to find the railing, the servant appeared with a light at the top of the stairs.

"Who is there?" she asked, holding the lantern before her.

"Ah!" I replied, "tell the doctor to come immediately; we have a child sick, very sick."

I could not restrain my sobs.

"Come up, Monsieur Moses," said the girl: "the doctor has just come in, and has not gone to bed. Come up a moment and warm yourself!"

But Father Steinbrenner had heard it all.

"Very well, Theresa!" said he, coming out of his room; "keep the fire burning. I shall be back in an hour at latest."

He had already put on his large three-cornered cap, and his goat's-hair great-coat.

We walked across the square without speaking. I went first; in a few minutes we ascended our stairs.

Sorlé had placed a candle at the top of the stairs; I took it and led M. Steinbrenner to the baby's room.

All seemed quiet as we entered. Zeffen was sitting in an arm-chair behind the door, with her head on her knees, and her shoulders uncovered; she was no longer crying but weeping. The child was in bed. Sorlé, standing at its side, looked at us.

The doctor laid his cap on the bureau.

"It is too warm here," said he, "give us a little air."

Then he went to the bed. Zeffen had risen from her chair, as pale as death. The doctor took the lamp, and looked at our poor little David; he raised the coverlet and lifted out the little round limbs; he listened to the breathing. Esdras having begun to cry, he turned round and said: "Take the other child away from this room—we must be quiet! and besides, the air of a sick-room is not good for such small children."

He gave me a side look. I understood what he meant to say. It was the typhus! I looked at my wife; she understood it all.

I felt at that moment as if my heart were torn; I wanted to groan, but Zeffen was there leaning over, behind us, and I said nothing; nor did Sorlé.

The doctor asked for paper to write a prescription, and we went out together. I led him to our room, and shut the door, and began to sob.

"Moses," said he, "you are a man, do not weep! Remember that you ought to set an example of courage to two poor women."

"Is there no hope?" I asked him in a low voice, afraid of being heard.

"It is the typhus!"said he. "We will do what we can. There, that is the prescription; go to Tribolin's; his boy is up at night now, and he will give you the medicine. Be quick! And then, in heaven's name, take the other child out of that room, and your daughter too, if possible. Try to find someone out of the family, accustomed to sickness; the typhus is contagious."

I said nothing.

He took his cap and went.

Now what can I say more? The typhus is a disease engendered by death itself; the prophet speaks of it, when he says:

Hell from beneath is moved for thee, to meet thee at thy coming!

How many have I seen die of the typhus in our hospitals, on the Saverne Hill, and elsewhere!

When men tear each other to pieces, without mercy, why should not death come to help them? But what had this poor babe done that it must die so soon? This, Fritz, is the most dreadful thing, that all must suffer for the crimes of a few. Yes, when I think that my child died of this pestilence, which war had brought from the heart of Russia to our homes, and which ravaged all Alsace and Lorraine for six months, instead of accusing God, as the impious do, I accuse men. Has not God given them reason? And when they do not use it—when they let themselves rage against each other like brutes—is He to blame for it?

But of what use are right ideas, when we are suffering!

I remember that the sickness lasted for six days, and those were the cruellest days of my life. I feared for my wife, for my daughter, for Sâfel, for Esdras. I sat in a corner, listening to the babe's breathing. Sometimes he seemed to breathe no longer. Then a chill passed over me; I went to him and listened. And when, by chance, Zeffen came, in spite of the doctor's prohibition, I went into a sort of fury; I pushed her out by the shoulders, trembling.

"But he is my child! He is my child!"she said.

"And art thou not my child too?" said I. "I do not want you all to die!"

Then I burst into tears, and fell into my chair, looking straight before me, my strength all gone; I was exhausted with grief.

Sorlé came and went, with firm-closed lips;she prepared everything, and cared for everybody.

At that time musk was the remedy for typhus; the house was full of musk. Often the idea seized me that Esdras, too, was going to be sick. Ah, if having children is the greatest happiness in the world, what agony is it to see them suffer! How fearful to think of losing them!—to be there, to hear their laboured breathing, their delirium, to watch their sinking from hour to hour, from minute to minute, and to exclaim from the depths of the soul:

"Death is near at hand! There is nothing, nothing more that can be done to save thee, my child! I cannot give thee my life! Death does not wish for it!"

What heart-rending and what anguish, till the last moment when all is over!

Then, Fritz, money, the blockade, the famine, the general desolation—all were forgotten. I hardly saw the sergeant open our door every morning, and look in, asking:

"Well, Father Moses, well?"

I did not know what he said; I paid no attention to him.

But, what I always think of with pleasure, what I am always proud of, is that, in the midst of all this trouble, when Sorlé,

Zeffen, myself, and everybody were beside ourselves, when we forgot all about our business, and let everything go, little Sâfel at once took charge of our shop. Every morning we heard him rise at six o'clock, go down, open the warehouse, take up one or two pitchers of brandy, and begin to serve the customers.

No one had said a word to him about it, but Sâfel had a genius for trade. And if anything could console a father in such troubles, it would be to see himself, as it were, living over again in so young a child, and to say to himself: "At least the good race is not extinct; it still remains to preserve commonsense in the world." Yes, it is the only consolation which a man can have.

Our *schabesgoïe* did the work in the kitchen, and old Lanche helped us watch, but Sâfel took the charge of the shop; his mother and I thought of nothing but our little David.

He died in the night of the eighteenth of March, the day when the fire broke out in Captain Cabanier's house.

That same night two shells fell upon our house; the blindage made them roll into the court, where they both burst, shattering the laundry windows and demolishing the butcher's door, which fell down at once with a fearful crash.

It was the most powerful bombardment since the blockade began, for, as soon as the enemy saw the flame ascending, they fired from Mittelbronn, from the Barracks, and the Fiquet lowlands, to prevent its being extinguished.

I stayed all the while with Sorlé, near the babe's bed, and the noise of the bursting shells did not disturb us.

The unhappy do not cling to life; and then the child was so sick! There were blue spots all over his body.

The end was drawing near.

I walked the room. Without they were crying "Fire! Fire!"

People passed in the street like a torrent. We heard those returning from the fire telling the news, the engines hurrying by, the soldiers ranging the crowd in the line, the shells bursting at the right and left.

Before our windows the long trails of red flame descended upon the roofs in front, and shattered the glass of the windows.

Our cannon all around the city replied to the enemy. Now and then we heard the cry: "Room! Room!"as the wounded were carried away.

Twice some pickets came up into my room to put me in the line, but, on seeing me sitting with Sorlé by our child, they went down again.

The first shell burst at our house about eleven o'clock, the second at four in the morning; everything shook, from the garret to the cellar; the floor, the bed, the furniture seemed to be upheaved; but, in our exhaustion and despair, we did not speak a single word.

Zeffen came running to us with Esdras and little Sâfel, at the first explosion. It was evident that little David was dying. Old Lanche and Sorlé were sitting, sobbing. Zeffen began to cry.

I opened the windows wide, to admit the air, and the powder-smoke which covered the city came into the room.

Sâfel saw at once that the hour was at hand. I needed only to look at him, and he went out, and soon returned by a side street, notwithstanding the crowd, with Kalmes the chanter, who began to recite the prayer of the dying:

The Lord reigneth! The Lord reigneth! The Lord shall reign everywhere and forever!
Praise, everywhere and forever, the name of His glorious reign!
The Lord is God! The Lord is God! The Lord is God!
Hear, oh Israel, the Lord our God is one God!
Go, then, where the Lord calleth thee—go, and may His mercy help thee!
May the Lord, our God, be with thee; may His immortal angels lead thee to heaven, and may the righteous be glad when the Lord shall receive thee into His bosom!
God of mercy, receive this soul into the midst of eternal joys!

Sorlé and I repeated, weeping, those holy words. Zeffen lay as if dead, her arms extended across the bed, over the feet of her child. Her brother Sâfel stood behind her, weeping bitterly, and calling softly, "Zeffen! Zeffen!"

But she did not hear; her soul was lost in infinite sorrows.

Without, the cries of "Fire!"the orders for the engines, the tumult of the crowd, the rolling of the cannonade still continued; the flashes, one after another, lighted up the darkness.

What a night, Fritz! What a night!

Suddenly Sâfel, who was leaning over under the curtain, turned round to us in terror. My wife and I ran, and saw that the child was dead. We raised our hands, sobbing, to indicate it. The chanter ceased his psalm. Our David was dead!

The most terrible thing was the mother's cry!

She lay, stretched out, as if she had fainted; but when the chanter leaned over and closed the lips, saying "Amen!" she rose, lifted the little one, looked at him, then, raising him above her head, began to run toward the door, crying out with a heart-rending voice:

"Baruch! Baruch! save our child!"

She was mad, Fritz! In this last terror I stopped her, and, by main force, took from her the little body which she was carrying away. And Sorlé, throwing her arms round her, with ceaseless groanings, Mother Lanche, the chanter, Sâfel, all led her away.

I remained alone, and I heard them go down, leading away my daughter.

How can a man endure such sorrows?

I put David back in the bed and covered him, because of the open windows. I knew that he was dead, but it seemed to me as if he would be cold. I looked at him for a long time, so as to retain that beautiful face in my heart.

It was all heart-rending—all! I felt as if my bowels were torn from me, and in my madness I accused the Lord, and said:

"I am the man that hath seen affliction by the rod of Thy wrath. Surely against me is He turned. My flesh and my skin hath He made old: He hath broken my bones. He hath set me in dark places. Also when I cry and shout He shutteth out my prayer. He was unto me as a lion in secret places! "

Thus I walked about, groaning and even blaspheming. But God in His mercy forgave me; He knew that it was not myself that spoke, but my despair.

At last I sat down, the others came back. Sorlé sat next to me in silence. Sâfel said to me:

"Zeffen has gone to the rabbi's with Esdras."

I covered my head without answering him.

Then some women came with old Lanche; I took Sorlé by the, hand, and we went into the large room, without speaking a word.

The mere sight of this room, where the two little brothers had played so long, made my tears come afresh, and Sorlé, Sâfel, and I wept together. The house was full of people; it might have been eight o'clock, and they knew already that we had a child dead.

CHAPTER 19

The Passover

Then, Fritz, the funeral rites began. All who died of typhus had to be buried the same day: Christians behind the church, and Jews in the trenches, in the place now occupied by the riding-school.

Old women were already there to wash the poor little body, and comb the hair, and cut the nails, according to the law of the Lord. Some of them sewed the winding-sheet.

The open windows admitted the air, the shutters struck against the walls. The *schamess* [1] went through the streets, striking the doors with his mace, to summon our brethren.

Sorlé sat upon the ground with her head veiled. Hearing Desmarets come up the stairs, I had courage to go and meet him, and show him the room. The poor angel was in his little shirt on the floor, the head raised a little on some straw, and the little *thaleth* in his fingers. He was so beautiful, with his brown hair, and half-opened lips, that I thought as I looked at him: "The Lord wanted to have thee near his throne!"

And my tears fell silently: my beard was full of them.

Desmarets then took the measure and went. Half an hour afterward, he returned with the little pine coffin under his arm, and the house was filled anew with lamentations.

I could not see the coffin closed! I went and sat upon the sack of ashes, covering my face with both hands, and crying in my heart like Jacob, "Surely I shall go down to the grave with this

---

1. Beadle.

child; I shall not survive him."

Only a very few of our brethren came, for a panic was in the city; men knew that the angel of death was passing by, and that drops of blood rained from his sword upon the houses; each emptied the water from his jug upon the threshold and entered quickly. But the best of them came silently, and as evening approached, it was necessary to go and descend by the postern.

I was the only one of our family. Sorlé was not able to follow me, nor Zeffen. I was the only one to throw the shovelful of earth. My strength all left me, they had to lead me back to our door. The sergeant held me by the arm; he spoke to me and I did not hear him; I was as if dead.

All else that I remember of that dreadful day, is the moment when, having come into the house, sitting on the sack, before our cold hearth, with bare feet and bent head, and my soul in the depths, the *schamess* came to me, touched my shoulder and made me rise; and then took his knife from his pocket and rent my garment, tearing it to the hip. This blow was the last and the most dreadful; I fell back, murmuring with Job:

Let the day perish wherein I was born, and the night in which it was said, there is a man child conceived! Let a cloud dwell upon it, let the blackness of the day terrify it! For mourning, the true mourning does not come down from the father to the child, but goes up from the child to the father. Why did the knees prevent me? or why the breasts that I should suck? For now I should have lain still in the tomb and been at rest!

And my grief, Fritz, had no bounds; "What will Baruch say," I exclaimed, "and what shall I answer him when he asks me to give him back his child?"

I felt no longer any interest in our business. Zeffen lived with the old rabbi; her mother spent the days with her, to take care of Esdras and comfort her.

Every part of our house was opened; the *schabesgoïé* burned sugar and spices, and the air from with- out had free circulation. Sâfel went on selling.

As for myself, I sat before the hearth in the morning, cooked some potatoes, and ate them with a little salt, and then went out, without thought or aim. I wandered sometimes to the right, sometimes to the left, toward the old gendarmerie, around the ramparts, in out-of-the-way places.

I could not bear to see any one, especially those who had known the child.

Then, Fritz, our miseries were at their height; famine, cold, all kinds of sufferings weighed upon the city; faces grew thin, and women and children were seen, half-naked and trembling, groping in the shadow in the deserted byways.

Ah! such miseries will never return!"We have no more such abominable wars, lasting twenty years, when the highways looked like ruts, and the roads like streams of mud; when the ground remained untilled for want of husbandmen, when houses sank for want of inhabitants; when the poor went barefoot and the rich in wooden shoes, while the superior officers passed by on superb horses, looking down contemptuously on the whole human race.

We could not endure that now!

But at that time everything in the nation was destroyed and humiliated; the citizens and the people had nothing left; force was everything. If a man said, "But there is such a thing as justice, right, truth!"the way was to answer with a smile, "I do not understand you!"and you were taken for a man of sense and experience, who would make his way.

Then, in the midst of my sorrow, I saw these things without thinking about them; but since then they have come back to me, and thousands of others; all the survivors of those days can remember them, too.

One morning, I was under the old market, looking at the wretches as they bought meat. At that time they knocked down the horses of Rouge-Colas and those of the *gendarmes*, as flesh-less as the cattle in the trenches, and sold the meat at very high prices.

I looked at the swarms of wrinkled old women, of hollow-eyed citizens, all these wretched creatures crowding before Frantz Sépel's stall, while he distributed bits of carcass to them.

Frantz's large dogs were seen no longer prowling about the market, licking up the bloody scraps. The dried hands of old women were stretched out at the end of their fleshless arms, to snatch everything; weak voices called out entreatingly, "A little more liver, Monsieur Frantz, so that we can make merry!"

I saw all this under the great dark roof, through which a little light came, in the holes made by the shells. In the distance, among the worm-eaten pillars, some soldiers, under the arch of the guard-house, with their old capes hanging down their thighs, were also looking on;—it seemed like a dream.

My great sorrow accorded with these sad sights. I was about leaving at the end of a half hour, when I saw Burguet coming along by Father Brainstein's old country-house, which was now staved in by the shells, and leaning, all shattered, over the street.

Burguet had told me several days before our affliction, that his maid-servant was sick. I had thought no more of it, but now it came to me.

He looked so changed, so thin, his cheeks so marked by wrinkles, it seemed as if years had passed since I had seen him. His hat came down to his eyes, and his beard, at least a fortnight old, had turned gray. He came in, looking round in all directions; but he could not see me where I was, in the deep shadow, against the planks of the old fodder-house; and he stopped behind the crowd of old women, who were squeezed in a semicircle before the stall, awaiting their turn.

After a minute he put some *sous* in Frantz Sépel's hand, and received his morsel, which he hid under his cloak. Then looking round again, he was going away quickly, with his head down.

This sight moved my heart: I hurried away, raising my hands to heaven, and exclaiming: "Is it possible? Is it possible? Burguet too! A man of his genius to suffer hunger and eat carcasses! Oh, what times of trial!"

I went home, completely upset.

We had not many provisions left; but, still, the next morning, as Sâfel was going down to open the shop, I said to him:

"Stop, my child, take this little basket to M. Burguet; it is some potatoes and salt beef. Take care that nobody sees it, they would take it from you. Say that it is in remembrance of the poor deserter."

The child went. He told me that Burguet wept.

This, Fritz, is what must be seen in a blockade, where you are attacked from day to day. This is what the Germans and Spaniards had to suffer, and what we suffered in our turn. This is war!

Even the siege rations were almost gone; but Moulin, the commandant of the place, having died of typhus, the famine did not prevent the lieutenant-colonel, who took his place, from giving balls and fetes to the envoys, in the old Thévenot house. The windows were bright, music played, the staff-officers drank punch and warm wine, to make believe that we were living in abundance. There was good reason for bandaging the eyes of these envoys till they reached the very ball-room, for, if they had seen the look of the people, all the punch-bowls and warm wines in the world would not have deceived them.

All this time, the grave-digger Mouyot and his two boys came every morning to take their two or three drops of brandy. They might say "We drink to the dead!" as the veterans said "We drink to the Cossacks!"

Nobody in the city would willingly have undertaken to bury those who had died of typhus; they alone, after taking their drop, dared to throw the bodies from the hospital upon a cart, and pile them up in the pit, and then they passed for grave-diggers, with Father Zébéde.

The order was to wrap the dead in a sheet. But who saw that it was done? Old Mouyot himself told me that they were buried in their cloaks or vests, as it might be, and sometimes entirely naked.

For every corpse, these men had their thirty-five *sous*; Father Mouyot, the blind man, can tell you so; it was his harvest.

Toward the end of March, in the midst of this fearful want, when there was not a dog, and still less a cat, to be seen in the streets, the city was full of evil tidings; rumours of battles lost, of marches upon Paris, etc.

As the envoys had been received, and balls given in their honour, something of our misfortunes became known either through the family or the servants.

Often, in wandering through the streets which ran along the ramparts, I mounted one of the bastions, looking toward Strasburg, or Metz, or Paris. I had no fear then of stray balls. I looked forth upon the thousand bivouac fires scattered over the plain, the soldiers of the enemy returning from the villages with their long poles hung with quarters of meat, at others crouched around the little fires which shone like stars upon the edge of the forest, and at their patrols and their covered batteries from which their flag was flying.

Sometimes I looked at the smoke of the chimneys at Quatre-Vents, or Bichelberg, or Mittelbronn. Our chimneys had no smoke, our festive days were over.

You can never imagine how many thoughts come to you, when you are so shut up, as your eyes follow the long white highways, and you imagine yourself walking there, talking with people about the news, asking them what they have suffered, and telling them what you have yourself endured.

From the bastion of the guard, I could see even the white peaks of the Schneeberg; I imagined myself in the midst of foresters, wood-cutters, and wood-splitters. There was a rumour that they were defending their route from Schirmeck; I longed to know if it were true.

As I looked toward the Maisons-Rouges, on the road to Paris, I imagined myself to be with my old friend Leiser; I saw him at his hearth, in despair at having to support so many people, for the Russian, Austrian, and Bavarian staff-officers remained upon this route, and new regiments went by continually.

And spring came! The snow began to melt in the furrows and behind the hedges. The great forests of La Bonne-Fontaine and the Barracks began to change their tents.

The thing which affected me most, as I have often remembered, was hearing the first lark at the end of March. The sky was entirely clear, and I looked up to see the bird. I thought of little David, and I wept, I knew not why.

Men have strange thoughts; they are affected by the song of a bird, and sometimes, years after, the same sounds recall the same emotions, so as even to make them weep.

At last the house was purified, and Zeffen and Sorlé came back to it.

The time of the Passover drew near; and the floors must be washed, the walls scoured, the vessels cleansed. In the midst of these cares, the poor women forgot, in some measure, our affliction; but as the time drew nearer our anxiety increased; how, in the midst of this famine, were we to obey the command of God:

This month shall be the first month of the year to you.

In the tenth day of this month they shall take to them every man a lamb, according to the house of their fathers, a lamb for a house.

Ye shall take it out from the sheep or from the goats.

And ye shall keep it until the fourteenth day of the same month.

And they shall eat the flesh in that night, roast with fire, and unleavened bread; and with bitter herbs shall they eat it.

But where was the sacrificial lamb to be found? Schmoûlé alone, the old *schamess*, had thought of it for us all, three months before; he had nourished a male goat of that year in his cellar, and that was the goat that was killed.

Every Jewish family had a portion of it, small indeed, but the law of the Lord was fulfilled.

We invited on that day, according to the law, one of the poorest of our brethren, Kalmes. We went together to the synagogue; the prayers were recited, and then we returned to partake of the feast at our table.

Everything was ready and according to the proper order, notwithstanding the great destitution; the white cloth, the goblet of vinegar, the hard egg, the horseradish, the unleavened bread, and the flesh of the goat. The lamp with seven burners shone above it; but we had not much bread.

Having taken my seat in the midst of my family, Sâfel took the jug and poured water upon my hands; then we all bent forward, each took a piece of bread, saying with heavy hearts:

This is the bread of affliction which our fathers ate in Egypt. Whosoever is hungry, let him come and eat with us. Whosoever is poor, let him come and make the Passover!

We sat down again, and Sâfel said to me:

"What mean ye by this service, my father?"

And I answered:

"We were slaves in Egypt, my child, and the Lord brought us forth with a mighty hand and an outstretched arm!"

These words inspired us with courage; we hoped that God would deliver us as He had delivered our fathers, and that the Emperor would be His right arm; but we were mistaken, the Lord wanted nothing more of that man!

CHAPTER 20

Peace

The next morning, at daybreak, between six and seven o'clock, when we were all asleep, the report of a cannon made our windows rattle. The enemy usually fired only at night. I listened; a second report followed after a few seconds, then another, then others, one by one.

I rose, opened a window, and looked out. The sun was rising behind the arsenal. Not a soul was in the street; but, as one report came after another, doors and windows were opened; men in their shirts leaned out, listening.

No shells hissed through the air; the enemy fired blank cartridges.

As I listened, a great murmur came from the distance, outside of the city. First it came from the Mittelbronn Hill, then it reached the Bichelberg, Quatre-Vents, the upper and lower Barracks.

Sorlé had just risen also; I finished dressing, and said to her:

"Something extraordinary is going on—God grant that it may be for good!"

And I went down in great perturbation.

It was not a quarter of an hour since the first report, and the whole city was out. Some ran to the ramparts, others were in groups, shouting and disputing at the corners of the streets. Astonishment, fear, and anger were depicted upon every face.

A large number of soldiers were mingled with the citizens, and all went up together in groups to the right and left of the

French gate.

I was about following one of these groups, when Burguet came down the street. He looked thin and emaciated, as on the day when I saw him in the market.

"Well!"said I, running to meet him, "this is something serious!"

"Very serious, and promising no good, Moses!"said he.

"Yes, it is evident," said I, "that the allies have gained victories; it may be that they are in Paris!"

He turned around in alarm, and said in a low voice:

"Take care, Moses, take care! If anyone heard you, at a moment like this, the veterans would tear you in pieces!"

I was dreadfully frightened, for I saw that he was right, while, as for him, his cheeks shook. He took me by the arm and said:

"I owe you thanks for the provisions you sent me; they came very opportunely."

And when I answered that we should always have a morsel of bread at his service, so long as we had any left, he pressed my hand; and we went together up the street of the infantry quarters, as far as to the ice-house bastion, where two batteries had been placed to command the Mittelbronn Hill. There we could see the road to Paris as far as to Petite Saint Jean, and even to Lixheim; but those great heaps of earth, called *cavaliers*, were covered with people; Baron Parmentier, his assistant Pipelingre, the old curate Leth, and many other men of note were there, in the midst of the crowd, looking on in silence. We had only to see their faces to know that something dreadful was happening.

From this height on the talus, we saw what was riveting everybody's attention. All our enemies, Austrians, Bavarians, Wurtemburgers, Russians, cavalry and infantry mixed together, were swarming around their intrenchments like ants, embracing each other, shaking hands, lifting their shakos on the points of their bayonets, waving branches of trees just beginning to turn green. Horsemen dashed across the plain, with their *colbacs* on the point of their swords, and rending the air with their shouts.

The telegraph was in operation on the hill of Saint Jean; Burguet pointed it out to me.

"If we understood those signals, Moses," said he, "we should know better what was going to happen to us in the next fortnight."

Some persons having turned round to listen to us, we went down again into the streets of the quarters, very thoughtfully.

The soldiers at the upper windows of the barracks were also looking out. Men and women in great numbers were collecting in the street.

We went through the crowd. In the street of the Capuchins, which was always deserted, Burguet, who was walking with his head down, exclaimed:

"So it is all over! What things have we seen in these last twenty-five years, Moses! What astonishing and terrible things! And it is all over!"

He took hold of my hand, and looked at me as if he were astonished at his own words; then he began to walk on.

"This winter campaign has been frightful to me," said he; "it has dragged along—dragged along—and the thunder-bolt did not come! But tomorrow, the day after tomorrow, what are we going to hear? Is the Emperor dead? How will that affect us? Will France still be France? What will they leave us? What will they take from us?"

Reflecting on these things, we came in front of our house. Then, as if suddenly wakened, Burguet said to me:

"Prudence, Moses! If the Emperor is not dead, the veterans will hold out till the last second. Remember that, and whoever they suspect will have everything to fear."

I thanked him, and went up, promising myself that I would follow his advice.

My wife and children were waiting breakfast for me, with the little basket of potatoes upon the table. We sat down, and I told them in a low voice what was to be seen from the top of the ramparts, and charged them to keep silent, for the danger was not over; the garrison might revolt and choose to defend itself, in spite of the officers; and those who mixed themselves in these matters, either for or against, even only in words, ran the risk of destruction without profit to anyone.

They saw that I was right, and I had no need of saying more.

We were afraid that our sergeant would come, and that we should be obliged to answer him, if he asked what we thought of these matters; but he did not come in till about eleven, when we had all been in bed for a long time.

The next day the news of the entrance of the allies to Paris was affixed to the church doors and the pillars of the market; it was never known by whom! M. de Vablerie, and three or four other emigrants, capable of such a deed, were spoken of at the time, but nothing was known with certainty.

The mounted guard tore down the placards, but unfortunately not before the soldiers and citizens had read them.

It was something so new, so incredible, after those ten years of war, when the Emperor had been everything, and the nation had been, so to speak, in the shadow; when not a man had dared to speak or write a word without permission; when men had had no other rights than those of paying, and giving their sons as conscripts,—it was such a great matter to think that the Emperor could have been conquered, that a man like myself in the midst of his family shook his head three or four times, before daring to breathe a single word.

So everybody kept quiet, notwithstanding the placards. The officials stayed at home, so as not to have to talk about it; the governor and council of defence did not stir; but the last recruits, in the hope of going home to their villages, embracing their families, and returning to their trades or farming, did not conceal their joy, as was very natural. The veterans, whose only trade and only means of living was war, were full of indignation! They did not believe a word of it; they declared that the reports were all false, that the Emperor had not lost a battle, and that the placards and the cannon firing of the allies were only a stratagem to make us open the gates.

And from that time, Fritz, the men began to desert, not one

at a time, but by sixes, by tens, by twenties. Whole posts filed off over the mountain with their arms and baggage. The veterans fired upon the deserters; they killed some of them, and were ordered to escort the conscripts who carried soup to the outposts.

During this time, the flag of truce officers did nothing but come and go, one after another. All, Russian, Austrian, Bavarian, staff-officers stayed whole hours at the head-quarters, having, no doubt, important matters to discuss.

Our sergeant came to our room only for a moment in the evening, to complain of the desertions, and we were glad of it; Zeffen was still sick, Sorlé could not leave her, and I had to help Sâfel until the people went home.

The shop was always full of veterans; as soon as one set went away another came.

These old, gray-headed men swallowed down glass after glass of brandy; they paid by turns, and grew more and more downhearted. They trembled with rage, and talked of nothing but treason, while they looked at you as if they would see through you.

Sometimes they would smile and say:

"I tell you! if it is necessary to blow up the fortress, it will go!"

Sâfel and I pretended not to understand; but you can imagine our agony; after having suffered all that we had, to be in danger of being blown up with those veterans!

That evening our sergeant repeated word for word what the others had said: "It was all nothing but lies and treason. The Emperor would put a stop to it by sweeping off this rabble!"

"Just wait! Just wait!" he exclaimed, as he smoked his pipe, with his teeth set. "It will all be cleared up soon! The thunderbolt is coming! And, this time, no pity, no mercy! All the villains will have to go then—all the traitors! The country will have to be cleansed for a hundred years! Never mind, Moses, we'll laugh!"

You may well suppose that we did not feel like laughing.

But the day when I was most anxious was the eighth of April, in the morning, when the decree of the Senate, deposing the Emperor, appeared.

Our shop was full of marine artillerymen and subalterns from the storehouses. "We had just served them, when the secretary of the treasury, a short stout man, with full yellow cheeks, and the regulation cap over his ears, came in and called for a glass; he then took the decree from his pocket.

"Listen!"said he, as he began calmly to read it to the others. It seems as if I could hear it now:

Whereas, Napoleon Bonaparte has violated the compact which bound him to the French nation, by levying taxes otherwise than in virtue of the law, by unnecessarily ad-journing the Legislative Body, by illegally making many decrees involving sentence of death, by annulling the authority of the ministers, the independence of the judiciary, the freedom of the press, etc.; Whereas, Napoleon has filled up the measure of the country's misfortunes, by his abuse of all the means of war committed to him, in men and money, and by refusing to treat on conditions which the national interest required him to accept; Whereas, the manifest wish of all the French demands an order of things, the first result of which shall be the re-establishment of general peace, and which shall also be the epoch of solemn reconciliation between all the States of the great European family, the Senate decrees: Napoleon Bonaparte has forfeited the throne; the right of succession is abolished in his family; the people and the army are re-leased from the oath of allegiance to him.

He had scarcely begun to read when I thought: "If that goes on they will tear down my shop over my head."

In my fright, I even sent Sâfel out hastily by the back door. But it all happened very differently from what I expected. These veterans despised the Senate; they shrugged their shoulders, and the one who read the decree sniffed at it, and threw it under the counter. "The Senate!"said he. "What is the Senate? A set of hangers-on, a set of sycophants that the Emperor has bribed, right and left, to keep saying to him—'God bless you!'"

"Yes, major," said another; "but they ought to be kicked out all the same."

"Bah! It is not worth the trouble," replied the sergeant-major; "a fortnight hence, when the Emperor is master again, they will come and lick his boots. Such men are necessary in a dynasty-men who lick your boots—it has a good effect!—especially old nobility, who are paid thirty or forty thousand *francs* a year. They will come back, and be quiet, and the Emperor will pardon them, especially since he cannot find others noble enough to fill their places."

And as they all went away after emptying their glasses, I thanked heaven for having given them such confidence in the Emperor.

This confidence lasted till about the eleventh or twelfth of April, when some officers, sent by the general commanding the fourth military division, came to say that the garrison of Metz recognized the Senate and followed its orders.

This was a terrible blow for our veterans. We saw, that evening, by our sergeant's face, that it was a death-blow to him. He looked ten years older, and you would have wept merely to see his face. Up to that time he had kept saying: "All these decrees, all these placards are acts of treason! The Emperor is down yonder with his army, all the while, and we are here to support him. Don't fear, Father Moses!"

But since the arrival of the officers from Metz, he had lost his confidence. He came into our room, without speaking, and stood up, very pale, looking at us.

I thought: "But this man loves us. He has been kind to us. He gave us his fresh meat all through the blockade; he loved our little David; he fondled him on his knees. He loves Esdras too. He is a good, brave man, and here he is, so wretched!"

I wanted to comfort him, to tell him that he had friends, that we all loved him, that we would make sacrifices to help him, if he had to change his employment; yes, I thought of all this, but as I looked at him his grief seemed so terrible that I could not say a word.

He took two or three turns and stopped again, then suddenly went out. His sorrow was too great, he would not even speak of it.

At length, on the sixteenth of April, an armistice was concluded for burying the dead. The bridge of the German gate was lowered, and large numbers of people went out and stayed till evening, to dig the ground a little with their spades, and try to bring back a few green things. Zeffen being all this time sick, we stayed at home.

That evening two new officers from Metz, sent as envoys, came in at night as the bridges were being raised. They galloped along the street to the head-quarters. I saw them pass.

The arrival of these officers greatly excited the hopes and fears of every one; important measures were expected, and all night long we heard the sergeant walk to and fro in his room, get up, walk about, and lie down again, talking confusedly to himself.

The poor man felt that a dreadful blow was coming, and he had not a minute's rest. I heard him lamenting, and his sighs kept me from sleeping.

The next morning at ten the assembly was beat. The governor and the members of the council of defence went, in full dress, to the infantry quarters.

Everybody in the city was at the windows.

Our sergeant went down, and I followed him in a few minutes. The street was thronged with people. I made my way through the crowd; everybody kept his place in it, trying to move on.

When I came in front of the barracks, the companies had just formed in a circle; the quartermasters in the midst were reading in a loud voice the order of the day; it was the abdication of the Emperor, the disbanding of the recruits of 1813 and 1814, the recognition of Louis XVIII., the order to set up the white flag and change the cockade!

Not a murmur was heard from the ranks; all was quiet, terrible, frightful! Those old soldiers, their teeth set, their moustaches shaking, their brows scowling fiercely, presenting arms in silence; the voices of the quartermasters stopping now and then as if choking; the staff-officers of the place, at a distance under the arch, sullen, with their eyes on the ground; the eager attention of all that crowd of men, women, and children, through the whole length of the street, leaning forward on tiptoe, with open mouths and listening ears; all this, Fritz, would have made you tremble.

I was on cooper Schweyer's steps, where I could see everything and hear every word.

So long as the order of the day was read, nobody stirred; but at the command:—Break ranks! a terrible cry arose from all directions; tumult, confusion, fury burst forth at once.

People did not know what they were doing. The conscripts ran in files to the postern gates, the old soldiers stood a moment, as if rooted to the spot, then their rage broke forth; one tore off his epaulettes, another dashed his musket with both hands against the pavement; some officers doubled up their sabres and swords, which snapped apart with, a crash.

The governor tried to speak; he tried to form the ranks again, but nobody heard him; the new recruits were already in all the rooms at the barracks, making up their bundles to start on their journey; the old ones were going to the right and left, as if they were drunk or mad.

I saw some of these old soldiers stop in a corner, lean their heads against the wall, and weep bitterly.

At last all were dispersed, and protracted cries reached from the barracks to the square, incessant cries, which rose and fell like sighs.

Some low, despairing shouts of "*Vive l'Empereur!*" but not a single shout of "*Vive le Roi!*"

For my part, I ran home to tell about it all; I tad scarcely gone up, when the sergeant came also, with his musket on his shoulder. We should have liked to congratulate each other on the ending of the blockade, but on seeing the sergeant standing at the door, we were chilled to the bones, and our attention was fixed upon him.

"Ah, well!"said he, placing the butt-end of his musket upon the floor, "it is all ended!"

And for a moment he said no more.

Then he stammered out: "This is the shabbiest piece of business in the world—the recruits are disbanded—they are leaving—France remains, bound hand and foot, in the grip of the *kaiserlichs*! Ah! the rascals! the rascals!"

"Yes, sergeant," I replied with emotion, seeing that his thoughts must be diverted: "now we are going to have peace, sergeant! You have a sister left in the Jura, you will go to her—"

"Oh!"he exclaimed, lifting his hand, "my poor sister!"

This came like a sob; but he quickly recovered himself, and went and placed his musket in the corner by the door.

He sat down at the table with us for a moment;, and took up little Sâfel, drawing him to him and caressing his cheeks. Then he wanted to hold Esdras also. We looked on in silence.

"I am going to leave you, Father Moses," said he, "I am going to pack my bag. Thunder and. lightning! I am sorry to leave you!"

"And we are sorry, too, sergeant," said Sorlé, mournfully; "but if you will live with us—"

"It is impossible!"

"Then you remain in the service?"

"Service of whom—of what?" said he; "of Louis XVIII.? No! no! I know no one but my general—but that makes it hard to go when a man has done his duty—"

He started up, and shouted in a piercing voices "*Vive l'Empereur*!"

"We trembled, we did not know why.

I reached out my hand to him, and rose; we embraced each other like brothers.

"Goodbye, Father Moses," said he, "goodbye for a long while."

"You are going at once, then?"

"Yes!"

"You know, sergeant, that you will always have friends here. You will come and see us. If you need anything—"

"Yes, yes, I know it. You are true friends excellent people!"

He shook my hand vehemently.

Then he took up his musket, and we were all following him, expressing our good wishes, when he turned, with tears in his eyes, and embraced my wife, saying:

"I must embrace you, too; there is no harm in it, is there, Madame Sorlé?"

"Oh, no!" said she, "you are one of the family, .and I will embrace Zeffen for you!"

He went out at once, exclaiming in a hoarse voice, "Goodbye! Farewell!"

I saw him go into his room at the end of the little passage.

Twenty-five years of service, eight wounds, and no bread in his old age! My heart bled at the thought of it.

About a quarter of an hour after, the sergeant came down with his musket. Meeting Sâfel on the stairs, he said to him, "Stay, that is for your father!"

It was the portrait of the *landwehr's* wife and children. Sâfel brought it to me at once. I took the poor devil's gift, and looked at it for a long time, very sadly; then I shut it up in the closet with the letter.

It was noon, and, as the gates were about to be opened, and abundance of provisions were to come, we sat down before a large piece of boiled beef, with a dish of potatoes, and opened a good bottle of wine.

We were still eating when we heard shouts in the street. Sâfel got up to look out.

"A wounded soldier that they are carrying to the hospital!" said he.

Then he exclaimed, "It is our sergeant!"

A horrible thought ran through my mind. "Keep still!" I said to Sorlé, who was getting up, and I went down alone.

Four marine gunners were carrying the litter by on their shoulders; children were running behind.

At the first glance I recognized the sergeant; his face perfectly white and his breast covered with blood. He did not move. The poor fellow had gone from our house to the bastion behind the arsenal, to shoot himself through the heart.

I went up so overwhelmed, so sad and sorrowful, that I could scarcely stand.

Sorlé was waiting for me in great agitation.

"Our poor sergeant has killed himself," said I; "may God forgive him!"

And, sitting down, I could not help bursting into tears!

CHAPTER 21

Conclusion

It is said with truth that misfortunes never come singly; one brings another in its train. The death of our good sergeant was, however, the last.

That same day the enemy withdrew his outposts to six hundred yards from the city, the white flag was raised on the church, and the gates were opened.

Now, Fritz, you know about our blockade. Should I tell you, in addition, about Baruch's coming, of Zeffen's cries, and the groanings of us all, when we had to say to the good man: "Our little David is dead—thou wilt never see him again!"

No, it is enough! If we were to speak of all the miseries of war, and all their consequences in after years, there would be no end!

I would rather tell you of my sons Itzig and Frômel, and of my Sâfel, who has gone to join them in America.

If I should tell you of all the wealth they have acquired in that great country of freemen, of the lands they have bought, the money they have laid up, the number of grandchildren they have given me, and of all the blessings they have heaped upon Sorlé and myself, you would be full of astonishment and admiration.

They have never allowed me to want for anything. The greatest pleasure I can give them is to wish for something; each of them wants to send it to me! They do not forget that by my prudent foresight I saved them from the war.

I love them all alike, Fritz, and I say of them, like Jacob:

May the God of Abraham and Isaac, our fathers, the God which fed me all my life long unto this day, bless the lads; let them grow into a multitude in the midst of the earth, and their seed become a multitude of nations!

The Invasion of France in 1814

Contents

Introductory Note

The invasion of France by the allied armies after the battle of Leipsic had proved the German campaign even more disastrous than that of Russia the year before, was not only essentially the death-blow to the power of Napoleon, but was the first real taste France had had for many years of an experience she had so often previously meted out to her neighbours. In spite of all she had suffered from the conscription, and from exhaustion of men and treasure in offensive war—or at least war waged outside her own territory—the great Invasion meant for her something far more terrible than any reverses she had yet undergone.

Napoleon was not only not invincible, it appeared, he was not even able to defend the frontiers he had found firmly established on his accession to power. The allies had announced that they were warring not against France but against the French Emperor—"against the preponderance that Napoleon had too long exercised beyond the limits of his empire." Everywhere in France except in the official world of Paris, the once enchanted name of Napoleon had become recognized as a synonym of national disaster.

Nevertheless nothing—except, perhaps, the similar circumstances of the Prussian invasion in 1870—has ever so well attested the fundamental and absorbing patriotism of the French people as their heroic resistance to this invasion and their instinctive and universal refusal to separate in this crisis the cause of their Emperor from their own. The presence of a foreign foe on whatever pretext within their boundaries sufficed to arouse them *en masse*. No such enthusiasm had been known since the days of the Republic's and the Consulate's victories as was awakened, in the thick of national disaster and amid the ruin of all ambitious hopes, by the thought of an enemy within the borders of *la patrie*.

And in *The Invasion* of MM. Erckmann-Chatrian this enthusiasm and devotion find a chronicle which is most realistically impressive. So soon as the peasants of the outlying villages of the eastern frontier learn of the impending descent of the Cossacks and Germans, without thought of their own comfort and safety—which it is, however, impartially pointed out they know would hardly be better secured by submission—they organize for resistance. They blockade the highways and defend the mountain passes. Women and children aid in the work.

While the siege of Phalsbourg goes on the heights are occupied by sturdy peasants who oppose for a while an effective obstacle to the passage of the invaders. The worst hardships, the most perilous adventures, are accepted by them with the heroic courage of regulars. Outlaws and smugglers work and fight hand to hand with the respected worthies of the neighbourhood. They watch their farms burn from their outlook on the hilltops, they suffer the pangs of starvation when their supplies are Intercepted by the enemy, they fight to desperation when their position is finally turned by the treachery of a crazy German they have long harboured—and whose vagaries give, by the way, a most romantic colour to the narrative—and they are finally slain or captured just as Paris capitulates and peace is made. None of the National Novels is more graphic or more significant historically than *The Invasion*.

CHAPTER 1

The Old Shoemaker and
His Daughter

If you would wish to know the history of the great invasion of 1814, such as it was related to me by the old hunter Frantz du Hengst, you must transport yourself to the village of Charmes, in the Vosges. About thirty small houses, covered with shingles and dark-green houseleeks, stand in rows along the banks of the Sarre: you can see the gables carpeted with ivy and withered honeysuckles, for winter is approaching; the beehives closed with corks of straw, the small gardens, the palings, the hedges which separate them one from the other.

To the left, on a high mountain, arise the ruins of the ancient *château* of Falkenstein, destroyed two hundred years ago by the Swedes. It is now only a mass of stones and brambles; an old "timber-way," with its worn-out steps, ascends to it through the pine-trees. To the right, on the side of the hill, one can perceive the farm of Bois-de-Chênes—a large building, with granaries, stables, and sheds, the flat roof loaded with great stones, in order to resist the north wind. A few cows are grazing in the heather, a few goats on the rocks.

Everything is calm and silent.

Some children, in gray stuff trousers, their heads and feet bare, are warming themselves around their little fires on the outskirts of the woods; the spiral lines of blue smoke fade away in the air, great white clouds remain immovable above the valley; behind these clouds arise the arid peaks of the Grosmann and Donon.

You must know that the end house of the village, whose square roof is pierced by two loophole windows, and whose low door opens on the muddy street, belonged, in 1813, to Jean-Claude Hullin, one of the old volunteers of '92, but now a shoe-maker in the village of Charmes, and who was held in much consideration by the mountaineers. Hullin was a short stout man, with gray eyes, large lips, a short nose, and thick eyebrows.

He was of a jovial, kind disposition, and did not know how to refuse anything to his daughter Louise, a child whom he had picked up among some miserable gypsies—farriers and tin-sell-ers—without house or dwelling-place, who go from village to village mending pots and pans, melting the ladles, and patching up cracked utensils. He considered her as his own daughter, and never seemed to remember she came of a strange race.

Besides this natural affection, the good old fellow possessed others still: he loved above all his cousin, the old mistress of the farm of Bois-de-Chênes, Catherine Lefèvre, and her son Gasp-ard, who had been carried off that year by the conscription—a handsome young fellow, the *fiancé* of Louise, and whose return was expected by all the family at the end of the campaign.

Hullin recalled always with enthusiasm his campaigns of the Sambre-et-Meuse, of Italy and of Egypt. He often thought of them, and sometimes in the evening, when the work was over, he would go to the sawmills of Valtin, that dark manufactory formed of trunks of trees still bearing their bark, and which you can perceive down there at the end of the valley.

He sat down among the woodcutters and charcoal-gatherers, and sledges, in front of the great fire; and while the heavy wheel turned, the dam thundered and the saws grinded, he, his elbow on his knee, and his pipe in his mouth, would speak to them of Hoche, of Kleber, and finally of General Bonaparte, whom he had seen hundreds of times, and whose thin face, piercing eyes, and eagle profile, he would depict as though he were present.

Such was Jean-Claude Hullin.

He was one of the old Gallic stock, fond of extraordinary

adventures and heroic enterprises, but constant to his work, out of a sentiment of duty, from New Year 's Day until Saint Sylvester's.

As for Louise, the child of the tramp, she was a slender creature, with long delicate hands, eyes of such a soft deep blue that they seemed to penetrate to the depths of your soul, skin of a snowy whiteness, hair of a pale straw-colour, like silk in texture, and drooping shoulders like those of a virgin praying. Her ingenuous smile, pensive forehead—in fact, her whole appearance—recalled the old *Lied* of the Minnesinger Erhart, when he said:

I have seen a ray of light pass by: my eyes are still dazzled by it. Was it a moonbeam piercing the foliage? Was it a smile from the dawn in the forests? No, it was the beautiful Edith, my love, who passed by. I have seen her, and my eyes are still dazzled.

Louise only cared for fields, gardens, and flowers. In springtime, the first notes of the skylark made her shed tears of delight. She went to gee the budding hawthorn and blue cornflowers behind the hedges on the hillsides; she watched for the return of the swallows, from the little windows of the garret. She was always the true child of the homeless vagrants, only less wild. Hullin forgave her everything; he understood her nature, and would sometimes say, laughingly:—"My poor Louise, with the booty that thou bringest us,—thy fine sheaves of flowers and golden wheat-ears—we should die of hunger in three days!"

Then she would smile so tenderly at him and embrace him so willingly, that he would go on with his work, saying:—"Bah! Why need I grumble? She is right: she loves the sunshine. Gaspard will work for two—he will have the happiness of four. I do not pity him: on the contrary. One can find plenty of women who work, and that does not improve their beauty; but loving woman! What luck to have found one—what luck!"

Thus reasoned the good old fellow; and days, weeks, and months wore away in the expectation of Gaspard's return.

Madame Lefèvre, an extremely energetic woman, partook of

Hullin's ideas on the subject of Louise.

"As for me," she said, "I only want a daughter who loves us; I do not wish her to have anything to do with my household affairs. So long as she is contented! Thou wilt not bother me—is it not so, Louise?"

And then they would embrace each other. But Gaspard did not return, and for two months they had had no tidings of him.

On that same day, toward the middle of December, 1813, between three and four o'clock in the afternoon, Hullin, bending over his bench, was finishing a pair of nailed shoes for the woodcutter Rochart. Louise had just put an earthenware porringer down on the little iron stove, which sang and crackled in a plaintive manner, while the old clock counted the seconds in its monotonous tic-tac. Outside, all along the street, could be perceived small pools of water, covered with a coating of thin white ice, announcing the approach of intense cold.

At times the sound of great wooden shoes, running along the hardened road, could be heard, and a felt hat, a cape, or a woollen cap would pass by: then the noise would cease, and the plaintive hissing of the green wood in the flames, the humming of Louise's spinning-wheel, and the boiling of the porridge-pot again prevailed. This had gone on for about two hours, when Hullin, glancing accidentally through the little window-panes, stopped his work, and remained with his eyes wide open, staring, as though absorbed by some unusual spectacle.

In fact, at the corner of the street, in front of the "Trois Pigeons," there advanced, in the midst of a crowd of whistling, jumping, and shouting boys, who called out "The King of Diamonds! The King of Diamonds!"—There advanced, I say, one of the strangest personages imaginable. Picture to yourself a red-headed, red-bearded man, with a grave face, gloomy expression, straight nose, the eyebrows meeting on the forehead, a circle of tin on the head, a gray dog-skin floating over the back, its forepaws tied around the neck; the chest covered with little copper crosses, the legs clothed with a sort of gray cloth trousers fastened above the ankle, and the feet bare. A great raven, with black wings glossed over with white, was perched on his shoulder. From his imposing gait one would have taken him for one of the ancient Merovingian kings, such as are represented by the images of Montbéliard; he held in the left hand a short thick stick in the shape of a sceptre, and with the right he made ostentatious gestures, raising his finger toward heaven, and apostrophizing his retinue.

All the doors opened on his passage; behind every pane appeared inquisitive faces. Some few old women on the outer stairs of their houses, called out to the madman, who would not deign to turn his head; others went down into the streets and tried to prevent him passing; but he, lifting his head and raising his eyebrows, with one word and a sign, forced them to make way.

"Hullo!" said Hullin, "here is Yégof. I did not expect to have seen him again this winter. It is not one of his customs. What on earth can bring him back in such weather?"

And Louise, laying down her distaff, hurried away to contemplate "The King of Diamonds." It was a great event, the arrival of Yégof the madman at the commencement of winter: some rejoiced over it, hoping to keep him and make him relate his glory and fortunes in the inns; others, and especially the women, were filled with a sort of vague uneasiness, for madmen, as all know, have ideas from another world: they know the past and the future—they are inspired by God: the only thing is to know how to understand them—their words bearing always two meanings: one for the ordinary run of people, the other for more refined and delicate souls, and the wise.

This madman besides, more than another, had truly some sublime and extraordinary thoughts. None knew from whence he came, nor where he went, nor what he wanted; for Yégof wandered about the country like some troubled spirit. He spoke of extinct races, and pretended that he was Emperor of Australasia, of Polynesia, and of other lands besides. Great books could have been written on his palaces, castles, and strongholds—of which he knew the number, the situation, the architecture— and whose beauty, riches, and grandeur, he would celebrate in a simple and modest manner.

He spoke of his stables, of his hunts, of his crown-officers, ministers, counsellors, of the heads of his provinces; he never made any mistakes as to their names or different merits; but he bitterly bewailed having been dethroned by the accursed race: and the old midwife, Sapience Coquelin, every time that she heard him groan over this subject, would cry bitterly, and others also did the same. Then he would raise his arms to heaven and cry out,—"O women, women! remember, remember! The hour approaches—the spirits of darkness flee! the old race—the masters of your masters—advance like the waves of the sea!"

And every spring he was in the habit of making a survey of all the old owls' nests, the ancient castles, and all the ruins which crown the Vosges in the depths of their forests, at Nideck, Géroldseck, Lutzelbourg, and Turkestein, saying that he was going to visit his territories, talking of re-establishing the past splendour of his states, and of putting all mutinous people into slavery, with the aid of his cousin the "Grand Gôlo."

Jean-Claude Hullin made light of these things, from not having a soul elevated enough to enter into the invisible spheres; but Louise was much troubled by them—above all, when the raven napped its wings and gave its hoarse cry.

Yégof, then, descended the street, without stopping anywhere; and Louise, all excitement, seeing that he looked toward their little house, said aloud,—"Papa Jean-Claude, I believe he is coming our way."

"It is quite possible," replied Hullin. "The poor devil must be in need of a pair of good lined shoes for the great cold, and if he were to ask me, I should hardly be able to refuse them to him."

"Oh, how kind you are!" said the young girl, embracing him affectionately.

"Yes, yes! thou art flattering me," said he, laughing, "because I do what thou wishest. Who will pay me for my wood and work? It will not be Yégof!"

Louise kissed him again, and Hullin, looking lovingly at her, murmured,—"This payment is worth the other."

Yégof was then about fifteen yards from their door: the tumult still kept increasing; the boys hung on to the tatters of his coat, crying out, "Diamond! Club! Spade!" Suddenly he turned, raised his sceptre, and called out in a dignified though furious manner,—"Go back, accursed race! Go back, deafen me no longer, or I will loose my bloodhounds against you!"

This menace only made the shouts of laughter and hisses redouble; but as at that moment Hullin appeared on the threshold with a long strap in his hand, and distinguishing five or six of the most obstinate among them, he warned them that that evening he would go and pull their ears during their supper—a feat which he had already performed several times with the consent of the parents, the whole band dispersed in great consternation. Then, going toward the madman,—"Enter, Yégof," said the shoemaker, "come and warm thyself by the fire."

"I do not call myself Yégof," replied the unhappy man, looking offended. "I call myself Luitprandt, King of Australasia and Polynesia."

"Yes, yes, I know," said Jean-Claude—"I know! Thou hast already told me all that. But what does it matter that thou callest thyself Yégof, or Luitprandt? come in all the same. It is cold; try to warm thyself."

"I come in," replied the madman; "but it is for a much more serious affair: it is for a state affair—to form an indissoluble alliance between the Germans and the Triboques."

"Well, we will talk of that."

Yégof, stooping under the door, entered as though in a reverie, and saluted Louise by bowing and lowering his sceptre; but the raven would not come in. Opening his great wings, he made a circuit around the house, and came and fastened himself onto the window-panes to break them.

"Hans," shouted the madman, "take care! I am coming!"

But the bird did not detach its sharp claws from the casement, and never ceased fluttering its great wings so long as its master remained in the cottage. Louise did not take her eyes off it: she was afraid. As for Yégof, he sat down in the old leathern armchair behind the stove, his legs stretched out as though on a throne; and gazing around him in a triumphant manner, he cried out,—"I come direct from Jérome, to conclude an alliance with thee, Hullin. Thou art not ignorant that I have deigned to cast my eyes on thy daughter, and I come to ask her of thee in marriage."

At this proposition Louise blushed to the roots of her hair, and Hullin burst into a loud laugh.

"Thou laughest!" cried the madman, in a hollow voice. "Well! thou art wrong to laugh. This alliance may alone save thee from the impending ruin of thyself, thy house, and all thy belongings.

At this moment my armies are advancing. They are countless—they cover the earth. What can you do against me? You will be vanquished, annihilated, or reduced to slavery, as you have already been for centuries: for I, Luitprandt, King of Australasia and of Polynesia—I have decided that everything shall be as it once was. Remember!"—here the madman raised his finger solemnly—"remember what has passed! You have been beaten! And we, the old northern races—we have put our yokes upon you. We have burdened you with the largest stones for building our strong castles and our subterraneous prisons; we have harnessed you to our ploughs; you have been before us as the straw before the hurricane. Remember, remember, Triboque, and tremble!"

"I remember very well," said Hullin, still laughing; "but we had our revenge. Thou knowest?"

"Yes, yes," interrupted Yégof, frowning; "but that time has gone by. My warriors are more numerous than the leaves in the forests; and your blood flows like the water of the brooks. Thou, I know thee—I knew thee a thousand years ago!"

"Bah!" said Hullin.

"Yes, it was this hand—dost thou hear?—this hand that has vanquished thee, when, for the first time, we entered your forests. It has made thy head bow beneath the yoke—it will make it bend again! Because you are brave, you believe your- selves masters of this country and of all France forever. Well, you are wrong! We have spoiled you, and we will spoil you again. We will restore Alsace and Lorraine to Germany, Brittany and Normandy to the men from the North, with Flanders and the South to Spain. We will make France into a little kingdom around Paris—a very little kingdom with a descendant of the ancient race at your head. And you will no longer agitate yourselves-you will be very tranquil. Ha, ha, ha!" Yégof began to laugh.

Hullin, who had no knowledge of history, was astonished that he should know so many names.

"Bah! stop that, Yégof," said he; "and come, take a little soup to warm thy inside."

"I do not ask thee for soup; I ask thee for this girl in marriage—the most beautiful on my estates. Give her to me willingly, and I raise thee to the steps of my throne: else my armies shall take her by force, and thou shalt not have the merit of giving her to me."

While thus speaking, the unhappy creature regarded Louise with an air of profound admiration.

"How beautiful she is! I destine her to the greatest honours. Rejoice, young girl, rejoice! Thou shalt be queen of Australasia."

"Listen, Yégof," said Hullin. "I am very much flattered by thy demand: it shows that thou canst appreciate beauty. It is well. But my daughter is already affianced to Gaspard Lefèvre."

"And I," said the madman, greatly irritated—"I will not hear of such a thing!" Then rising up,—"Hullin," said he, in solemn tones, "it is my first demand. I will renew it yet twice again-dost thou hear—twice! And if thou wilt persist in thy obstinacy—misfortune, misfortune on thee and thy race!"

"What! thou wilt not take any soup?"

"No, no! I will accept nothing from thee so long as thou hast not consented. Nothing, nothing!" And then marching toward the door, much to the satisfaction of Louise, who was intent on the raven, fluttering its wings against the windowpanes, he said, raising his sceptre,—"Twice again!" and departed.

Hullin went off into a shout of laughter. "Poor devil!" he exclaimed. "In spite of himself, his nose turned toward the porringer. He has nothing in his inside—his teeth chatter with hunger. Well! his madness is stronger than either cold or hunger."

"Oh, how he frightened me!" said Louise.

"Come, come, my child, calm thyself. He is gone. He thinks thou art pretty, fool though he is; do not let that terrify thee."

But although the madman had left, Louise still trembled, and felt herself blushing when she thought of how he had looked at her.

Yégof had taken the road to Valtin. He could still be seen, his raven on his shoulder, walking slowly along and making curious gestures, although no one was near him. The night was drawing on, and soon the tall figure of "The King of Diamonds" disappeared in the gray shadows of the winter twilight.

CHAPTER 2

The Shoemaker's Visitor

In the evening of that same day, after their supper, Louise, having taken her spinning-wheel, was gone for a little diversion to the Mother Rochart's where all the good women and young girls of the neighbourhood used to assemble till near midnight. They spent their time in relating old legends, talking of the rain, of the weather, of marriages, baptisms, of the departure or return of the conscripts, and what not, that enabled them to pass the hours agreeably.

Hullin remained alone before his little copper lamp, nailing the shoes of the old woodcutter. He no longer thought of the madman Yégof. His hammer rose and fell, driving the great nails into the thick wooden shoes quite mechanically, by force of habit. In the meantime thousands of ideas came into his head; he was thoughtful without knowing why. Now it was Gaspard, who gave no signs of being alive; then it was the campaign, which was being indefinitely prolonged. The lamp threw its yellowish light around the smoky little room. Outside, not a sound. The fire began to die away. Jean-Claude rose to put on a fagot, then sat down again, muttering,—"Bah! this cannot last; we shall receive a letter one of these days."

The old clock began to strike nine; and as Hullin was recommencing his work, the door opened and Catherine Lefèvre, the mistress of Bois-de-Chênes, appeared on the threshold, to the great stupefaction of the shoemaker, for it was not her custom to arrive at such a time.

Catherine Lefèvre might have been sixty years old, but she was as upright and strong as at thirty. Her clear gray eyes and beaked nose resembled those of a bird of prey; the corners of her mouth turned down, and made her look somewhat gloomy and sad; two or three locks of gray hair fell over her forehead; a brown striped hood reached from her head, over her shoulders and down to her elbows. Her physiognomy announced a steadfast, tenacious character, with something indescribably grand and mournful about it, which inspired both respect and fear.

"Can it be you, Catherine?" said Hullin, in astonishment.

"Yes, it is I," replied the old dame, calmly.

"I am come to talk with you, Jean-Claude. . . . Louise is away?"

"She has gone for a little amusement to Madeleine Rochart's."

"It is well."

Then Catherine pushed back her hood from her head, and sat down at the end of the bench. Hullin looked fixedly at her: he perceived something extraordinary and mysterious about her which fascinated him.

"What has happened, then?" said he, putting down his hammer.

Instead of answering this question, she turned toward the door, and seemed to be listening; then hearing no sound, her serious expression came back.

"Yégof the madman spent last night at the farm," said she.

"He came to see me this afternoon," rejoined Hullin, without attaching any importance to this fact, which was totally indifferent to him.

"Yes," replied the old dame, in a low voice, "he spent the night with us; and yesterday evening, about this time, in the kitchen, before us all, this madman related terrible things!"

Then she relapsed into silence, and the corners of her mouth seemed to turn down more than ever.

"Terrible things!" murmured the shoemaker, excessively astonished: for he had never seen Catherine Lefèvre in such a condition before. "But what then? say, what?"

"Dreams I have had!"

"Dreams? You certainly want to make fun of me!"

"No!"

Then, after a short pause, she slowly continued—"Yesterday evening, all our people were assembled in the kitchen around the large fireplace after supper; the table still remained covered with empty dishes, plates, and spoons. Yégof had partaken of it with us, and had amused us with the history of his treasures, castles, and provinces. It might have been toward nine o'clock: the madman was sitting at one end of the blazing fire; old Duchêne, my ploughboy, was mending Bruno's saddle; the herdsman, Robin, was plaiting a basket; Annette arranged her pans on the shelves: and I had brought my wheel nearer the fire to finish spinning a distaff-ful before going to bed.

Out of doors, the dogs were barking at the moon; the cold was very great. We were all there, talking of the coming winter. Duchêne said it would be very severe, for he had seen several flocks of wild-geese. And Yégof's raven, on the edge of the mantelpiece, its head buried in its ruffled feathers, seemed to sleep; but now and then it would elongate its neck and watch us, listen a moment and then cover itself again in its plumes."

She remained silent a moment, as though to collect her ideas; her eyelids drooped, her great beaked nose seemed to bend down on to her lips, and a strange pallor came over her face.

"What the devil is coming next?" thought Hullin.

The old woman continued: "Yégof near the fire, with his tin crown, and his short stick on his knees, was dreaming of something. He looked at the great black chimney, the stone mantelpiece, which is carved with different figures and trees, and the smoke which went up in great clouds around the sides of bacon: when suddenly he struck with the end of his stick on to the tiles and called out, as though in a dream—'Yes, yes, I have seen that long ago—long ago!' And as we all looked at him speechless—'In those times,' he went on to say, 'the pine-forests were forests of oak. The Nideck, the Dagsberg, Falkenstein, Géoldseck, all those old ruined castles did not exist. In those times the bison could be hunted in the depths of the woods, the salmon caught in the Sarre, and you, the fair men, were buried in snow six months of the year.

"'You lived on milk and cheese, for you had many flocks and herds on the Hengst, the Schnéeberg, the Grosmann, the Donon. In the summer you hunted: you came down to the Rhine, the Moselle, the Meuse. I can recall it all!'

"And wonderful to relate, Jean-Claude, as the madman spoke, I seemed to see also these countries of years gone by, and to remember them as I should a dream. I had let fall my distaff, and Duchêne, Robin, Jeanne—in fact, everybody—listened. 'Yes, it was long ago,' he continued. 'In those days you were already building these great chimneys; and all around, at a distance of two or three hundred yards, you planted palisades fifteen feet high, and with the points hardened by the fire. And inside them you kept your big dogs with their hanging cheeks, who barked day and night.'

"We could see what he said, Jean-Claude; we could see it all. But he paid no heed to us: he regarded the figures on the chimney-piece with his mouth open; but, in an instant, having stooped his head and seeing how attentive we all were, he laughed with a wild, mad laughter, and cried out:—'In those days you believed yourselves the lords of the country, O fair men, with your blue eyes and white skins, fed on milk and cheese, and only tasting blood in the autumn, at the great hunts: you believed yourselves the masters of the plains and mountains, when we, the red men, with the green eyes, out of the sea—we who drank always blood and only liked battles one fine morning we arrived with our axes and spears, and ascended the Sarre under the shadows of the old oaks.

"Ah! it was a cruel war, which lasted weeks and months. And the old woman—there—' said he, pointing at me, with a singular smile, 'the Margareth of the clan of Kilberix, that old woman with her beaked nose, in her palisades, in the midst of her dogs and warriors—she fought like a wolf. But when five moons had passed, hunger arrived. The doors of the palisades opened for flight, and we, in ambush in the stream—we massacred all!—all—except the children and the beautiful young girls. The old woman, alone, defended herself to the last with her teeth and nails; and I, Luitprandt, clove her head in two; and I took her father, the aged man and blind, to chain him at the door of my castle like a dog!'

"Then, Hullin," continued the old woman, "the madman began to chant a long song—the lamentation of the old man chained to his doorway. Wait till I can recall it, Jean-Claude. It was mournful—mournful as a *Miserere*. No, I cannot remember it; but I seem still to hear it. It made our blood curdle; and, as he laughed without ceasing, at last all our servants gave a terrible cry, rage seized them. Duchêne sprang on the madman to strangle him; but he, with more strength than one could suppose he possessed, threw him back, and raising his stick furiously, said to us: 'On your knees, slaves on your knees! My armies are advancing! Do you hear? The earth trembles with them. These castles, the Nideck, the Haut-Barr, the Dagsberg, the Turkestein, you shall build them up again! On your knees!'

"I never saw a more fearful face than Yégof's at that moment; but, seeing for the second time my servants rising against him, I was obliged to defend him myself. 'It is a madman,' I said to them. 'Are you not ashamed to believe in the words of a madman?' They stopped on my account; but I could not close my eyes that night. The words of that wretched man kept recurring to me. I seemed to hear the chant of the old prisoner, the barking of our dogs, and the sounds of battle. For years I have never felt so uneasy. That is why I came to see you, Jean-Claude. What do you think of it?"

"I?" exclaimed the shoemaker, in whose ruddy face both irony and pity were visible. "If I did not know you so well, Catherine, I should say you were deranged:—you, Duchêne, Robin, and the rest of you. All that has about the same effect on me as one of Geneviève de Brabant's tales—made up to terrify little children, and which shows us how foolish our ancestors were."

"You do not comprehend these things," said she, in a calm, grave voice; "you have never had any of those ideas."

"Then you believe all that Yégof has said to you?"

"Yes, I believe it."

"What, you, Catherine?—you, a sensible woman? If it were the mother of Rochart I should say nothing; but you!"

He rose as though annoyed, took off his apron, shrugged his shoulders, then sat down again quickly, and called out:—"This madman, do you know what he is? I will tell you. He is most assuredly one of those German school-masters who stuff their brains with 'Old Mother Goose' tales, and then gravely relate them to others. By dint of studying, dreaming, ruminating, their wits get out of order; they have visions, many-sided ideas, and take their dreams for realities. I have always looked upon Yégof as one of those poor wretches.

"He knows lots of names, he speaks of Brittany and Australasia, of Polynesia and the Nideck, and then of Géroldseck, of the Turkestein, of the Rhine—in fact of everything at hazard; and it ends by having the appearance of something when it is nothing. In ordinary times you would think as I do, Catherine; but you are troubled at not receiving any tidings from Gaspard. These rumours of war and of invasion that are going about torment and unsettle you. You cannot sleep; and what a poor madman says, you regard as Bible truths."

"No, Hullin; it is not that. If you yourself had heard Yégof—"

"Get along!" exclaimed the good old fellow. "If I had, I should have laughed at him as I did just now. Do you know that he came to ask Louise of me in marriage, to make her queen of Australasia?"

Catherine Lefèvre could not restrain a smile; but, regaining almost at once her serious expression—"All your reasonings, Jean-Claude," said she, "cannot convince me; but, I confess it, the silence of Gasper frightens me. I know my son: he would certainly have written to me. Why have his letters never reached me? The war is going on badly, Hullin—we have all the world against us. They don't want our revolution—you know it as well as I do. So long as we were masters, and won victory after victory, they looked kindly on us; but since our Russian misfortunes, things wear a bad aspect."

"*Là, Là*, Catherine, how you get carried away. You see everything gloomily."

"Yes, I see everything gloomily, and I am right. What makes me so uneasy is, that we never get any news from the outer world; we live here as in a savage country: one knows of nothing that goes on. The Austrians and the Cossacks could be upon us at any time, and we should be taken by surprise."

Hullin observed the old dame, whose expression was very animated; and even he began to be influenced by the same fears.

"Listen, Catherine," said he, suddenly. "When you speak in a reasonable manner, it is not I who would say anything against it. All you now tell me is possible. I do not believe in it; but one might as well make sure. I had intended to go to Phalsbourg in a week, to buy sheepskins for trimming some shoes: I will go tomorrow. At Phalsbourg, a garrison and post town, there must be some reliable news. Will you believe those I shall bring you on my return from that place?"

"Yes."

"Good; it is then arranged. I shall leave tomorrow early. There are five leagues in all. I shall return about six o'clock. You will see, Catherine, that all your dismal ideas have no sense in them."

"I hope so," she replied, rising. "I hope so. You have somewhat reassured me, Hullin. Now I will go to the farm, and may I sleep better than I did last night. Goodnight, Jean-Claude."

CHAPTER 3

At Phalsbourg

The next day at dawn, Hullin, wearing his blue cloth Sunday breeches, his large brown velvet jacket and red waistcoat with brass buttons, and a broad beaver mountaineer's hat turned up like a cockade above his ruddy face—started on his way to Phalsbourg, a stout stick in his hand.

Phalsbourg is a small fortress, half-way on the imperial road from Strasbourg to Paris; it dominates Saverne, the denies of Haut-Barr, Roche-Platte, Bonne-Fontaine, and of the Graufthâl. Its bastions, outposts, and *demilunes* are cut out in zig-zags on a rocky plain: from afar, the walls look as though they might be cleared at a jump; but on coming closer one perceives the moat, a hundred feet wide, thirty deep, and the dark ramparts hewn in the face of the rock. That makes one stop suddenly.

Besides, with the exception of the church, the town-hall, the two gateways of France and Germany, in shape of mitres, and the peaks of the two powder-magazines, all the rest is hidden behind the fortifications. Such is Phalsbourg, which is not without a certain imposing effect, especially when one crosses its bridges and piers, under its thick gates, garnished with iron-spiked portcullis. In the interior, the houses are distributed in regular quarters; they are low, in straight lines, built of freestone: everything bears a military aspect.

Hullin, owing to his robust constitution and jovial disposition, never had any fears for the future, and considered all rumours of retreat, rout, and invasion, which circulated in the country, as so many lies propagated by dishonest individuals; so that one may judge of his stupefaction when, on leaving the mountains and from the outskirts of the woods, he saw the whole surroundings of the town laid as bare as a pontoon: not a garden, not an orchard, not a promenade, or a tree, or even a shrub—all was destroyed within cannon-range. A few poor creatures were picking up the last remnants of their little houses, and carrying them into the town. Nothing was to be seen on the horizon but the line of ramparts standing out clearly above the hidden roads. It had the effect of a thunderbolt on Jean-Claude.

For some moments he could neither articulate a word nor make a step forward.

"Oh, ho!" said he, at last, "this is bad—this is very bad. They expect the enemy."

Then his warlike instincts prevailed; a dark flush came over his brown cheeks. "It is those rascally Austrians, Prussians, and Russians, and all the other wretches picked up out of the dregs of Europe, who are the cause of this," cried he, waving his stick. "But beware! we will make them pay for the damages!"

He was possessed with one of those white rages such as honest people feel when they are driven to extremities. Woe to him who annoyed Hullin just then!

Twenty minutes later he entered the town, at the rear of a long file of carriages, each harnessed to five or six horses, pulling, with much trouble, enormous trunks of trees, destined to construct block-houses on the *place-d'armes*. Among the conductors, the peasants, and neighing, stamping horses, marched gravely a mounted *gendarme*—Father Kels—who did not seem to hear anything, and said, in a rough voice, "Courage, courage, my friends! We will make two more journeys before evening. You will have deserved well of your country!"

Jean-Claude crossed the bridge.

A new spectacle opened before him in the town.

There reigned the ardour of defence: all the doors were open; men, women, and children came and ran, helping to transport the powder and projectiles. They stopped in groups of three, four, six, to make themselves acquainted with the news.

"*Hé* neighbour!"

"What then?"

"A courier has just arrived in great speed. He entered by the French gate."

"Then he has come to announce the National Guard from Nancy."

"Or, perhaps, a convoy from Metz."

"You are right. We want sixteen-pounders, and shot also. The stoves are to be broken up to make some."

A few worthy tradespeople in their shirt-sleeves, standing on tables along the pavement, were busying themselves with barricading their windows with large pieces of wood and mattresses; others rolled up to their doors tubs of water. This enthusiasm reanimated Hullin.

"Excellent!" said he; "everybody is making holiday here. The allies will be well received."

In front of the College, the squeaky voice of the Sergeant-de-ville Harmentier was proclaiming:—

Let it be known that the casemates are to be opened: therefore everybody may take a mattress there, and two blankets each. And the commissaries of this place are going to commence their rounds of inspection, to ascertain that each inhabitant possesses food for three months in advance, which he must certify.—This day, 20th December,—1813. Jean Pierre Meunier, Governor.

All this Hullin saw and heard in less than a minute, for the whole town was in the greatest excitement. Strange, serious, and comic scenes succeeded each other without interruption.

Near the narrow street leading to the Arsenal, a few National Guards were drawing a twenty-four pounder. These honest fellows had a very steep ascent to climb; they could do no more. "Ho! all together! *Mille tonnerres*! Once again! Forward!" They all shouted at once, pushing the wheels, and the great cannon, stretching out its long neck over its immense carriage, above their heads, rolled slowly along, making the pavement tremble.

Hullin, quite rejoiced, was no longer the same man. His soldier-like instincts, the remembrance of the bivouac, of the marches, of the firing, and of the battles—all returned. His eyes sparkled, his heart beat faster, and already thoughts of defence, of entrenchments, of death-struggles came and went in his head.

"Faith!" said he, "all goes well! I have made enough shoes in my life, and since the occasion to take up the musket presents itself, well, so much the better: we will show the Prussians and Austrians that we have not forgotten to charge at the double."

Thus reasoned the good man, carried away by his warlike instincts; but his joy did not last long.

Before the church, on the *place-d'armes*, were standing fifteen or twenty carts, full of wounded, arrived from Leipzig and Hanau. These unhappy creatures, pale, ghastly, heavy-eyed, some whose limbs were already amputated, others with their wounds still untouched, tranquilly awaited death. Near them, a few worn-out jades were eating their meagre allowance, while the conductors, poor wretches, who had been brought into requisition in Alsace, wrapped in their old mantles, slept notwithstanding the cold—their great hats turned down over their faces and their arms folded on the steps of the church.

One shuddered to see these sad groups of men, with their gray hoods, heaped up on the bloody straw—one carrying his broken arm on his knees; another with his head bandaged in an old handkerchief; a third, already dead, being used as a seat for the living, his black hands hanging down the ladder. Hullin, in front of this mournful spectacle, stopped rooted to the ground.

He could not lift his eyes from it. Great human suffering has this strange power of fascination over us: we look to see men perish, how they regard death: the best among us are not exempt from this frightful curiosity. It seems as though eternity is going to deliver up its secret!

There, then, near the shafts of the first cart, to the right of the file, were crouched two *carbineers* in little sky-blue vests, veritable giants, whose powerful natures gave way under the clutch of pain: like two caryatides crushed by the weight of some heavy mass. One, with great red moustaches and ashy cheeks, looked at you out of his sunken eyes, as though from the depths of some fearful night- mare; the other, bent double, with blue hands, and shoulder torn by shot, sank more and more; then would raise himself with a jerk, talking softly as though dreaming.

Behind lay stretched, two and two, some infantry soldiers, the greater number struck by ball, with a leg or an arm broken. They seemed to support their fate with more firmness than the giants. These poor creatures said nothing: a few only, the youngest, furiously demanded water and bread; and in the next cart, a plaintive voice—the voice of a conscript—called, "My mother! my mother!" while the older men smiled gloomily, as though to say: "Yes, yes, she will come, thy mother!" Perhaps they did not think of anything all the time.

Now and then a shudder would pass along the whole of them. Then several wounded could be seen half lifting themselves, with deep groans, and falling back as if death had gone its rounds at that moment.

And again everything relapsed into silence. While Hullin was watching, and feeling sick to his heart's core, a shopkeeper in the vicinity, Some the baker, came out of his house carrying a large basin of soup. Then you should have seen all these spectres move, their eyes sparkle, their nostrils dilate; they seemed born again. The unhappy fellows were dying of hunger!

Good Father Sôme, with tears in his eyes, approached, saying, "I am coming, my children. A little patience! It is I, you know me!"

But hardly was he near the first cart, when the great *carbineer* with the ashy cheeks, reviving, plunged his arm up to the elbow in the boiling basin, seized the meat, and hid it under his vest. It was done with the rapidity of lightning. Savage yells arose on all sides: those men, if they had had strength to move, would have devoured their comrade. He, his arms pressed tightly to his chest, the teeth on his prey, and glaring round him, appeared to hear nothing. At these cries an old soldier, a sergeant, rushed out of the nearest inn. He was an old hand; he understood at once what it was about, and, without useless reflections, he tore away the meat from the wild beast, saying to him, "Thou dost not deserve any! It must be divided into parts. We will cut ten rations!"

"We are only eight!" said one of the wounded, very calm to all appearance, but with eyes gleaming out of their bronze mask.

"How, eight?"

"You can see, sergeant, that those two are dying fast: it would be so much food lost!"

The old sergeant looked.

"Right," said he; "eight rations!"

Hullin could bear it no longer. He went over to the inn-keeper Wittmann's opposite, as white as death; Wittmann was also a fur and leather merchant. Seeing him enter, "*Hé*! is it you, Master Jean-Claude?" he exclaimed. "You arrive sooner than usual; I did not expect you till next week." Then seeing how he staggered—"But say, you are ill?"

"I have just seen the wounded."

"Ah, yes! the first time, it shocks you; but if you had seen fifteen thousand pass, as we have, you would not think anything more about it."

"A glass of wine, quick?" said Hullin, who felt badly. "Oh, mankind, mankind! And to think that we are brothers!"

"Yes, brothers until it touches your purse," replied Wittmann. "Come, drink! that will set you right."

"And you have seen fifteen thousand go by?" rejoined the shoemaker.

"At the least, for two months, without speaking of those who have remained in Alsace and the other side of the Rhine; for, you comprehend, they cannot find carts enough for all, and then many are not worth the trouble of being carried away."

"Yes, I comprehend! But why are they there, those poor crea-tures? Why do they not go into the hospital?"

"The hospital! What is one hospital, ten hospitals, for fifty thousand wounded? Every hospital, from Mayence and Coblentz as far as Phalsbourg, is crowded. And, besides, that terrible fever, typhus, you see, Hullin, kills more than the bullet. All the villages of the plain twenty leagues round are infected with it; they die everywhere like flies. Luckily the town has been in a state of siege these three days; the gates will be closed, and no more will enter. I have lost, for my part, my Uncle Christian and my Aunt Lisbeth, as healthy, solid people as you and I, Master Jean-Claude. At last the cold has arrived; last night there was a white frost."

"And the wounded remained on the pavements all night?"

"No, they came from Saverne this morning; in an hour or two, when the horses are rested, they will leave for Sarrebourg."

At that moment, the old sergeant, who had re-established order in the carts, came in rubbing his hands.

"*Hé! hé!*" said he, "it freshens, Papa Wittmann. You did well to light the fire in the stove. A little glass of cognac to drive away the fog. Hum! hum!"

His small half-closed eyes, his beaked nose, the cheek-bones being separated from it by two flourishing wrinkles, which were lost to sight in a long reddish imperial—everything looked gay in his face, and told of a jovial, kind disposition. It was a regular military face, scorched, burnt by the open air, full of frankness, but also of a cheery slyness; his great shako, his blue-gray cloak, the shoulder-belt, the epaulette, seemed to partake of his individuality.

One could not have represented him without them. He walked up and down the room, continuing to rub his hands, while Wittmann poured him a glass of brandy. Hullin, seated near the window, had at once noticed the number of his regiment—6th Light Infantry. Gaspard, the son of Madame Lefèvre, served in this regiment. Jean-Claude could now obtain some tidings of the lover of Louise; but, as he was going to speak, his heart beat loud. If Gaspard was dead; if he had perished like so many others!

The worthy shoemaker felt nearly suffocated; he kept silent. "Better to know nothing," thought he. However, a few minutes later, he could do so no longer. "Sergeant," said he, in a hoarse voice, "you are in the 6th Light Infantry?"

"Yes, my citizen," said the other, turning round in the middle of the room.

"Do you know one called Gaspard Lefèvre?"

"Gaspard Lefèvre, of the 2nd division of the 1st? *Parbleu*, if I know him! It is I who taught him his drill. A brave soldier! hardened against fatigue. If we had a hundred thousand of that stamp—"

"Then he lives? he is well?"

"Yes, citizen. Eight days ago I left the regiment at Fredericsthal to escort this convoy of wounded. You understand, it is hot there—one cannot answer for anything. From one moment to the other, each of us may have his business settled for him. But eight days ago, at Fredericsthal—the 15th December Gaspard Lefèvre still answered to the roll-call."

Jean-Claude breathed. "But then, sergeant, have the goodness to tell me why Gaspard has not written to his village for two months?"

The old soldier smiled, and blinked his little eyes. "Ah! now, citizen, do you then believe that one has nothing else to do on the march but to write?"

"No. I have served; I was in the campaigns of Sambre-et-Meuse, of Egypt and Italy, but that did not prevent me from giving some news of myself."

"One instant, comrade," interrupted the sergeant. "I have passed through Egypt and Italy also; the campaign we are finishing is altogether different."

"It has then been very severe?"

"Severe! one must have one's soul driven into every part of one's members, so as not to leave one's bones there. All was against us: sickness, traitors, peasants, townsfolk, our allies—in fact all! From our company, which was complete when we quitted Phalsbourg, the 21st of last January, only thirty-four men remain. I believe Gaspard Lefèvre is the only conscript left. Those poor conscripts! they fought well; but they were not accustomed to endure hardships: they melted like butter in an oven." So saying, the old sergeant approached the counter and drank his glass off at one draught. "To your health, my citizen. Are you perchance the father of Gaspard?"

"No, I am a relation."

"Well, you can pride yourselves on being stoutly built in your family. What a man at twenty! He has gone through everything—he has, while the others fell away in dozens."

"But," rejoined Hullin, after an instant's silence, "I cannot see anything so very different in this last campaign; for we also had sickness and traitors."

"Anything different!" exclaimed the sergeant. "Everything was different! Formerly, if you have gone through the war in Germany, you ought to remember that, after one or two victories, it was over: the people received you well; one drank the little white wines, and ate *sauerkraut* and ham with the townsfolk; one danced with the buxom wives. The husbands and grandpapas laughed heartily, and when the regiment left, everybody cried. But this time, after Lutzen and Bautzen, instead of feeling kindly, the people regarded us with diabolical faces; we could get nothing out of them but by force; one could have fancied one's self in Spain or Vendée.

"I do not know what stuff they had in their heads against us. Better had we only been French, had we not had Saxons and other allies, who only awaited the moment to spring at our throats: we should then have pulled through all the same, one against, five! But the allies don't talk to me of the allies! Why, at Leipzig, the 18th of October last, in the hottest part of the battle, our allies turned against us and shot at us from behind; those were our good friends the Saxons.

"A week later, our former friends the Bavarians came and threw themselves across our retreat: we had to pass over them at Hanau. The day after, near Frankfort, another column of good friends presented themselves, and we had to crush them. The more one kills, the more they come! Here we are now this side of the Rhine. Well, there are decidedly more of these good friends marching from Moscow. Ah! if we could have foreseen it after Austerlitz, Jena, Friedland, Wagram!"

Hullin had become very thoughtful. "And now how do we stand, sergeant?"

"We have had to repass the Rhine, and all our strongholds on the other side are blockaded. The 10th of November last the Prince of Neufchâtel reviewed the regiment at Bleckheim. The 3rd battalion had been amalgamated with the 2nd, and the '*cadre*' received orders to be in readiness to leave for the depot. Cadres are not wanting, but men. As for twenty years we have been Bléd on all sides, it is not astonishing. All Europe is down upon us. The Emperor is at Paris; he is laying down a plan of the campaign. If we may only have breathing time till the spring—"

Just then Wittmann, who was standing by the window, said,—"Here is the governor come from inspecting the clearings around the town."

It was the commandant, Jean-Pierre Meunier, wearing a three-cornered hat, and a tricolour scarf around his waist, who crossed over the square.

"Ah," said the sergeant, "I must get him to sign my papers. Pardon, citizen; I must leave you."

"Do so, sergeant: and thank you. If you meet Gaspard, tell him that Jean-Claude Hullin embraces him, and that they expect tidings from him in the village."

"Good—good. I will not fail to do so."

The sergeant went out, and Hullin finished his wine in a reverie.

"Father Wittmann," said he, after a pause, "what of my parcel?"

"It is ready, Master Jean-Claude." Then, looking into the kitchen, "Grédel! Grédel! bring Hullin's parcel"

A little woman appeared, and put down on the table a roll of sheepskins. Jean-Claude passed his stick through it, and lifted it over his shoulder.

"What, you are going to leave us so soon?"

"Yes, Wittmann. The days are short, and the roads difficult

through the forests after six o'clock. I must get back early."

"Then a safe journey to you, Master Jean-Claude."

Hullin left, and crossed the square, turning away his face from the convoy, which still remained before the church.

The innkeeper from his window watched him hurrying away, and thought to himself, "How white he looked on entering; he could hardly keep upright. It is queer that such a sturdy man, and an old soldier too, should not have energy enough for a cat. As for me, I would see fifty regiments go by on those carts without minding it any more than I did my first pipe."

Chapter 4

Madame Lefèvre

While Hullin was learning the disaster of our armies, and was walking slowly, his head bent, and an anxious expression on his face, toward the village of Charmes, everything went on as usual at the farm of Bois-de-Chênes. No one thought of Yégof's wonderful stories, or of the war: old Duchêne led his oxen to their drinking-place, the herdsman Robin turned over their litter; Annette and Jeanne skimmed their curdled milk. Only Catherine Lefèvre was silent and gloomy—thinking of days gone by—all the while superintending with an impassible face the occupations of her domestics.

She was too old and too serious to forget from one day to another what had so much troubled her. When night came on, after the evening's repast, she entered the great room, where her servants could hear her drawing the large register-book from the closet and putting it on the table, to sum up her accounts, as she was in the habit of doing.

They soon began to load the cart with corn, vegetables, and poultry: for the next day there was a market at Sarrebourg, and Duchêne had to start early.

Picture to yourself the great kitchen, and all these worthy folks hurrying to finish their work before going to rest: the black kettle, full of beetroot and potatoes destined for the cattle, boiling on an immense pinewood fire; the plates, dishes, and soup-tureens shining like suns on the shelves; the bunches of garlic and of reddish-brown onions hung up in rows to the beams of the ceiling, among the hams and flitches of bacon; Jeannie, in her blue cap and little red petticoat, stirring up the contents of the kettle with a big wooden spoon; the wicker cages, with the cackling fowls and great cock, who pushed his head through the bars and looked at the flames with a wondering eye and raised crest; the bull-dog Michel, with his flat head and hanging jowl, in search of some forgotten dish; Dubourg coming down the creaking staircase to the left, his back bent with a sack on his shoulder; while outside, in the dark night, old Duchêne, upright on the cart, lifted his lantern and called out, "That makes the fifteenth, Dubourg; two more."

One could see also, hanging against the wall, an old hare, brought by the hunter Heinrich to be sold at the market, and a fine grouse, with its purple and green plumage, dimmed eye, and a drop of blood at the end of its beak.

It was about half-past seven when the sound of footsteps was heard at the entrance to the yard. The bull-dog went toward the door growling. He listened, sniffed the night air, then went back quietly, and began licking his dish again.

"It is someone belonging to the farm," said Annette. "Michel does not move."

Nearly at the same time, old Duchêne from outside called,- "Goodnight, Master Jean-Claude. Is it you?"

"Yes. I come from Phalsbourg; and I am going to rest myself a minute before going down to the village. Is Catherine here?

And then the good man came forward to the light, his hat pushed off his face, and his roll of sheepskins on his back.

"Goodnight, my children," said he; "good night! Always at work!"

"Yes, Monsieur Hullin, as you see," replied Jeanne, laughing. "If one had nothing to do, life would be very wearisome."

"True, my pretty girl, true. It is only work which gives you your roses and brilliant eyes."

Jeanne was going to answer, when the door of the great room opened, and Catherine Lefèvre advanced, looking piercingly at Hullin, as though to guess beforehand what news he brought.

"Well, Jean-Claude, you have returned."

"Yes, Catherine; with good tidings and bad."

They entered the large room—a high and spacious apartment wainscoted with wood to the ceiling, with its oak closets and their shining clasps, its iron stove opening into the kitchen, its old clock counting the seconds in its walnut-wood case, and the leathern armchair, worn and used by ten generations of aged men. Jean-Claude never went into this room without its bringing back to his remembrance Catherine's grandfather, whom he seemed still to see, with his white head, sitting behind the oven in the dark.

"Well?" demanded the old dame, offering a chair to the old shoemaker, who was just putting his pack down on the table.

"Well, from Gaspard the tidings are good; the boy is in good health. He has had hardships. All the better: it will be the making of him. But for the rest, Catherine, it is bad. The war! the war!"

He shook his head, and the old woman, her lips pressed, sat down facing him, upright in the armchair, her eyes attentively fastened on him.

"So things look badly—decidedly—we shall have the war among us?"

"Yes, Catherine, from day to day we may expect to see the allies in our mountains."

"I thought so. I was sure of it; but speak, Jean-Claude."

Hullin, then, his elbows on his knees, his red ears between his hands, and lowering his voice, began to relate all he had seen: the clearing of everything around the town, the placing of batteries on the ramparts, the proclamation of the state of siege, the cart-loads of wounded on the great square, his meeting with the old sergeant at Wittmann's, and the story of the campaign. From time to time he paused, and the old mistress of the farm blinked her eyes slowly, as though to impress more deeply the various circumstances on her mind. When Jean-Claude told about the wounded, the good woman murmured softly—"Gaspard has then escaped it all!"

Then, at the end of this mournful tale, there was a long silence, and both looked at each other without pronouncing a word.

How many reflections, how many bitter feelings filled their souls!

After some seconds, Catherine recovering from these terrible thoughts—"You see, Jean-Claude," said she, in a serious tone. "Yégof was not wrong."

"Certainly, certainly, he was not wrong," replied Hullin; "but what does that prove? A madman, who goes from village to village, who descends into Alsace, and from thence to Lorraine-who wanders from right to left—it would be very astonishing if he saw nothing, and if he did not sometimes tell the truth in his madness. Everything gets muddled in his head, and others believe they understand what he does not understand himself. But what of these wild stories, Catherine? The Austrians are upon us. It only concerns us to know if we shall allow them to pass, or if we shall have courage to defend ourselves."

"To defend ourselves!" cried the old woman, whose white cheeks trembled: "if we shall have courage to defend ourselves! Surely it is not to me that you speak, Hullin. What! are we not worthy of our ancestors? Did they not defend themselves? Were they not exterminated—men, women, and children?"

"Then you are for the defence, Catherine?"

"Yes, yes; so long as there remains to me a bit of skin on my bones. Let them come! The oldest of the women is ready!"

Her masses of gray hair shook on her head, her pale rigid cheeks quivered, and her eyes sent forth lightnings. She was beautiful to see—beautiful, like that old Margareth of whom Yégof had spoken.

Hullin held out his hand silently, and gave an enthusiastic smile.

"Excellent," said he—"excellent! We are always the same in this family. I know you, Catherine: you are ready now; but be calm and listen to me. We are going to fight, and in what way?"

"In every way; all are good—axes, scythes, pitchforks."

"No doubt; but the best are muskets and the balls. We have

muskets: every mountaineer keeps his above his door; unfortunately powder and balls are scarce."

The old dame became quieter all of a sudden; she pushed her hair back under her cap, and looked anxiously about.

"Yes," she rejoined brusquely; "the powder and balls are wanting, it is true, but we shall have some. Marc Divès, the smuggler, has some. You shall go and see him tomorrow from me. You shall tell him that Catherine Lefèvre will buy all his powder and balls; that she will pay him; that she will sell her cattle, her farm, land, everything—everything—to have some. Do you understand, Hullin?"

"I understand. What you would do, Catherine, is noble."

"Bah I it is noble—it is noble!" replied the old dame. "It is quite simple; I wish to revenge myself. These Austrians—these red men who have already exterminated us well!—I hate them, I detest them, from father to son. There! you will buy powder, and these mad ruffians shall see if we will rebuild their castles."

Hullin then perceived that she still thought of Yégof's tale; but seeing how exasperated she was, and that, besides, her idea contributed to the defence of the country, made no observation on that subject, and said calmly,—"So, Catherine, it is settled; I am to go over to Marc Divès's tomorrow!"

"Yes! you shall buy all his powder and lead. Someone ought also to go the round of the mountain villages, to warn the people of what is coming, and to arrange a signal beforehand for bringing them together in case of attack."

"Do not fear," said Jean-Claude. "I will undertake to charge myself with that."

Both rose and turned toward the door. For about half an hour no sounds were heard in the kitchen; the farm-servants had gone to bed. The old dame put down her lamp on the corner of the hearth, and drew the bolts. Outside the cold was intense, the air still and clear. All the peaks round, and the pine-trees of the Jägerthal, stood out against the sky in dark or light masses. In the distance, far away behind the hillside, a fox giving chase could be heard yelping in the valley of Blanru.

"Goodnight, Hullin," said Catherine.

"Goodnight."

Jean-Claude walked quickly away on the heath-covered slopes, and the mistress of the farm, after watching him for a second, shut her door again.

I leave you to imagine the joy of Louise when she learnt that Gaspard was safe and sound. The poor child had hardly been living for two months. Hullin took care not to show her the dark cloud which was coming over the horizon.

Through the night he could hear her prattling in her little room, talking as though congratulating herself, murmuring Gaspard's name, opening her drawers and boxes, without doubt so as to hunt up some relics in them and tell them of her love.

So the linnet drenched in the storm, will, while yet shivering, begin to sing and hop from branch to branch with the first sunbeam.

CHAPTER 5

The Depot

When Jean-Claude Hullin, in his shirt-sleeves, opened the shutters of his little house the next morning, he saw all the neighbouring mountains—the Jägerthal, the Grosmann, the Donon—covered with snow. This first appearance of winter, coming in our sleep, is very striking to us: the old pines, the mossy rocks, adorned only the night before with verdure, and now sparkling with rime, fill our souls with an indefinable sadness. "Another year gone by," one says to one's self; "another hard season to pass before the return of the flowers!" And one hastens to put on the great-coat and to light the fire. Your sombre habitation is filled with a white light, and outside, for the first time, you hear the sparrows—the poor sparrows huddled under the thatch, their feathers ruffled—calling, "No breakfast this morning—no breakfast!"

Hullin drew on his big iron-nailed, double-soled shoes, and over his vest a great thick cloth waistcoat.

He heard Louise walking overhead in the little garret.

"Louise," he cried, "I am going."

"What! you are going away today also?"

"Yes, my child: it must be so: my affairs are not yet finished."

Then, having doffed his large hat, he went up the stair, and said, in a low tone: "Thou must not expect me back so soon, my child. I have to make some distant rounds. Do not be uneasy. If anyone ask where I am, thou art to reply, 'He is with Cousin Mathias at Saverne.'"

"You will not have breakfast before leaving?"

"No: I have a crust of bread and the small flask of brandy in my pocket. *Adieu*, my child! Rejoice, and dream of Gaspard."

And, without waiting for fresh questions, he took his stick and left the house, going in the direction of the hill of Bouleaux to the left of the village. In a quarter of an hour he had passed it by. and reached the path of the Trois-Fontaines, which winds round the Falkenstein along by a little wall of dry stones. The first snow, which never lasts in the damp shades of the valleys, was beginning to melt and run down the path. Hullin got on the wall to climb the ascent.

On giving an accidental look toward the village, he saw a few women sweeping before their doors, a few old men wishing each other the "Good-day" while smoking their first pipes on the threshold of their cottages. The deep calm of life, in presence of his agitating thoughts, affected him much. He continued his way pensively, saying to himself, "How quiet everything is down there! Nobody has any idea of anything; yet in a few days, what clamours, what rolls of musketry, will rend the air!"

As the first thing to be done was to procure powder, Catherine Lefèvre had very naturally cast her eyes on Marc Divès the smuggler, and his virtuous spouse, Hexe-Baizel.

These people lived on the other side of the Falkenstein, under the base of the old ruined castle. They had hollowed inside a sort of den, very comfortable, possessing one door and two sky-lights, but according to certain rumours, communicating with ancient caves by a rift in the rock. The custom-house officers had never been able to discover these caves, notwithstanding numerous domiciliary visits for that purpose. Jean-Claude and Marc Divès had known each other from infancy; they had gone nesting together after hawks and owls, and since that time had seen each other nearly every week at the saw-mills of Valtin.

Hullin, therefore, believed himself sure of the smuggler, but he had some doubts of Madame Hexe-Baizel, a most cautious person, who would not, in all probability, have the war-like instinct sufficiently developed. "But we shall see," he said to himself as he went along.

He had lit his pipe, and from time to time turned round to contemplate the immense landscape, whose limits were extending more and more.

Nothing could be grander than those wooded mountains, rising one above the other in the pale sky—those vast heather plains, stretching as far as the eye could see, white with snow; those black ravines, shut in between the woods, with torrents at the bottom, dashing over the greenish pebbles polished like bronze.

And then the silence—the great silence of winter! The soft snow falling from the top of the loftiest pine-trees onto their lower drooping branches: the birds of prey circling in couples above the forests, screaming out their war-cry: all this ought to be seen for it cannot be described.

An hour after his departure from the village of Charmes, Hullin, climbing the summit of the peak, reached the base of the rock of the Arbousiers. All round this granite mass extends a sort of rugged terrace, three or four feet wide. This narrow passage, surrounded by the tall pines growing out from the precipice, looks dangerous, but it is safe; unless one feels dizzy, there is no danger in going along it. Overhead projects, in a vaulted arch, the rock covered with ruins.

Jean-Claude was approaching the retreat of the smuggler. He halted a minute on the terrace, put back his pipe into his pocket, then advanced along the passage, which forms a half-circle, and ends on the other side with a chasm. Quite at the farthest extremity of it, and almost on the edge of the chasm, he perceived the two skylight windows of the den and the partly opened door. A great heap of manure was collected in front of it.

At the same time Hexe-Baizel appeared, tossing, with a broom made of green furze, the manure into the abyss. This woman was small and hard-looking; she had shaggy red hair, hollow cheeks, pointed nose, little eyes, bright like two sparks, thin lips, very white teeth, and a florid complexion. As for her costume, it was composed of a short dirty woollen petticoat, and a coarse but clean chemise; her brown, muscular arms, covered with yellow hairs, were bare to the elbows, notwithstanding the excessive cold of the winter at this height; and, lastly, all she had on her feet were a pair of long shoes hanging in shreds.

"Ha! good-day, Hexe-Baizel," Jean-Claude called out, good naturedly but with a tone of raillery. "You are always fair and fat, happy and lively! It gives me pleasure!"

Hexe-Baizel turned sharply, like a weasel surprised on the watch; her red hair stiffened, and her little eyes flashed fire. However, she calmed down immediately, and exclaimed, in a curt voice, as though speaking to herself, "Hullin—the shoe- maker! What does he want?"

"I am come to see my friend Marc, fair Hexe-Baizel," replied Jean-Claude; "we have some business to settle together."

"What business?"

"Ah, it only concerns us. Here let me pass that I may speak to him."

"Marc is asleep."

"Well, he must be awakened then; the time is precious."

So saying, Hullin stooped under the door, and penetrated into a cavern, whose vault, instead of being round, was composed of irregular curves, scored with fissures. Close to the entrance, two feet from the ground, the rock formed a sort of natural fireplace, on which burned a few coals and branches of juniper. Hexe-Baizel's culinary utensils consisted of an iron kettle, a stone pot, two broken plates, and three or four tin forks; her furniture comprised a wooden stool, a hatchet to split wood, a salt box fastened to the rock, and her large furze broom. To the left of this kitchen was another cavern, with a curious door, larger at the top than at the bottom, closing by aid of two planks and a cross-bar.

"Well, where is Marc?" said Hullin, seating himself near the hearth.

"I have already told you that he is asleep. He returned home late yesterday. My husband must sleep, don't you hear?"

"I hear very well, dear Hexe-Baizel; but I have no time to

wait."

"Then go away!"

"Go away? It is easy said; only I won't go away. I did not walk three miles, to turn back with my hands in my pockets."

"Is it thou, Hullin?" interrupted a brusque voice coming from the neighbouring cavern.

"Yes, Marc."

"Ah! I'm coming."

The sound of straw in motion could be heard; then the wooden barrier was withdrawn; and a huge frame, three feet broad from one shoulder to the other, wiry, bony, with neck and ears brick-colour, and thick brown hair, appeared in the doorway, and Marc Divès drew himself up before Hullin, yawning and stretching his long arms with a short sigh.

At first sight, the physiognomy of Marc Divès seemed peaceable enough: his low broad forehead, bare temples, short curly hair coming down in a point almost to the eyebrows, his straight nose and long chin—above all the quiet expression in his brown eyes—would have caused him to be classed among the ruminating rather than the wilder animals; but one would have been wrong in thinking so.

Certain rumours were prevalent in the country that Marc Divès, when attacked by the custom-house people, had never any hesitation to use his axe or carbine to decide the dispute; to him were attributed several serious accidents which had happened to tire fiscal agents; but proofs were completely wanting. The smuggler, owing to his thorough knowledge of all the mountain defiles and by-roads from Dagsburg to Sarrbrück, and from Raon-l'Etape to Bâle in Switzerland, was always fifteen leagues from any place where a wicked action had been committed. And then he had such an ingenuous look! and those who connected him with sinister tales generally finished badly: which clearly shows the justice with which Providence sways the world.

"Faith, Hullin," said Marc, after having left his lair, "I was thinking of thee yesterday evening, and if thou hadst not appeared, I should have gone expressly to the saw-mills of Valtin to meet thee. Sit down! Hexe-Baizel, give a chair to Hullin!"

Then he placed himself on the hearth, his back to the fire, in front of the open door, which was raked by all the winds of Alsace and Switzerland.

Through this opening there was a magnificent view: it might be compared to a picture framed in the rock—an enormous picture, embracing the whole valley of the Rhine, and the mountains beyond, which melted away in the mist. And then one could breathe so freely! and the little fire, which glimmered in the owl's-nest, was a place to look on, with its red light, after one had gazed into the azure expanse.

"Marc," said Hullin, after a short pause, "may I speak before thy wife?"

"We are as one, she and I."

"Well, Marc, I am come to buy powder and lead of thee."

"To kill hares, is it not so?" observed the smuggler, winking.

"No, to fight against the Germans and Russians."

There was a moment's silence.

"And thou wilt want much powder and lead?"

"All that thou canst supply."

"I can supply as much as three thousand francs' worth today," said the smuggler.

"Then I'll take it."

"And as much more in a week," added Marc, with the same calm manner and eager look.

"I take that also."

"You will take it!" cried Hexe-Baizel. "You will take it! I should think so! But who is to pay?"

"Hold thy tongue!" said Marc, roughly, "Hullin takes it: and his word is enough for me." And holding out his large hand cordially: "Jean-Claude, here is my hand: the powder and lead are thine: but I must have my price, dost thou understand?"

"Yes, Marc: only I intend paying thee at once."

"He will pay, Hexe-Baizel, dost thou hear?"

"Eh, I am not deaf, Baizel. Go and find a bottle of '*brimbelle-*

wasser' for us, so that we may warm our hearts a little. What Hullin tells me rejoices me. These rascally *'kaiserlichs'* will not have the easy game against us that I thought. It appears that we are going to defend ourselves, and right well."

"Yes, right well!"

"And there are people who can pay?"

"Catherine Lefèvre pays, and she it is who sends me," said Hullin.

Then Marc Divès rose, and in a solemn tone, and pointing toward the precipice, exclaimed, "She is a woman indeed—a woman as grand as that rock down there, the Oxenstein, the greatest I have ever seen in my life. I drink to her health. Drink also, Jean-Claude."

Hullin drank, then Hexe-Baizel.

"Now everything has been said," continued Divès; "but listen, Hullin. Do not believe that it will be an easy matter to check the enemy: all the hunters, all the sawyers, all the woodcutters and carriers on the mountains will not be too many. I come from the other side of the Rhine. They are so many those—Russians, Austrians, Bavarians, Prussians, Cossacks, and Hussars—they are so many, that the earth is black with them. The villages cannot hold them: they camp on the plains, in the valleys, on the hills, in the towns, in the open air—they are to be found everywhere."

At that moment a shrill cry was heard.

"It is a buzzard chasing something," said Marc, stopping.

But just then a shadow came over the rock. A cloud of chaffinches cleared the abyss, and hundreds of buzzards and hawks fought above them in their rapid flight, uttering loud screams to terrify their prey, while the mass seemed stationary, so dense was it. The regular movement of these thousands of wings produced, in the silence, a sound like that of dead leaves blown in the wind.

"That is the departure of the chaffinches of the Ardennes," said Hullin.

"Yes, it is the last passage: the beech-nuts are buried under the snow, and the seeds also. Well, then, look! there are more men over there than birds in this pass. All the same, Jean-Claude, we will get over them, so long as everyone bears a hand in it! Hexe-Baizel, light the lantern: I am going to show Hullin our supplies of powder and lead."

Hexe-Baizel made a face at this proposition. "For twenty years," said she, "no one has gone into the cave. He can surely believe our word. We believe, for our part, that he will pay us. I will not light the lantern—no, indeed!"

Marc, without saying anything, put out his hand and caught up a cudgel from the pile of wood; thereupon the old woman darted into the nearest hole like a weasel, and, two seconds later, came out with a big horn lantern, which Divès quietly lit at the fire on the hearth.

"Baizel," said he, replacing the stick in its corner, "thou must know that Jean-Claude is an old friend of my childhood, and that I confide much more in him than in thee,. old wench; for wert thou not afraid of being hanged the same day as myself, I should long ago have been swinging to a rope's end. Come, Hullin, follow me."

They went out, and the smuggler, turning to the left, walked straight toward the chasm, which projected over the Valtin two hundred feet in the air. He pushed aside the branches of a little oak, which had its roots down below, put forth his leg, and disappeared as though pitched into the abyss. Jean-Claude shuddered, but directly after he saw, against the side of the rock, the head of Divès, who called to him,—"Hullin, put out thy hand to the left there is a hole. Stretch thy leg out boldly—thou wilt feel a step, and then turn around."

Master Jean-Claude obeyed, with some trepidation. He could feel the hole in the rock, he found the step, and turning slightly, was face to face with his comrade in a sort of arched niche, evidently abutting on a sally-port in times past. At the end of the niche there was a low vault.

"How the devil didst thou discover that?" exclaimed Hullin, much astonished.

"In seeking after nests thirty-five years ago. I was one day on the rock, and I had often observed flying from there a horned-owl and its mate, two splendid birds: their heads were the size of my fists, and the wings six feet broad. I could hear their young calling, and I said to myself, 'They are near the cavern, at the end of the terrace. If I could get round a little beyond the chasm I should have them!'

By dint of looking and bending over, I perceived at last a corner of the step above the precipice. There was a strong holly-bush at one side. I caught hold of it, put out my leg, and, faith, I found myself here. What a fight, Hullin! The old birds wanted to tear out my eyes. Luckily, it was broad daylight. They went at me like cocks, opened their beaks and hissed, but the sun dazzled them. I kicked them.

Finally, they fell on to the top of an old pine-tree down there, and all the jays in the country, the thrushes, chaffinches and tom-tits, flew about them till nightfall, plucking out their feathers. Thou canst not imagine, Jean-Claude, the quantity of bones, rat-skins, leverets, and carrion of all sorts that they had heaped up in this niche. It was pestilential. I threw it all into the Jäger-thal, and I discovered this passage. But I must also tell thee that there were two young ones. I twisted their necks and poked them into my bag. Afterward, I quietly entered, and thou shalt see what I found. Come!"

They slipped under the narrow archway, formed of enormous red stones, where the light threw only a nickering glimmer.

Thirty paces farther on, a vast circular cave, low in the middle, and formed in the rock itself, appeared to Hullin. About fifty little casks were arranged at the bottom in shape of pyramids, and, at the sides, a large number of ingots of lead and bales of tobacco, which filled the air with its smell. Marc deposited his lantern at the entrance of the vault, and regarded his hiding-place with gratification and a smile upon his lips.

"That is what I discovered," said he; "the cave was empty, only in the centre of it was the carcass of an animal, snowy white,—no doubt some fox, dead of old age. The rascal had known of the passage before I had. He slept safely here. Who on earth would have dreamed of pursuing him? In those days, Hullin, I was twelve years old. I immediately thought that this place might one day be of use to me. I did not know then what use. But, later on, when I had begun my first attempts at smuggling—at Landau, Kehl, Bâle—with Jacob Zimmer, and during two winters all the custom-house people were after us, the idea of my old cavern began to haunt me from morning till evening. I had made the acquaintance of Hexe-Baizel, who was then one of the farm-servants at Bois-de-Chênes with Catherine's father. She brought me twenty-five *louis* as marriage-portion, and we settled ourselves in the cavern of the Arbousiers."

Divès paused; and Hullin, who had become very thoughtful, asked him,—"This hole, then, pleases thee much, Marc?"

"Pleases me! Why, I would not go and live in the most beautiful house in Strasbourg for two thousand pounds a year. For twenty-three years I have here hidden my wares: sugar, coffee, powder, tobacco, brandy—everything goes in here. I have eight horses always travelling."

"But thou hast no happiness."

"I have no happiness! Dost thou think it is nothing to laugh at the *gendarmes*, excisemen, custom-house people; to enrage them, to outdo them, to hear on all sides, 'That rascally Marc —isn't he a sharp one! How he manages his business! He can do as he likes with the law and its agents,' and this and that. *Hé!* hé! hé! I can tell thee, I can, that it is the greatest pleasure in the world. And then the people like il: they get everything half price; one helps the poor, and keeps himself warm and well-off."

"Yes, but what dangers!"

"Bah! a customs'-guard would never think of crossing the chasm."

"I should suppose not," thought Hullin, remembering that he must cross the precipice again.

"At the same time thou art not altogether wrong, Jean-Claude. When I first had to enter this place with those little barrels on my back, I streamed with perspiration; now I am accustomed to it."

"And if thy foot slipped?"

"There would be an end of me! I would as soon die, spiked on a pine, as to cough weeks and months on a mattress."

Divès then shed the light of his lantern on the piles of kegs reaching to the top of the vault.

"It is the finest English powder," said he; "it runs like silver grains in the hand, and fires like Old Nick. No need to use much of it—a thimbleful is enough. And here is lead, unmixed with tin. From this very evening, Hexe-Baizel shall begin casting balls. She knows all about it, thou wilt see."

They were beginning to return by the path leading to the chasm, when suddenly a confused murmur of words began to fill the air. Marc blew out his lantern, and they stopped still in the darkness.

"Someone is walking up there," the smuggler softly said. "Who on earth has been able to climb up the Falkenstein in such snow?"

They listened, holding their breath, and their eyes fixed on the ray of bluish light which came down through a small chink into the cavern. Around the cleft grew a few shrubs, sparkling with frost; above, could be perceived the ridge of an old wall. While they were watching, keeping profound silence, there appeared at the foot of the wall a large shaggy head bound round with a shining circle, a long face, then a pointed red beard,—the whole standing out in curious relief against the white winter sky.

"It is 'The King of Diamonds,'" observed Marc, laughing.

"Poor devil!" said Hullin, gravely; "he has come to walk about his castle, his bare feet on the ice, and a tin crown on his head! But look! he is speaking: he is giving orders to his courtiers; he points with his sceptre to the north and to the south—all belongs to him; he is master of the heavens and earth! Poor devil! merely to see him in those trousers of his, with his dog-skin on his back, makes me cold all over."

"Yes, Jean-Claude, it produces on me the effect of a *burgomaster* or village mayor, who puffs himself out like a bullfinch, and blows his cheeks up, saying, 'I am Hans Aden; I have ten acres of fine meadows; I have two houses; I have a vineyard, an orchard, a garden, h-m! h-m! I have this and that!' The next day a little fit lays hold of him, and—good-evening. Mad, mad! who is not mad? Let us go, Hullin; the sight of this unfortunate who talks to the winds, and of his raven that croaks of famine, makes my teeth chatter."

They entered the passage, and the daylight almost blinded Hullin. Happily, the great height of his companion standing in front of him, prevented his becoming giddy.

"Lean firmly," said Marc; "imitate me: the right hand in the hole, the right foot on the step, turn a bit—here we are!"

They returned to the kitchen, where Hexe-Baizel told them that Yégof was in the ruins of the old Burg.

"We knew it," replied Marc: "we have just seen him breathing the fresh air over there. Each man to his taste."

Just then the raven Hans, sailing above the abyss, passed the door with a hoarse cry; they heard the frost crackling on the bushes, and the madman appeared upon the terrace. He was haggard; and after glancing toward the hearth, cried out—"Marc Divès, clear out quickly. I warn thee I am tired of this disorder. The fortifications of my domains ought to be free. I cannot allow vermin to lodge where I am; consequently, thou must make thy arrangements."

Then perceiving Jean-Claude, his face brightened—"Thou here, Hullin?" said he, "Art thou at length clear-sighted enough to accept the proposals that I have condescended to make thee? Dost thou feel that an alliance such as mine, is the only resource to preserve thee from the total destruction of thy race? If it is so, I congratulate thee; thou showest more sense than I gave thee credit for."

Hullin could not help laughing.

"No, Yégof, no! heaven has not yet enlightened me, or I might accept the honour thou wouldst make me. Besides, Louise is not old enough to be married."

The madman became again serious and gloomy. Standing on

the edge of the terrace, his back to the abyss, he seemed quite at home, and his raven, hovering from right to left, did not trouble him.

He raised his sceptre, frowned, and exclaimed:

"Then this is the second time, Hullin, that I have made my demand, and for the second time thou darest refuse me. Now, I will renew it once again—once, dost thou hear? Then the fate shall be accomplished!"

Hullin, Marc Divès, and Hexe-Baizel herself burst into fits of laughter.

"He is a great madman," said Hexe-Baizel.

"I think them art right there," replied the smuggler. "Poor Yégof! decidedly he is out of his wits. But never mind! Baizel, attend to me. Thou must commence melting balls of all sizes. I am going to start for Switzerland. In a week, at latest, the remainder of our ammunition will be here. Give me my boots."

Then stamping down his heels, and twisting round his neck a thick scarf of red wool, he unhooked from the wall one of those dark-green mantles such as herdsmen wear, threw it over his shoulders, put on an old worn hat, took a gourd, and shouted: "Don't forget what I have been telling thee, old woman, or beware! Let us go, Jean-Claude!"

Hullin followed him on the terrace without wishing good-bye to Hexe-Baizel, who, for her part, did not deign even to go to the doorstep to see them depart. When they were come to the base of the rock, Marc Divès drew up and said, "Thou art going into the mountain villages, art thou not, Hullin?"

"Yes: that must first be done. I must warn the woodcutters, charcoal-burners, and others, of what is going on."

"Without doubt. Do not forget Materne of Hengst and his two boys, Labarbe of Dagsburg, and Jérome of St. Quirin. Tell them that there will be powder and balls; that we are of the number, Catherine Lefèvre, myself, Marc Divès, and all the honest folks of the country."

"Calm thyself, Marc—I know my men."

"Then goodbye for the present."

They shook hands warmly.

The smuggler took the path to the right, toward Donon; Hullin that to the left, toward the Sarre.

They were now at some distance from each other, when Hullin called out to his comrade: "*Hé!* Marc, inform Catherine Lefèvre, as thou passest by, that all goes on well. Tell her I am going into the mountains."

The other assented by a nod, and they both continued their different ways.

CHAPTER 6

Among the Mountaineers

An extraordinary agitation reigned at that time all along the line of the Vosges: the tidings of the invasion which was approaching spread from village to village, and among the farmhouses and woodmen's cottages of the Hengst and the Nideek. The hawkers, wagoners, tinkers, all that floating population which is continually moving from the mountains to the plains and from the plains to the mountains, brought every day, from Alsace and the borders of the Rhine, many strange reports.

"The towns," so these people said, "were being put into a state of defence; expeditions were being made to provision them with corn and meat; the roads to Metz, Nancy, Huningue, and Strasbourg were swarming with convoys. Everywhere you met powder and ammunition wagons, cavalry, infantry, artillery, going to their posts. Marshal Victor still held the route to Saverne; but the bridges of the fortresses were already raised from seven in the evening to eight in the morning."

No one thought that all this could bode any good. Nevertheless, though many were seriously afraid of war, and though the old women lifted up their hands to heaven, crying, "Jesus! Mary! Joseph!" the greater number were preparing the means of defence. Under such circumstances, Jean-Claude Hullin was well received by all.

The same day, toward five in the evening, he reached the summit of the Hengst, and halted with the patriarch of forest-hunters, old Materne. He spent the night there; for in winter the days are short and the roads difficult. Materne promised to keep watch over the defile of the Zorn, with his two sons Kasper and Frantz, and to reply to the first signal which was made from the Falkenstein.

On the following day, Jean-Claude started early for Dagsburg, so as to come to an understanding with his friend Labarbe, the woodcutter. They visited together the nearest hamlets, re-animating the love of country in the people's hearts; and the next day Labarbe accompanied Hullin into Christ-Nickel's, the anabaptist farmer of Painbach—a sensible and respectable man, but who could not be prevailed upon to participate in their glorious enterprise. Christ-Nickel had only one reply for all their observations: "It is well, it is just, but the Bible saith, *Put up thy sword into its place. He who lives by the sword shall perish by the sword.*" He promised them, however, to pray for the good cause: it was all they could obtain.

They went from there to Walsch, and had some hearty shakes of the hand with Daniel Hirsch, a former marine gunner, who agreed to collect all the people of his district.

At this place Labarbe left Jean-Claude to make his way by himself.

For eight days longer he beat about the mountain, from Soldatenthal, to Léonsberg, Meienthal, Abreschwiller, Voyer, Loëttenbach, Cirey, Petit-Mont, and Saint-Sauveur; and on the ninth day he reached St. Quirin and saw the bootmaker Jérome. They visited the pass of Blanru together; after which Hullin, satisfied with what he had done, took his way to the village.

He had been walking briskly for about two hours, picturing to himself the life of the camp, the bivouac, marches and counter-marches—all that life of a soldier which he had so often regretted, and which he now saw returning with enthusiasm—when in the far distance, amidst the shades of the twilight, he perceived the hamlet of Charmes in a bluish mist, his little cottage sending forth a scarcely perceptible line of smoke, the small gardens surrounded with palisades, the stone-covered roofs, and to the left, bordering the hill, the great farm of Bois-de-Chênes, with the saw-mills of Valtin at the end of the now dark ravine.

Then suddenly, and without knowing why, his soul was filled with a great sadness.

He slackened his pace, and thought of the calm, peaceable life he was abandoning—perhaps forever; of his little room, so warm in the winter, and cheerful in spring when he opened his windows to the breath of the woods; of the tic-tac of the old timepiece, and then of Louise, his good little Louise, spinning in the silence with downcast eyes, and in the evenings singing some quaint strain with her pure penetrating voice when they were both feeling weary.

These reflections laid such hold of him that the slightest objects, every instrument used in his profession,—the long shining augers, the round-handled hatchet, the mallets, the little stove, the old closet, the platters of varnished wood, the ancient figure of Saint Michael nailed to the wall, the old four-post bed at the bottom of the alcove, the stool, the trunk, the copper lamp,- all these things impressed themselves on his mind like a living picture, and the tears came into his eyes.

But it was Louise, his darling child, whom he pitied. How she would weep, and implore him to renounce the war! And how she would hang on his neck, saying:—"Oh! do not leave me, Papa Jean-Claude! Oh, I will love you so much! Oh, surely you will not abandon me!"

And the honest fellow could see the terror in her beautiful eyes—he could feel her arms round his neck. For a moment he fancied that he might deceive her, make her believe anything, no matter what, and so account for his absence to her satisfaction; but such means were not in accordance with his character, and his sadness increased the more.

Arrived at the farm of Bois-de-Chênes, he went in to tell Catherine Lefèvre that all was going well, and that the mountaineers were only awaiting the signal.

A quarter of an hour after, Master Jean-Claude came down by the Houx road in front of his own little house.

Before pushing open the creaking door, the idea struck him

to see what Louise was about at that moment. He glanced into the little room through the window: Louise was standing by the curtains of the alcove; she seemed very animated, arranging, folding and unfolding clothes on the bed. Her sweet face beamed with happiness, and her large blue eyes sparkled with a sort of enthusiasm; she even talked aloud. Hullin listened; but a cart happening to pass at the time in the street, he could hear nothing. Making a firm resolve, he entered, saying quietly: "Louise, I have returned."

Immediately the young girl, joyous and skipping like a deer, ran to embrace him.

"Ah! it is you, Papa Jean-Claude! I was expecting you. *Mon Dieu! Mon Dieu!* how long you stayed away! At length you are back."

"It was, my child," replied the honest fellow, in a more undecided tone, putting his stick behind the door and his hat on the table, "it was because—"

He could say nothing else.

"Yes, yes, you went to see our friends," said Louise, laughing: "I know all about it—Mamma Lefèvre has told me everything."

"What! thou knowest? And dost thou not mind? So much the better, so much the better! it shows thy sense. And I, who fancied thou wouldst have cried!"

"Cry! and what for, Papa Jean-Claude? Oh, I am courageous; you don't know me yet—go!" She put on a resolute air, which made Hullin smile; but he did not smile long when she continued: "We are going to war—we are going to fight—we are going to pass up the mountain!"

"Hullo! we are going! we are going!" exclaimed he in astonishment.

"Certainly. Then are we not going?" said she, regretfully.

"That is to say—I must leave thee for a little time, my child."

"Leave me—oh, no! I go with thee; it is all agreed upon. Look, see! my small parcel is ready, and here is yours, which I have arranged. Don't trouble yourself, let me alone, and you will be satisfied!"

Hullin could not get over his stupefaction. "But, Louise," he exclaimed, "thou canst not think of such a thing. Consider: we must pass nights abroad, and march and run; consider the cold, the snow, the musketry! It cannot be."

"Come," said the young girl, in a tearful voice, throwing herself into his arms, "do not pain me! You are only making fun of your little Louise. You cannot forsake her!"

"But thou wilt be much safer here—thou wilt be warm-thou wilt hear from us every day."

"No, no. I will not—I must go too. The cold does not harm me. Only too long have I been shut up. I, too, must breathe a little. Are not the birds out of doors? The robins are out all the winter. Have I not known what cold was when I was quite tiny? and hunger also?"

She stamped, and, for the third time, putting her arms round Jean-Claude's neck, "Come then, Papa Hullin," said she softly, "Mamma Lefèvre said yes. "Would you be more naughty than she was? Ah, if you only knew how much I love you!"

The good man had sat down and turned away his head, so as not to yield, and did not allow himself to be embraced.

"Oh, how naughty you are today, Papa Jean-Claude!"

"It is for thy sake, my child."

"Well, all the worse. I will run away after you. Cold—what is cold? And if you are wounded—if you ask to see your little Louise for the last time, and she is not there—near you, to take care of you, and love you to the end—oh, you must think me very cold-hearted."

She sobbed, and Hullin could not stand it any longer.

"Is it true that Mamma Lefèvre consents?"

"Oh, yes—oh, yes—she told me so. She said to me,—'Try and make Papa Jean-Claude decide. I am willing, and quite satisfied.'"

"Well, what can I do against two of you. Thou shalt come with us; it is quite decided."

She gave a scream of delight which ran through the cottage,- "Oh, how kind you are!"

And with one rub she wiped all her tears away,—"We are going to be off, to take to the woods and to make war."

"Ah," said Hullin, shaking his head, "I see it now; thou art always the little gypsy. As soon try to tame a swallow."

Then making her sit on his knees:—"Louise, it is now twelve years since I found thee in the snow: thou wast blue, poor little one. And when we were in the cottage, near a good fire, and thou wert slowly reviving, the first thing thou didst was to smile at me. And since that time thy will has always been mine. With that smile thou hast led me wherever thou wouldst."

Then Louise began again to smile at him, and they embraced each other. "Now we will look at the packages," he said, sighing. "Are they well made, I wonder?"

He approached the bed, and was surprised to see his warmest clothes, his flannel-waistcoats, all well brushed, folded, and packed; and Louise's bundle, with her best dresses, petticoats, and stout shoes, in nice order. At last he could not help laughing and crying out—"O gypsy, gypsy! you are the one for making fine bundles, and going away without ever turning the head."

Louise smiled. "Are you satisfied?"

"I suppose I must be. But during all this piece of work, I will venture to say thou hast never thought of preparing my supper."

"Oh, it will soon be ready. I did not know you would return this evening, Papa Jean-Claude."

"That is true, my child. Bring me something—no matter what—quickly, for I am hungry. Meanwhile I shall smoke a pipe."

"Yes, that's it; smoke a pipe."

He sat down on the side of the bench and struck the tinder-box quite dreamily. Louise rushed right and left like a sprite, seeing to the fire, breaking the eggs, and turning out an omelette with surprising celerity. Never had she appeared so lively, smiling, and pretty. Hullin, his elbow on the table and his face in his hand, watched her gravely, thinking how much will, firmness, and resolution there was in this girl—as light as a fairy, yet determined as a hussar. In a few seconds she served him with the omelette on a large china plate, with bread, and the glass and bottle.

"There, Papa Jean-Claude, be hungry no longer." She observed him eating with a look of tenderness.

The flame sprang up in the stove, lighting clearly the low beams, the wooden stair in the shadow, the bed at the end of the alcove, the whole of the abode, so often cheered by the joyous humour of the shoemaker, the little songs of his daughter, and the industry of both. And all this Louise was leaving without any hesitation: she cared only for the woods, the snow-covered paths, and the endless mountains, reaching from the village into Switzer- land, and even beyond. Ah, Master Jean-Claude had reason to cry "gypsy, gypsy!" The swallow cannot be tamed: it needs the open air, the broad sky—continual motion. Neither storms, nor wind, nor rain in torrents frighten it, when the hour of its departure is at hand. It has only one thought, one desire, one cry—"Let us away! Let us away."

The meal finished, Hullin rose and said to his daughter, "I am tired, my child; kiss me, and let us go to bed."

"Yes; but do not forget to awake me, Papa Jean-Claude, if you start before daybreak."

"Do not trouble thyself. It is understood thou shalt come with us." And seeing her mount the stair and disappear in the garret: "Isn't she afraid of stopping in the nest, that's all!" said he to himself.

The silence was great outdoors. Eleven o'clock had struck from the village church. The good man was sitting down to take off his boots, when he caught sight of his musket suspended above the door: he took it down, wiped it, and drew the trigger. His whole soul was intent on the business in hand.

"It is all right," he murmured: and then in a grave tone: "It is curious. . . . The last time I held it … at Marengo . . . was fourteen years ago, and yet it seems like yesterday!"

Suddenly the hardened snow cracked under a quick footstep. He listened: "Someone!" At the same time two little sharp taps resounded on the panes. He ran to the window and opened it. The head of Marc Divès, with his broad hat stiff with the frost, bent forward from the darkness.

"Well, Marc, what news?"

"Hast thou warned the mountaineers—Materne, Jérome, Labarbe?"

"Yes, all."

"It was time: the enemy has passed."

"Passed?"

"Yes, along the whole line. I have walked fifteen leagues through the snow since this morning to announce it to thee."

"Good; the signal must be given: a great fire on the Falkenstein."

Hullin was very pale. He put on his boots.

Two minutes later, his large blouse on his shoulders and his stick in his hand, he softly opened the door, and with long strides followed Mark Divès on the way to the Falkenstein.

CHAPTER 7

Rising of the Partisans

From midnight till six in the morning a flame shone through the darkness on the summit of the Falkenstein, and the whole mountain was on the alert.

All the friends of Hullin, Marc Divès, and of Mother Lefèvre, their long gaiters on their legs and old muskets on their shoulders, journeyed, through the silent woods, toward the gorges of the Valtin. The thought of the enemy traversing the plains of Alsace to surprise the passes, was present to the minds of all. The tocsins of Dagsburg, Abreschwiller, Walsch, and St. Quirin, and of all the other villages, began to call the defenders of the country to arms.

Now-you must picture to yourself the Jägerthal, at the foot of the old castle, in unusually snowy weather, at that early hour when the clumps of trees begin to creep out of the shadow, and when the extreme cold of night softens at the approach of day. Picture, also, to yourself the old Sawyerie, with its flat roof, its heavy wheel burdened with icicles, the low interior dimly lit up by a pine-wood fire, whose blaze fades away in the glimmer of the coming dawn; and, around the fire, fur bonnets, caps, and black profiles, gazing one over the other, and squeezing close together like a wall; and farther on, in the woods, more fires lighting up groups of men and women squatting in the snow.

The agitation began to decrease. As the sky became grayer the people recognized each other.

"Ah, it is Cousin Daniel of Soldatenthal. You have come

too?"

"Yes, as you see, Heinrich, with my wife also."

"What, Cousin Nanette! Where is she?"

"Down there, near the old oak, by Uncle Hans' fire."

They shook hands. Many could be heard yawning loudly: others threw on the fire bits of planks. The gourds went round; some retired from the circles to make room for their shivering neighbours. Meanwhile the crowd began to grow impatient.

"Ah," cried some, "we did not come here only to get our feet warmed. It is time to see and come to an understanding."

"Yes, yes! Let them hold a council, and name the chiefs."

"No; everybody is not yet arrived. See, there are more coming from Dagsburg and St. Quirin."

Indeed, the lighter it became, the more people could be seen hastening along all the mountain paths. At that time there must have been many hundreds of men in the valley—woodcutters, char- coal-burners, raftsmen—without counting the women and children.

Nothing could be more picturesque than that gathering in the midst of the snows, in the depths of the defile, closed in as it was by tall pines losing themselves in the clouds. To the right, the valleys opening away into each other as far as the eye could reach; to the left, the ruins of the Falkentein rising into the sky. From a distance one would have said it was a flock of cranes settled on the ice; but, nearer, these hardy men could be distinguished, with stiff beards bristling like a boar, gloomy fierce eyes, broad square shoulders, and horny hands.

Some few, taller than the rest, belonged to the fiery race of red men, white-skinned, and hairy to the tips of their fingers, with strength enough to pull an oak up by the roots. Among this number was old Materne of Hengst, with his two sons Kasper and Frantz. These sturdy fellows—all three armed with little rifles from Innsprück—having blue cloth gaiters with leathern buttons reaching above their knees, their loins girdled with goat-skin, and their felt hats coming down low over their necks—did not deign to approach the fire. For an hour they had been sitting on a trunk by the riverside, on the watch, with their feet in the snow. From time to time the old man would say to his sons, "What do they shiver for over there? I never knew a milder night for the season: it is nothing—the rivers are not even touched."

All the forest-hunters of the country passing by came to shake hands with them, then congregated round them and formed a circle apart. These fellows spoke little, being used to silence for whole days and nights, for fear of frightening away their game.

Marc Divès, standing in the middle of another group, a head taller than any of them, spoke and gesticulated—pointing now to one part of the mountain, now to another. In front of him was the old herdsman Lagarmitte, with his large gray smock, a long bark trumpet on his shoulder, and his dog at his feet. He listened to the smuggler, open-mouth, and kept on bowing his head. The others all seemed attentive: they were composed of charcoal-burners and wood-carriers, with whom the smuggler had daily intercourse.

Between the saw-mills and the first fire, on the bridge over the dam, sat the bootmaker Jérome of St. Quirin—a man of from fifty to sixty years of age, with a long brown face, hollow eyes, big nose—his ears covered with a badger-skin cap—and a yellow beard reaching to his waist in a peak. His hands, enveloped in great green woollen gloves, were clasped over an immense stick of knotty service-tree. He wore a long sackcloth hood; and might easily have been taken for a hermit. At every rumour that arose, Father Jérome would slowly turn his head, and try to catch what it was, frowning.

Jean Labarbe, grasping his axe, remained immovable. He was a white-faced man, with an aquiline nose and thin lips. He exercised great influence over the men of Dagsburg, owing to his resolution and the clearness of his ideas. When they shouted around him, "We must deliberate; we cannot stay here doing nothing," he simply contented himself with saying, "Let us wait: Hullin has not arrived, nor Catherine Lefèvre. There is no hurry." Everybody then was silenced, and looked impatiently toward the path from Charmes.

The sawyer Piorette—a small, brisk, thin, energetic man, whose black eyebrows met above his eyes—stood on the threshold of his hut, with his pipe between his teeth, contemplating the general appearance of this scene.

Meanwhile, the impatience increased every moment. Some village mayors—in square-cut coats and three-cornered hats-advanced in the direction of the saw-mills, calling on their communes to come and decide what was to be done. Most fortunately, at last Catherine Lefèvre's cart appeared, and a thousand enthusiastic shouts arose on all sides:

"There they are! they come!"

Old Materne gravely mounted on a trunk and quietly descended, saying, "It is they."

Great agitation showed itself. The farthest groups gathered together in one crowd. A sort of impatient shiver passed over the mass. Scarcely has the old farmer's wife become visible, whip in hand, on her straw box with little Louise, than from all parts came cries of "*Vive la France! Vive la mère Catherine!*"

Hullin, who had remained behind, his broad hat pushed back, his musket slung across his shoulder, was now crossing the meadow of Eichmath, distributing vigorous shakes of the hand: "Good-day, Daniel; good-day, Colon. Good-day—good- day!"

"Ah! it is going to be warm, Hullin."

"Yes—yes; we are going to hear the chestnuts popping this winter. Good-day, my old Jérome! We have serious business on hand."

"Yes, Jean-Claude. "We must hope to pull through it by the grace of God."

Catherine, on arriving at the saw-works, told Labarbe to set on the ground a keg of brandy which she had brought away from the farm, and to get a jug from the sawyer's cottage.

Soon after, Hullin, coming up to the fire, met Materne and his two sons.

"You have come late," said the old hunter.

"Ah! yes. What was to be done? I had to descend the Falkenstein, get my gun, and start the women. But as we are now here, let us lose no more time; Lagarmitte, blow thy horn, so that all the men may assemble. The first thing is to appoint the leaders."

Lagarmitte blew his long trumpet, his cheeks puffed out to his ears: then those who were still on the hillsides or paths hastened their pace to be in time. Soon all those brave fellows were assembled in front of the saw-works. Hullin got up on a pile of tree-trunks, and looking seriously upon the crowd, said, amidst deep silence: "The enemy crossed the Rhine the day before yesterday: they are marching over the mountain into Lorraine: Strasbourg and Huningue are blockaded. We may expect to see the Germans and Prussians in three or four days."

There was a loud shout of "*Vive la France!*"

"Yes, *vive la France!*" continued Hullin; "for if the allies enter Paris they can do what they choose; they can re-establish statute-labour, tithes, convents, monopolies, and the gallows. If you wish to see that over again, you have only to let them pass."

It would be impossible to depict the savage fierceness of the audience at that moment.

"That is what I had to tell you," cried Hullin, quite white. "Since you are here, it can only be to fight."

"Yes, yes."

"It is well; but listen to me. I will be open with you. Among you are fathers of families. We shall be one against ten, against fifty: we must expect to perish. So let the men who have not reflected on it, who feel they have not heart to do their duty to the end, go—none will take notice of them. Each man is free."

Then he paused and looked around him. Everybody remained stationary: then with a firmer voice, he concluded thus: "No one goes away; you are all, all resolved to fight. Well, I am rejoiced to see there is not one coward among us. Now a leader must be chosen. In great dangers, the first thing is order and discipline. The leader you are going to name will have the right of commanding and being obeyed. So reflect seriously, for on that man will hang the fate of you all."

THERE WAS A GENERAL SHOUT OF "LONG LIVE FRANCE!"

So saying, Jean-Claude descended from the treetrunk, and the agitation became extreme. Every village deliberated apart by itself—every mayor proposed his friend—and the hours wore on. Catherine Lefèvre was burning with impatience. At length she could no longer contain herself, and standing up on her bench, signed that she was going to speak.

Catherine was held in great esteem. At first only a few, then a larger number approached to know what she wished to communicate.

"My friends," said she, "we are losing time. What do you wish for? A trustworthy man, is it not so? a soldier—a man who has seen service, and who knows how to profit by our positions? Well, why do you not choose Hullin? Can anyone find a better? If so, let him speak, and we will decide. I propose Jean-Claude Hullin. *Hé*! do you hear—over there? If this continues, the Austrians will have arrived before a leader has been decided on."

Yes—yes! Hullin!" shouted Labarbe, Divès, Jérome, and several others. "Let us see how many are for and against him."

Then Marc Divès, clambering on to the trunks, cried out in a voice like thunder: "Those who do not want Jean-Claude Hullin for leader must lift up their hands."

Not one hand was uplifted.

"Those who want Jean-Claude Hullin for their leader must raise their hands."

Every hand was put up.

"Jean-Claude," said the smuggler, "mount up here, look-they have chosen you for their leader."

Master Jean-Claude having done so, saw he was named, and said immediately in a stern voice: "Good! you name me to be your chief . I accept! Let Materne the elder, Labarbe of Dagsburg, Jérome of St. Quirin, Marc Divès, Piorette the sawyer, and Catherine Lefèvre, come into the saw-works. We are going to take counsel. In a quarter of an hour or twenty minutes, I shall give my orders. Meanwhile, each village must put two men under the orders of Marc Divès, to fetch powder and ball from the Falkenstein."

CHAPTER 8

The Leader

The persons indicated by Jean-Claude Hullin met together in the shed of the Sawyerie, before the great fireplace; a species of good-humour beaming on their faces.

"For twenty years have I heard speak of the Russians, Austrians, and Cossacks," said old Materne, smiling, "and I shall not be sorry to see a few within reach of my musket: it gives a change to one's ideas."

"Yes," replied Labarbe, "we shall see queer things; the little children of the mountains will be able to relate something of what their fathers and grandfathers did! And the old women, of an evening—won't they tell long tales in fifty years' time?"

"Comrades," said Hullin, "you know the whole country: you have the mountain under your eyes from Thann to Wissembourg. You know that the great roads, imperial roads—traverse Alsace and the Vosges. They both commence at Bâle: one runs along the Rhine to Strasbourg, from whence it ascends to Saverne and enters Lorraine. Huningue, Neuf-Brisach, Strasbourg, and Phalsbourg defend it. The other turns to the left and passes by Schlestadt: at Schlestadt it enters the mountain and reaches Saint-Dié, Raon-l'Etape, Baccarat, and Lunéville.

"The enemy will want to force these two roads first,—being the best for cavalry, artillery, and baggage,—but as they are defended, we need not trouble ourselves about them. If the allies besiege the fortresses—which would lengthen the campaign— we have nothing to fear; but it is not probable they will do so.

After having summoned Huningue to surrender, Belfort, Schlestadt, Strasbourg, and Phalsbourg, on this side the Vosges-
Bitsche, Lutzelstein, and Sarrebrück on the other—I imagine
they will fall upon us. Now attend to me. Between Phalsbourg
and Saint-Dié, there are several defiles for the infantry; but there
is only one way practicable for cannon: this is the road from
Strasbourg to Raon-les-Leaux by Urmatt, Mutzig, Lutzelhouse,
Phramond, Grandfontaine.

"Once masters of this passage, the allies will be able to come
out on Lorraine. This road passes the Donon, two leagues from
here, on our right. The first thing to be done is to make a firm
stand there, in the most favourable part for defence, that is to say,
on the plateau of the mountain; to intersect it, to break down
the bridges, and to erect solid breastworks across it. A few hundreds of great trees across the road with all their branches are
worth as much as ramparts. They are the best ambuscades: one is
well sheltered behind them and can see everything coming.

"Those large trees hold like death. They must be taken away
piece by piece; bridges cannot be thrown over them:—in fact
it is the best thing to be done. All that, comrades, must be accomplished tomorrow evening, or next day at the latest. I charge
myself with it. But it is not sufficient to occupy a position and
put it in a good state of defence: it must be so managed that the
enemy shall not be able to turn it."

"I was just thinking of that," said Materne.. "Once in the valley of Bruche, the Germans can march with their infantry into
the hills of Haslach and turn our left. Nothing can prevent their
trying the same manoeuvre on our right, if they reach Raon-
l'Etape."

"Yes, but to take these ideas out of their heads, we have a very
simple thing to do: it is to occupy the defiles of the Zorn and
the Sarre on our left, and that of Blanru on our right. One can
only keep a defile by holding the heights; that is why Piorette
must place himself with a hundred men on the side of Raon-
les-Leaux; Jérome on the Grosmaun, with the same number,
to close the valley of the Sarre; and Labarbe, at the head of the

remainder on the great slopes to watch over the hills of Haslach. You must choose your men from those of the nearest villages. The women ought not to have a long distance to carry provisions; and then the wounded will be nearer their homes, which must also be thought of.

"There is all I have to say to you just now. The chiefs of posts must take care to send me every day on the Donon, where I shall establish our head-quarters this evening, a good walker, to inform me of what happens, and to receive the countersign. We shall also organize a reserve; but as we must make haste, we will speak of that when you are all in position, and there is no longer cause to fear a surprise from the enemy."

"And I," exclaimed Marc Divès, "I shall have nothing to do then? I am to remain with my arms folded, watching the others fight?"

"Thou—thou art to survey the transport of ammunition. None of us know how to treat the powder as thou dost, to preserve it from fire and damp, to melt the balls, and make cartridges."

"But it is woman's work, that is," exclaimed the smuggler. "Hexe-Baizel could do it as well as I. What! am I not even to fire once?"

"Softly, Marc," replied Hullin, laughing; "occasions will not be wanting. In the first place, the Falkenstein is the centre of our line; it is our arsenal and our retreating place in case of misfortune. The enemy will know through his spies that our convoys come from there; he will try, probably, to take them: the balls and bayonet-thrusts will come in thy way. Besides, to have thee in safety will be all the better, for thy cellars and caves must not be confided to the first comer. But if thou really wouldst like—"

"No," said the smuggler, who had been touched by Hullin's reference to his caves—"no! all things considered, I believe thou art right, Jean-Claude. I have my men—they are well armed—we will defend the Falkenstein; and if the opportunity of firing a shot should present itself, I shall be all the freer."

"Then that is a decided and well-understood business?" demanded Hullin.

"Yes, yes, it is decided."

"Well, comrades," said the worthy fellow, joyously, "let us warm ourselves with a few good glasses of wine. It is ten o'clock; let each one return to his village, and make his preparations. To-morrow morning all the defiles must be vigorously occupied."

They quitted the shed, and Hullin, in the presence of his followers, named Labarbe, Jérome, and Piorette chiefs of the defiles: then he told those of the Sarre to assemble as soon as possible near the farm of Bois-de-Chênes, with axes, mattocks, and muskets. "We shall leave at two o'clock, and encamp on the Donon across the route," said he to them. "Tomorrow, at dawn, we will begin the breastworks."

He retained Materne and his two sons Frantz and Kasper, announcing to them that the battle would commence undoubtedly on the Donon, and that good shots would be wanted on that side, which gave them pleasure.

Mistress Lefèvre had never looked happier than when she got into her cart again, and, kissing Louise, said in her ear: "All goes well. Jean-Claude is a man: he sees everything; he draws people to him. I have known him forty years, yet he surprises even me." Then turning round—"Jean-Claude," cried she, "we have a ham waiting for us down there and a few old bottles, which the Germans shall not drink."

"No, Catherine, they shall not drink them. Go on. I am coming."

But just as they were starting, and when already a number of mountaineers were climbing the hillsides to regain their villages, quite in the distance, on the path of Trois-Fontaines, appeared a large thin man on a big roan cob, with a flat-brimmed cap of rabbit-skin covering the whole back of his neck: a great sheep-dog with a black shaggy coat bounded along near him; and the ends of his enormous surtout flapped behind him like wings. Every one cried out,—"It is Doctor Lorquin from the plain the one who attends poor people *gratis*. He comes with his dog Pluto. He is a good man."

DOCTOR LORQUIN

In fact he it was. He galloped on, shouting, "Halt! stop! halt!" And his red face, sharp eyes, red-brown beard, broad shoulders, great horse and dog, all cleaved the air and grew upon the view. In two seconds he had reached the foot of the mountain, crossed the meadow, and appeared at the bridge, before the shed. Instantly, in breathless tones, he began to say:—"Ah! the cunning rogues who want to enter on a campaign without me; they shall pay for it!"

And tapping a small box he carried at his crupper,—"Listen, my good fellows, listen! I have something inside there of which you shall give me an account: every description of knife, large, small, round and pointed, to take from you the balls and shot of all kinds which you are going to be regaled with!" Whereupon he burst out laughing, and all those near him felt a cold shiver in all their veins.

Having delivered himself of this pleasantry, Doctor Lorquin continued in a graver tone:—"Hullin, I must pull your ears! What, when the country has to be defended, you forget me! others have to warn me. It appears to me, however, that a doctor will not be out of the way here. I must call you to account."

"Pardon me, doctor, I was wrong," said Hullin, squeezing his hand. "During the last week so many things have happened! One does not always think of everything; and besides, such a man as you are, need not be told how to fulfil his duty."

The doctor was appeased.

"All that is right and good," he cried; "but nevertheless by your fault I am too late; the good places are taken, the crosses distributed. Come, where is the general, that I may make complaints to him?"

"I am the general."

"Oh! oh! really?"

"Yes, doctor, I am the general; and I promote you to be our head surgeon."

"Chief surgeon of the partisans of the Vosges! Well, it suits me. No malice now, Jean-Claude."

Approaching the cart, the worthy man told Catherine that he

relied on her for the organization of the ambulances.

"Everything shall be ready, doctor," replied the farm-mistress. "Louise and I are going to set to work this evening. Is it not so, Louise?"

"Oh, yes, Mamma Lefèvre," said she, enchanted to perceive that the campaign was going to begin. "We shall work well; we will spend the night at it even. M. Lorquin shall be well pleased, with us."

"Well, then, let us go. You will dine with us, doctor?"

They trotted away. While keeping pace with them, the good doctor related to Catherine laughingly how the tidings of the general rising had reached him; the affliction of his old house-keeper, Mario, who wanted to prevent his going to be massacred by the "*kaiserlichs*," and the various episodes of his journey from Quibolo to the village of Charmes. Hullin, Materne, and his sons were coming on behind, their carbines on their shoulders; and thus they ascended the hillside toward the farm of Bois-de-Chênes.

CHAPTER 9

The Conscript

You can imagine the animation at the farm, the bustling of the domestics, the shouts of enthusiasm, the chinking of glasses and forks, the joy depicted on all faces, when Jean-Claude, Doctor Lorquin, the Maternes, and all those who had followed the cart of Catherine Lefèvre were installed in the large room around a magnificent ham, and began to celebrate their future triumphs, glass in hand.

It was on a Tuesday, baking-day at the farm. Excitement had prevailed in the kitchen all the morning: old Duchêne, with shirt-sleeves turned up and a cotton cap on his head, was taking out of the oven numberless loaves of bread, the good odour of which pervaded the whole house. Annette received them and piled them on the hearth; Louisa waited on the guests; and Catherine Lefèvre superintended everything, crying out,—"Make haste, my children—make haste! The third batch must be ready when the men from the Sarre arrive. It will make six pounds of bread for each man."

Hullin, from his seat, watched the movements of the old farm-mistress.

"What a woman!" said he; "what a woman! She forgets nothing. Could one find another such in the whole country? To the health of Catherine Lefèvre!"

"To the health of Catherine Lefèvre!" replied the others.

The glasses met together, and they began again to talk over combats, assaults, and intrenchments. Each one felt animated with an invincible confidence; every one said in himself, "All will go well!"

But heaven had in store for them yet another satisfaction on that day, especially for Louise and the Mother Lefèvre. About noon, just as a beautiful gleam of winter sunshine whitened the snow and made the frost melt on the window-panes, and the great cock, putting his head out of his coop, uttered his triumphant crow, flapping his wings—just then the watch-dog, old "Yohan," half blind and toothless, began to bark so joyously and plaintively, that everyone listened with the greatest attention. The kitchen was all excitement with the fourth batch coming out of the oven, and even Catherine Lefèvre herself stopped.

"Something is going on," said she, in a low voice; and then added, all trembling, "Since my boy left, Yohan has never barked like that."

At the same moment, rapid steps traversed the court. Louise sprang toward the door, crying,—"It is he! It is he!" and almost immediately a hand tried to hasp. The door opened, and a soldier appeared on the threshold; but such a soldier, so worn, so bronzed, so emaciated! his gray hood, with its pewter buttons, so ragged—his high leathern gaiters so torn, that all present were astonished.

He appeared unable to advance a step farther, and slowly put the butt-end of his musket on the ground. The tip of his aquiline nose—the nose of Mother Lefèvre—shone like bronze; his red moustaches shook like one of those great lean hawks which are forced by hunger to come to the very doors of the stables in winter. He looked into the kitchen, pale beneath the brown coating of his cheeks, and with his great hollow eyes filled with tears, he seemed unable to advance or say a word.

Outride, the old dog leaped, whined, and shook his chain; in the interior, one could hear the fire blazing, so great was the silence; but soon Catherine Lefèvre, with a piercing voice, exclaimed,—"Gaspare!! my child! It is thou!"

"Yes, my mother," replied the soldier, softly, as though suffocating.

And at the same moment Louise began to weep, while in the great room there arose a shout like thunder. All the friends ran out, Master Jean-Claude at their head, crying,—"Gaspard! Gaspard Lefèvre!"

Then they saw Gaspard and his mother embracing each other. This strong, courageous woman was weeping: he did not weep; he held her pressed to his breast, his red moustaches mingling with her gray locks, and murmured,—"My mother!—my mother! Ah, how often have I thought of you!"

Then, in a louder voice, he said, "Louise! Where is Louise? I saw Louise!" And Louise threw herself into his arms, and their kisses were mingled together. "Ah, thou didst not recognize me, Louise!"

"Oh, yes!—oh, yes! I knew thee, even by thy step!"

Old Duchêne, with his cotton cap in his hands, stammered out by the fireplace,—"Lord! is it possible? My poor child! What does he look like?"

He had brought up Gaspard, and always fancied him, ever since his departure, fresh and ruddy in a beautiful uniform with red facings. It completely deranged his ideas to see him otherwise.

At that moment Hullin, raising his voice, said,—"And the rest of us, Gaspard,—thy old friends art thou not going to take notice of us?"

Then the brave fellow turned round and exclaimed with enthusiasm,—"Hullin! Doctor Lorquin! Materne! Frantz! Why, they are all here!"

And the embraces recommenced, but this time more joyously, with shouts of laughter and shaking of hands that seemed endless.

"Ah, doctor, it is you! Ah, my old father, Jean-Claude!"

They looked closely at each other, with bright, beaming faces, and went arm-in-arm up and down the great room; and Mother Catherine with the knapsack, Louise with the gun, and Duchêne with the shako, followed them, laughing and drying their cheeks and eyes—nothing had ever been seen like it before.

"Let us sit down and drink!" exclaimed Doctor Lorquin. "This is the bouquet of the feast."

"Ah, my poor Gaspard, how happy I am to behold thee safe and sound," said Hullin. "Ha, ha! Without flattery, I like thee better as thou art now than with thy great red cheeks. *Parbleu!* thou art a man now. Thou remindest me of the old fellows of my time, those of the Sambre and Egypt—ha, ha, ha! we had not round noses, we were not sleek and fat; we looked like lean rats watching a cheese, and our teeth were long and white!"

"Yes, yes, that does not surprise me, Papa Jean-Claude. Come, let us sit down; we can talk more at ease. Ah, now, why are you all at the farm?"

"What, dost thou not know? All the country is up, from Houpe to Saint-Sauveur, to defend itself."

"Yes, the anabaptist of Painbach just mentioned it as I passed. It is then true?"

"It is true. Everybody is in it; and I am the general in chief."

"Excellent—excellent! That these rogues of *kaiserlichs* should not carry everything with a high hand in our own country gives me pleasure. But hand me the knife. Anyway one is happy to find one's self at home again. *Hé!* Louise, come here and sit down a little while. Look, Papa Jean-Claude: with this girl on one side of me, the ham on the other, and the bottle to the front, I should not need a fortnight to pick up again; and my comrades would not know me when I joined the company."

Everybody was now sitting down and astonished to see with what appetite the brave fellow ate and drank, while regarding Louise and his mother tenderly, and replying to one and the other, without losing a single mouthful.

The farm-people, Duchêne, Annette, Robin, and Dubourg, arranged in a half-circle, watched Gaspard in ecstasies; Louise refilled his glass; the Mother Lefèvre, seated by the stove, got up and went to his knapsack, and, on only finding two old black shirts with holes wide enough to put one's hand through, with worn-out shoes and a bit of wax for cartridges, a comb with two teeth and an empty bottle, she lifted her hands to heaven and hastening to open the linen chest, saying, "Lord, can one be astonished that so many die of sheer want!"

Doctor Lorquin, in presence of such a vigorous appetite, rubbed his hands joyfully, and murmured to himself, "What a sturdy fellow! What a digestion! What a set of teeth! He could crunch pebbles like nuts."

And even old Materne said to his sons:—"In other days, after two or three days of hunting in the high mountains in winter, I also used to feel the hunger of a wolf, and to eat a haunch of venison right off: now I am getting old, one or two pounds of meat are sufficient for me—which shows what age does."

Hullin had lit his pipe, and seemed in a reverie: evidently something worried him. After a few minutes, seeing that Gaspard's appetite was less lively, he brusquely asked, "Say, then, Gaspard, without interrupting thyself, how the devil hast thou managed to come?" We believed that thou wast still on the borders of the Rhine, on the Strasbourg side."

"Ah! ah! old soldier, I comprehend," said young Lefèvre, winking. "There are so many deserters, are there not?"

"Oh! such an idea would never enter my head, and yet—"

"You would not be sorry to know that I had done nothing wrong? I cannot blame you, Papa Jean-Claude: you are right. He who is missing at the roll-call when the *kaiserlichs* are in France, deserves to be shot. Be composed, here is my leave."

Hullin, who possessed no false delicacy, read,—

Leave for twenty-four hours to the grenadier Gaspard Lefèvre, of the 2nd of the 1st. This day, 3rd January, 1814.—Gemeau, Head of Battalion.

"Good, good," exclaimed he. "Put that carefully in thy knapsack, thou mightest lose it."

All his good-humour had returned:—"Do you see, my children, I know what love is? There is both good and bad in it: but it is particularly bad for young soldiers who come too close to their village after a campaign. They are capable of forgetting themselves and of not returning unless in company of two or three *gendarmes*. I have seen it. But come, since everything is in order, let us drink a glass of *rikevir*. What say you, Catherine? The men of the Sarre may arrive at any moment, and we have not an instant to lose?"

"You are right, Jean-Claude," replied the old farm-mistress sadly. "Annette, go down and bring three bottles from the small cellar."

The servant obeyed quickly.

"But this leave, Gaspard," continued Catherine—"how long has it lasted?"

"I received it yesterday, at eight in the evening, at Yasselonne, my mother. The regiment is retreating on Lorraine; I must re-join it this evening at Phalsbourg."

"It is well; thou hast still seven hours; thou wilt not need more than six to reach there, although there is much snow on the Foxthal."

The good woman came and sat down again by her son, with a full heart. Everyone was moved. Louise, with her arm on the old tattered epaulet of Gaspard and her cheek against his, was sobbing. Hullin emptied the ashes from his pipe at the end of the table, frowning, without saying anything, but when the bottles arrived and were uncorked, "Come, Louise," said he, "take courage! this cannot last forever; it must end in one way or an-other, and I venture to affirm that it will end well. Gaspard will come back to us, and then we shall have the wedding."

He refilled the glasses, and Catherine dried her eyes, mur-muring, "To think that those brigands are the cause of all this. Ah! let them come—let them come here!"

They all drank with a melancholy air; but the old *rikevir*, en-tering the hearts of these brave people quickly enlivened them. Gaspard, stronger than he had appeared at first, began to re-late the terrible battles of Bautzen, Lutzen, Leipzig, and Hanau, where the conscripts had fought like tried soldiers, winning vic-tory after victory, till traitors began to appear.

Every one listened in silence. Louise, when he spoke of any great danger—of the passage over rivers under the enemy's fire, or the taking of a battery by the bayonet—squeezed his arm as though to defend him. Jean-Claude's eyes sparkled; the doctor demanded each time the position of the ambulance; Materne and his sons stretched out their necks and clinched their jaws; and with help of the old wine the enthusiasm increased every moment. "Ah, the rascals! ah, the brigands! But look out! it is not over yet."

Mother Lefèvre admired the courage and luck of her son in the midst of these events, which will be remembered centuries to come. But when Lagarmitte, looking solemn and grave in his long gray cloth coat, with his broad black felt on his white head, and with his bark trumpet on his shoulder, crossed the kitchen, and appeared at the entrance to the large room, saying,—"The men of the Sarre are come,"—then all this enthusiasm disappeared, and the company rose, thinking of the terrible struggle which would soon take place in the mountains.

Louise, throwing her arms round Gaspard's neck, cried, "Gaspard, do not go away! Remain with us!"

He became very pale.

"I am a soldier," said he. "I am called, Gaspard Lefèvre. I love thee a thousand times more than my own life; but a Lefèvre only knows his duty."

And he unwound her arms. Louise then, sinking on the table, began to moan aloud. Gaspard rose. Hullin stood between them, and grasping his hands tightly, with trembling lips, said: "Excellently well! Thou hast spoken like a man."

His mother came forward with a calm countenance to buckle his knapsack on his shoulders.

She did it with knitted eyebrows and pressed lips, without one sigh escaping her; but two great tears slowly ran down the wrinkles of her cheeks. And when she had done it, she turned away, and with her sleeve over her eyes, said: "It is well! Go—go, my child! thy mother blesses thee. Whatever thy fortune thou wilt yet not be lost to us. Look, Gaspard: there is thy place—there between Louise and myself—thou wilt always be there. This poor child is not old enough yet to know that to live is to suffer."

Everybody left; only Louise remained lamenting in the room. A few seconds later, as the butt end of the musket sounded on the slabs of the kitchen, and the outer door was opened, she gave a piercing shriek, and darted after him.

"Gaspard, Gaspard, look! I will be courageous; I will not cry; I will not keep thee back. Oh, no; but do not leave me in anger. Have pity on me!"

"Angry! angry with thee, my Louise! Oh, no! But to see thee so unhappy breaks my heart. Ah! if thou wert a little braver now, I should feel happier."

"Well, I am. Let us kiss each other! See, I am no longer the same. I would be like Maman Lefèvre."

They calmly gave each other a parting embrace, Hullin held the gun; Catherine motioned with her hands, as though to say, "Go, go! it is enough!" And he, suddenly seizing his musket, walked away resolutely, without looking back.

On the other side, the men of the Sarre, with their axes and hatchets, were climbing the steep ascent of the Valtin.

Five minutes later, on, passing by the great oak, Gaspard turned round, lifting his hands. Catherine and Louise replied to it. Hullin advanced to meet his people. Doctor Lorquin alone remained with the women; and when Gaspard, continuing his way, had disappeared, he exclaimed, "Catherine Lefèvre, you can pride yourself on having an affectionate son. God grant him good fortune!"

And the distant voices of the newcomers could be heard laughing among themselves, as they were marching to war as gayly as to a wedding.

LOUISE THROWING HER ARMS ROUND GESPARD'S NECK

CHAPTER 10

Robin's Vision

As Hullin, at the head of the mountaineers, was taking his measures for the defence of his country, the madman Yégof, with his tin crown, that sad spectacle of humanity shorn of its noblest attribute, intelligence—the madman Yégof, his breast exposed to the fierce wind, his feet bare, reckless of cold, like the reptile in his prison, was wandering from mountain to mountain, in the midst of the snows of winter. How comes it that the madman is able to resist the sharpest severity of the atmosphere, while an intelligent being would succumb to it? Does it arise from a more powerful concentration of life, a more rapid circulation of the blood, a state of continued fever? Or is it the effect of the extraordinary excitement of the senses, or any other unknown cause?

Science tells us nothing. She admits only material causes, without giving an account of such phenomena.

So Yégof went on at random, and night came. The cold was redoubled, the fox gnashed his teeth in the pursuit of an invisible prey; the famished buzzard fell back with empty claws among the bushes, uttering a cry of distress. He, with his raven on his shoulder, gesticulating, jabbering, as if in a dream, kept walking on, from Holderloch to Sonneberg, from Sonneberg to Blut-feld.

Now, on this particular night, the old shepherd, Robin, of the farm of Bois-de-Chênes, was destined to be the witness of a most strange and fearful sight.

Some days ago, having been overtaken by the first fall of snow at the bottom of the ravine of the Blutfeld, he had left his cart there to conduct his flock back to the farm; but having discovered that he had forgotten his sheepskin, and left it in a shed there, he had on this day, when his work was done, set out about four o'clock in the afternoon to go and fetch it. The Blutfeld, situated between the Schnéeberg and the Grosmann, is a narrow gorge, bounded by rocks. A narrow stream of water winds through it, under shadow of the tall shrubs, and in its depths extends a vast pasturage, all covered with large gray stones, that lie thickly scattered about.

This gorge is very little frequented, for there is a wild look about the Blutfeld, especially by the light of a winter moon. The learned folks of these regions, the school-master of Dagsburg, and he of Hazlach, say that in that spot occurred the famous battle of the Triboques against the Germans, who wished to penetrate into Gaul, under the command of a leader named Luitprandt. They say that the Triboques, from the neighbouring heights, hurling upon their enemies huge masses of rocks, crushed them there as in a mortar, and that, on account of this great carnage, the gorge has preserved to this day the name of Blutfeld, Fragments of broken pots, of rusty lances, of helmets, and long swords with cross hilts, are often found there.

At night, when the moon sheds her light upon this field and those immense stones, all covered with snow, when the north wind blows among the frost-covered branches, making them rattle and clatter like cymbals, you might fancy you heard the wild cry of the Germans at the moment of surprise, the shrieks of the women, the neighings of the horses, the rumbling of the chariots in the defile; for it seems that these people brought with them, in their skin-covered carriages, women, children, old men, and all that they possessed in gold, and silver, and movables, like the Germans setting out for America.

The Triboques never ceased to massacre them during two days, and on the third day they returned to the Donon, the Schnéeberg, the Grosmann, the Giromani, the Hengst, their broad shoulders stooping under the weight of their booty.

This is what is related concerning the Blutfeld, and certainly to see this gorge enclosed within the mountains like an immense trap, without any other outlet than a narrow footpath, it is easy to understand how the Germans were taken at a disadvantage and fell an easy prey to their conquerors.

Robin did not reach the spot till between seven and eight o'clock, just as the moon was rising.

The worthy fellow had descended the precipice a hundred times, but never had he beheld the place so brightly illuminated, and at the same time of so gloomy an aspect.

At a distance, his white cart, at the bottom of the abyss, looked to him exactly like one of those enormous stones, covered with snow, beneath which the Germans had been buried. It was at the entrance of the gorge, behind a thick cluster of shrubs, and beside it the little torrent ran murmuring in a slender stream, bright as steel, and sparkling like diamonds.

When he arrived there, the shepherd began to look for the key of the padlock; then, having un- locked the shed, he crept in on his hands and knees, and found, very fortunately, not only his sheepskin, but an old hatchet, which he had quite forgot ten.

But judge of his surprise when, on issuing from it, he saw the madman Yégof appear at the turn of the footpath, and come straight toward him in the bright moonlight.

The honest man immediately remembered the fearful story told in the kitchen of Bois-do-Chênes, and he felt afraid; but quite another feeling came over him when behind the fool, at fifteen or twenty-paces, he beheld, stealthily approaching in their turn, five gray wolves, two big and three smaller ones.

At first he took them for dogs, but they were wolves. They followed Yégof step by step, and he did not appear to see them; his raven hovered overhead, flitting from the full moonlight to the shadow of the rocks, and then returning; the wolves, with flaming eyes, their sharp muzzles turned up, were sniffing the air; the fool raised his sceptre.

The shepherd pulled-to the door of the shed as quick as lightning, but Yégof did not see him. He advanced into the gorge as into a spacious chamber, to the right and left rose the steep rocks, above which myriads of stars were shining. You might have heard a fly move; the wolves made no noise in walking; all was silent, and the raven had just perched on the top of an old withered oak that grew upon one of the rocks opposite; his shining plumage looked still darker than usual, as he turned his head, and seemed to be listening.

It was a strange sight.

Robin said to himself:—"The fool sees nothing, hears nothing; they will devour him. If he stumbles, if his foot slips, it is all over with him."

But in the middle of the gorge, Yégof, having turned round, sat down upon a stone, and the five wolves round him, still sniffing the air, squatted on their haunches in the snow.

And then, a really terrible sight—the fool raising his sceptre, made them a speech, calling them each by his name.

The wolves answered him with dismal howls.

Now this is what he said to them:—"*Hé*, Child, Bléd, Merweg, and thou, Sirimar, my ancient, we are met together, then, once again! You have returned fat. There has been good cheer in Germany, eh?"

Then, pointing to the snow-covered gorge:—"You remember the great battle?"

First one of the wolves began to howl slowly in a dismal voice, then another, then all the five together.

This lasted a good ten minutes.

The raven, perched on the withered branch, did not stir.

Robin would gladly have fled. He put up his prayers, invoked all the saints, and, in particular, his own patron, for whom all the shepherds of the mountain have the highest veneration.

But the wolves still continued howling, awakening all the echoes of the Blutfeld.

At last one, the oldest of the number, was silent, then another, then all, and Yégof continued:—"Yes, yes: that is a dismal story. Look! there is the river down which our blood flowed

THE LUNATIC WAVING HIS SCEPTRE, MADE THEM A DISCOURSE

in streams! No matter, Merweg, no matter; the others have left their bones to whiten on the common, and the cold moon has seen their women tearing their hair for three days and three nights! Oh, that frightful day! Oh, the dogs! were they proud of their great victory? Let them be accursed—accursed."

The fool had cast his crown to the ground. He now picked it up, groaning as he did so.

The wolves, still crouching round, listened to him like attentive spectators. The biggest among them began to howl, and Yégof answered his complaint.

"You are hungry, Sirimar; take comfort, take comfort; you will not want for food much longer; the men of our side are coming, and the strife will begin afresh."

Then rising, and striking his sceptre on a stone, "See," said he, "behold thy bones!"

He approached another. "And thine, Merweg, behold them!" said he.

All the troop followed him, while he, raising himself upon a low rock, and glancing round upon the silent gorge, exclaimed:-
"Our war-song is silent! our war-song is now a groan! The hour is near; it will reawaken, and you will be among the warriors; you will possess once more these valleys and these mountains. Oh! that sound of wheels, those cries of women, those blows from crushing rocks and stones; I hear them; the air is full of them. Yes, yes; they fell on us from above, and we were surrounded. And now all is dead; hear! all is dead; your bones sleep, but your children are on their way, and your turn will come. Sing! sing!"

And this time he himself began to howl, while the wolves took up again their savage song.

These dismal howls grew more and more loud and appalling; and the silence of the rocks around, some plunged in darkness, while others were fully revealed in the moon's rays, the solemn stillness of every tree and shrub beneath its weight of snow, the distant echoes replying with a sad voice to the mournful concert, all were calculated to strike terror into the breast of the old shepherd.

But by degrees his fears grew less, for Yégof and his gloomy procession were getting farther and farther away from him, and gradually retreating toward Hazlach.

The raven, in his turn, with a hoarse cry unfurled his wings, and took his flight through the sky.

The whole scene vanished like a dream.

Robin heard for a long while after the howlings of the retreating wolves. They had completely ceased for more than twenty minutes. The silence of winter reigned on all sides, when the worthy man felt himself sufficiently recovered from his fright to come out of his hiding-place, and take his way back at full speed to the farm.

On arriving at Bois-de-Chênes, he found everybody stirring. They were preparing to kill an ox for the troops from the Donon. Hullin, Doctor Lorquin, and Louise were already set out with those from the Sarre. Catherine Lefèvre was loading her great four-horse wagon with bread, meat, and brandy. People were coming and going in all directions, and all lending a helping hand in the preparations.

Robin could not bring himself to relate to anyone all that he had seen and heard. Besides, it seemed to himself so incredible that he really dared not open his mouth about it.

When he had retired to rest in his crib in the middle of the stable, he said to himself that no doubt Yégof had, during the winter, tamed a litter of young wolves, and that he talked nonsense to them just as one talks sometimes to one's dog.

But, for all that, this strange encounter left a superstitious dread upon his mind, and even when he had arrived at a great age, the old fellow never spoke of these things without shuddering.

CHAPTER 11

A Reconnaissance

Hullin's orders had all been carried out; the defiles of the Zorne and of the Sarre were well guarded; while that of Blanru, the extreme point of the position, had been put into a state of defence by Jean-Claude himself and the three hundred men who composed his principal force.

We must now transport ourselves to the southern slopes of the Donon, two kilometres from Grandfontaine, and await further events.

Above the high-road which winds round the hillside up to within two-thirds of the summit, was a farm, surrounded with a few acres of tilled land, the freehold of Pelsly the anabaptist: it was a large building with a flat roof, much needed, so as to prevent its being blown away by the high winds. The outhouses and pigsties were situated at the back, toward the summit of the mountain.

The partisans were encamped near: at their feet lay Grandfontaine and Framont; in a narrow gorge farther on, at the point where the valley takes a turn, rose Schirmeck and its old mass of feudal ruins; lastly, among the undulations of the chain, the Bruche disappears in a zigzag, under the grayish mists of Alsace. To their left arose the arid peak of the Donon, covered with rocks and a few stunted pines. Before them was the rugged road, its shelving banks thrown down over the snow, and great trees flung across it with all their branches.

The melting snow let the yellow soil be seen in patches here and there, or else formed great drifts, heaped up by the north wind.

It was a grand and severe spectacle. Not a single traveller, not a carriage appeared along the whole length of the road in the valley, winding as far as the eye can reach: it was like a desert. The fires scattered round the farmhouse sent up their puffs of damp smoke to the sky, and alone indicated the position of the bivouac.

The mountaineers, seated by their kettles, with their hats slouched over their faces, were very melancholy: three days they had been awaiting the enemy. Among one of the groups, sitting with their legs doubled up, bent shoulders, and pipes in their mouths were old Materne and his two sons.

From time to time Louise appeared on the step of the farm, then quickly re-entered, and set herself again to her work. A great cock was scratching up the manure with his claws, and crowing hoarsely; two or three fowls were strutting up and down among the bushes. All that was pleasant to look upon; but the chief pleasure of the partisans was to contemplate some magnificent quarters of bacon, with red-and-white sides, which were spitted on greenwood sticks, the fat melting drop by drop on to the small coals—and to fill their flasks at a small cask of brandy placed on Catherine Lefèvre's cart.

Toward eight o'clock in the morning a man suddenly appeared between the great and little Donon; the sentinels perceived him at once; he descended, waving his hat.

A few minutes later Nickel Bentz, the old forest-keeper of the Houpe, was recognized.

The whole camp was roused; they ran to awaken Hullin, who had been sleeping for an hour in the farmhouse, on a great straw mattress, side by side with Doctor Lorquin and his dog Pluto.

The three came out, accompanied by the herdsman Lagarmitte, nicknamed Trumpet, and the anabaptist Pelslys—a silent man, having his arms buried to the elbows in the deep pockets of his gray woollen tunic trimmed with pewter clasps, with an immense beard, and the tassel of his cotton cap half way down his back.

Jean-Claude seemed light-hearted. "Well, Nickel, what is going on down there?" cried he.

"At present, nothing new, Master Jean-Claude; only on the Phalsbourg side one hears something like the rumbling of a storm. Labarbe says that it is cannon, for all night we have seen flashes through the forest of Hildehouse, and since the morning gray clouds have been spreading over the plain."

"The town is attacked," said Hullin; "but what about the Lutzelstein side?"

"One can hear nothing," replied Bentz.

"Then the enemy is trying to turn the place. In any case, the allies are down there: there must be hosts of them in Alsace." And turning toward Materne, who was standing behind him, "We cannot remain any longer in uncertainty," said he; "thou, with thy two sons, go on a reconnaissance."

The old hunter's face brightened. "So be it! I can stretch my legs a little," said he, "and see if I can't knock over one of those rascally Austrians or Cossacks."

"Stop an instant, my old fellow! it is not now a question of knocking anybody over; we want to see what is going on. Frantz and Kasper will remain armed; but I know thee: thou must leave thy carbine here, thy powder-flask, and thy hunting-knife."

"What for?"

"Because thou wilt have to go into the villages, and if thou art taken in arms, thou wilt be shot directly."

"Shot?"

"Certainly. "We do not belong to the regular troops; they do not take us prisoners; they shoot us. Thou wilt follow, then, the road to Schirmeck, stick in hand, and thy sons will accompany thee at a distance, in the underwood, within musket-range. If any marauders attack thee, they will come to thy rescue; if it is a column, or a handful of troops, they must allow thee to be taken."

"They are to let me be taken!" cried the old hunter, indignantly. "I should like to see that."

"Yes, Materne; it will be the best plan: for an unarmed man would be released, an armed shot. I do not need to tell thee not to sing out to the Germans that thou art come to spy upon them."

"Ah, ah! I comprehend. Yes, yes, that is not badly planned. As for me, I never quit my gun, Jean-Claude, but war is war. Hold! there is my carbine, and my powder-flask, and my knife. Who will lend me his blouse and his stick?"

Nickel Bentz handed him his blue blouse and his cap. They were surrounded by an admiring crowd.

After he had changed his clothes, notwithstanding his large gray moustaches, one would have taken the old hunter for a simple peasant from the high mountains.

His two sons, proud to be of this first expedition, looked to the priming of their muskets, and fixed to the end of the barrel a boar-spear, straight and long as a sword. They felt their hunting-knives, flung their bags upon their backs, and confident that all was in order, they glanced proudly round them.

"Ah," said Doctor Lorquin, laughing, "do not forget Master Jean-Claude's advice. Be careful. One German more or less in a hundred thousand would not make much difference in our affairs; whereas if one or the other of you came back to us injured, you would be replaced with difficulty."

"Oh, fear nothing, doctor: we shall have our eyes open."

"My boys," replied Materne, haughtily, "are true hunters; they know how to wait the moment and profit by it. They will only fire when I call. You can rest assured! and now, let us start; we must be back before night."

They departed.

"Good luck to you I" shouted Hullin, while they mounted the snow in order to avoid the breastworks.

They soon descended toward the narrow path, which turns sharply on the right of the mountain.

The partisans watched them. Their red frizzy hair, long muscular legs, their broad shoulders, and supple, quick movements, all showed that in case of an encounter, five or six *kaiserlichs* would have little chance against such fine fellows.

In a quarter of an hour they had reached the pine-forest and disappeared.

Then Hullin quietly returned to the farm, talking to Nickel Bentz.

Doctor Lorquin walked behind, followed by Pluto, and all the others returned to their places round the bivouac fires.

CHAPTER 12

The Landlord of the "Pineapple"

Materne and his two boys walked for some time in silence. The weather had become fine; the pale winter sun shone over the brilliant snow without melting it, and the ground remained firm and hard.

In the distance, along the valley, stood out, with surprising clearness, the tops of the firtrees, the reddish peaks of the rocks, the roofs of the hamlets, with their icy stalactites hanging from the eaves, their small sparkling windows, and sharp gables.

People were walking in the street of Grandfontaine. A troupe of young girls were standing round the washing-place; a few old men in cotton caps were smoking their pipes on the doorsteps of the little houses. All this little world, lying in the depths of the blue expanse, came, and went, and lived, without a sound or sigh reaching the ears of the foresters.

The old hunter halted on the outskirts of the wood, and said to his sons: "I am going down to the village to see Dubreuil, the innkeeper of the 'Pineapple.'"

And he pointed with his stick to a long white building, the doors and windows of which were surrounded with a yellow bordering, a pine-branch being suspended to the wall as a sign-board.

"You must await me here. If there is no danger, I will come out on to the doorstep and raise my hat; you can then come and take a glass of wine with me."

He immediately descended the snowy slopes to the little gardens lying above Grandfontaine, which took about ten minutes; he then made his way between two furrows, reached the meadow, and crossed the village square: his two sons, with their arms at their feet, saw him enter the inn. A few seconds after he reappeared on the doorstep and raised his hat.

Fifteen minutes later they had rejoined their father in the great room of the "Pineapple." It was a rather low room with a sanded floor, and heated by a large iron stove.

Excepting the innkeeper Dubreuil, the biggest and most apoplectic landlord in the Vosges, with immense paunch, round eyes, flat nose, a wart on his left cheek, and a triple chin reaching over his collars—with the exception of this curious individual, seated near the stove in a leather armchair, Materne was alone. He had just filled the glasses. The clock was striking nine, and its wooden cock flapped its wing with a peculiar scraping sound.

"Good-day, Father Dubreuil," said the two youths in a gruff voice.

"Good-day, my brave fellows," replied the innkeeper, trying to smile.

Then, in an oily voice, he asked them, "Nothing new?"

"Faith, no!" replied Kasper; "here is winter, the time for hunting boars."

And they both, putting their carbines in the corner of the window, within reach, in case of attack, passed one leg across the bench, and sat down, facing their father, who was at the head of the table.

At the same time they drank, saying, "To our healths!" which they were always very careful to do.

"Thus," said Materne, turning to the fat man, as though taking up the threads of an interrupted conversation, "you think, Father Dubreuil, that we have nothing to fear from the wood of Baronies, and that we may hunt boar peaceably?"

"Oh, as to that, I know nothing!" exclaimed the innkeeper; "only at present the allies have not passed Mutzig. Besides, they harm no one; they receive all well-disposed people to fight against the usurper."

"The usurper? Who is he?"

"Why, Napoleon Bonaparte, the usurper, to be sure. Just look at the wall."

He pointed to a great placard stuck on the wall, near the clock.

"Look at that, and you will see that the Austrians are our true friends."

Old Materne's eyebrows nearly met, but, repressing his feelings, "Oh, ah!" said he.

"Yes, read that."

"But I do not know how to read, Monsieur Dubreuil, nor my boys either. Explain to us what it is."

Then the old innkeeper, leaning with his hands on the arms of his chair, arose, breathing like a calf, and placed himself in front of the placard, with his arms folded on his enormous paunch; and in a majestic tone he read a proclamation from the allied sovereigns, declaring "that they made war on Napoleon personally, and not on France. Therefore everybody ought to keep quiet and not meddle in their affairs, under pain of being burnt, pillaged, and shot."

The three hunters listened, and looked at each other with a strange air.

"When Dubreuil had finished, he reseated himself and said, "Now do you see?"

"And where did you get that?" demanded Kasper.

"That, my boy, is put up everywhere!"

"Well, we are pleased with that," said Materne, laying his hand on Frantz's arm, who had risen with sparkling eyes. "Dost thou want a light, Frantz? Here is my flint."

Frantz sat down again, and the old man continued, good-naturedly: "And our good friends the Germans take nothing from anyone?"

"Quiet, orderly people have nothing to fear; but as to the rascals who rise, all is taken from them. And it is justs—the good ought not to suffer for the wicked. For example, instead of doing you any harm, the allies would receive you well at their head-quarters. You know the country: you would serve as guides, and you would be richly paid."

There was a slight pause. The three hunters again looked at each other: the father had spread his hands on the table, as though to recommend calm to his sons; but even he was very pale.

The innkeeper, observing nothing, continued: "You would have much more to fear in the woods of Baronies from those brigands of Dagsburg, Sarre, and Blanru, who have all revolted, and wish to have '93 over again."

"Are you sure of that?" demanded Materne, making an effort to control himself.

"Am I sure! You have only to look out of the window and you will see them on the road to the Donon. They have surprised the anabaptist Pelsly, and bound him to the foot of his bed. They pillage, rob, break up the roads. But beware! In a few days they will see strange things. It is not with a thousand men that they will be attacked, not with ten thousand, but with millions. They will all be hung."

Materne rose.

"It is time for us to be going," said he briefly. "At two o'clock we must be at the wood, and here we are talking quietly like magpies! *Au revoir*, Father Dubreuil." They rushed out hastily, no longer able to contain their passion.

"Think of what I have said," cried the innkeeper to them from his chair.

Once in the open air, Materne, turning round, said, with trembling lips: "If I had not restrained myself, I should have broken the bottle on his head."

"And I," said Frantz, "should have run him through with my bayonet."

Kasper, one foot on the step, seemed about to re-enter the inn; he grasped the handle of his hunting-knife, and his face bore a terrible expression. But his father took him by the arm and dragged him off, saying: "Come, come, we will deal with him later on. To counsel me to betray the country! Hullin told us to be on our guard: he was right."

They went down the street, looking to the right and left with haggard eyes. The people asked among themselves: What is the matter with them?

On reaching the end of the village, they halted, in front of the old cross, close to the church, and Materne in a calmer tone, pointing out the path which winds round Phramond over the heath, said to his sons: "You must take that road. I shall follow the route to Schirmeck. I shall not go too fast, so that you may have time to come up with me."

They parted, and the old hunter, with bowed head, walked on thoughtfully for a long time, asking himself by what inward strength he had been able to keep from breaking the fat inn-keeper's head. He said to himself that no doubt it was from fear of compromising his sons.

While thinking over these things, Materne kept continually meeting herds of cattle, sheep and goats, which were being led into the mountain. Some came from Wisch, Urmatt, and even from Mutzig; the poor beasts could scarcely stand.

"Where the devil are you running so fast?" shouted the old hunter to the melancholy herdsmen. "Have you then no confidence in the proclamation of the Austrians and Russians?"

And they angrily answered: "It is easy for you to laugh. Proclamations! we know what they are worth now. They pillage and rob everything, make forced contributions, carry off the horses, cows, oxen, and carts."

"Nonsense! impossible! What are you talking about?" said Materne. "You astound me! Such worthy people, such good friends, the saviours of France. I cannot believe you. Such a beautiful proclamation as it was."

"Well, go down to Alsace, and you will see."

The poor creatures went on, shaking their heads in extreme indignation, and he laughed slyly.

The farther Materne advanced, the number of herds became greater. There were not only troops of cattle bellowing and low-ing, but flocks of geese, as far as the eye could reach, screeching and cackling, dragging themselves along the road with wings spread and half-frozen feet: it was piteous to see.

It was worse still on approaching Schirmeck. The people were flying in crowds, with their great wagons loaded with barrels, smoked meats, furniture, women and children. They were lashing their horses almost to death on the road, and screaming in terrified voices: "We are lost; the Cossacks are coming."

The cry of "The Cossacks! the Cossacks!" ran along the whole line like a puff of wind; the women turned round open-mouthed, and the children stood up on the wagons to get a better view. You never beheld anything like it before; and Materne, angered, blushed for the terror of these people, who might have defended themselves; while selfishness and their desire to save their property, made them fly like cowards.

At the crossing of the Fond-des-Saules quite close to Schirmeck, Kasper and Frantz rejoined their father, and the three entered the "Golden Key" tavern, kept by the Widow Faltaux, on the right side of the road. The poor woman and her two daughters were watching from a window the great migration with streaming eyes and clasped hands.

In fact, the tumult increased every minute; the cattle, wagons, and people seemed eager to get away over each other's shoulders. They no longer had any command of themselves: they were howling and striking about them in their desire to escape.

Materne pushed the door open, and seeing the women more dead than alive, white and dishevelled, he shouted, striking his stick on the ground: "What, mother, have you too gone mad? What! you, who owe a good example to your daughters,—have you lost courage? it is a shame."

The old woman turned round and said in a broken voice: "Ah, my poor Materne, if you only knews—if you only knew!"

"Well, what then? The enemy is coming: they won't eat you."

"No; but they devour everything without mercy. Old Ursula, of Schlestadt, came here yesterday evening. She says that the Austrians only want *Knopfe* and *Nudel*, the Russians *Schnapps*, and the Bavarians *Sauerkraut*. And when they have stuffed all that down their throats, they cry out with their mouths still full, *Schocolat! schocolat!* O Lord, how can we feed all these people?"

"I know well that is difficult," said the old hunter: "you can never satisfy a jay with white cheese. But, first of all, where are these Cossacks, these Bavarians, these Austrians? All the way from Grandfontaine we have not met even one."

"They are in Alsace, on the Urmatt side, and they are coming here."

"While waiting for them," said Kasper, "give us a bottle of wine. Here is a three-crown piece: you will hide it easier than your barrels."

One of the girls went to the cellar, and, at the same time, several other persons entered: an almanac-seller from Strasbourg, a wagoner from Sarrebrück in a blouse, and two or three townspeople from Mutzig, Wisch, and Schirmeck, who were flying with their herds, and were exhausted with shouting.

All sat down at the same table, before the windows overlooking the road. Wine was served them, and each began to relate what he knew. One said the allies were in such numbers that they had to sleep side by side in the valley of Hirschenthal, and they were so covered with vermin that, after their departure, the dead leaves walked of themselves in the woods; another, that the Cossacks had set fire to a village in Alsace, because they had been refused candles for dessert after dinner; that some of them, especially the Calmucks, ate soap like cheese and bacon-rind like cake; that many drank brandy by the pint, after having taken care to season it with handfuls of pepper; and that it was necessary to hide everything from them, for nothing came amiss to them for eating and drinking.

The wagoner said, at this point, that three days before, a Russian *corps-d'armée* having passed the night under the ramparts of Bitsch, it had been compelled to remain more than an hour on the ice in the little village of Rorbach, and that the whole of this army corps had drunk out of a warming-pan left on the windowsill of an old woman's house; that this race of savages broke the ice to bathe, and afterward crept into the brick-kilns to dry;

lastly, that they only feared Corporal Knout.

These worthy folks communicated such singular things to each other, which they pretended to have seen with their own eyes, or heard from trustworthy sources, that one could with difficulty believe them.

Outside, the tumult, rolling of wagons, lowing of herds, shouts of the drivers, and clamours of the fugitives, continued unceasingly, and produced the effect of a vast murmur.

Toward noon Materne and his sons were going to leave, when a more prolonged shout than any of the others was heard: "The Cossacks! the Cossacks!"

Then everybody rushed outside, except the hunters, who contented themselves with opening a window and looking out: they all ran away across the fields: men, herds, wagons and all, were dispersed like leaves in autumn. In less than two minutes the road was deserted, except in Schirmeck, which was so encumbered, that it would have been impossible to walk four steps. Materne, gazing far away along the road, cried, "I look in vains—I can see nothing."

"Nor do I," rejoined Kasper.

"Come, come," cried the old hunter, "I see clearly that the fear of all these people gives more strength to the enemy than he in fact possesses. It is not in such a way we shall receive the Cossacks in the mountains; they will find who they have to deal with."

Then, shrugging his shoulders with an expression of disgust, he said: "Fear is an odious thing, and after all we have only one poor life to lose. Let us go."

They quitted the inn and the old man having taken the road to the valley, in order to climb the summit of the Hirschberg in front of them, his sons followed him. They soon reached the outskirts of the wood, when Materne said that they must mount as high as possible, so as to see the whole plain, and bring back some positive news to the bivouac; that all the accounts of those cowards were not worth one good look by themselves.

Kasper and Frantz agreed, and all three began to climb the

slope, which forms a sort of advanced promontory commanding the plain. When they reached the peak they distinctly saw the enemy's position, three leagues distant, between Urmatt and Lutzelhouse. They formed great black lines on the snow: farther off were a few dark massess—no doubt, the artillery and baggage. Other surrounded the villages, and, notwithstanding the distance, the sparkling of the bayonets announced that a column had just commenced marching toward Visch.

After having contemplated this spectacle in silence for some minutes, the old man said, "We have decidedly thirty thousand men under our eyes. They are advancing in our direction; we shall be attacked tomorrow, or the day after at the latest. It will not be a trumpery affair, my boys; but if they are numerous we have the best of the position. And then it is always agreeable to fire into a heap; there are no balls lost."

Having made these judicious reflections, he looked at the height of the sun, and added: "It is now two o'clock; we know all we want. Let us return to the bivouac."

The youths slung their carbines crossways, and leaving to their left the valley of the Brocque, Schirmeck, and Framont, they climbed the steep banks of the Hengsbach, which overlook the Little Donons—two leagues distants—and came down again on the other side, without following any regular path through the snow, and only guiding themselves by the peaks in order to take a short cut.

They continued thus for about two hours: the winter sun was going down to the horizon, night was approaching, bright and calm. They had now only to descend, and then mount, on the other side, the solitary gorge of Riel, forming a large circular basin in the midst of the woods, and enclosing a bluish pond, where the deer came sometimes to quench their thirst.

Suddenly, as they were coming out from the underwood, not dreaming of anything, the old man, stopping behind a thick screen of shrubs, said "*Chut!*" and lifting his hand, pointed to the little lake, which was covered with thin clear ice.

The two young fellows needed only to glance toward it to

be greeted by a most strange sight. About twenty Cossacks, with yellow shaggy beards, heads covered with old fur caps in the shape of stove-pipes, their lean legs draped in long rags, and their feet in rope stirrups, were seated on their little horses, with long floating manes and thin tails, their bodies speckled yellow, black and white, like goats.

Some had for their only weapon a long lance, others a sword, others an axe suspended by a cord to their saddle, and a large horse-pistol passed through their belts. Several were looking upward with ecstasy on the green tops of the pines, rising by stages above each other into the clouds. One great lanky fellow had broken the ice with the butt-end of his lance; and his little horse was drinking with outstretched neck and overhanging mane. A few having dismounted, were clearing the snow and pointing to the woods—no doubt to indicate that it was a good place for encamping. Their comrades on horseback were conversing and pointing to the bottom of the valley on their right, which descends in the form of a gap toward Grinderwald.

Anyway it was a halt. It is impossible to describe the strange and picturesque aspect of these fellows from a strange country, with their copper-coloured faces, long beards, black eyes, flat heads, squat noses, and grayish tatters, on the banks of this lake, under the lofty perpendicular rocks lifting up their green pines to the skies.

It seemed a new world in ours,—a sort of unknown and strange game, which the three red hunters at first contemplated with intense interest. Having remained so for about five minutes, Kasper and Frantz fixed their long bayonets at the muzzle of their carbines, and then retired about twenty paces into the underwood. They reached a rock, fifteen or twenty feet high, which Materne climbed, having no arms; then, after a few words exchanged in whispers, Kasper examined his priming and raised his musket slowly to his shoulder, while his brother stood by in readiness.

One of the Cossacks—he who was letting his horse drink-was about two hundred paces from them. The gun went off, awakening the deep echoes of the gorge; and the Cossack, spinning over his horse's head, plunged through the ice of the lake.

It is impossible to describe the stupor of the party at this report. They looked round them in every direction: the echo replied as though it had been a general fusillade; while a puff of smoke rose above the clump of trees where the hunters were hiding.

Kasper had reloaded his piece in a moment; but in the same space of time the dismounted Cossacks had bounded on their horses, and all took flight over the slope of the Hartz, one after the other, like roebucks, screaming wildly, "Hourah! hourah!"

This flight was but the work of a moment: the instant Kasper took aim for the second time, the tail of the last horse disappeared in the bushes.

The horse of the dead Cossack alone remained at the water's edge, held there by a singular circumstance: his master, whose head and part of whose body was in the water, had his foot still in the stirrup.

Materne listened from his rock, then said joyously—"They are gone! Well, let us go and see. Frantz, remain here. Suppose any of them should return—?"

Notwithstanding this recommendation, they all three approached near the horse. Materne immediately took the bridle, saying:—"Come, old fellow, we are going to teach you to speak French."

"Let us be off," exclaimed Kasper.

"No, we must see what we have shot. Don't you see that will be good for our comrades? Dogs who have not sniffed the skin of the game are never well trained."

Whereupon they fished the Cossack out of the pool, and having placed him across the horse, began to climb the side of the Donon by such a steep path, that Materne repeated, a hundred times at least,—"The horse will never go up there." But the horse, with its long goat-like legs, passed more easily than they did; so that the old hunter wound up by remarking—"These Cossacks have famous horses. If ever I grow old, I will keep him to go after the deer with. We have a famous horse, my boys; with all his look of a cow, he is strong as a carthorse."

From time to time he also made reflections on the Cossack:– "What a queer face, eh! A round nose and a forehead like a cheese-box. There are certainly queer folks in the world! Thou hast hit him well, Kasper; right in the middle of the chest.

And look! the ball came out at the back. Capital powder! Divès always keeps good articles."

Toward six they heard the first shout of their sentinels: "Who goes there?"

"France," replied Materne, advancing.

Everybody ran to meet them. "Here is Materne!"

Hullin himself was as curious as the rest, and could not help hastening toward them with Doctor Lorquin. The partisans were soon collected round the horse, with outstretched necks and open mouths, by the side of a large fire where the supper was cooking.

"It is a Cossack," said Hullin, squeezing Materne's hand.

"Yes, Jean-Claude; we caught him at the pond of Riel: it was Kasper who shot him."

They stretched the corpse out near the fire. His yellow face had strange shadows on it in the firelight.

Doctor Lorquin, having looked at him, said: "It is a fine specimen of the Tartar race; if I had time, I should put it in a lime-bath, so as to obtain a skeleton of this tribe."

He then knelt down, and opening the long tunic,—"The ball has traversed the pericardium, and has produced almost the same effect as aneurism of the heart."

The others kept silence.

Kasper, with his hand on the muzzle of his rifle, seemed quite contented with his game; and old Materne, rubbing his hands, said: "I was sure I would bring you back something: my boys and I never return empty-handed. There now!"

Hullin then pulled him aside. They entered the farm together, and after the first surprise was over, every man began to make his own personal reflections on the Cossack.

Chapter 13

Round the Watchfires

That night, which was on a Friday, the anabaptist's little farm-house never ceased for an instant to be filled with people coming in and going out.

Hullin had established his head-quarters in the large room on the ground floor, to the right of the barn, facing Framont: on the other side of the passage was the ambulance: the upper part was inhabited by the farm people.

Although the night was very still and the stars were shining in myriads, the cold was so intense that there was nearly an inch of ice on the panes.

Outside, one could hear the challenge of the sentinel, the passing of the patrols, and, on the surrounding peaks, the howling of the wolves, who followed our armies in hundreds since 1812. These wild beasts crouched on the ice, their sharp muzzles between their paws, with hunger at their entrails, calling each other, from the Grosmann to the Donon, with moaning sounds like that of the north wind.

It made more than one mountaineer grow pale.

"It is Death who calls," thought they; "he scents the battle, he summons us!"

The oxen lowed in the stables, and the horses gave frightful neighs.

About thirty fires blazed on the plateau; all the anabaptist's wood was taken; fagots were heaped one upon another. Their faces were scorched, and their backs frozen; they warmed their backs, and the ice hung from their moustaches.

Hullin, alone, before the great pinewood table, was taking thought for all. According to the latest tidings of the evening, announcing the arrival of the Cossacks at Framont, he was convinced that the first attack would take place the next day. He had distributed cartridges, doubled the sentries, appointed patrols, and marked all the posts along the outworks. Everyone knew beforehand what place he was to occupy.

Hullin had also sent orders to Piorette, Jérome of St. Quirin, and Labarbe, to send him their best marksmen.

The little dark pathway, lit by a dim lantern, was full of snow, and passing under the immovable light every instant one could see the chiefs of the ambush, with their hats pressed down to their ears, the ample sleeves of their great-coats pulled down over their wrists, with their dark eyes and beards stiffened with ice.

Pluto no longer growled at the heavy step of these men. Hullin, with his head between his hands and his elbows on the table, listened thoughtfully to all their reports:—

"Master Jean-Claude, there is a movement in the direction of Grandfontaine; and the sounds of galloping are distinguishable."

"Master Jean-Claude, the brandy is frozen."

"Master Jean-Claude, many of the men are in want of powder."

"They are in want of this: they are in want of that."

"Let someone be sent to watch Grandfontaine, and let the sentries on that side be changed every half-hour."

"Let the brandy be brought to the fire."

"Wait until Divès comes: he brings us ammunition. Let the remainder of the cartridges be distributed. Let those who have more than twenty give some to their comrades."

And so it went on all the night.

At five in the morning, Kasper, Materne's son, came to tell Hullin that Marc Divès, with a load of cartridges, Catherine Lefèvre on a cart, and a detachment from Labarbe, had just arrived together, and that they were already on the plateau.

317

The tidings pleased him, especially on account of the cartridges, for he had feared delay.

He immediately rose and went out with Kasper. The plateau presented a curious spectacle.

On the approach of day, clouds of mist began to rise from the valley, the fires hissed with the damp, and all around could be seen sleeping men: one stretched on his back, with his arms thrown under his hat, a blue face, and doubled-up legs; another with his cheek on his arm and his back to the fire; the greater number seated, with bent heads and their muskets slung across their shoulders. All was silent, wrapped in purple light or gray tints, just as the fire blazed or smouldered. Then, in the distance, could be discerned the profile of the sentinels, with their muskets across their arms or clubbed upon the ground, gazing into the cloud-filled abyss beneath them.

To the right, fifty paces from the last fire, could be heard the neighing of horses, and people stamping with their feet to warm themselves, and talking aloud.

"Master Jean-Claude is coming," said Kasper, going toward them.

One of the partisans having thrown a few sticks of dry wood on to the fire, there was a bright blaze; and Marc Divès's men on horseback, twelve tall fellows, wrapped in their long gray cloaks, their felts slouched back over their shoulders, with their long moustaches either turned up or falling down to their necks, their sabres in their grasp, stood motionless round the load of cartridges. Farther on Catherine Lefèvre crouched down in her cart, her hood over her face, her feet in the straw, her back against a large barrel. Behind her was a caldron, a grid-iron, a fresh-killed pig, scalded all white and red, with some strings of onions and cabbages for making soup. All stood out of the darkness for a second, and then relapsed into night.

Divès, having quitted the convoy, advanced on his powerful horse.

"Is it you, Jean-Claude?"

"Yes, Marc."

"I have some few thousand cartridges there. Hexe-Baizel is working day and night."

"Good!"

"Yes, old fellow. And Catherine Lefèvre brings provisions as well; she killed yesterday."

"All right, Marc: we shall want all that. The battle is impending."

"Yes, yes, I thought so; we came quickly. Where is the powder to be put?"

"There, under the cart-house behind the farm. Ah, is that you, Catherine?"

"Of course, Jean-Claude. It is dreadfully cold this morning!"

"You are always the same. Have you no fear?"

"What! should I be a woman if I were not curious? I must poke my nose everywhere."

"Yes, you always make excuses for the fine and noble things you do."

"Hullin, you are wearisome with your repetitions; let me alone with your compliments. Must not all those people eat? Can they live on air in such weather as this? And is not air fattening on a day so cold—like needles and razors. So I took my measures. Yesterday we slaughtered an ox—poor Schwartz, you know—he weighed a good nine hundred. I have brought his hindquarters for this morning's soup."

"Catherine, it is in vain I have known you so long," cried Jean-Claude, quite touched; "you are always astonishing me. No sacrifice is too great for you, neither money, care, nor trouble."

"Ah," replied the old farm-wife, rising and springing from her cart, "you tease and worry me, Jean-Claude. I am going to warm myself."

She gave Dubourg the reins of her horse, and looking back, said, "Jean-Claude, those fires are a pleasure to behold. But where is Louise?"

"Louise spent the night cutting and sewing bandages with Pelsly's two daughters. She is at the ambulance: over there you see, where the light is shining."

"Poor child!" said Catherine, "I will go and help her. That will warm me."

Hullin watched her retreating figure, and made a gesture, as though saying, "What a woman!"

At this moment, Divès and his people were carrying the powder into the shed, and as Jean-Claude approached the nearest fire, what was his surprise to see, among the crowd of partisans, Yégof the madman, crowned as usual, gravely seated on a stone, with his feet in the ashes, and draped in his rags as though they were a royal mantle.

Anything more strange than this figure by the firelight could not be imagined. Yégof was the only one awake of the crowd, and might readily have been taken for some barbarian king musing in the midst of his sleeping horde.

Hullin only saw in him a madman, and laying his hand softly on his shoulder, said, ironically:

"I salute thee, Yégof! Thou art come, then, to lend us the help of thy invincible arm and of thy countless armies?"

The madman, without showing the least surprise, replied: "That depends on thee, Hullin; thy fate, and that of all these people, is in thy hands. I have suspended my anger, and I will allow thee to pronounce sentence."

"What sentence?" demanded Jean-Claude.

The other, without replying, continued, in a low solemn voice: "Behold us two on the eve of a great battle, as we were sixteen hundred years ago. At that time, I, the chief of so many people, came among thy tribe to ask a passage."

"Sixteen hundred years ago!" said Hullin. "Zounds! Yégof, that makes us terribly old! But it is of no consequence—each to his taste."

"Yes," rejoined the madman, "but, with thy usual obstinacy, thou wouldst hear nothing. Men died on the Blutfeld men-who now call for vengeance!"

"Ah, the Blutfeld!" said Jean-Claude. "Yes, yes, an old story; I seem to have heard it before."

Yégof reddened, and his eyes sparkled.

"Thou pridest thyself on thy victory!" cried he; "but take care—take care! blood calls for blood!" And in a calmer tone, "Listen," he added. "I am not angry with thee. Thou art brave; the children of thy race might mingle with those of mine. I am anxious for an alliance with thee—thou knowest it."

"There, he is going to begin about Louise," thought Jean-Claude. And, foreseeing a formal demand, he said: "Yégof, I am sorry, but I must leave thee. I have so much to see after—"

The madman did not wait the end of this leave-taking, and rising, with his face distorted by indignation, "Thou refusest me thy daughter?" cried he, lifting his finger solemnly.

"We will talk of that later on."

"Thou refusest!"

"Yégof, thy shouts will awaken everyone."

"Thou refusest, and it is for the third time! Beware! beware!"

Hullin, despairing of making him become more reasonable, walked rapidly away, but the madman furiously pursued him with these strange words:

"Huldrix, woe on thee! Thy last hour is at hand; the wolves are coming to feed upon thy carcass. All is over. I let loose the tempests of my wrath; and neither to thee nor thine shall mercy, pity, or pardon be shown. Thou hast so willed it."

And, flinging his rags over his shoulder, the poor wretch went away in the direction of the peak of Donon.

Some of the volunteers, awakened by his cries, looked up drowsily, and saw him disappearing in the darkness. They heard the fluttering of wings round the fire; then, as though it were a dream, they turned round and fell asleep again.

About an hour later, Lagarmitte sounded the *reveille*; and in a few minutes all were on their feet.

The chiefs of the ambuscade collected their men: some went toward the shed, to obtain cartridges; others filled their gourds with brandy from the cask. All this was done in good order, their chiefs being at the head of each body of men; then the several companies disappeared in the gray morning light toward the out-posts on the hillsides.

When the sun rose, the plateau was quite deserted, and, with the exception of five or six fires which were still burning, there was no sign that the partisans were in possession of all the posts on the mountain, or in what place they had passed the night.

Hullin hurriedly ate a crust and drank a glass of wine with his friends Doctor Lorquin and Pelsly the anabaptist.

Lagarmitte was with them, for he was not allowed to leave Master Jean-Claude all day, and had to transmit his orders in case of need.

CHAPTER 14

"Forward! Forward!"

At seven o'clock there was no sign of any movement in the valley.

From time to time, Doctor Lorquin opened one of the windows in the large room and looked out. Nothing was stirring; the fires had smouldered away; all was still.

In front of the farm, on a bank, about a hundred feet distant, the Cossack could be seen who had been killed the previous evening by Kasper. He was white with the frost, and as hard as a stone.

In the interior, a fire had been made in the great iron stove.

Louise sat near her father, looking at him with an inexpressible affection, as though she feared never to see him again. Her red eyes showed that she had been crying.

Hullin, though firm, looked not a little moved. The doctor and the anabaptist, both grave and serious, talked over the present position of affairs, and Lagarmitte, from behind the stove, listened to them with deep interest.

"We are not only right, but it is our duty to defend ourselves," said the doctor. "Our fathers cleared these woods and cultivated them: they are our legitimate inheritance."

"No doubt," returned the anabaptist, sententiously; "but it is written, *Thou shalt not kill. Thou shalt not shed thy brother's blood!*"

Catherine Lefèvre, who was in the act of cutting a slice of ham, evidently felt impatient at this conversation, and, turning round sharply, replied to him: "If that were true, and your religion were right, the Germans, Russians, and all these red men might take the clothes off our backs. 'Tis fine, that religion of yours; yes, fine, for it gives the rogues such an advantage! It helps them to pillage people of substance. I am sure the allies would wish for us no better religion than yours. Unfortunately, everybody does not care to live like sheep.

As for me, Pelsly—and I say it without wishing to annoy you—I consider it folly to grow rich for the benefit of others. But, after all, you are honest folks; one cannot be angry with you: you have been brought up from father to son in the same notions: what the grandfather thought, the grandson thinks also. But we will defend you in spite of yourselves; and afterward we will let you tell us of the peace eternal. I am fond of discourses on peace, when I have nothing else to do, and when I am thinking after dinner: then it rejoices my heart."

After having said this, she turned round and went on carving her ham.

Pelsly opened his mouth and eyes, and Doctor Lorquin burst out laughing.

Just then the door opened, and one of the sentries who had been stationed on the edge of the plateau, cried out, "Master Jean-Claude, come and see. I believe they are mounting the hill."

"It is well, Simon; I am coming," said Hullin, rising. "Louise, kiss me. Have courage, my child. Do not fear; all will go well."

He pressed her to his breast, her eyes swollen with tears. She seemed more dead than alive.

"Above all," said the worthy man, addressing Catherine, "let no one go outside or near the windows."

Then he darted out into the road.

All those present turned pale.

When Master Jean-Claude had reached the verge of the hill, and cast his eyes over Grandfontaine and Framont, three thousand metres below, the following sight presented itself to his eyes:

The Germans, who had arrived the evening before, a few

hours after the Cossacks, and had passed the night (about five or six thousand of them) in the barns, stables, and sheds, were moving about like ants. They appeared on all sides in bodies of ten, fifteen, and twenty, buckling their knapsacks and swords, and fixing their bayonets.

Besides these, the cavalry—the Uhlans, Cossacks, Hussars-in green, blue, and gray uniforms striped with red and yellow-with their glazed linen and sheepskin caps, *colbacks*, and helmets—were saddling their horses and hastily rolling up their long cloaks.

Meanwhile the officers, in their great military cloaks, came down the small staircase: some were looking up at the country; others were embracing the women on the doorsteps.

Trumpeters, with their hands on their sides, were sounding the roll-call at all the corners of the streets, and the drummers tightening the cords of their instruments.

In short, through the broad expanse, one could see all their military attitudes as they were on the point of starting.

A few peasants, leaning out of their windows, were watching the scene; women were showing themselves at the loopholes of the garrets; and the innkeepers were filling the gourds, Corporal Knout watching them meanwhile.

Hullin's sight was keen, and nothing escaped him; besides, for years he had been accustomed to this sort of thing; but Lagarmitte, who had never seen anything like it, was stupefied: "There are great numbers of them," he exclaimed, shaking his head.

"Bah! what does that matter?" said Hullin. "In my days we exterminated three armies of them, of fifty thousand each, in six months; we were not one against four. All that thou seest there would not have been a breakfast for us. And besides, you may be sure, we shall not have to kill them all; they will run like hares. I have seen it before."

After these remarks, he resolved to inspect his men. "Come on," he said to the herdsman.

Then the two made their way behind the abatis, following a trench made two days before in the snow, which had been fro-

Big Dubreuil, the friend of the Allies

zen as hard as ice: the felled trees in front of it, formed an insurmountable barrier, which extended about six hundred metres. Below this was the broken-up road.

On coming near, Jean-Claude saw the mountaineers of Dagsburg crouching at distances of twenty paces from each other, in a sort of round nests which they had dug out for themselves.

All these fine fellows were sitting on their knapsacks, with their gourds to their right hand, their felts or foxskin caps drawn down upon their heads, and their guns between their knees. They had only to rise to have a clear view of the road fifty feet below, at the foot of a slippery descent.

Jean-Claude's arrival pleased them much.

"Ho, Master Hullin, shall we soon begin?"

"Yes, my boys, never fear; before an hour we shall be at it."

"Ah, so much the better!"

"Yes, but take care to aim at the breast: do not hurry, and show yourselves no more than you can help."

"You may rest assured, Master Jean-Claude."

He passed on; but everywhere he met with a like reception.

"Do not forget," said he, "to stop firing when Lagarmitte sounds his horn: it would be only powder lost."

Coming up to old Materne, who commanded all these men numbering about two hundred and fifty—he found him smoking his pipe, his nose fiery red, and his beard stiffened with the cold.

"Ah, it is thou, Jean-Claude."

"Yes, I have come to shake your hand."

"In good time. But why are they so slow in coming—tell me that? Are they going to march off in another direction?"

"Don't be afraid: they need the road for their artillery and baggage. Hark! they are sounding 'to horse.'"

"Yes, I have seen already that they are preparing." Then, chuckling to himself: "Thou dost not know, Jean-Claude, what a funny thing I saw, a few minutes ago, as I was looking toward Grandfontaine."

"What was it, my old friend?"

"I saw four Germans lay hold of big Dubreuil, the friend of the allies: they stretched him on the stone bench by his door, and one great lanky fellow gave him I know not how many cuts with a stick across his back. Ha, ha, ha, he must have yelled, the old rascal! I will wager that he re- fused something to his good friends,—his wine of the year 11 for instance."

Hullin heard no more: for, casting his eyes accidentally down the valley, he caught sight of an infantry regiment coming up the road. Farther back in the street, cavalry were seen coming, five or six officers galloping in front of them.

"Ah? ah! there they come!" cried the old soldier, whose face glowed suddenly with an expression of strange energy and enthusiasm. "At last they have made up their minds!" Then he rushed out of the trench, shouting: "Attention, my children!"

Passing by, he saw Riffi, the little tailor of Charmes, bending over a long musket: the little man had been piling up the snow to give him a better position for aiming. Farther up, he saw the old woodcutter Rochart, his great shoes trimmed with sheep-skin: he had taken a gulp at his gourd, and was rising deliberately, having his carbine under his arm and his cotton cap over his ears.

That was all: for in order to command the whole of the action, he had to climb almost to the summit of the Donon, where there is a rock.

Lagarmitte followed, striding till his long legs looked like stilts. Ten minutes after, when they had reached the top of the rock, half-breathless, they perceived, fifteen hundred metres below them, the enemy's column, three thousand strong, with white great-coats, leather belts, cloth gaiters, tall shakos, and red moustaches; and in the spaces formed by the companies, the young officers, with flat caps, waving their swords, and shouting in shrill voices: "Forward! forward!"

These troops were bristling with bayonets, and advancing at the charge toward the breastworks.

Old Materne, his beaked nose rising above a juniper branch and his brow erect, was also watching the arrival of the Germans; and as he was very clear-sighted, he could distinguish even faces among the crowd, and choose the man he wished to knock over.

In the centre of the column, on a large bay horse, an old officer was advancing right ahead, with a white wig, a three-cornered hat trimmed with gold, his waist encircled with a yellow scarf, and his breast decorated with ribbons. When this personage raised his head, the peak of his hat, surmounted by a tuft of black plumes, formed a visor. He had great wrinkles along his cheeks, and looked sufficiently stern.

"There is my man!" thought the old hunter, deliberately taking aim.

He fired, and when he looked again the old officer had disappeared.

Immediately the whole hillside became enveloped in fire all along the intrenchment; but the Germans, without replying, continued to advance toward the breastworks, their guns on their shoulders, and as steadily as though on parade.

To tell the truth, more than one brave mountaineer, father of a family, seeing this forest of bayonets coming up, and notwithstanding the excitement of battle, felt that he would have done better had he remained in his village, than to have mixed himself up in such an affair. But, as the proverb says, "The wine was drawn, and it had to be drunk."

Riffi, the little tailor, recalled the words of his wife Sapience: "Riffi, you will get yourself crippled, and it will serve you right."

He vowed a costly offering to St. Léon's Chapel should he return from the war; but at the same time he resolved to make good use of his musket.

When they were about two hundred feet from the breastworks, the Germans halted and began a rolling fire, such as had never been heard in the mountain before. It was a regular storm of shot: the balls in hundreds tore away the branches, sent bits of broken ice flying in all directions, or flattened themselves on the rocks on every side, leaping up with a strange hissing noise, and passing by like flocks of pigeons.

All this did not stop the mountaineers from continuing their fire, but it could no longer be heard. The whole hillside was wrapped in blue smoke, which prevented their taking any aim.

About ten minutes later, there was the rolling of a drum, and all this mass of men made a rush at the breastworks, their officers shouting, "Forward!"

The earth shook with them.

Materne, springing up in the trench, with quivering lips and in a terrible voice, cried out, "To your feet! to your feet!"

It was time: for a good number of these Germans,—nearly all students in philosophy, law, and medicine, heroes of the taverns of Munich, Jena, and other places—who fought against us, because they had been promised great things after Napoleon's fall—all these intrepid fellows were climbing the icy slope, and endeavouring to jump into the intrenchment.

But they were received with the butt-end of the musket, and fell back in disorder.

It was then that the gallant conduct of the old woodcutter Rochart was observable, knocking over, as he did, more than ten *kaiserlichs*, whom he took by the shoulder and hurled down the incline. Old Materne's bayonet was red with blood; and little Riffi never ceased loading his musket and firing into the mass of Germans with great spirit. Joseph Larnette, who unluckily received a bullet in his eye; Hans Baumgarten, who had his shoulder smashed; Daniel Spitz, who lost two fingers by a sabre-cut, and many others, whose names should be honoured and revered for ages—all these never once left off firing and reloading their guns.

Below the slope fearful cries were heard, while above nothing but bristling bayonets and men on horseback were to be seen.

This lasted a good quarter of an hour. No one knew what the Germans would do, since there was no passage; when they suddenly decided on going away. Most of the students had fallen, and the others—old campaigners used to honourable retreats-no longer fought with the same steadiness.

At first they retreated slowly, then more quickly. Their officers struck them from behind with the flat end of their swords; the musketry-fire pursued them; and, finally, they ran away with as much precipitation as they had been orderly in advancing.

Materne, and fifty others, rose upon the barricades, the old hunter brandishing his carbine, and bursting into hearty roars of laughter.

At the foot of the bank were heaps of wounded dragging themselves along the ground. The trodden-down snow was red with blood. In the midst of the piles of dead were two young officers, still alive, but unable to disengage themselves from their dead horses.

It was horrible! But men are, in fact, savages: there was not one among the mountaineers who pitied those poor wretches; but, on the contrary, they seemed to rejoice at the sight.

Little Riffi, transported with a noble enthusiasm, just then glided out along the bank. To the left, underneath the breastworks, he had caught sight of a superb horse, which had belonged to the colonel killed by Materne, and had retired unhurt into his nook.

"Thou shalt be mine," said he to himself. "Sapience will be astonished!"

All the others envied him. He seized the horse by the bridle and sprang upon him; but judge of the general stupefaction, and of Riffi's in particular, when this noble animal began to shape his course toward the Germans in full gallop.

The little tailor lifted his hands to heaven, imploring God and all the saints.

Materne would have liked much to fire; but he dared not, the horse went so fast.

At last Riffi disappeared amid the bayonets of the enemy.

Everybody thought he had been killed. However, an hour later, he was to be seen passing along the main street of Grandfontaine, his hands tied behind him, and Corporal Knout at his back, bearing his emblem of office.

Poor Riffi! He alone did not partake of the triumph, and his

As they climbed up they were clubbed with muskets

comrades laughed at his misfortune, as though he had been but a *kaiserlich.*

Such is the character of men; so long as they are happy themselves, the misery of others grieves them but little.

CHAPTER 15

The Battle Renewed

The mountaineers were almost beside themselves with enthusiasm: they lifted their hands and bepraised one another, as if they were the cream of mankind.

Catherine, Louise, Doctor Lorquin and all the others came out of the farm, cheering and congratulating each other, gazing at the marks of the bullets and at the bank blackened with powder; then at Joseph Larnette stretched in his hole, having his head smashed; at Baumgarten, who, with his arm hanging down, walked in great pallor toward the ambulance; and then at Daniel Spitz, who, in spite of his sabre-cut, wanted to stay and fight; but the doctor would not hear of it, and forced him to enter the farm.

Louise came up with the little cart, and poured out brandy for the combatants; while Catherine Lefèvre, standing at the edge of the sloping bank, watched the dead and wounded scattered over the road, and led up to by long lines of blood. There were both young and old among them, with faces white as wax, wide-opened eyes, and outstretched arms. Some few tried to raise themselves, but no sooner had they done so than they fell back again; others looked up as though they were afraid of receiving some more bullets, and dragged themselves along the bank in order to get under shelter.

Many of them seemed resigned to their fate, and were looking for a place to die, or else watching their retreating regiment on its way to Framont—that regiment with which they had quitted their homes, with which they had made a long campaign, and which was now abandoning them!

"It will see old Germany again!" they thought. "And when someone asks the captain or the sergeant, 'Did you know such a one—Hans, Kasper, Nickel, of the 1st or of the 2nd company?' they will reply, 'Ah! I think so. Had he not a scar on the ear, or on the cheek? fair or dark hair? five feet six in height? Yes, I know him. He was buried in France, near a little village whose name I do not remember. Some mountaineers killed him the same day big Major Yéri-Peter was killed. He was a fine fellow!' And then it is, 'Good-day to you.'"

Perhaps, too, there were some of them who dreamed of their mother, or of a pretty girl left behind them, Gretchen or Lotchen, who had given them a ribbon, and shed hot tears when they left: "I will await thy return, Kasper. I will only marry thee! Yes, yes, thou wilt have to wait long!"

It was not pleasant to think of.

Madame Lefèvre, seeing this, thought of Gaspard. Hullin, who came up with Lagarmitte, cried out in a joyous tone, "Well, my boys, you have been under fire. Bravo! everything goes well. The Germans will have no occasion to boast of this day."

Then he embraced Louise, and hurried up to Catherine.

"Are you satisfied, Catherine? There! our success is certain. But what is the matter? You do not smile."

"Yes, Jean-Claude, all goes well. I am satisfied. But look down at the road. "What a butchery!"

"It is only what happens in war," replied Hullin, gravely.

"Could we not go and help that little fellow down there, who watches us with his large blue eyes? He makes me feel so sad. Or that tall, dark man, who is binding his leg with his handkerchief?"

"Impossible, Catherine. I am very sorry. We should have to cut steps in the ice to get down, and the Germans, who will be back in an hour or two, would take advantage of them. Let us go. The victory must be announced in all the villages—to Labarbe, Jérome, and Piorette. Ho! Simon, Niklo, Marchal, come here.

335

You will have to set out immediately, and carry the great tidings to our comrades. Materne, keep thy eyes open, and warn me at the slightest movement."

They approached the farm, and, as he passed, Jean-Claude took a look at the reserve, Marc Divès being on horseback surrounded by his men. The smuggler complained bitterly of being left with nothing to do, as if his honour were tarnished thereby.

"Bah!" said Hullin, "so much the better! Besides, thou keepest guard over our right. Look at that flat ground down there. If we are attacked from that point, thou wilt have to march!"

Divès made no answer; he looked both sad and indignant, nor did his stalwart smugglers, wrapped in their cloaks, their long swords hanging by their sides, seem at all in a better humour; one might have said that they were meditating some revenge.

Hullin, not succeeding in consoling them, entered the farmhouse. Doctor Lorquin was extracting the ball from Baumgarten's wound, who was making terrible cries.

Pelsly, on the doorstep, was trembling all over. Jean-Claude asked him for paper and ink, in order to transmit his orders through the mountain; but the poor anabaptist could hardly give them to him, so great was his trouble. However, he succeeded at last, and the messengers departed, proud of being charged to announce the first battle and victory.

A few mountaineers were in the large room, warming themselves at the oven and talking animatedly. Daniel Spitz had already undergone amputation of his two fingers, and sat behind the stove with his hand bound up.

Those who had been posted behind the abatis before daybreak, not having breakfasted, were now eating a crust of bread and drinking a glass of wine, shouting, gesticulating, and making great bravado meanwhile. Then they went out, looked at the intrenchments, came back to warm themselves again, and laughed fit to split their sides when they spoke of Riffi, and his wails and cries on horseback.

It was eleven o'clock. These incomings and outgoings lasted till twelve, when Marc Divès suddenly came into the room, calling out:—"Hullin! Where is Hullin?"

"Here I am."

"Well, then, come!"

The smuggler's tone had something remarkable about it: from being a moment before furious at having. taken no part in the fight, he had now become triumphant. Jean-Claude followed him, feeling very uneasy: and the large room was immediately deserted, everybody being convinced, from Marc's manner, that there was something serious the matter.

To the right of the Donon extends the ravine of Minières, through which runs a foaming torrent when the snows melt-descending from the summit of the mountain to the valley.

Exactly in front of the plateau defended by the partisans, and on the other side of this ravine, at a distance of five or six hundred metres, projects a sort of open terrace with rugged sides, which Hullin had considered unnecessary to occupy for the time, wishing not to divide his forces, and seeing, besides, that it would be easy for him to turn this position by the pine-clumps, and to establish himself there, if the enemy showed any intention to take it.

Now imagine the consternation of the worthy man when, on reaching the door of the farmhouse, he saw two companies of Germans climbing this ascent, among the gardens of Grandfontaine, having two field-pieces yoked to powerful horses, which appeared to hang over the precipice. A troop was pushing at the wheels, and in a few seconds the guns would have reached the plateau.

It was like a thunder-bolt for Jean-Claude; he turned pale, and then into a great passion with Divès.

"Couldst thou not have warned me sooner?" he cried. "Did I not command thee to watch over the ravine? Our position is turned. They will hem us in, and cut us off from the road farther on. Everything is going to the deuce."

The people present, and old Materne himself, who had come up in great haste, were startled by the glance he darted at the smuggler; who, notwithstanding his usual audacity, was quite confused, not knowing what to reply.

"Come, come, Jean-Claude," said he at last, "be calm. It is not so serious as thou sayest. We have not fought—yet we others; and besides, we have no cannons—so it will be the very thing for us."

"Yes, the very thing for us, imbecile! Thy self-love made thee wait till the last minute, did it not? Thou wert too eager to fight, and have an opportunity for boasting and making bravado; and for that thou didst not hesitate to risk all our lives. Look! there are other troops being got ready at Framont."

In fact, another column, much stronger than the first, was just then marching out of Framont at the charge, and advancing against the breastworks. Divès did not say a word. Hullin controlled his anger, and became suddenly calm in the presence of danger.

"Go back to your posts," he said briefly to those around him. "Let all be ready for the coming attack. Materne, listen!"

The old hunter inclined his head. Meanwhile, Marc Divès had recovered his self-possession.

"Instead of screaming like a woman," said he, "thou wouldst do better to give me orders to attack down there, by turning the ravine at the pine-clumps."

"Then do it!" replied Jean-Claude; and in a calmer tone: "Listen, Marc! I am very angry with thee. We were conquerors; and by thy fault the battle has to be fought over again. If thou failest in thy attack, all is lost for us."

"Good! good! The affair is altogether mine: I will answer for it."

Then, springing on his horse, and throwing the end of his mantle over his shoulder, he drew his long blade with a defiant air. His men did the same.

He then turned to the reserve, composed of five hundred mountaineers, and showing the plateau to them with the point of his sword, said, "Look there, my men! we must carry that position. The men of Dagsburg must not say that they are braver than the men of the Sarre. Forward!" And, full of ardour, they advanced, skirting the ravine. Hullin shouted to them—"At the point of your bayonets!"

The big smuggler, on his great sleek roan, turned round, laughing out of the corners of his moustache, and waved his sword in a significant way; then the whole body dashed into the pine-wood.

At the same time the Germans, with their eight-pounders, had gained the plateau, and were putting them in position, while the column from Framont was ascending the hillside. Thus everything was in the same condition as before the battle,—with this difference, that the enemies' bullets would now come into play and take the mountaineers in the rear.

One could see distinctly the two field-pieces with their cramp-irons, levers, sponges, artillerymen, and the officer commanding, a great lanky fellow, with broad shoulders and fair moustaches floating in the wind. The blue shades of the valley seeming to diminish the distance, they looked as though you might have touched them; but Hullin and Materne were not to be deceived; it was a good six hundred metres across. No carbine could reach so far. Nevertheless, the old hunter, before returning to the abatis, wished to have his mind set quite at rest, he advanced as close as possible to the ravine, followed by his son Kasper and a few mountaineers; and, leaning against a tree, he raised his gun deliberately and took aim at the tall officer with the fair moustaches. All those about him held their breath for fear of balking the attempt.

Materne fired, but when he laid down his weapon to see what had occurred, no change had taken place.

"It is astonishing how age weakens the sight," he said.

"Your weakened sight!" cried Kasper. "There is not a man from the Vosges to Switzerland who can boast of hitting his mark at two hundred metres like you!"

The old hunter knew well it was the case, but he did not wish to discourage the others.

"Well," he replied, "we have no time for disputing. Here is the enemy again; let each do his duty." Although these words seemed simple and calm enough, Materne was very much troubled in reality. On entering the trench confused sounds met his ear—the clattering of arms and the regular tramp of many feet. He looked down over the steep bank, and now saw the Germans, who this time carried long ladders with hooks at the end.

It was not a pleasant sight for the brave fellow: he made a sign to his son to approach, and said to him, in a low voice, "Kasper, that looks bad—very bad; the rascals are coming with ladders. Give me thy hand! I should like to have thee near me, and Frantz as well; but we must defend ourselves with steadiness."

At this moment a great explosion shook the abatis, and a hoarse voice was heard crying out, "Ah, my God!" Then a hundred paces distant there was a heavy sound, and a fine tree bent down slowly and fell into the abyss. It was the first cannon-ball: it had cut off old Rochart's legs. It was followed by another immediately after, which covered all the mountaineers with broken ice, and made a great rumbling. Old Materne himself had bent down under the force of the explosion, but raising himself quickly, he shouted, "Let us revenge ourselves, my children. They are before you. To conquer or die!"

Fortunately the panic of the mountaineers only lasted a second: they all understood that the slightest hesitation and they were lost. Two ladders had already been raised, notwithstanding the fusillade, and were being attached to the bank by their iron hooks. This sight made the partisans furious, and the fight became more terrible and desperate than before.

Hullin had noticed the ladders before Materne had, and his wrath against Divès increased; but as in such a case indignation is of no avail, he had sent Lagarmitte to tell Frantz Materne, who had been posted on the other side of the Donon, to come to him quickly with half his men. We may well believe the brave fellow, warned of the danger his father was in, lost not a moment. Already their large black hats could be seen climbing the hillside amid the snows, their carbines slung across their shoulders. They came with all despatch, nevertheless Jean-Claude met them, with a haggard expression in his eyes, and shouted in a vibrating voice, "Come quicker! at that rate you will never reach us."

He was in a towering passion, and attributed all the misfortune to the smuggler.

Meanwhile Marc Divès, in about half an hour, had gone round the ravine, and, from the back of his tall horse, began to perceive the two companies of Germans, with grounded arms, about a hundred feet behind the guns, which were being fired upon the trench. Then, approaching the mountaineers, he said to them, in a stifled voice, while the reports of the cannon were re-echoed in the gorge and in the distance the noise of battle was heard: "Comrades, you must attack the infantry with your bayonets: I and my men will be answerable for the rest. Is it understood?"

"Yes, it is understood."

"Then, forward!"

The whole troop advanced in good order toward the outskirts of the wood, big Piercy of Soldatenthal at their head. Nearly at the same instant the *Wer da*? ("Who there?") of a sentinel was heard; then two shots; a loud cry of "*Vive la France!*" and the trampling of many feet in a charge. The brave mountaineers threw themselves like wolves on the enemy.

Divès stood up in his stirrups and watched them with great glee. "That is well," said he.

The *mêlée* was a terrible one; the ground trembled with it. The Germans were firing no more than the partisans: the affair was passing in silence; the clashing of bayonets and the sound of sabre-strokes, with here and there a rifle-shot, shouts of anger and a great tumult: except these, one could hear nothing else. The smugglers, with outstretched necks and sword in hand, sniffed the carnage and awaited the signal from their chief with impatience.

"Now, it is our turn," said Divès, at length. "The guns must be ours."

And out of the underwood they sprang, and their large cloaks flying behind them like wings, they dashed forward, bending in their saddles and pointing their swords.

"Never mind cutting! Run them through!" cried Divès once more.

That was all he said.

In a second, the twelve vultures were down upon the guns. Among their number were four old Spanish dragoons and two *cuirassiers* of the guard, whom a life of danger had attached to Marc: so I leave you to imagine how they fought. Blows from lever, rammer, and sabre, the only arms the gunners had to hand, rained upon them like hail; they parried them all, and every cut they made brought down a man.

Marc Divès received two pistol-shots, of which one singed his left cheek and the other carried away his hat. But, at the same time, bending over his saddle, his long arms stretched out, he transfixed the big officer with the fair moustaches to his gun; then raising himself deliberately, and gazing round him with a frown, said, in a sententious manner: "We have cleared out the rubbish! the guns are ours."

To get a good idea of this terrible scene, you must imagine the crowd on the plateau of Minières. The cries, the neighings of horses, the flight of some, who threw down their arms in order to run the faster, the desperation of others;—beyond the ravine, the ladders covered with white uniforms and bristling with bayonets; the mountaineers above the escarpment defending themselves with obstinacy; the hillsides, the road, and, above all, the space outside the breastworks, encumbered with dead and wounded;—the great numbers of the enemy, their muskets over their shoulders and their officers in the midst of them, pressing forward into action; and, finally, Materne standing on the crest of the hill, his bayonet in the air, his mouth opened wide, shouting wildly to his son Frantz, who was advancing with his troop, Master Jean-Claude at their head, to aid the mountaineers.

You should have heard the fusillade, the platoon and file firing, and, above all, the distant confused shouts, intermixed with sharp wails dying away among the mountain echoes. To gain a good idea of the scene, you should imagine all these as concentrated into one moment and surveyed with a rapid glance.

But Divès was not of a contemplative turn: he lost no time in making poetical reflections on the uproar and savagery of the battle. With one look he had taken in the whole situation; so, springing from his horse, he went up to the first gun, which was still loaded, aimed it at the ladders, and fired.

Then there arose wild clamours, and the smuggler, peering through the smoke, saw that fearful havoc had been made in the enemy's ranks. He waved his hands in sign of triumph, and the mountaineers on the breastworks answered with a general hurrah.

"Now then, dismount," said he to his men, "and don't go to sleep. A cartridge, a ball, and some turf. We will sweep the road. Look out!"

The smugglers put themselves in position, and continued to fire with enthusiasm upon the white coats. The bullets rained into their ranks. At the tenth discharge there was a general *sauve-qui-peut*.

"Fire! fire!" shouted Marc.

And the partisans, now supported by Frantz's troop, regained, under Hullin's directions, the positions which they had for the moment lost.

The whole of the hillside was soon covered with dead and wounded. It was then four in the evening; night was approaching. The last ball fell into the street of Grandfontaine, and rebounding on the angle of the pavement, knocked down the chimney of the "Red Ox."

About six hundred men perished that day: there were, of course, many mountaineers among them, but the greater number were *kaiserlichs*. Had it not been for the fire of Marc Divès's cannon, all would have been lost; the partisans were not one against ten, and the enemy had already begun to gain on the trenches.

CHAPTER 16

Painful Scenes

The Germans, huddled together in Grandfontaine, fled in crowds in the direction of Framont, on foot and on horseback, hurrying, dragging along their ammunition-wagons, strewing the road with their knapsacks, and looking behind as though they feared to find the partisans at their heels.

In Grandfontaine they destroyed everything out of sheer revenge; they smashed in doors and windows, maltreated the people, demanded food and drink indiscriminately. Their shouts and curses, the commands of their officers, the murmurs of the townsfolk, the artillery rolling over the bridge of Framont, the shrill cries of the wounded horses, were heard as a confused murmur at the breastworks.

The hillside was covered with arms, shakos, and dead; in fact, with all the signs of a great rout. In front was Marc Divès's cannon directed down the valley, ready to fire in case of a fresh attack.

All was finished, and finished well. Yet no shout of triumph rose from the intrenchments: the losses of the mountaineers, in this last assault, had been too great for that. There was something solemn in this silence succeeding to the uproar; all these men who had escaped the carnage, looked grave, as though astonished to see each other again. Some few called a friend, others a brother, who did not answer; and then they searched for them in the trenches, along the breastworks, or on the slopes, calling "Jacob, Philip, is it thou?"

Night came on; and the gray shadow creeping over everything, added mystery to these fearful scenes. The people came and went among the wrecks of the battle without recognizing each other.

Materne, having wiped his bayonet, called hoarsely to his boys:—"Kasper! Frantz!" and seeing them approach in the darkness, he asked, "Is that you?"

"Yes, we are here."

"Are you safe? are you wounded?"

"No."

The old hunter's voice became hoarser and more trembling still:—"Then we are all three united once more," said he, in a low tone.

And he, whom none would have thought to be so tender, embraced his sons warmly. They could hear his chest heaving with suppressed sobs. They were both much moved, and said to each other,—"We never dreamed that he loved us so much!"

But the old man, soon recovering from his emotion, called out, "It was a hard day, though, my boys. Let us have something to drink, for I am thirsty."

Then, casting one last look on the dark slopes, and seeing that Hullin had placed sentinels at short distances apart, they proceeded toward the farmhouse.

As they were picking their way carefully through the trenches, encumbered with the dead, they heard a stifled voice, which said to them, "Is it thou, Materne?"

"Ah! forgive me, my poor old Rochart," replied the hunter, bending over him, "if I touched thee. What, art thou still here?"

"Yes, I cannot get away, for I have no longer any legs to carry me."

They remained silent for a moment, when the old woodcutter continued,—"Thou wilt tell my wife that in a bag behind the closet, there are five pieces of six. I have saved them up, in case we either of us fell ill. I no longer need them."

"That is to say—that is to say—But thou mayst recover still, my poor old fellow. We will carry thee away."

"No; it is not worth the trouble: I cannot last more than an hour. It would only make me linger."

Materne, without answering, signed to Kasper to place his carbine with his own, so as to form a stretcher, and Frantz placed the old woodcutter upon them, notwithstanding his moans. In this way they arrived at the farm.

All the wounded who during the combat had had strength to drag themselves to the ambulance were now assembled there; and Doctor Lorquin and his comrade Dubois, who had arrived during the day, had work enough to do. But all was far from being over yet.

As Materne, his boys, and Rochart were traversing the dark alley under the lantern, they heard to their left a cry which made their blood run cold, and the old woodcutter, half dead, called out, "Why do you take me there? I will not go; I will not have anything done to me."

"Open the door, Frantz," said Materne, his face streaming with perspiration. "Open it! Be quick!"

Frantz having pushed open the door, they beheld in the centre of the low room with its large brown beams, Colard's son stretched out full length on a great kitchen-table, a man at each arm and a bucket beneath him. Doctor Lorquin, his shirtsleeves turned up to his elbows, and a short saw in his hand, was cutting off the poor fellow's leg, while Dubois stood by with a large sponge. The blood trickled into the pail. Colard was as white as death.

Catherine Lefèvre was there with a roll of lint on her arm. She seemed calm; but her teeth were clinched, and she fastened her eyes on the ground as though determined to witness nothing.

"It is finished," said the doctor, turning round; and perceiving the newcomers, "Ha! it is you, Father Rochart!" he exclaimed.

"Yes, it is I; but I will not let any one touch me. I would rather die as I am."

The doctor lifted up a candle, looked at him, and made a grimace.

"It is time to see to you, my poor old fellow. You have lost much blood, and if we wait longer it will be too late."

"So much the better! I have suffered enough in my life."

"As you like. Let us pass on to another."

He cast his eyes over a long line of straw mattresses at the end of the room; the two last were empty, but covered with blood. Materne and Kasper laid the old woodcutter down on the last, while Dubois, approaching another wounded man, said, "Nicolas, it is thy turn!"

Nicolas Cerf raised his pale face and his eyes glistened with fright.

"Let him have a glass of brandy," said the doctor.

"No, I would rather smoke my pipe."

"Where is thy pipe?"

"In my waistcoat pocket."

"Good, I have found it. And the tobacco?"

"In my trousers."

"All right. Fill his pipe, Dubois. He is a plucky fellow; it gives one pleasure to see a man like that. We are going to take off thy arm in a trice."

"Is there no way of saving it, Monsieur Lorquin, to bring up my poor children? It is their only resource."

"No; it is no use; the bone is smashed. Light the pipe, Dubois. Now, Nicolas, smoke away."

The unhappy fellow began, though evidently without relish.

"Is all ready?" asked the doctor.

"Yes," replied Nicolas, in a husky voice.

"Good. Attention, Dubois! Sponge away."

And he made a rapid turn in the flesh with a great knife. Nicolas ground his teeth. The blood spurted up, and Dubois bound up something tightly. The saw grated for two seconds, and the arm fell heavily on the boards.

"That is what I call a well-performed operation," said Lorquin.

Nicolas was no longer smoking; the pipe had fallen from his lips. David Schlosser, of Walsch, who had held him, let go. They

347

bound up the stump with linen, and, all unaided, Nicolas went to lie down on the straw.

"One more finished! Sponge the table well, Dubois, and let us go on to another," said the doctor, washing his hands in a large bowl.

Each time that he said, "Let us go on to another," the wounded moved uneasily, terrified by the screams they heard and the glittering knives they saw. But what was to be done? Every room in the farm, the granary, and the lofts was full. They were thus obliged to operate under the eyes of those who would soon in their turns come beneath the painful knife.

The operation had taken but a few seconds. Materne and his sons looked on for the same reason as one looks at other horrible things,—to know what they are like. Then in the corner, under the old china clock, they saw a heap of amputated limbs.

Nicolas's arm had already been cast among them, and a ball was now being extracted from the shoulder of a red-whiskered mountaineer of the Harberg. They opened deep gashes in his back; his flesh quivered, and the blood coursed down his powerful limbs.

The dog Pluto, behind the doctor, looked on with an attentive air, as though he understood, and from time to time stretched himself and yawned loudly.

Materne could look on no longer.

"Let us get out of this," said he.

Hardly were they outside the door, when they heard the doctor exclaim, "I have got the ball!" which must indeed have been satisfactory to the man from the Harberg.

Once outside, Materne, inhaling the cold air with delight, exclaimed: "Only think that the same might have happened to us!"

"True," said Kasper; "to get a ball in one's head is nothing; but to be cut up in that style, and then to beg one's bread for the rest of one's days!"

"Bah! I should do the same as old Rochart," said Frantz. "I should die quietly. The old fellow was right. When one has done

one's duty, why should one be afraid?"

Just then the hum of voices was heard on their fight.

"It is Marc Divès and Hullin," said Kasper, listening.

"Yes; they must be just returning from throwing up breast-works behind the pine-wood, to protect the cannon," added Frantz.

They listened again; the footsteps came nearer.

"Thou must be very much bothered with these three prisoners," said Hullin, roughly. "Since thou returnest to the Falkenstein tonight to get ammunition, what prevents thee from taking them away?"

"Where are they to be put?"

"Why, in the communal prison of Abreschwiller, to be sure. We cannot keep them here."

"All right, I understand, Jean-Claude. And if they try to escape on the way, I am to use my sword?"

"Just so."

By this time they had reached the door, and Hullin, perceiving Materne, could not suppress a shout of enthusiasm: "Ah! Is it thou, old fellow? I have been searching for thee an hour. Where the devil wert thou?"

"We have been carrying poor Rochart to the ambulance, Jean-Claude."

"Ah! it is a sad affair, isn't it?"

"Yes; it is sad."

There was a moment's pause, and the satisfaction of the worthy man again became visible.

"It is not at all lively," said he; "but what is to be done when one goes to the war? You are not hurt any of you?"

"No; we are all three safe and sound."

"So much the better. Those who are left can boast of being lucky."

"True," cried Marc Divès, laughing. "At one time I thought Materne was going to give way. Without those cannon-balls at the finish, things would have gone badly."

Materne coloured, and glanced sideways at the smuggler.

349

"Perhaps so," said he, dryly; "but without the cannon-balls at the beginning, we should not have needed those at the end. Old Rochart, and fifty other brave men, would still have had their arms and legs, and our victory would not have been clouded."

"Bah!" interrupted Hullin, anticipating a dispute between the two brave fellows, neither of whom was remarkable for his conciliatory disposition. "Leave that alone. Everyone has done his duty; and that is the chief thing."

Then, addressing Materne: "I have just sent a flag of truce to Framont, to bid the Germans carry away their wounded. In an hour, I dare say, they will be here. Our sentries must be warned to let them approach if they come without arms and with torches. If in any other way, let them be received with a volley."

"I will go at once," answered the old hunter.

"Materne, thou wilt afterward sup at the farm with thy boys."

"Agreed, Jean-Claude."

And he went off.

Hullin then bade Frantz and Kasper light great bivouac fires; Marc was at once to feed his horses, so that he might go without delay to procure ammunition. Seeing them hurrying away, Hullin turned into the farm.

CHAPTER 17

Round the Festive Board

At the end of the dark alley was the yard of the farm, into which one descended by five or six well-worn steps. On the left were the granary and the wine-press; to the right the stables and pigeon-cot, the gables of which stood out black on the dark cloudy sky; and in front of the door was the laundry.

No sound from the outside reached the yard. After so many tumultuous scenes, Hullin was impressed by the deep silence. He looked up at the piles of straw hanging from the beams of the granary roof, the ploughs and carts in the shadows of the outhouses, and an inexpressible feeling of calm and repose came over him. A cock was roosting quietly among the hens on the wall. A big cat, darting quickly by, disappeared through a hole into the cellar. Hullin thought himself in a dream.

After a few moments spent in silent contemplation, he walked slowly toward the laundry, the three windows of which shone brightly in the darkness: for the farm-kitchen not being large enough for preparing food for three or four hundred men, it was now being used for the purposes of cooking.

Master Jean-Claude heard Louise's clear voice giving orders in a resolute tone, which astonished him.

"Now, Katel, quick! supper-time is near. Our people must be hungry. Since six in the morning they have taken nothing, and have been fighting all the time. They must not be kept waiting. Come, bestir yourself, Lesselé; bring the salt and pepper!"

Jean-Claude's heart leaped within him at the sound of this

voice. He could not help gazing for a minute through the window before entering.

The kitchen was large, with low whitewashed ceiling. A beechwood fire crackled on the hearth, its red flames encircling the sides of an immense kettle. The charming figure of Louise, wearing her short petticoat so as to move unimpeded, a bright colour in her face, the short red body of her dress leaving uncovered her round shoulders and white neck, stood out clearly in the foreground. She was in all the bustle of the occasion, coming and going, tasting the soup and sauces with a knowing air, and approving and criticising everything.

"A little more salt! Lesselé, have you almost done plucking that great lean cock? At this rate we shall never have finished!"

It was delightful to see her thus busily commanding. It brought tears into Hullin's eyes.

The two daughters of the anabaptist—one tall, thin, and pale, with her large flat feet encased in round shoes, her red hair fastened up in a little black cap, her blue stuff dress falling in folds to her heels; the other fat, slowly lifting up one foot after the other, and waddling along like a duck—forming a striking contrast to Louise.

The stout Katel went panting about without saying a word, while Lesselé performed everything in her sleepy methodical way.

The worthy anabaptist himself, seated at the end of the room, with his legs crossed on a wooden chair, his cotton cap on his head, and his hands in his blouse pockets, looked on with a wondering air, addressing to them sententious exhortations from time to time: "Lesselé, Katel! be obedient, my children. Let this be for your instruction. You have not yet seen the world. You must be quicker and sharper."

"Yes, yes, you must bestir yourselves," added Louise. "Gracious! what should become of us if we stood thinking months and weeks before putting a little onion into a sauce! Lesselé, you are the tallest, unhook me that parcel of onions from the ceiling."

The girl obeyed.

Hullin had never felt prouder in his life.

"How she makes them move about!" thought he. "Ah! ha! ha! she is like a little hussar. I never should have believed it."

After having watched them for five minutes, he went into the room.

"Well done, my children!"

Louise was holding a soup-ladle at the time. She let it fall, and threw herself into his arms, crying: "Papa Jean-Claude, is it you? you are not wounded? Nothing is the matter with you?"

At the sound of this voice, Hullin turned pale, and could make no reply. After a long silence, pressing her to his heart, he said: "No, Louise, I am quite well; I am very happy."

"Sit down, Jean-Claude," said the anabaptist, seeing him trembling with emotion; "here, take my chair."

Hullin sat down, and Louise, with her arms on his shoulder, began to cry.

"What is the matter, my child?" said the worthy man, kissing her. "Come, calm thyself. Only a few seconds ago thou wert so courageous."

"Oh, yes, but I was only acting; I was very much afraid. I thought, 'Why does he not come?'"

She threw her arms round his neck. Then a strange idea came into her head. She took him by the hand, crying: "Papa Jean-Claude, let us dance, let us dance!"

And they made three or four turns. Hullin could not help laughing, and turning toward the grave anabaptist, said: "We are rather mad, Pelsly; do not let that astonish you."

"No, Master Hullin, it is quite natural. King David himself danced before the ark after his great victory over the Philistines."

Jean-Claude, astonished to find that he was like King David, made no reply.

"And thou, Louise," he continued, stopping, "thou wert not afraid during this last battle?"

"Oh, at first, with all the noise and the roaring of the cannons;

but afterward I only thought of you and of Mamma Lefèvre."

Master Jean-Claude grew silent again.

"I knew," thought he, "that she was a brave girl. She has everything in her favour."

Louise taking him by the hand, then led him to a regiment of pans around the fire, and showed him with delight her kitchen.

"Here is the beef and roast mutton, here is General Jean-Claude's supper, and here is the soup for our wounded. Haven't we been busy! Lesselé and Katel would tell you so. And here is our bread," said she, pointing to a long row of loaves arranged on the table. "Mamma Lefèvre and I mixed up the flour."

Hullin looked on astonished.

"But that is not all," said she; "come over here."

She took off the lid of a saucepan, and the kitchen was immediately filled with a savoury odour which would have rejoiced the heart of a gourmand.

Jean-Claude was deeply touched by all these proofs of attention to the wants of his men.

Just then Mother Lefèvre came in.

"Well," said she, "prepare the table; everybody is waiting over there. Come, Katel, go and lay the cloth."

The girl went running out to do so.

They all crossed the dark yard and made their way toward the large room. Doctor Lorquin, Dubois, Marc Divès, Materne, and his two boys, all very hungry, were awaiting the soup impatiently.

"How about our wounded, doctor?" said Hullin, on entering.

"They have all been attended to, Master Jean-Claude. You have given us plenty of work to do; but the weather is favourable; there is nothing to fear from putrid fevers; things wear a pleasant aspect."

Katel, Lesselé, and Louise soon came in bearing an immense tureen of smoking soup and two sirloins of roast beef, which they deposited on the table. They all sat down without ceremony—old Materne to the right of Jean-Claude, Catherine

Lefèvre to the left; and from that time the clatter of spoons and forks and the gurgling of the bottles took the place of conversation till half-past eight in the evening. The glow which might be seen from the outside upon the windows, proved that the volunteers were doing justice to Louise's cookery, which contributed greatly to the enjoyment of her guests.

At nine o'clock Marc Divès was on his way to Falkenstein with the prisoners. At ten everybody was asleep at the farm, on the plateau, and around the watchfires. The silence was only broken by the passing of the patrols and the challenge of the sentinels.

Thus terminated this great day, after the mountaineers had proved that they had not degenerated from their ancestors.

Other events, not less important, were soon to succeed those which had already taken place: for in this world, when one obstacle is surmounted, others present themselves. Human life resembles a restless sea: one wave follows another from the old world to the new, and nothing arrests its everlasting movement.

CHAPTER 18

The Cave of Luitprandt

All through the battle, till the close of night, the good people of Grandfontaine had observed the poor crazy Yégof standing upon the crest of the Little Donon, and, his crown on his head, with his sceptre held aloft, like a Merovingian king, shouting commands to his phantom armies. What passed through his mind when he saw the utter rout of the Germans no one can say; but at the last cannon-shot he disappeared. Where did he betake himself? On this point the people of Tiefenbach have the following story:—

At that time there lived upon the Bocksberg two singular creatures—sisters—one named "little Kateline," and the other "great Berbel." These creatures, who were almost in tatters, had taken up their abode in the "Cave of Luitprandt," so called, according to old chronicles, because the German king, before invading Alsace, had caused to be interred in that immense vault of red sandstone the savage chiefs who had fallen in the battle of Blutfeld. The hot spring which always bubbles in the middle of the cavern protected the eerie sisters from the sharp colds of winter; and the woodcutter, Daniel Horn, of Tiefenbach, had been good enough to fill up the largest entrance to the rock with heaps of brushwood.

By the side of the hot spring there is another, cold as ice and clear as crystal. Kateline, who always drank of its waters, was scarce four foot high, thick-set and bloated; and her cowering figure, her round eyes and enormous *goître*, rendered her whole appearance peculiarly suggestive of a big turkey-hen in a reverie. Every Sunday she carried into Tiefenbach a great basket, which the people of the place filled with boiled potatoes, crusts of bread, and occasionally, on high days, with cakes and other remains of their festivals;—with which she reascended breathlessly to her rocky home, muttering, gibbering, and behaving in the absurdest way. Meanwhile Berbel took care to drink from the cold spring: she was gaunt, one-eyed, scraggy as a bat, with a flat nose, large ears, a gleaming eye, and thrived upon the booty obtained by her sister.

Seldom did she descend from the Bocksberg, except in July, at the time of greatest heat—when she proceeded to launch her incantations—her enchanting-wand a withered thistle—against the crops of those who had failed to contribute to her sister's basket. These imprecations were always believed to be followed by dire storms, hail, and destructive vermin without stint: whence they came to be dreaded as the plague, and the hag herself to be regarded as a weather-witch (*Wetterhexe*), while "little Kateline" was looked upon as the good genius of Tiefenbach and its neighbourhood. In such wise Berbel folded her arms and took her ease in her cave, while her sister went gibbering along the highways.

Unfortunately for the sisters, Yégof had for many years established his winter-quarters in "Luitprandt's cavern;" and it was thence he set forth every spring on a visit to his innumerable *châteaux* and feudatories, as far as Geierstein in the Hundsriick. Every year, therefore, toward the end of November, after the first snows, he arrived with, his raven, to the accompaniment of piercing cries from *Wetterhexe*.

"What have you to grumble at?" he would say, while installing himself in the place of honour. "Are you not intruders upon my domain, and am I not truly good to permit two such useless old hags (*Valkyries*) to stay in the Valhalla of my fathers?"

Then Berbel, in a rage, used to overwhelm him with abuse, while Kateline gave vent to her dissatisfaction in thick unintelligible utterances; but he, regardless of both, lit his old box pipe and set him- self to describe his endless peregrinations to the ghosts of the German warriors buried in the cavern sixteen centuries before, calling upon each of them by name, and addressing them as personages still living. From this it will be understood with what disgust the arrival of the maniac came to be regarded by Kateline and Berbel; in fact for both it was nothing less than a calamity.

Now in the year we are speaking of, Yégof, having failed to return to them at the proper time, induced the sisters to believe that he was dead and to rejoice at the idea of seeing no more of him. But for many days *Wetterhexe* had remarked an extraordinary movement going on in the neighbouring gorges, and men marching off in bodies, shouldering their muskets, from the sides of Falkenstein and Donon.

Clearly something was taking place out of the common. Recollecting that the year before Yégof had informed the phantoms of the cave that his armies, in countless hosts, were coming to invade the country, the sorceress was seized with a vague apprehension and anxiety to learn the cause of so much agitation; but no one came up to the cave, and Kateline having made her rounds on the previous Sunday, could not have been induced to stir out for the gift of a kingdom.

In this state of apprehension, *Wetterhexe* went and came upon the side of the mountain and became hourly more restless and irritable. During the whole of that Saturday events assumed quite another aspect. From nine o'clock in the morning deep and heavy explosions began to growl like a continuous storm among the thousand echoes of the mountain; while far away in the direction of Donon, the swift lightnings swept up across the sky among the peaks; then toward night the discharges deepening in intensity filled the silent gorges with an indescribable tumult. At every report the Hengst, the Gantzlee, the Giromani, and the Grosmann cliffs seemed to echo to their lowest depths.

"What can it be?" cried Berbel. "Has the end of the world come?"

Then re-entering her lurking-place, and finding Kateline

crouched in her corner and munching a potato, Berbel shook her roughly and hissed out:—"Fool! have you got no ears? Is there anything that you fear? You are good for nothing but eating, drinking, and mumbling. Oh, you idiot!"

She snatched away the potato in a rage, and then seated herself by the side of the hot spring, which was sending up its gray fumes to the roof. Half an hour after, the darkness having become intense and the cold excessive, she made a fire of brushwood, which shed its pale gleams upon the blocks of red sandstone and lit up the farthest corner of the cave, where Kateline was now asleep, huddled in the straw, with her chin upon her knees.

Without, the noisy tumult had ceased. Then withdrawing the brush-wood curtain from the mouth of the cave, she peered out into the darkness, and returned to crouch down by the spring. With her large lips compressed, her eyes closed, and the great round wrinkles playing upon her cheeks, she drew round her knees an old woollen covering, and appeared to fall asleep. Throughout the cavern there was no sound, except that of the congealed vapour, which fell back at long intervals into the spring with a strange splashing noise.

This silence lasted for about two hours; midnight was approaching, when all of a sudden a distant sound of footsteps, mingled with discordant cries, was heard outside the cave. Berbel listened, and at once perceived that they were human cries. Then she rose, trembling, and, armed with her thistle-wand, proceeded to the entrance of the cave; whence, through the screen of brushwood, she saw, at fifty paces distant, Yégof advancing toward her in the moonlight. He was alone, but gesticulating and waving his sceptre, as if myriads of invisible beings were about him.

"Hark, ye red men!" he was shrieking, with beard sticking up on end, his hair streaming about his head, and his dog-skin upon his arm. "Hark, ye red men! Roog! Bléd! Adelrik! hark! Will ye not hear me at last? Do you not see they are coming? Behold them cleaving the sky like vultures. Hark to me. Let this miserable race be annihilated! Ha, ha! it is you, Minau! it is you, Rochart . . . ha! ha!" And addressing the dead upon the Donon, he called upon them defiantly, as if they were standing before him; and then fell back a step at a time, striking the air, uttering imprecations, encouraging his phantoms, and casting about him as if in close fight.

The sight of this terrible struggle against beings who were invisible caused Berbel to shudder with fright, and to fancy her hair stiffening upon her head. She sought to hide herself; but just at the moment a strange noise from, behind drew her attention, and her terror may be imagined when she saw the hot spring bubbling with more than usual activity and sending out clouds of steam, which rose and broke away in separate masses toward the entrance of the cavern; and while these clouds like phantoms were slowly advancing in close order, Yégof appeared upon the scene, shouting hoarsely:—

"You come at last! you heard me then!"

Thus saying, he removed with an impatient effort all obstructions from the mouth of the cave: the cold air rushed down the vault and the steaming vapours rose far into the sky, writhing and glancing above the cliff, as if the slain of that day and those of the ages gone by had recommenced beyond the earth a battle that would never end.

Yégof, with face which appeared shrunken in the pale moonlight, his sceptre held high, his great beard flowing down his breast, and his eyes flaming, saluted each phantom with a wave of the hand, ad- dressing it by name:

"Hail, Bléd! Roog, hail! and you, my brave men, all hail! The hour you have been expecting for ages is at hand: the eagles are whetting their beaks and the soil is thirsting for blood. Remember Blutfeld!"

At this point Berbel's terror seemed to hold her transfixed; but soon the last volumes of gray mist disappeared out of the cavern and melted into the sky. Seeing which the crazy *montagnard* marched fiercely into the cave, and seating himself by the spring, with his great head between his hands, and his elbows on his knees, looked down into the boiling water with a haggard stare.

Kateline was now awake and venting her guttural moans; while *Wetterhexe*, more dead than alive, was furtively watching the maniac from the farthest corner of the cave.

"They have all gone up from the earth!" exclaimed Yégof, suddenly. "All, all! They have gone to reanimate the courage of my youths, and inspire them with contempt of death!"

And again lifting up his face, which seemed impressed with deep anguish, he cried, fixing his wolfish eyes on *Wetterhexe*:—

"Oh, thou descendant of the sterile *valkyries*, thou who hast nurtured within thy bosom no life-breath of warriors, nor ever filled their deep goblets at the festive board, nor regaled them with the smoking flesh of the wild boar, for what purpose art thou good? To spin shrouds for the dead. Ha! take thy distaff and spin night and day; for thousands of brave men are slumbering in the snow! . . . They fought well. . . . Yes, they did all that men could do; but the time had not come, . . . now the ravens are fighting for their carcasses!"

Then in accents of uncontrollable rage, snatching the crown off his head together with handfuls of hair—"Ah, cursed race," he exclaimed, "will you always be barring our passage? Were it not for you we had already conquered Europe; the red men would have been masters of the world. . . . And I have bowed my head before the leader of this race of curs. ... I asked him for his daughter, instead of seizing and carrying her away as the wolf carries the lamb! . . . Ah! Huldrix, Huldrix!"

Then changing this rhapsody—"Listen, listen, *valkyrie*!" he cried in a hoarse voice, and pointing his finger with great solemnity.

Wetterhexe listened. A great gust of wind rose up through the night, shaking the old forest-trees heavy with their load of frost. Often and often had the sorceress in the winter nights heard the soughing of the north wind and paid it no attention, but now she was overwhelmed with fear! And as she stood there all trembling, a hoarse cry was heard without; and almost at the same

YÉGOF SALUTED EACH PHANTOM WITH SPARKLING EYES

time the raven Hans, sweeping beneath the rock, set himself to describe great circles overhead, flapping his wings with a frightened air, and uttering melancholy cries.

Yégof became pale as death. "*Vod, Vod*! what has thy son Luitprandt done for thee? Why choose him rather than another?"

For some seconds he stood as though amazed then, suddenly transported by savage enthusiasm and brandishing his sceptre, he dashed out of the cavern.

Two minutes afterward, *Wetterhexe*, standing at the entrance of the rock, followed him with anxious eyes.

He went straight on, with neck stretched forward and long strides. You would have thought him a wild beast upon the prowl. Hans went before him, hopping from place to place.

In a moment they disappeared down the Blutfeld Gorge.

CHAPTER 19

Gaspard's Letter

Toward two o'clock the next morning, snow began to fall. At daybreak the Germans had left Grandfontaine, Framont, and even Schirmeck. In the distance, on the plains of Alsace, could be seen the black lines, which indicated their retreating battalions.

Hullin arose early and made the round of the bivouacs. He stopped for a few seconds on the plateau, to look at the cannons in position, the sleeping partisans, and the watchful sentries; then, satisfied with his inspection, he re-entered the farm, where Louise and Catherine were still asleep.

The gray light was spreading everywhere. A few wounded in the next room were growing feverish; they were calling for their wives and children. Soon the hum of voices and the noise of busy feet broke the stillness of the night. Catherine and Louise awoke. They saw Jean-Claude sitting in a corner of the window watching them, and ashamed of having slept longer than he, they arose and approached him.

"Well?" asked Catherine.

"Well, they have left; and we are masters of the field, as I expected."

This assurance did not appear to satisfy the old dame. She looked through the window to see for herself that the Germans were retreating into Alsace; and during the whole of that day she seemed both anxious and troubled.

Between eight and nine the *curé* Saumaize came in from the

village of Charmes. Some mountaineers then descended the slopes to pick up the dead, and dug a deep pit to the right of the farm, where partisans and *kaiserlichs*, with their clothes, hats, shakos, and uniforms, were laid side by side. The *curé* Saumaize, a tall old man with white hair, read the prayers for the dead in that solemn, mysterious voice which seems to penetrate to the depths of one's soul, and to summon from the tomb the spirits of extinct generations to attest to the living the terrors of the grave.

All day carts and sledges continued to arrive to carry away the wounded, who demanded, with loud cries, to be allowed to see their villages once more. Doctor Lorquin, fearing to increase their irritation, was forced to consent. And toward four o'clock, Catherine and Hullin were alone in the great room: Louise had gone out to prepare the supper. Outside, large flakes of snow continued to fall, and, from time to time, a sledge might be seen silently passing along, bearing a wounded man laid in straw. Catherine, seated near the table, was folding bandages with an absent air.

"What ails you, Catherine?" demanded Hullin. "You have seemed so thoughtful since morning: and yet our affairs are going on well."

The old dame, pushing the linen slowly away from her, replied,—"Yes, Jean-Claude, I am uneasy."

"Uneasy about what? The enemy is in full retreat. Only this moment, Frantz Materne, whom I had sent to reconnoitre, and all the messengers from Piorette, Jérome, and Labarbe, told me that the Germans are returning to Mutzig. Old Materne and Kasper, having gathered up the dead, learned at Grandfontaine that nothing is to be seen in the direction of Saint-Blaize-la-Roche. All this proves that our Spanish dragoons gave the enemy a warm reception on the way to Senones, and that they fear an attack from Schirmeck. "What is it, then, Catherine, that troubles you?"

And seeing that Hullin looked at her inquiringly, "You may laugh at me," said she; "but I have had a dream."

"A dream?"

"Yes, the same as at the farm of Bois-de-Chênes." And getting animated, she continued, in an almost angry tone, "You may say what you like, Jean-Claude, but a great danger menaces us. Yes, yes! you don't see any sense in all this; but it was not a dream, it was like an old tale which comes back to one: something one sees in sleep and remembers. Listen! We were as we are now, after a great victory—in some place—I don't know where—in a sort of large wooden shed, with beams across it, and palisades around. We were not thinking of anything: all the faces I saw I knew: you were among them, Marc Divès, Duchêne, and old men already dead: my father and old Hugues Rochart of Harberg, the uncle of him who has just died: and they all had coarse gray cloth blouses, with long beards and bare necks.

"We had won a like victory, and were drinking out of red earthenware pots, when a cry arose: 'The enemy is coming!' And Yégof, on horseback, with his long beard and pointed crown, an axe in his hand, and with his eyes gleaming like a wolf's, appeared before me in the darkness. I rushed on him with a club, he waited for me—and from that moment I saw no more. I only felt a great pain in my neck; a cold wind passed over my face, and my head seemed to be dangling at the end of a cord: it was that wretched Yégof who had hung my head to his saddle and was galloping away!"

There was a short pause; and then Jean-Claude, rousing from his stupor, replied: "It is a dream. I also have had dreams. Yesterday you were agitated, Catherine, by all that tumult, that noise."

"No," she exclaimed in a firm tone, taking up her task again: "no, it was not that. And to tell you the truth, during the battle, and even when the cannons were thundering against us, I was not afraid; I was certain beforehand that we should not be beaten; I had seen it long ago. But now I am afraid."

"But the Germans have evacuated Schirmeck; the whole line of the Vosges is defended. We have more men than we need; they are coming every minute in great numbers."

"No matter."

Hullin shrugged his shoulders.

"Come, come! you are feverish, Catherine; try to be calm, and think of pleasanter things. As for all these dreams, you see, I make no more account of them than I do of the Grand Turk, with his pipe and blue stockings. The chief thing is to keep a good look-out, and to have plenty of ammunition, men, and guns: that is infinitely better than the most rose-coloured dreams."

"You are mocking me, Jean-Claude."

"No; but to hear a sensible, courageous woman speak as you do, reminds one in spite of himself of Yégof, who pretends to have lived sixteen hundred years ago."

"Who knows?" said the old woman, in an obstinate tone; "it is possible he may remember what others have forgotten."

Hullin was going to relate to her his conversation of the evening before at the bivouac-fire with the madman, thus hoping to overthrow all her gloomy fancies; but seeing she agreed with Yégof about the sixteen hundred years, the worthy man said no more, but resumed his walk up and down, with his head bent and an anxious face: "She is mad," thought he; "one more shock and it is all over with her!"

Catherine after a pause was going to speak, when Louise entered like a swallow, calling out, in her sweetest voice, "Maman Lefèvre, Maman Lefèvre, a letter from Gaspard!"

Whereupon the old farm-wife, whose hooked nose almost touched her lips, so angry was she to see Hullin turning her dream into ridicule, raised her head, the long wrinkles in her face relaxing.

She took the letter, looked at the red seal, and said to the young girl: "Embrace me, Louise: it is a good letter!" And Louise at once embraced her with joy.

Hullin came close up to them, delighted at this incident; and the postman Brainstein, his big boots dyed red with the snow, his two hands on his stick, and drooping his shoulders, stationed himself at the door with a tired look.

The old dame put on her spectacles, slowly opened the letter under the impatient eyes of Jean-Claude and Louise, and read aloud:—

This, my mother, is to announce to you that all goes well, and that I reached Phalsbourg on Tuesday evening just as the gates were being closed. The Cossacks were already on the Saverne road; we had to fire all night against their advanced guard. The following day, an envoy was sent demanding the surrender of the place. The commandant, Meunier, told him to go and be hanged; and three days after great showers of bombs and shells began to rain upon the town. The Russians have three batteries—one on the side of Mittelbronn, the other at the Baraques above, and the third behind the tilery of Pernette near the drinking-tank; but the red-hot shot do us the most harm: they burn down the houses, and when a fire has broken out the bombs then come in quantities and prevent the people from extinguishing it.

The women and children do not leave the block-houses; the townsmen remain with us on the ramparts: they are fine fellows. Among them are some old soldiers of the Sambre-et-Meuse, Italy, and Egypt, who have not forgotten how to manage the guns. I felt sorry to see the graybeards bending over the carronades to take aim. I will answer for it that there are no balls lost with them; but all the same, when one has made the world tremble, it is hard to be obliged, in one's old days, to fight for one's home and last morsel of bread.

"Yes, it is hard," exclaimed Catherine, drying her eyes. "Only to think of it makes one's heart bleed."

Then she continued:—

The day before yesterday, the governor decided on our making a sortie against the tile-kiln battery. You must know that these Russians break the ice of the tank, and bathe in it, in groups of from twenty to thirty; afterward drying themselves in the oven of the brick-kiln. Well! about four o'clock, as the day was closing, we went out by the Arsenal gateway, ascending the covered way, and filing along the Allée-des-Vaches, with our muskets under our arms, and marching at the double. Ten minutes after we commenced a rolling fire on the men that were in the tank.

Then their comrades rushed out of the brick-kilns: they had only time to put on their cartouche-boxes, seize their muskets, and form, all naked as they were, on the snow, like regular savages. Notwithstanding that, the rogues were ten times more numerous than we, and they began a movement to the right, in the direction of the little chapel of St. John, in order to surround us, when the guns from the Arsenal began to send such a storm of shot at them as I never saw before; it carried whole files clean off.

A quarter of an hour later they retreated in a body to Quatre-Vents, without waiting to pick up their breeches—their officers at their head, and the hail from the fortress bringing up the rear. Papa Jean-Claude would have laughed at the rout immensely. At last, toward nightfall, we returned to the town, having destroyed one of their batteries and thrown two eight-pounders into the well of the kiln. It was our first sortie. I am now writing to you from the Baraques du Bois-de-Chênes, where we have been sent to get provisions for the fortress.

All this may last months. It is said that the allies are reascending the valley of Dosenheim as far as Weschem, and that thousands of them are marching on Paris. Oh, if the Emperor once obtained the upper hand in Lorraine and Champagne, not one of them would escape! But who lives will see. They are sounding the retreat on Phalsbourg. We have collected a pretty good number of oxen, cows, and goats about here; but shall have to fight in order to get them in safely. Goodbye, my good mother, my dearest Louise, and Papa Jean-Claude. I embrace you as though I held you in my arms.

At the close of the letter, Catherine Lefèvre was overwhelmed with emotion.

"What a brave boy!" said she. "He only knows his duty. There! thou hearest, Louise? He embraces thee!"

Louise then throwing herself into her arms, they embraced each other; and Catherine, notwithstanding the firmness of her character, could not keep back two large tears from trickling down her cheeks; then, recovering herself, "Come," said she, "all is well! Come, Brainstein, you must eat some meat and drink a glass of wine. And here is a crown-piece for your journey; I would give you the same sum every day of the week for such a letter."

The postman, delighted with his present, followed the old dame. Louise walked after them, and Jean-Claude, also, being eager to interrogate Brainstein as to what he had learnt on the road, touching the events taking place; but he could get nothing new out of him, except that the allies were besieging Bitsche and Lutzelstein, and that they had lost some hundreds of men in trying to force the Graufthal Pass.

CHAPTER 20

The Surprise

Toward ten o'clock, Catherine Lefèvre and Louise, after having wished Hullin goodnight, went up to sleep in the room over the large kitchen; in which there were two feather-beds, with curtains, striped with blue and red, reaching to the ceiling.

"Come," exclaimed the old woman, climbing up to hers on a chair—"come, sleep well, my child. As for me, I am tired out, and almost asleep already."

She drew the bedclothes round her, and five minutes after was sound asleep. Louise soon followed her example.

Now this had lasted about two hours, when the old dame was awakened suddenly by a tremendous noise.

"To arms! to arms! Ho! this way quick! A thousand thunders! they are upon us!"

Five or six shots then followed each other, lighting up the dark windows.

"To arms! to arms!"

Then there was more firing, and the noise of people rushing about everywhere.

Hullin's voice, sharp and vibrating, could be heard giving orders.

Then, to the left of the farm, a great way off, there came a low dull crackling sound, from the gorges of the Grosmann.

"Louise! Louise!" cried the old farm-wife,—"dost thou hear?"

"Yes! Oh, my God! it is terrible."

Catherine sprang out of bed.

"Get up, my child," said she, "and let us dress."

The firing redoubled, and flashed like lightning upon the panes.

"Attention!" shouted Materne.

One could also hear the neighing of a horse outside, and the tramping of a great crowd in the alley, the yard, and before the farm: the house seemed shaken to its foundations.

Suddenly, the firing came from the windows of the large room on the ground-floor. The two women dressed in haste. Just at that moment, a heavy foot creaked on the stairs; the door opened, and Hullin appeared with a lantern, showing signs of great agitation.

"Make haste!" cried he; "we have not an instant to lose."

"What has happened then?" asked Catherine.

The fusillade came nearer.

"Eh!" exclaimed Jean-Claude, throwing up his arms, "have I time now to explain to you?"

The old dame understood that the only thing to be done was to obey. She put on her hood and descended the staircase with Louise. By the flickering light of the shots, Catherine saw Materne, bare-necked, and his son Kasper, firing from the entrance of the alley upon the abatis, and ten others behind handing them muskets, so that they had only to aim and fire. All these men, in a throng, loading, shouldering, and firing, had a terrible aspect. Three or four dead bodies lying against the old wall added to the horror of the scene. The smoke was at the point of reaching the dwelling.

Coining down the stairs, Hullin cried, "Here they are, thank heaven!" And all the brave fellows who were there, looking up, cried out, "Courage, Mother Lefèvre!"

Whereupon the poor old lady, worn out by her emotions, began to weep and lean on Jean-Claude's shoulder; but he lifted her up like a feather, and ran along by the wall to the right. Louise followed, sobbing loudly.

Out of doors, one could only hear the whizzing of bullets

and the dull heavy blows against the wall; the bricks and mortar were tumbling down, the tiles rolling about; while in front, near the abatis, and three hundred yards off, one could see the white uniforms in line, lit up by their own fire in the dark night; and, to their left, on the other side of the ravine of Minières, the mountaineers attacking them in flank.

Hullin disappeared at the corner of the farm,—where all was in darkness;—Doctor Lorquin, on horseback in front of a sledge, having a large cavalry sword in his hand and two pistols passed through his belt, with Frantz Materne and a dozen other armed men, being barely distinguishable. Hullin placed Catherine in the sledge, on some straw, and Louise by her side.

"There you are!" exclaimed the doctor. "It is well for you."

And Frantz Materne added:—"If it were not for you, Mother Lefèvre, you may well believe that not one of us would quit the plateau this night; but there is nothing to be said since you are in the case."

"No," cried the others, "there is nothing to be said!"

Just at that moment, a tall fellow, with legs long as a heron's and a round back, came running behind the wall and shouting, "They are coming! Fly! fly!"

Hullin turned pale.

"It is the big knife-grinder of the Harberg!" he exclaimed, grinding his teeth.

Frantz without saying a word put his musket to his shoulder, aimed and fired; and Louise saw the grinder at thirty yards in the dim light, throw up his arms and fall face downward on the ground. Frantz reloaded, smiling grimly.

Hullin then said: "Comrades, here is our mother—she who has given us powder and furnished us with food for the defence of our country; and here is my child: save them!"

They all replied: "We will save, or die with them."

"And do not forget to warn Divès to stay at the Falkenstein till further orders."

"All right, Jean-Claude."

"Then forward, doctor, forward!" cried the gallant man.

"And you, Hullin?" exclaimed Catherine.

"My place is here; our position must be defended till death!"

"Papa Jean-Claude!" cried Louise, holding out her arms to him.

But he had already turned the corner,—the doctor flicked his horse, and the sledge passed quickly along the snow. Frantz Materne and his men, with their muskets on their shoulders, marched behind; while a rolling fire of musketry was still kept up around the farm.

That was what Catherine Lefèvre and Louise saw in the space of a few minutes. No doubt something strange and terrible had happened in the night. The old farm-mistress, recalling her dream, became very thoughtful. Louise dried her eyes and looked toward the plateau, which was lighted up as by a fire. The horse bounded away under the doctor's whip, so that the mountaineers could hardly keep up. For some distance the tumult and clamour of the battle, the explosions, and whizzing of the balls among the branches, were distinctly heard; but all this grew fainter and fainter, and soon, at the descent of the path, vanished as in a dream.

The sledge had reached the opposite side of the mountain, and was flying like an arrow through the darkness. The only sounds which broke the silence were the galloping of the horse, the quick breathing of the escort, and from time to time the doctor's cry, "Here, Bruno! here then!"

A current of cold wind, coming up from the valley of the Sarre, carried upon its breeze, like a great sigh, the endless roar of the torrents and soughing of the woods. The moon was peering out from behind a cloud, and looking down on the black forests of Blanru, with their tall pines loaded with snow.

Ten minutes later the sledge had gained an angle of the woods, and Doctor Lorquin, turning round in his saddle, exclaimed,-

"Now, Frantz, what have we to do? Here is the way which leads toward the hills of St. Quirin, and there is another road which descends to Blanru. Which shall we take?"

Frantz and the men of the escort came up. As they were then on the western slope of the Donon, they began to see again, high in the air, on the other side of the hill, the fusillade of the Germans, who were advancing by way of the Grosmann. First they saw the flashes, and then heard the rolling echoes in the depths of the valleys.

"The road by the hills of St. Quirin," said Frantz, "is the shortest cut to the farm of Bois-de-Chênes; it would save at least three-quarters of an hour."

"Yes," rejoined the doctor, "but we should risk being stopped by the Germans, who now occupy the defile of the Sarre. See, they are already masters of the heights; they have no doubt sent detachments to the Sarre-Rouge in order to turn the Donon."

"Let us take the Blanru road, then," said Frantz; "it is longer, but safer."

The sledge passed down the left along the woods. The partisans, gun in hand, advanced one after the other along the top of the bank, while the doctor on his horse swept along the snow in the roadway. Above, the great pine-branches met across the road, and enveloped it with their deep shadows, while the moon lit up the surrounding scenery. This road was so majestic and picturesque, that, under any other circumstances, Catherine would have been astonished at it, and Louise would not have failed to admire the garlands of icicles, looking like crystals in the pale rays of the moon; but just then they were filled with uneasiness; and, moreover, when the sledge entered the gorge, all the brightness vanished, and only the summits of the high mountains around remained visible.

They had been going in this way for a quarter of an hour, when Catherine, having kept silence for some time, at last could contain herself no longer, but exclaimed: "Doctor Lorquin, now that you have us in the depths of Blanru, and can do with us what you please, will you explain to me why we have been dragged away by force? Jean-Claude carried me off, and flung me on this heap of straw—and here I am!"

"Up, Bruno," cried the doctor.

Then he gravely answered her: "This night, Dame Catherine, a great misfortune has overtaken us. You must not attribute it to Jean-Claude: it is by another's fault that we have lost the fruit of all our sacrifices!"

"Through whose fault?"

"That unlucky Labarbe's, who did not guard the defile of the Blutfeld. He died afterward fulfilling his duty; but that does not repair the disaster; and if Piorette does not come up in time to aid Hullin, all is lost; it will be necessary to abandon the road and to fight retreating."

"What! the Blutfeld is taken?"

"Yes, Mistress Catherine. Who the deuce could ever have thought that the Germans would enter that? A defile almost impracticable for foot-passengers, enclosed by rugged rocks, where the goatherds can barely descend with their flocks. Well, they marched that way, two at a time; they turned Roche-Creuse, crushed Labarbe, and then fell upon Jérome, who defended himself like a lion till nine in the evening; but, at last, he was obliged to take refuge in the pine-woods, and leave the pass to the *kaiserlichs*. That is the whole story. It is shocking. Indeed, there must be someone among us base and vile enough to have guided the enemy, and would deliver us over to him bound hands and feet. Oh, the wretch!" cried Lorquin, furiously. "I am not revengeful, but if he came into my clutches, how I would serve him! Up, Bruno! up, then!"

The partisans were marching along the bank like spectres, without saying a word.

The old farm-mistress became silent in order to collect her ideas.

"I begin to understand," said she at last. "We were attacked tonight on both sides."

"Exactly so, Catherine. Fortunately, ten minutes before the attack, one of Marc Divès's smugglers, Zimmer, the old dragoon, had come full gallop to warn us. Had it not been for that, we would have been lost. He fell in with our vanguard, after having run the gauntlet of a detachment of Cossacks on the plateau of

Grosmann. The poor fellow had received a terrible sabre-thrust; and his bowels were protruding over the saddle—was it not so, Frantz?"

"Yes," replied the hunter, sadly.

"And what did he say?" demanded Catherine.

"He had only time to cry, 'To arms! We are hemmed in! Jérome sends me. Labarbe is dead! The Germans have passed the Blutfeld!'"

"He was a gallant fellow," exclaimed Catherine.

"Yes, a gallant fellow," replied Frantz, with his head bent down.

Then they relapsed into silence, and for some time the sledge swept through the winding valley. Now and then they were obliged to stop, the snow was so deep—when three or four mountaineers would take the horse by the bridle—and so they continued their way.

"All the same," said Catherine, suddenly rousing up from her reverie, "Hullin might have told me."

"But if he had mentioned these two attacks," interrupted the doctor, "you would have wanted to remain."

"And who can hinder me from doing what I like? If it pleased me to get out of the sledge this very moment, should I not be free? I had forgiven Jean-Claude, but I am sorry for it!"

"Oh, Maman Lefèvre, supposing he is killed while you are saying that!" murmured Louise.

"She is right, poor child," thought Catherine; and then quickly added, "I said I was sorry for it; but he is such a good man, that one cannot be angry with him. I forgive him with all my heart; in his place I should have done the same."

Two or three hundred yards farther on they entered the defile of Roches. The snow had ceased falling, and the moon was shining between great white clouds. The narrow gorge, hemmed in by steep precipices, expanded in the distance, its sides covered with tall pines. Nothing disturbed the deep calm of the woods; one could have imagined one's self far away from all human agitation. The silence was so great that every step the horse made in the snow could be heard, and even his sharp quick breathing. Frantz Materne halted at times to gaze upon the black slopes, and then hurried on to overtake the others.

They crossed valley after valley; the sledge mounted and descended, now to the right and then to the left; and the partisans, with their bayonets fixed, followed continually.

Toward three in the morning they reached the meadow of Brimbelles, where at the present day an old oak can still be seen bending over the valley. To the left, in the midst of the snow-covered heather, behind a low stone wall, stood the old house of the guard Cuny. Three beehives were placed on a bench, a gnarled vine hung down from the roof and a small pine-bough was suspended over the door lay way of sign-board, for Cuny carried on the business of innkeeper in this solitary place.

At this spot the road runs close under the meadow wall, and as a large cloud obscured the light of the moon, the doctor, fearing to be upset, halted beneath the oak.

"We have only one hour's journey more, Mother Lefèvre," said he; "take courage; there is no hurry."

"Yes," said Frantz; "the heaviest part of the road is over, and the horse may breath a while."

The small party collected round the sledge, and the doctor got down. Some lit their pipes; but no one spoke: they were all busy thinking of the Donon. What was going on there? Would Jean-Claude be able to defend the plateau till Piorette arrived? So many dread thoughts and dismal reflections passed through the minds of the worthy people, that not one seemed able to speak.

They had been standing thus about five minutes, when the black cloud passed slowly away, and the pale moonlight lit up the gorge. Suddenly, a dark figure on horseback appeared two hundred paces from them, in the path between the pine-trees. By the light of the moon they quickly perceived that it was the figure of a Cossack with his sheepskin cap, and bearing a lance under his arm.

He was advancing slowly; Frantz was already taking aim,

when other Cossacks with their lances appeared behind him. They advanced deliberately in the direction of the sledge, like people on the search, some with their heads turned upward, others peering into the shrubs from their saddles. They numbered more than thirty.

Imagine the feelings of Louise and Catherine, seated in the middle of the road. They looked on open-mouthed. In another minute they would be surrounded by these bandits. The mountaineers were stupefied; it was impossible to return: they were hemmed in on one side by the meadow wall, on the other by the mountain-side. The old farm-wife seized Louise by the hand, and said, in a stifled voice, "Let us escape to the woods!"

She sprang from the sledge, leaving her shoe in the straw.

Suddenly one of the Cossacks uttered a guttural cry, which was repeated along the whole line.

"We are discovered!" exclaimed the doctor, as he drew his sword.

The words had scarcely escaped his lips when twelve musket-shots lit up the path from end to end; a regular savage whoop answered the report of the muskets. The Cossacks made off from the path to the meadow in front, gave their horses the reins, bent down in their saddles, and flew toward the guard-house like deer.

"Ha! they are off like the devil!" said the doctor.

But the worthy man was too hasty. Suddenly, when they had gone two or three hundred yards along the valley, the Cossacks again wheeled round and massed themselves firmly together; then, with their lances in rest, and bending over their horses' heads, they rushed straight at the partisans, shouting in hoarse voices—"Hourah! hourah!"

It was a terrible moment.

Frantz and the others sprang toward the wall, to protect the sledge.

In another second, the clashing of lances and screams of rage could alone be heard, mingled with imprecations. Under the shadow of the old oak, through the straggling moonbeams, could be seen the horses prancing with tossing manes, as they endeavoured to clear the meadow wall; while the barbarian Cossacks, with gleaming eyes and uplifted arms, struck furiously with their lances, advancing, retreating, and uttering piercing yells.

Louise, deathly pale, and Catherine, with her gray dishevelled hair, stood up in the straw.

Doctor Lorquin, in front of them, parried the strokes with his sabre, and all the time kept shouting to them—"Lie down! lie down!" But they did not hear him.

Louise, in the midst of the tumult and shouting, thought only of sheltering Catherine; and the old dame, in the midst of her terror, had recognized Yégof, on a tall, gaunt horse—Yégof, with his tin crown, bristling beard, long lance, and dog-skin floating from his shoulders. She saw him as distinctly as though it were broad daylight. He stood about ten feet distant, with sparkling eyes, brandishing his blue lance in the darkness, and striving to reach her.

What could she do? Submit to her fate! Thus do the most resolute characters succumb to inevitable destiny. The old dame thought her fate was sealed. She saw all these people tearing like wolves, thrusting and parrying in the moonlight. She saw some fall; and horses running, riderless through the fields. She saw the topmost window of the guard-house thrown open; and old Cuny, in his shirtsleeves, shoulder his gun, though not daring to fire into the crowd. All passed before her eyes with wonderful clearness.

"The madman has returned," she said to herself. "Do what they will, he will hang my head to the side of his saddle. It will end as I saw in my dream."

And, indeed, everything seemed to justify her fears: the mountaineers, inferior in numbers, were giving way. The Cossacks had cleared the wall, and were already on the footpath. A well-aimed thrust passed through the old dame's back-hair, and she felt the cold iron against her neck.

"Oh, the murderers!" she screamed, falling back and clutching fast at the reins.

Doctor Lorquin himself had been hurled against the sledge. Frantz and the others, surrounded by twenty Cossacks, could afford them no help. Louise felt a hand on her shoulder: it was the hand of the madman, seated on his great horse.

At this fearful moment, the poor child, mad with terror, uttered a scream of distress; then she saw something gleaming in the darkness: it was Lorquin's pistols. Quick as lightning, tearing them from the doctor's belt, she fired them off both at once, singeing Yégof's beard, and blowing out the brains of a Cossack who was bending toward her with flaming eyes. She then seized Catherine's whip, and pale as death, lashed the horse, who bounded away. The sledge flew through the bushes, swaying from right to left. Suddenly there was a shock. Catherine, Louise, the straw, and all rolled in the snow on the slopes of the ravine. The horse stopped short on its haunches, its mouth full of bloody foam. It had struck against an oak-tree.

Rapid as was the fall, Louise had seen figures passing like the wind behind the underwood. She had heard a powerful voice, that of Divès, crying out, "Forward! Cut them down!"

It was like a vision—one of those confused apparitions which pass before the eyes in moments of supreme danger; but, on rising, the young girl had no longer any doubts. Fighting was going on only a few paces distant behind the cover of some trees, and the voice of Marc was heard shouting, "Go it, my old fellows! Give them no quarter!"

Then she saw a dozen Cossacks clambering up the hill in front, like hares among the heather; below Yégof was crossing the valley in the moonlight with the speed of a terrified bird on the wing. Several shots were sent after him, but the madman remained unscathed, and, standing upright in his stirrups, with his horse at full gallop, he turned, waving his lance with bravado, and shouting "Hourah!" Two more shots whizzed by from the guard-house; a bit of rag fell from his loins, but the madman continued his course, crying "Hourah!" in a hoarse tone, and toiled up the path which his companions had taken before him.

All this passed before Louise like a dream.

Then, turning round, she saw Catherine by her side, stupefied and absorbed like herself. They gazed at each other for a moment, and then embraced with an inexpressible feeling of happiness.

"We are saved!" murmured Catherine; and they both wept. "Thou hast behaved bravely. Jean-Claude, Gaspard, and I have good reason to be proud of thee!"

Louise was deeply agitated and trembled all over. The danger being passed, her gentle nature again resumed its sway, and she could not understand whence came her courage of a few minutes before.

They were recovering from their fright and about to get into the sledge, when they saw five or six partisans with the doctor coming toward them.

"Ah! you may cry as much as you like, Louise," said Lorquin; "but, for all that, you are a regular dragoon, a real little warrior. Though you now look so gentle, we have all seen you at work. But where are my pistols?"

At that moment the shrubs were pushed aside, and Marc Divès, sword in hand, appeared.

"Ah, Mistress Catherine, these are rough adventures for you. Zounds! what luck that I happened to come up. Those villains were spoiling you right and left."

"Yes," replied she, pushing her hair under her cap again; "it was very fortunate."

"Very fortunate! I should think so. It is only ten minutes since I arrived with my wagon at Cuny's. 'Do not go to the Donon,' said he; 'the sky has been red for an hour in that direction; there is certainly fighting going on up there.'

"'You think so?'

"'Faith! yes.'

"'Then Joson must go out and reconnoitre a little and we others will drink a glass while waiting.'

"'Good!' Hardly had Joson left, when I heard shouts as though five hundred devils were let loose.

"'What is it, Cuny?'

"'I don't know.' We pushed open the door, and saw the fray. Ha!" exclaimed the big smuggler, "we did not wait long. I jumped on my brave horse Fox, and dashed forward. What luck!"

"Ah!" said Catherine, "if we were only sure that our affairs go as well on the Donon, we might then rejoice."

"Yes, yes! Frantz told me about that:—it is the devil—there must always be something wrong," replied Marc. "But—but why stay here with our feet in the snow? Let us hope that Piorette will not allow his comrades to be crushed, and let us go and empty our glasses, which we left half full."

Four other smugglers then arrived, saying that that rascally Yégof would probably come back, with some more brigands like himself.

"Very likely," replied Divès. "We will return to the Falkenstein, since, it is Jean-Claude's orders; but we can't bring our wagon with us: it would prevent our taking the short cuts; and in an hour all these bandits would be down upon us. Let us go first to Cuny's. Catherine and Louise will not be sorry to drink a little wine; and the others too. It will put their hearts in the right place again. Up Bruno!"

He led his horse by the bridle. Two wounded men had been laid in the sledge; two others having been killed, as well as seven or eight Cossacks stretched with their boots wide apart in the snow, were abandoned, and they went on toward the forester's house.

Frantz was consoling himself for not having been on the Donon: he had finished two Cossacks, and the sight of the inn made him feel in a good humour. Before the door stood the small wagon full of cartridges. Cuny came out, saying: "A hearty welcome, Mistress Lefèvre. What a night for women! Be seated! What is going on up there?"

While they were hastily drinking some wine, everything had to be explained over again. The worthy old man in a blouse and green breeches, with, his wrinkled face, bald head, and wide-open eyes, listened with clasped hands, exclaiming: "Good God!

Good God! in what times are we living? One can no longer follow the high-roads without risk of being attacked. It is worse than the old Swedish tales." And he shook his head.

"Come," said Divès, "time flies. We must continue our way."

Everybody being ready, the smugglers led the wagon, which contained some thousands of cartridges and two small kegs of brandy, about three hundred yards off, to the middle of the valley, and then unharnessed the horses.

"Go forward!" shouted Marc; "we will re- join you in a few minutes."

"But what art thou going to do with the cart?" said Frantz. "Since we have no time to take it to the Falkenstein, it had better be left under Cuny's shed than in the road."

"Yes, to get the poor old man hanged, when the Cossacks arrive, for they will be here in less than an hour. Do not trouble thyself; I have my own idea."

Frantz rejoined the sledge, which went on its way. In a short time they passed by the saw-works of the Marquis and turned sharp to the right, to reach the farm of Bois-de-Chênes, whose tall chimneys could be perceived three-quarters of a league distant on the plateau. They were on the hillside when Marc Divès and his men overtook them, shouting:

"Halt! Stop a bit! Look down there!"

And, looking down into the gorge, they saw the Cossacks capering round the wagon—about three hundred of them.

"They are coming! Let us fly!" cried Louise.

"Wait a bit," said the smuggler. "We have nothing to fear."

He was still speaking, when an immense sheet of flame sped out from one mountain to the other, illuminating the woods, rocks, and the little house of the forester fifteen hundred yards below; then there was a report so terrible that the earth seemed to tremble.

While those near him gazed in bewilderment and dumb terror at each other, Marc's bursts of laughter reached their ears, in spite of the din.

"Ha, ha, ha!" shouted he, "I was sure the rogues would stop

round the wagon, to drink up my brandy. I knew the match would have just time to reach the powder!"

"Do you think they will pursue us?"

"Their arms and legs are now hanging from the branches of the pine-trees! Come along! And may heaven grant the same fate to all those who have now crossed the Rhine!"

The whole escort, the partisans, the doctor, all had grown silent: so many terrible emotions had filled them with endless thoughts such as do not fall within the experience of everyday life. They said to themselves: "What are men that they destroy, harass, and ruin each other in this manner? Why do they hate each other so? And what spirit of evil is it that thus excites them?"

But Divès and his men were not at all troubled by these events: they galloped along, laughing and boasting.

"For my part," said the big smuggler, "I never saw such a farce before. Ha, ha, ha! if I lived a thousand years, I should laugh at it still." Then he became more serious, and exclaimed: "All the same, Yégof is the cause of this. One must be blind not to see that it was he who led the Germans to the Blutfeld. I shall be sorry if he has been struck down by a piece of my wagon; I have something better in store for him than that.

"All that I wish is that he may keep in good health till we meet somewhere in a lonely corner of the wood. It is no matter whether it be in one year, ten years, twenty years, provided only that we meet. The longer it is deferred, the more savage my determination becomes: the daintiest morsels are eaten cold, like a boar's head in white wine." He said this with an air of good-humour, but those who knew him perceived beneath it a serious danger for Yégof .

Half an hour later, they all reached the plateau on which the farm of Bois-de-Chênes was situated.

CHAPTER 21

"All is Lost"

Jérome of St. Quirin had managed to make good his retreat to the farm, and since midnight he had occupied the plateau.

"Who goes there?" cried his sentinels as the escort approached.

"It is we, from the village of Charmes," shouted Marc, in his stentorian voice.

The sentinels approached to examine them, and then they passed on their way.

The farm was silent; a sentry, his musket over his arm, was pacing before the granary, where about thirty partisans were asleep upon the straw. At the sight of these great dark roofs, the stables and outhouses belonging to the old building where she had spent her youth, where her father and grandfather had led their tranquil laborious lives in peace, and which she was now about to abandon, perhaps forever, Catherine felt a terrible wrenching at her heart; but no word escaped her. Springing from the sledge, as in other days when she returned from marketing, she said: "Come, Louise, here we are at home, thank God."

Old Duchêne pushed open the door, exclaiming: "Is that you, Madame Lefèvre?"

"Yes, it is I. Any news from Jean-Claude?"

"No, Madame."

They entered the large kitchen. Some cinders were still smouldering on the hearth, and in the dark, under the broad chimney, was sitting Jérome of St. Quirin, with his big horsehair hood, his great stick between his knees, and his carbine leaning against the wall.

"Good-day, Jérome," said the old farm-wife.

"Good-day, Catherine," replied the grave chief of the Grosmann. "Have you come from the Donon?"

"Yes: things are going badly, my poor Jérome. The *kaiserlichs* were attacking the farm when we left the plateau. Nothing but white uniforms was to be seen on every side. They were already beginning to cross the breastworks."

"Then you think Hullin will be compelled to abandon the road?"

"Possibly, if Piorette does not come to his assistance."

The partisans had approached near the fire. Marc Divès bent over the cinders to light his pipe; on rising, he exclaimed: "I ask thee one thing only, Jérome; I know beforehand that they fought well under thy command—"

"We have done our duty," replied the shoemaker. "There are sixty men stretched on the slopes of the Grosmann who will tell you so at the last day."

"Yes; but who, then, guided the Germans? They could not have discovered the pass of the Blutfeld by themselves."

"Yégof the madman—Yégof," said Jérome, whose gray eyes, encircled by deep wrinkles and thick white eyebrows, seemed to sparkle in the darkness.

"Ah! art thou certain of it?"

"Labarbe's men saw him climbing up; he led the others."

The partisans looked at each other with indignation.

At this moment Doctor Lorquin, who had remained outside to unharness the horse, opened the door, shouting: "The battle is lost! Here are our men from the Donon. I have just heard Lagarmitte's horn."

It is easy to imagine the emotion of the recipients of these tidings. Each thought of the relations and friends that he might never see again; and from the kitchen and the granary everybody at once rushed on to the "plateau." At the same time Robin and Dubourg, posted as sentinels above Bois-de-Chênes, cried out,

"Who goes there?"

"France!" replied a voice.

Notwithstanding the distance, Louise, fancying she could recognize her father's voice, was seized with such a fit of trembling that Catherine was compelled to support her.

Just then the noise of many footsteps resounded over the hardened snow, and Louise, unable to contain herself any longer, exclaimed, "Papa Jean-Claude!"

"I am coming," replied Hullin, "I am coming."

"My father?" exclaimed Frantz Materne, rushing to meet Jean-Claude.

"He is with us, Frantz."

"And Kasper?"

"He has received a slight scratch, but it is nothing. Thou wilt see them both again."

Catherine threw herself into Jean-Claude's arms.

"Oh, Jean-Claude, what joy to behold you once more!"

"Yes," replied the worthy man, in a suppressed voice, "there are many who will never see their friends again."

"Frantz," said old Materne, "here, this way!"

And one could only see, on all sides, people seeking each other in the dim light, squeezing hands, and embracing. Some called for, "Niclau! Sapheri!" but many did not answer to their names.

Then the voices became hoarse, as though stifled, and relapsed into silence. The joy of some, and the consternation of others, produced a terrible sensation. Louise was in Hullin's arms, sobbing bitterly.

"Ah, Jean-Claude," said Mother Lefèvre, "you will hear strange things about that child. I will say no more now, but we have been attacked—"

"Yes, we will talk of that later; our time is short," said Hullin. "The road to the Donon is lost, the Cossacks may be here at daylight, and we have many things to arrange."

He turned the corner and entered the farm, all following him. Duchêne had just thrown a fagot on the fire. All these people, with faces blackened by powder, still animated by the combat, their clothes torn by bayonet-thrusts, some blood-stained, advancing from the darkness into the light, presented a strange spectacle. Kasper, whose forehead was bandaged with his handkerchief, had received a sabre-cut; his bayonet, buff facings, and high blue gaiters, were stained with blood. Old Materne, thanks to his imperturbable presence of mind, returned safe and sound from the fray.

The remains of Jérome's and Hullin's troops were thus once more united. They wore the same wild physiognomies, animated by the same energy and desire for vengeance. But Hullin's men, harassed by fatigue, sat down right and left, on the fagots, on the stone sink, on the low pavement of the hearth—their heads in their hands and elbows on their knees; while Jérome's, who could not be convinced of the disappearance of Hans, Joson, and Daniel, looked about everywhere, exchanging questions, broken by long pauses. Materne's two sons held each other by the arm, as though afraid of losing one another, and their father, behind them, leaning against the wall, with his elbow on his gun, watched them with an expression of satisfaction.

"There they are, I see them," he seemed to say: "two famous fellows! They have saved their skins, both of them." If any one came to ask him about Pierre, Jacques, or Nicolas, his son or his brother, he would reply hap-hazard—"Yes, yes, there are several lying down there on their backs. What can you expect? It is war! Your Nicolas has done his duty. You must console yourself." Meanwhile he thought—"Mine are out of the scrimmage; that is the chief thing."

Catherine and Louise were busy preparing supper. Duchêne came up from the cellar with a barrel of wine on his shoulder. He set it down, and knocked out the bung; and each partisan presented his flask or cup to be filled with the purple liquid which glittered in the firelight.

"Eat and drink," said the old dame to them: "all is not lost yet; you will have need of your strength again. Here, Frantz, unhook those hams for me. Here is bread and knives. Sit down,

MANY OF THEM WILL NEVER AGAIN SEE THEIR FRIENDS

my children."

Frantz reached down the hams in the chimney with his bayonet.

The benches were brought forward; they sat down, and notwithstanding their sorrows, they eat with that vigorous appetite which neither present griefs nor thoughts for the future can make a mountaineer forget. But it did not prevent a bitter sadness from filling the hearts of these brave men; and first one and then another would stop suddenly, letting fall his fork, and leave the table, saying—"I have had enough!"

While the partisans were thus engaged in recruiting their strength, the chiefs were assembled in the next room to make some last resolutions for the defence. They sat round the table; on which was placed a tin lamp: Doctor Lorquin, with his dog Pluto, looking inquiringly into his master's face; Jérome, in the corner of the window to the right; Hullin to the left, very pale; Marc Divès, his elbow on the table and cheek in his hand, and his back turned to the door, showed only his brown profile and the tip of his long moustache. Materne alone remained standing, leaning, as was his custom, against the wall behind Lorquin's chair, with his carbine at his feet. The noise of the men in the kitchen could be distinctly heard.

When Catherine, summoned by Jean-Claude, entered the room, she heard a sort of groan which made her shudder. It was Hullin who was speaking.

"All these brave lads—all these fathers of families, who fell one after the other," he cried, in a heartrending voice, "do you think I did not feel it? Do you think that I would not rather a thousand times have been killed myself? You do not know what I have suffered this night! To lose one's life is nothing; but to bear alone the weight of such a responsibility—"

He paused: his trembling lips, the tear which trickled slowly down his cheek, his attitude, all is showed the scruples of the worthy man, in face of one of those situations where conscience itself hesitates and seeks further support. Catherine went and sat down quietly in the big armchair. A few seconds later

Hullin continued in a calmer tone:—"Between eleven o'clock and midnight, Zimmer came up, shouting, 'We are turned! The Germans are coming down the Grosmann! Labarbe is crushed! Jérome can hold out no longer!' What was to be done! Could I beat a retreat? Could I abandon a position which had cost us so much blood—the road to the Donon, the road to Paris?

"If I had done so, should I not have been a coward? But I had only three hundred men against four thousand at Grandfontaine, and I know not how many descending from the mountain! Well, I decided at any cost to hold it; it was our duty. I said to myself, ' Life is nothing without honour! We will all die; but they shall not say that we have yielded the high-road to France. No, no; they shall not say that.'"

At this moment Hullin's voice faltered, and his eyes filled with tears, as he continued—"We held out; my brave children held out till two o'clock. I saw them fall: they fell shouting, '*Vive la France!*' I had warned Piorette in the beginning of the action. He came up quickly, with fifty stout men. It was too late. The enemy poured in on every side; they held three parts of the plain, and forced us back among the pine-forests on the Blanru side; their fire burst upon us.

"All I could do was to assemble my wounded, those who could still drag along, and put them under Piorette's escort; a hundred of my men joined him. For myself, I only kept fifty to occupy the Falkenstein. We had to pass right through the Germans, who wanted to cut off our retreat. Happily, the night was dark; had it not been for that, not one of us would have escaped. That is how we are situated. All is lost! The Falkenstein alone remains ours, and we are reduced to three hundred men. Now the question is, shall we go on to the end?

"I have already told you that I dread to bear alone such a responsibility. So long as it concerned defending the road to the Donon, there was no doubt about it: every man belongs to his country. But this road is lost. "We should need ten thousand men to retake it; and at this very moment the enemy is entering Lorraine. Come, what is to be done?"

"We must go on to the end," said Jérome.

"Yes, yes!" cried the others.

"Is that your opinion, Catherine?"

"Certainly," exclaimed the old dame, whoso features expressed an inflexible tenacity.

Then Hullin, in a firmer tone, explained his plan:—"The Falkenstein is our point of retreat. It is our arsenal; it is there that we have our ammunition; the enemy knows it; he will attempt an attack on that side, therefore all of us here present must make an effort to defend it, so that the whole country may see us and say, 'Catherine Lefèvre, Jérome, Materne and his boys, Hullin, and Doctor Lorquin are there. They will not lay down their arms.'

"This idea will give fresh courage to all manly hearts. Besides, Piorette will remain in the woods; his troops will grow more numerous day by day: the country will be filled with Cossacks and marauders of every description; when the enemy's army shall have entered Lorraine I will signal to Piorette; he will throw himself between the Donon and the highway, so that all the laggers behind scattered over the mountains will be caught as in a trap. We shall also be able to profit by favourable chances to carry off the convoys of the Germans, to harass their reserves, and, if fortune aids us, as we must hope it will, and all these *kaiserlichs* are beaten in Lorraine by our army, then we can cut off their retreat."

Everybody got up, and Hullin going into the kitchen, pronounced this simple address to the mountaineers:—"My friends, we have decided that we must push our resistance to the end. Nevertheless, everyone is free to do as he likes; to lay down his arms and return to his village; but let those who wish to revenge themselves join us; they will share our last morsel of bread and our last cartridge."

Colon, the old wood-floater, arose and said, "Hullin, we are all with thee; we began to fight together, and so will we finish."

"Yes, yes!" they all shouted.

"Have you all decided? Well, listen. Jérome's brother will take the command."

"My brother is dead," interrupted Jérome; "he lies on the slopes of the Grosmann."

There was a moment's pause; then in a loud voice Hullin continued:"Colon, thou wilt take the command of all those that remain, with the exception of the men who formed Catherine Lefèvre's escort, and whom I shall keep with me. Thou wilt go and rejoin Piorette in the valley of Blanru, passing by the 'Two Rivers.'"

"And the ammunition?" said Marc Divès.

"I have brought up my wagon-load," said Jérome; "Colon can use it."

"Let the dray be loaded," said Catherine; "the Cossacks are coming, and will pillage everything. Our men must not leave empty-handed; let them take away the cows, oxen, and calves-everything: it will be so much gained on the enemy."

Five minutes later the farm was being ransacked; the dray was loaded with hams, smoked meats, and bread; the cattle were led out of the stables, the horses harnessed to the great wagon, and soon the convoy began its march, Robin at the head, blowing on his horn, with the partisans behind pushing at the wheels. When it had disappeared in the road, and silence had succeeded to all the noise, Catherine turning round, beheld Hullin behind her.

"Well, Catherine," said he, "all is finished! We are now going to make our way up there."

Frantz, Kasper, and those of the escort, with Marc Divès and Materne, all armed, were waiting in the kitchen.

"Duchêne," said the good woman, "go down to the village; you must not be ill-treated by the enemy on my account."

The old servant shook his white head, and, with his eyes full of tears, replied:—"I may as well die here, Madame Lefèvre. It is nearly fifty years since I came to the farm. Do not make me leave; it would be the death of me."

"Do as you like, my poor Duchêne," replied Catherine, softly; "here are the keys of the house."

And the poor old man sat down in the chimney-corner, on

a settee, with fixed eyes and half -open mouth, as though lost in some painful reverie.

Then began the journey to the Falkenstein. Marc Divès, on horseback, sword in hand, formed the rear-guard. Frantz and Hullin watched the plateau to the left; Kasper and Jérome the valley to the right: Materne and the men of the escort surrounded the women. It was a singular sight. Before the cottages of the village of Charmes, on the doorsteps, at the windows and loopholes, appeared the faces of young and old, looking at the flight of Mother Lefèvre; nor did their evil tongues spare her:- "Ah! they are turned out at last," cried some; "another time, do not meddle with what does not concern you."

Others reflected with a loud voice, that Catherine had been rich long enough, and that everyone should have his turn at poverty. As for the industry, wisdom, kind-heartedness, and all the virtues of the old farm-wife, or Jean-Claude's patriotism, or the courage of Jérome and the three Maternes, the disinterested motives of Doctor Lorquin or Marc Divès's self-sacrifice, nobody ever mentioned them; for were they not vanquished?

CHAPTER 22

On The Falkenstein

At the end of the valley of Bouleaux, two gunshots from the village of Charmes, to the left, the little troop began slowly to ascend the path to the old *burg*. Hullin, remembering how he had taken the same road when he went to buy powder of Marc Divès, could not help feeling very sad. Then, notwithstanding his journey to Phalsbourg, the spectacle of the wounded from Leipzig and Hanau, and the account given by the old sergeant, he did not despair or doubt of the success of the defence. Now all was lost; the enemy were descending into Lorraine, and the mountaineers were retreating. Marc Divès rode by the side of the wall in the snow; his horse, apparently accustomed to this journey, neighed loudly. The smuggler turned from time to time to look back on the plateau of Bois-de-Chênes. Suddenly he exclaimed, "Look! here come the Cossacks!"

They all halted to look. They were already high up on the mountain, above the village and farm of Bois-de-Chênes. The morning mists were giving way to the gray light of the winter's day, and, on the hillside could be distinguished the forms of several Cossacks, with their heads raised, and pistols pointed, stealthily approaching the old farmhouse. They were scattered after the manner of sharpshooters, as if they feared a surprise. A few minutes later more appeared, ascending the valley of Houx, then still more, all in the same attitude, upright in their stirrups, in order to see as far as possible. The first, having passed by the farm and observing nothing threatening, waved their lances and returned half way back. Whereupon the others galloped up at full speed like a flock of crows when they have sighted their prey. In a few minutes the farm was surrounded and the door opened. In another moment the windows were smashed, and the furniture, mattresses, and linen, thrown outside. Catherine calmly looked on at the pillage. She said nothing for some time; but, on seeing Yégof, whom she had not perceived before, strike Duchêne with the butt-end of his lance, and push him out of the farm, she could not restrain a cry of indignation.

"The wretch! Could anyone be cowardly enough to strike a poor old man unable to defend himself. Ah! brigand, if I only held thee!"

"Come along, Catherine," said Jean-Claude; "that's enough; what is the use of gazing at such a spectacle any longer?"

"You are right," said the old mistress; "let us go on, or I shall be tempted to go back and revenge myself."

On approaching the red rocks, incrusted with large white and black pebbles, overhanging the precipice like the arches of an immense cathedral, Louise and Catherine stopped in ecstasy. The magnificent view of the streams of Lorraine, and the blue ribbon of the Rhine to their right, with the distant woods and valleys, filled them with joy, and the old dame said piously, "Jean-Claude, He who created these rocks, and formed these valleys, forests, heaths, and mosses, He will render to us the justice we merit."

As they were gazing thus on the rugged precipices, Marc led his horse into a cavern close by, and, returning, began to climb up before them, saying, "Take care, or you may slip!"

At the same time he pointed to the blue precipice on their right, with pine-trees at the bottom. Everybody then relapsed into silence till the terrace was reached, where the Arch, commenced. There they breathed more freely. In the middle of the passage were the smugglers Brenn, Pfeifer, and Joubac, with their long gray mantles and black hats, sitting round a fire. Marc Divès said to them, "Here we are! The *kaiserlichs* are masters. Zimmer was killed last night. Is Hexe-Baizel up there?"

THERE GO UP IN SMOKE FORTY YEARS OF TOIL AND TROUBLE

"Yes," replied Brenn; "she is making cartridges."

"They may be of use," said Marc. "Keep your eyes open, and if any come up fire on them."

The Maternes halted at the corner of the rock; and these three sturdy men, with their powerful muscular limbs, their hats pushed back, and carbines on their shoulders, offered a curious spectacle in the blue mists of the abyss. Old Materne was pointing with outstretched hand to a small white speck in the distance, almost hidden in the midst of the pines. "Do you recognize that, my boys?" said he; and they all three peered through their half-closed eyes.

"It is our house," replied Kasper.

"Poor Margrédel!" rejoined the old hunter, after a short pause; "how uneasy she must have been these last eight days? What prayers does she not offer up for us to Saint-Odile?"

At that moment Marc Divès, who was walking on in front, uttered an exclamation of surprise.

"Mother Lefèvre," said he, stopping short, "the Cossacks are burning your farm."

Catherine received the tidings very calmly, and advanced to the edge of the terrace, Louise and Jean-Claude following. At the bottom of the abyss was a great white cloud, through which could be seen a bright spark, as it were, on the side of Bois-de-Chênes—that was all; but at intervals, when the wind blew strong, the flames shot up, the two high black gables, the hay-loft, the small stables burned brightly, then all disappeared once more.

"It is nearly finished," said Hullin, in a low voice.

"Yes," replied Catherine; "there are the labour and trouble of forty years vanishing in smoke; but they cannot burn my good land, nor the great meadow of Eichmath. We will begin our work over again. Gaspard and Louise will repair it all. I regret nothing I have done."

A quarter of an hour later thousands of sparks arose, and the building crumbled to the ground. The black gables alone remained standing. They continued to ascend the path. As they were ascending the higher terrace, they heard the sharp voice of Hexe-Baizel.

"Is it thou, Catherine?" she cried. "Ah, I never thought thou wouldst have come to see me in my wretched hole."

Baizel and Catherine Lefèvre had been at school together in former days, therefore they used the third person when speaking.

"Nor I neither," replied the old farm-mistress. "All the same, Baizel—one is glad to find in misfortune an old companion of one's childhood."

Baizel seemed touched by her words.

"All that is here, Catherine, is thine," she exclaimed; "everything!"

She pointed to her miserable stool, the furze broom, and the five or six fagots on the hearth. Catherine looked on a few moments in silence, and then said: "It is not grand, but it is solid; at least, they will not be able to burn down thy house."

"No, they will not burn it," said Hexe-Baizel, laughing; "they would need all the wood of the province of Dabo even to warm it a little. Ha! ha! ha!"

After so many fatigues, the partisans stood in need of repose. They all placed their guns against the wall, and lay down on the ground to sleep, Marc Divès having opened the second cavern to them, where they at least were sheltered. Marc then went out with Hullin to examine their position.

CHAPTER 13

Marc Divès's Mission

On the rock of the Falkenstein, high up in the clouds, stands a tower, somewhat sunken at its base. This tower, overgrown with brambles, hawthorn, and bilberries, is as old as the mountain; neither the French, Germans, nor Swedes have destroyed it. The stone and cement are so solidly combined that not even a fragment can be detached from it. It looks gloomy and mysterious, carrying one back to ancient times, beyond the memory of man.

At that time of the year when the wild-geese migrated in flocks, Marc Divès, when he had nothing better to do, used to await them hidden in the tower, and sometimes at nightfall, when the flocks came through the fogs flying in large circles before resting, he would bring down two or three, much to the satisfaction of Hexe-Baizel, who was always very willing to put them on a spit. Often, too, in the autumn, Marc laid traps in the bushes, where he caught thrushes. The old tower also served him as a wood-house.

Divès, perceiving that his wood, covered with snow and soaked by rain, gave more smoke than light, had covered in the old tower with a roof of planks. With reference to this occasion, the smuggler related a curious story. He pretended that, on laying the rafters, he had discovered, at the bottom of a fissure, a snow-white owl, blind and feeble, but supplied with quantities of bats and fieldmice. He therefore called it the "grandmother of the country," as he supposed that all the birds came to feed it on account of its extreme old age.

Toward the close of the day, the partisans posted round the rock saw the white uniforms appearing in the neighbouring gorges. They poured in on all sides in large numbers, thereby clearly showing their determination to blockade the Falkenstein. Perceiving this, Marc Divès became more thoughtful. "If they surround us," said he, "we shall not be able to procure food, and shall have to surrender or die of hunger."

The enemy's staff on horseback could be clearly distinguished, halting round the fountain of the village of Charmes. There also stood a tall chief with a large paunch, who was contemplating the rock through a telescope. Behind him was Yégof, whom from time to time he turned round to question. The women and children formed a circle beyond them, apparently highly delighted, and five or six Cossacks pranced about. The smuggler could not contain himself any longer, and, taking Hullin aside, "Look," said he, "at that long line of shakos gliding along the Sarre, and at the others who are scaling the valley on this side like hares; they are *kaiserlichs*, aren't they? Well, what are they going to do, Jean-Claude?"

"They are going to surround the mountain, that is clear. How many are there, dost thou think?"

"From three to four thousand men, without counting those who are walking over the country. Well, what can Piorette do against this pack of vagabonds with three hundred men? I ask thee frankly, Hullin."

"He can do nothing," replied the worthy man, simply. "The Germans know that our ammunition is on the Falkenstein; they dread an insurrection after they enter Lorraine, and wish to insure their rear. The enemy's general knows that we cannot be taken by mere force, he is deciding to reduce us by hunger. All that is true, Marc; but we are men: we will do our duty—we will die here!"

There was a short silence; Marc Divès frowned, and did not seem at all convinced.

"We will die!" he replied, scratching his head. "I do not see why we should die at all; it is not our intention to die: too many people would be gratified by it."

"What wouldst thou do?" said Hullin, dryly. "Wouldst thou surrender?"

"Surrender!" exclaimed the smuggler. "Dost thou take me for a coward?"

"Then explain thyself."

"This evening I start for Phalsbourg. I risk my skin in crossing the enemy's lines; but I like that better than folding my arms here, and perishing with hunger. I will enter the town on the first 'sortie,' or I will endeavour to climb one of the gates. The commandant, Meunier, knows me. I have sold him tobacco for three years. Like thyself, he has gone through the campaigns of Italy and Egypt. Well, I will explain everything to him. I shall see Gaspard Lefèvre. I will so arrange that they will give us, perhaps, a company. Dost thou see, Jean-Claude, that the uniform alone would save us? All the brave men who remain will join Piorette; and in any case we shall be delivered. That is my idea. What dost thou think of it?"

He looked at Hullin, whose gloomy, fixed expression made him uneasy.

"Dost thou not think that a chance?"

"It is an idea," said Jean-Claude at last. "I do not oppose it." And, looking full in the smuggler's face, "Swear to me to do thy best to enter the town."

"I will swear nothing," replied Marc, whose brown cheeks were covered with a flush. "I leave all my possessions here, my wife, my comrades, Catherine Lefèvre, and thee, my oldest friend! If I do not return, I shall be a traitor; but if I return, Jean-Claude, thou shalt explain what thou meanest by thy demand: we will settle this little affair between us."

"Marc," said Hullin, "forgive me! I have suffered much these last days. I was wrong. Misfortune makes one distrustful. Give me thy hand. Go! Save us, save Catherine, save my child! I say so now: our only resource is in thee."

Hullin's voice faltered. Divès relented; but he rejoined: "All

403

the same, Hullin, thou shouldst not have said that to me at such a time. Never let us speak of it again. I will leave my skin on the way, or return to deliver you. This evening, when darkness sets in, I will leave. The *kaiserlichs* surround the mountain already; but no matter, I have a good horse, and, besides, I have always been lucky."

By six o'clock the highest peaks were hid in darkness. Hundreds of fires, sparkling in the depths of the gorges, announced that the Germans were preparing their repasts.

Marc Divès felt his way down the narrow path. Hullin listened for a few seconds to the retreating steps of his comrade, then walked anxiously toward the old tower, where their headquarters were established. He lifted the thick woollen covering which closed the owl's-nest, and perceived Catherine, Louise, and the others crouching round a small fire. The old farm-mistress sat on an oak log, her hands clasped round her knees, watching the flames fixedly, with compressed lips. Louise leant dreamily against the wall. Jérome stood behind Catherine, his hands crossed on his stick, his otter-skin cap touching the mouldy roof. All were sad and discouraged. Hexe-Baizel, who was lifting the lid of a kettle, and Doctor Lorquin, who was scratching the softer parts of the old wall with the point of his sabre, alone preserved their usual expression.

"Here we are," said the doctor, "returned to the days of the Triboques. These walls are more than two thousand years old. A great deal of water must have flowed from the heights of the Falkenstein and Grosmann to the Sarre and Rhine since a fire was last kindled in this tower."

"Yes," replied Catherine, as though awaking from a dream; "and many besides ourselves have suffered cold, hunger, and misery here. Who knew of it? No one. And one, or two, or three hundred years hence, others, perhaps, will again come for shelter to this place. They will find, as we have, the wall cold, and the earth damp; they will make a fire; they will look as we look; and they will say, like us, 'Who suffered here before ourselves? Why did they suffer? They must have been pursued and hunted, like ourselves, to be obliged to come and hide in this wretched hole.' And they will think of past times; and no one will reply."

Jean-Claude came up to them. The old dame, raising her head, and looking at him, said, "Well! we are blockaded; the enemy wants to subdue us by famine."

"True, Catherine," replied Hullin; "but I did not expect that. I felt certain of a sudden attack; but the *kaiserlichs* have not gained all yet. Divès has just left for Phalsbourg. He knows the commandant of the place; and if they will only send a few hundred men to our help—"

"Do not count on that," interrupted the old woman. "Marc may be taken or killed by the Germans: and, if not, and suppose he manages to cross their lines, how will he be able to enter Phalsbourg? You well know that the town is besieged by the Russians."

Then everybody relapsed into silence. Hexe-Baizel brought up the soup, and they sat in a circle round the smoking bowl.

CHAPTER 24

A Flag Of Truce

Catherine Lefèvre came out of the ancient ruin about seven in the morning; Louise and Hexe-Baizel were still asleep; but broad daylight, the clear light of the high regions, was already penetrating the abysses. In the depths, through the azure, the woods, valleys, and rocks could be clearly traced, like the mosses and pebbles of a lake beneath the blue crystal water. Not a breath disturbed the air; and Catherine, gazing over this grand spectacle, felt a calmness and tranquillity beyond even that which comes of sleep.

"What are our miseries of a day," thought she, "our uneasinesses and our sufferings? Why pester heaven with our moans? why fear the future? All this lasts but a second; our sighs are of no more avail than the chirp of the grasshopper in autumn; and do its cries prevent winter from coming? Must not time pursue its course, and everything die to be renewed?"

Thus thought the old dame, and she had no longer any fears for the future. She had been thus musing for a few instants, when suddenly a hum of voices struck her ears: she turned, and saw Hullin with the three smugglers, talking seriously together on the other side of the plateau. They were engaged in a grave discussion, and had not noticed her. Catherine approached closer to them, and heard the following conversation:—

"Then you do not think it possible for anyone to get down either side?"

"No, Jean-Claude, it is quite impossible," replied Brenn;

"those brigands know the country thoroughly well: all the paths are guarded. Hold, look along the paths of that stream: we never dreamt of observing it even; well! they are defending that now. And over there, on the passage of the Rothstein, a path only for a goat, which is not trodden once in ten years—thou canst see a bayonet sparkle behind the rock, canst thou not? And that nearer path along which I have slipped with my bags for these eight years past without meeting a single *gendarme*, they occupy that also: the devil certainly must have showed them all the defiles."

"Yes," exclaimed Joubac, "if the devil has nothing to do with it, at least Yégof has!"

"But," continued Hullin, "it seems to me that three or four men might, if they liked, push through one of those posts."

"No, those posts lean one on the other; at the first shot one would have a whole regiment upon one's shoulders," replied Brenn. "Besides, supposing one had the luck to get through, how could one return with provisions? My opinion is, that it is impossible."

There was a pause.

"After that," said Joubac, "if Hullin likes we will try all the same."

"We will try what?" said Brenn. "To break our legs in escaping ourselves, and leave the others in the trap. I don't mind; if any others go, I will too. But as for pretending to return with provisions, it is impossible. Come, Joubac, by which way art thou going, and by which way wilt thou return? If thou knowest of a passage, tell me. For twenty years I have scoured the mountain with Marc. I know all the paths and roads ten leagues round, and I see no other way but through the sky!"

Hullin turned round at that moment and saw Mother Lefèvre, close behind, listening attentively.

"What! were you there, Catherine?" said he. "Our affairs are taking a bad turn."

"Yes, I heard; there is no means of renewing our provisions."

"Our provisions!" said Brenn with a queer laugh. "Are you aware, Mother Lefèvre, for how long we have them?"

"Why, for a fortnight," replied the old dame.

"For a week," said the smuggler, shaking out the ashes from his pipe.

"It is true," said Hullin, "Marc Divès and myself thought they would attack the Falkenstein; we never imagined the enemy would blockade it like a fortress. We have been deceived!"

"And what is to be done?" said Catherine, turning pale.

"We are going to put everybody on half rations. If, in a fortnight, Marc does not return we shall have nothing left—then we shall see."

So saying, Hullin, Catherine, and the smugglers, with bowed heads, took the path to the breach again. As they were coming down the slope, thirty feet below them they perceived Materne. He was climbing breathlessly among the ruins, and clutched hold of the bushes to help him along faster.

"Well," shouted Jean-Claude to him; "what is the matter, old fellow?"

"Ah! there thou art. I was coming to find thee; one of the enemy's officers has come forward on the wall of the old *burg.* with a little white flag; he looks as though he had something to say to us."

Hullin advanced immediately to the edge of the rock, and saw a German officer standing on the wall, and awaiting a signal to mount. He was about two gunshots distant; farther behind five or six soldiers were stationed with their arms shouldered. After having inspected this group, Jean-Claude turned and said: "It is a flag of truce. He comes no doubt to summon us to surrender."

"Fire upon them!" cried Catherine; "it is all we have to say."

All the others appeared of the same advice, excepting Hullin, who, without making any reply descended to the terrace, where the rest of the partisans were assembled.

"My children," said he, "the enemy sends us a flag of truce. We do not know what he wants of us. I suppose it is to order us to lay down our arms; but it may possibly be something else. Frantz and Kasper will go to meet him; they must blindfold the officer and lead him here."

No objection being made, Materne's sons shouldered their carbines and walked away under the lofty arch. About ten minutes later, the two red-haired hunters reached the officer; there was a rapid conference between them, after which all three began to climb to the Falkenstein. By degrees, as the party ascended, the uniform of the officer and his face could be distinguished: he was a thin man, with light brown hair, well made, and determined-looking. At the foot of the rock Frantz and Kasper blindfolded him, and soon the sound of their steps under the arch could be heard.

Jean-Claude going toward them, himself unbound the handkerchief, saying, "You desire to communicate something to me, sir; I am listening."

The partisans stood about fifteen paces away. Catherine Lefèvre, the foremost among them, frowned; her bony, angular face, long beaked nose, her three or four tresses of gray hair, falling down over her temples and hollow cheek-bones, her compressed lips, and the fixity of her gaze, appeared at first to rivet the attention of the German officer. Next to her stood Louise, with her sweet pale face. Jérome, with his long tawny beard, draped in his horse-hair tunic, and Materne, leaning on his short carbine, and the others around him completed the group.

The officer himself was the object of particular attention. One could see in him, his attitude, fine sunburnt features, clear gray eyes, handsome moustache, in the elegance of his limbs, hardened by the labours of war, a member of an aristocratic race: he combined the old soldier and the man of the world, the warrior and the diplomatist.

This reciprocal inspection being finished, the bearer of the flag of truce said, in good French, "I have the honour of addressing the Commandant Hullin?"

"Yes, sir," replied Jean-Claude.

And seeing the other gazing hesitatingly around the circle, he continued, "Speak loud, Sir, so that everybody may hear you. When honour and the country are in question all are concerned in France; the women are interested as well as ourselves. Have you any proposition to make me, and from whom?"

"From the General Commander-in-chief. Here is my commission."

"Good; we are listening to you, sir."

Then the officer, raising his voice, said in a resolute tone: "Permit me first, commandant, to remark that you have fulfilled your duty splendidly: you have called forth the esteem of your enemies."

"In the matter of duty," replied Hullin, "we have all done our best."

"Yes," added Catherine, dryly, "and since our enemies esteem us on that account, well, they will esteem us still more in eight or fifteen days, for we have not reached the end of the war yet. You will live to see more of us."

The officer turned his head, and looked with astonishment at the savage energy in the old woman's face.

"They are noble sentiments," he retorted, after an instant's silence: "but humanity has its rights, and to squander blood uselessly is returning evil for evil."

"Then why do you come into our country?" cried Catherine sharply. "Go away, and we will let you alone. You make war like brigands: you steal, pillage, and burn. You all deserve to be hanged. And to set a good example, you personally ought to be hurled over that rock."

The officer turned pale, for the old woman seemed quite capable of carrying out her threat; however he soon regained his composure, and replied calmly: "I am aware that the Cossacks have set fire to the farm in front of this rock. They are pillagers, such as are to be found in the rear of every army, and this isolated act proves nothing against the discipline of our troops. The French soldiers did the same in Germany, and particularly in the Tyrol; not content with pillaging and burning the villages, they mercilessly shot all mountaineers suspected of having taken up arms for the defence of their country. We might make reprisals, and should be justified in doing so; but we are not barbarians, we can understand that patriotism is noble and grand, even in its most ill-advised acts. Besides, we are not making war on the French people, but on the Emperor Napoleon. And the general, on learning the conduct of the Cossacks, has publicly punished this act of Vandalism; more, he has decided that an indemnity shall be accorded to the proprietor of the farm."

"I will not receive anything from you," Catherine hastily interrupted; "I will keep my injustice and revenge myself."

The officer understanding by the accent of the old woman's voice that he could make no impression upon her, and feeling that it was even dangerous for him to reply, turned toward Hullin, and said: "I am ordered, commandant, to offer you the homers of war if you will consent to give up this position. You have no provisions, we know that. In a few days you will be obliged to lay down your arms. The esteem felt for you by our general has alone caused him to make you honourable conditions. A longer resistance would be useless. We are masters of the Donon, our battalions are entering Lorraine; the campaign will not be concluded here, therefore you have no interest in defending such a position. We wish to spare you the horrors of famine on this barren rock. Come, commandant, decide."

Hullin turned toward the partisans and said to them: "You have heard? I refuse; but I will submit if everybody accepts the propositions of the enemy."

"We refuse, all of us," said Jérome.

"Yes, all," replied the others.

Catherine Lefèvre, who had looked inflexible till then, regarded Louise and seemed touched; she took her by the arm, and turning toward the officer, said to him: "We have a child with us; is there no means by which we could send her to one of our relations at Saverne?"

Hardly had Louise heard these words, than throwing herself into Hullin's arms with fear, she cried out: "No, no, I will remain with you, Papa Jean-Claude; I will die with you."

"Well," said Hullin; "go tell your general what you have seen: tell him that the Falkenstein will be ours till death! Kasper,

Frantz, reconduct the truce-bearer."

The officer appeared to hesitate, but as he opened his mouth to speak, Catherine, pale with rage, exclaimed, "Begone! you have not yet gained all the advantages you think. It is that brigand Yégof who has told you that we have no provisions; but we have for two months, and by that time our army will have exterminated you all. Traitors will not always have the best of it: bad luck to you."

Seeing she was becoming more and more excited, the officer thought it best to take his departure: he turned to his guides, who put the bandages over his eyes, and conducted him to the foot of the Falkenstein.

The instructions which Hullin had given concerning the provisions were executed on the same day, and each received his half ration. A sentry was placed before Hexe-Baizel's cavern, where the food was kept; the door was barricaded, and Jean-Claude decided that the distributions should be made in the presence of all, so as to prevent any injustice; but all these precautions were destined to fail in preserving the unfortunate people from the horrors of famine.

CHAPTER 25

"Battle of the Rocks"

For three days they had been entirely without food on the Falkenstein, and Divès had given no signs of life. How often, during those long days of agony, did the mountaineers turn their eyes toward Phalsbourg!—how often had they listened, fancying they could hear the smuggler's step, while the vague murmur of the wind alone filled the space!

The nineteenth day since the arrival of the partisans on the Falkenstein was passed amidst all the tortures of hunger. They no longer spoke; they remained crouched on the earth, with pinched faces, and lost in endless reveries. Sometimes they watched each other with sparkling eyes, as though about to devour one another, then relapsed into sullen calm.

Occasionally Yégof's raven, flying from crag to crag, would approach this place of misfortune. Then old Materne would take aim with his rifle, but the ill-omened bird would immediately take flight with dismal croakings, and the old hunter's arm fell helpless by his side. And as though the exhaustion of hunger was not enough to fill the measure of so much misery, the poor creatures only opened their mouths to accuse and menace one an- other.

"Do not touch me," cried Hexe-Baizel, in a shrill voice to those who looked at her—"do not look at me, or I will bite you!"

Louise was delirious; her great blue eyes, instead of living objects, saw only shadows flit across the plateau, touching the tops of the bushes, and resting on the old tower.

"Here is food!" she said. Then the others became enraged with the poor child, crying out with fury, that she was mocking them, and bidding her beware.

Jérome alone remained perfectly calm; but the great quantity of snow he had swallowed to appease the pangs of ravenous hunger, had inundated his whole body and bony face with a cold sweat. To appease the cravings of his stomach, Doctor Lorquin had bound a handkerchief round his loins, and tightened it more and more. He was seated with his back against the tower, and his eyes closed, though he now and then opened them to say, "We have reached the first the second the third stage. One more day, and all will be over!"

He then began to declaim about the Druids, Odin, Brahma, Pythagoras, quoting Latin and Greek, and announcing the near transformation of the people of Harberg into wolves, foxes, and animals of all sorts. "For myself," he exclaimed, "I will be a lion! I will eat fifteen pounds of beef every day!"

Then renewing his discourse:—"No, I will be a man. I will preach peace, brotherhood, justice. Ah, my friends, we suffer for our own faults. What have we done with the other side of the Rhine for the last ten years? With what right did we set up masters over those peoples? Why did we not exchange our ideas, our sentiments, the produce of our arts and of our industry with theirs? Why did we not approach them like brothers, in place of wishing to subject them to us? We should have been well received. What must they not have suffered, those unhappy people, during those ten years of violence and rapine! Now they are avenged, and it is just! May the malediction of heaven fall on the miserable wretches who get up divisions among peoples in order to oppress them!"

After these moments of excitement he would fall exhausted against the wall of the tower, and murmur—"Some bread; oh, only a morsel of bread!"

Materne's two sons, crouched in the brushwood, their carbines at their shoulders, seemed to expect the passage of some game which never arrived. Their ceaseless watching alone sustained their expiring strength.

Others, bent double with pain, were shivering with cold, and yet were burning with fever: they reproached Jean-Claude with having brought them to the Falkenstein.

Hullin, with a superhuman force of character, still went and came, observing what took place in the neighbouring valleys, but without saying anything.

Occasionally he would advance to the edge of the rock, and with his massive jaws clinched and shining eyes, looked at Yégof, seated before a large fire, on the plains of Bois-de-Chênes, in the midst of a band of Cossacks. Since the arrival of the Germans in the valley of the Charmes, the madman had never quitted his post, but appeared to be watching the agony of his victims.

Such was the position of these unfortunate people beneath the open heaven.

In the gloom of a prison the torture of hunger is doubtless frightful, but in the broad light of day, in the eyes of a whole country, in face of all the resources of nature, its sufferings are beyond all description.

At the close of the nineteenth day, between four and five o'clock in the afternoon, the weather was gloomy; large gray clouds rose behind the snowy summit of the Grosmann; the red sun, like a ball of fire, threw a few last rays into the misty horizon. The silence on the rock was unbroken. Louise no longer gave signs of life; Kasper and Frantz remained among the bushes immovable as stones; Catherine Lefèvre, crouching on the earth, her skinny arms clasped round her pointed knees, with hard, rigid features, her hair hanging over her clammy cheeks, looked like some old sibyl seated in the heather. She had ceased speaking.

That evening, Hullin, Jérome, old Materne, and Doctor Lorquin gathered themselves around the old farm-mistress to die. They were silent, and the last rays of twilight fell upon the wretched group. To the right, behind a jutting rock, a few German watchfires sparkled in the abyss. Suddenly the old dame,

FOR THREE DAYS PROVISIONS HAD COMPLETELY FAILED

rousing from her dreams, began to murmur some unintelligible words.

"Divès is coming," said she, in a low voice. "I see him. He goes out from the door to the right of the arsenal. Gaspard follows him, and—"

Then she began to count.

"Two hundred and fifty men," she exclaimed; "National Guards and soldiers. They cross the ditch; they mount behind the *demilune*. Gaspard is speaking with Marc. What does he say?"

She appeared to listen.

"Let us hurry!—yes, hurry! Time flies! There they are on the glacis!"

There was a long pause; then the old woman suddenly arose, with outstretched arms and hair on end, and screamed aloud in a terrible voice:—"Courage! Kill, kill! Ah, ah!" And she fell down heavily.

This fearful cry awoke them all; it would have aroused the dead. The besieged seemed born anew. Something was abroad. Was it hope, life, a spirit? I know not; but all rose up on their hands and knees, like wild beasts, holding their breath to hear. Louise even moved softly and lifted her head; Frantz and Kasper dragged themselves along; and, strange to say, Hullin, turning his eyes toward Phalsbourg, thought he saw through the darkness the flashes of a fusillade announcing a sortie.

Catherine had resumed her first appearance; but her cheeks, before still and pale as those of a corpse, trembled now. The others listened as though their salvation hung on her lips. A quarter of an, hour nearly had passed, when the old dame slowly recommenced:—"They have passed the enemy's lines; they are running toward Lutzelbourg. I see them! Gaspard and Divès are before, with Desmarets, Ulrich, Weber, and our friends of the town. They come! they come!"

She again became silent. Long did they listen; but the vision was gone. Seconds followed seconds slowly like centuries. At length, Hexe-Baizel, in an angry voice, began to say:—"She is mad! She saw nothing! Marc, I know him: he is making fun of us. What does it matter to him if we perish? So long as he has his bottle and tobacco and can smoke his pipe in peace by the fireside, all the rest is nothing. Ah, the wretch!"

Then all relapsed into silence, and the unhappy creatures, re-animated for an instant by hope of a speedy deliverance, again fell into despair.

"It is a dream," thought they; "Hexe-Baizel is right: we are condemned to die of hunger."

While this was going on night arrived. When the moon rose behind the high pine-trees, and lit up the gloomy group, Hullin alone kept watch, in spite of his raging fever. Far off—very far off in the gorges—he heard the voices of the German sentries; "*Wer da? Wer da ?*" the rounds of the patrols in the woods; the shrill neighing of the horses at the picket, and the shouts of their keepers. Toward midnight the worthy fellow fell asleep like the rest. When he awoke, the clock of the village of Charmes struck four. At the sound of the distant chimes, Hullin shook off his drowsiness, and he opened his eyes. As he gazed unconsciously into the darkness, trying to collect his thoughts, the vague glimmer of a torch passed before his eyes. A feeling of dread came over him, and he said to himself:—"Am I mad? The night is dark, and I see torches!"

Nevertheless, the flame reappeared; he looked at it, then raised himself quickly, resting his contracted face for a second in his hand. At length, hazarding one more look, he distinctly saw a fire on the Giromani, on the other side of Blanru—a fire which swept the heavens with its purple wings, causing the shadows of the pines to dance on the snow.

Recalling to himself that this signal had been agreed upon between him and Piorette to announce an attack, he trembled from head to foot, his face streamed with perspiration, and, walking in the dark, groping like a blind man with his hands outstretched, he stammered,—"Catherine, Louise, Jérome." But no one answered. Still groping about, thinking he was walking while he did not make a step, the unfortunate man fell down, exclaiming, "My children! Catherine! they come! We are saved!"

A vague sound immediately arose. One would have said that the dead were awaking. There was a shrill laugh: it was Hexe-Baizel, gone mad from her sufferings.

Then Catherine exclaimed: "Hullin! Hullin! who spoke?"

Jean-Claude, recovering from his emotion, said, in firmer tones: "Jérome, Catherine, Materne, and the others, are you dead? Do you not see that fire down there, in the direction of Blanru? It is Piorette, who is coming to our assistance."

At the same instant, a deep boom rolled along the gorges of the Jägerthal, like the rumbling of a storm. The summoning trumpet of the Judgment could not have produced a greater effect on the besieged: they suddenly awoke.

"It is Piorette! it is Marc!" cried broken, harsh voices, such as might have belonged to skeletons; "they are coming to our aid!"

And all the wretched creatures tried to rise: some sobbed; but they had no longer any tears to shed. A second report brought them upright.

"They are firing in detachments," said Hullin. "Ours are doing so too. We have soldiers in lines! France forever!"

"Yes," replied Jérome. "Mother Catherine was right; the Phalsbourgers are coming to our assistance; they are descending the hills of the Sarre; and there is Piorette, who is now attacking by Blanru."

Indeed, the fusillade now began to resound on both sides at once, toward the plateau of Bois-de-Chênes and the heights of Kilbèri.

The two chiefs embraced; and, as they groped along in the dark night, seeking to reach the edge of the rock, suddenly Materne cried out, "Take care, the precipice is near!"

They stopped short and looked down; but nothing was to be seen: a current of cold air ascending from the abyss alone warned them of the danger. The peaks and gorges round were all plunged in darkness.

On the hillsides in front the flashes of the fusillade passed like lightning, illuminating now an old oak, now the heather, or the black outline of some rock; and groups of men were coining and going, as though in the midst of a conflagration. Two thousand feet below, in the depth of the gorge, could be heard dull sounds of galloping horses, and the clamours of command. Now, the shout of a mountaineer hailing another was prolonged from peak to peak, and arose to the Falkenstein like a sigh.

"It is Marc!" said Hullin; "it is Marc's voice!"

"Yes, it is Marc, who bids us have courage," replied Jérome.

The others looked around them with outstretched necks, their hands grasping the rock. The fusillade continued with a vivacity that betrayed the fury of the battle; but nothing could be seen. Oh! how they wished to take part in this supreme struggle! With what ardour would they not have thrown themselves into the fire! The fear of being abandoned once more, of seeing by daylight their defenders retreating, rendered them speechless with, terror.

Day began to dawn; the pale light arose behind the black summits, and began to illumine the gloomy valleys, and soon the fog of the abyss turned to silvery mists. Hullin, looking across the openings of these clouds, at length made out the position. The Germans had lost the heights of Valtin, and the plain of Bois-de-Chênes. They were massed in the valley of Charmes, at the foot of the Falkenstein, so as to obtain shelter from their adversaries' fire. Piorette, master of Bois-de-Chênes, had thrown out outworks in front of the rock, on the side of the descent to Charmes. He was pacing to and fro, his pipe in his mouth, and carbine slung across his shoulders; and the blue axes of the woodcutters glistened in the rising sun.

On the left of the village, toward Valtin, in, the midst of the furze, Marc Divès, on a small black horse, with a long tail, his blade by his side, pointed to the ruins and the sledge road; while an infantry officer and a few National Guards were listening to him. Gaspard Lefèvre stood alone, in front of the group, leaning on his gun; and, on the summit of the hill, by the wood, two or three hundred men were keeping watch.

The sight of the small number of their defenders caused the

hearts of the besieged to grow fearful; all the more so, as the Germans were seven or eight times superior in numbers, and had already begun to form columns of attack, to regain the positions they had lost. Horsemen were conveying on all sides the general's orders, and the bayonets began to defile.

"It is all over," said Hullin to Jérome. "What are five or six hundred men to do against four thousand in line of battle? The Phalsbourgers will return to their houses and say, 'We have done our duty.' And Piorette will be crushed."

The others thought so too; and their despair was brought to a climax when they suddenly saw a long file of Cossacks riding furiously along the valley of Charmes, with Yégof the madman galloping like the wind at their head, his beard, horse's tail, dog-skin, and red hair floating wildly in the air. He looked up at the rock, and brandished his lance above his head. Reaching the bottom of the valley, he made at once for the enemy's staff, and coming up to the general, he indicated by gestures the other side of the plateau of Bois-de-Chênes.

"Ah, the brigand!" shouted Hullin. "See, he tells them that Piorette has no outworks on that side, that they must go round the mountain."

In fact, a column began immediately to march in that direction, while another went toward the outworks to mask the movement of the first.

"Materne," cried Jean-Claude, "is there no means of sending a ball into the madman?"

The old hunter shook his head.

"No," said he, "it is impossible; he is out of range."

Just then, Catherine Lefèvre gave a wild scream like a hawk.

"Crush them, crush them, as they did at the Blutfeld!"

And the old woman, an instant before so feeble, threw herself on a mass of rock, lifted it with both hands, advanced, with her streaming gray hair, bent over to the edge of the abyss, and the rock dashed through the space beneath.

A terrible crash resounded below, pieces of pine flew out on all sides, the great stone rebounded a hundred feet away, and

"LET US OVERWHELM THEM AS AT BLUTFELD!"

descending the steep slope with fresh impulse, struck Yégof, and crushed him at the feet of the enemy's general. This was but the work of a few seconds.

Catherine, upright on the edge of the rock laughed with a rattling sound, which seemed as though it would never end.

The others, as though all animated with new life, precipitated themselves on the ruins of the old castle, shouting: "Slay them! slay them! Crush them as at the Blutfeld!"

It is impossible to imagine a more terrible scene. These beings, at death's very door, lean and haggard as skeletons, found strength for the carnage. They no longer stumbled, they trembled no more; each one lifted his stone and threw it down the precipice, then returned to take another, without even looking to see what was passing below.

Imagine the stupor of the *kaiserlichs* at this deluge of ruins and rocks. All had turned at the sound of the stones bounding above through the bushes and clumps of trees. At first they stopped as though petrified; but looking higher up, and seeing more and more stones descending, and above it all the spectres coming and going, lifting their arms, and continually discharging fresh burdens—seeing their comrades crushed, fifteen or twenty at a time, an immense cry went up from the valley of Charmes to the Falkenstein, and, notwithstanding the fusillade which they kept up on every side, the Germans scampered away to escape this fearful death.

In the thickest of the rout, the enemy's general contrived to rally a battalion, and descend slowly toward the village.

There was something grand and dignified about this man, so calm in the midst of disaster. He turned from time to time with a gloomy look to watch the bounding rocks, which made ghastly havoc in his columns.

Jean-Claude observed him, and, notwithstanding the intoxication of his triumph and the certitude of having escaped famine, the old soldier could not suppress a feeling of admiration.

"Look," said he to Jérome, "he acts as he did on returning from the Donon and Grosmann: he is the last to retire, and yields only bit by bit. There are, indeed, brave fellows in every country!"

Marc Divès and Piorette, the witnesses of this stroke of fortune, then descended into the midst of the firtrees, to try and cut off the retreat of the enemy. But the battalion, reduced to half its strength, formed into square behind the village of Charmes, and slowly ascended the valley of the Sarre, stopping sometimes, like a wounded boar who turns to look at the huntsmen, whenever Piorette's men or those of Phalsbourg tried to press too nearly upon them.

Thus terminated the great battle of the Falkenstein, known in the mountains under the name of the Battle of the Rocks.

CHAPTER 26

Conclusion

The combat was hardly over, when, toward eight o'clock, Marc Divès, Gaspard, and about thirty mountaineers, laden with provisions, ascended the Falkenstein. What a spectacle awaited them! The besieged, stretched on the earth, appeared to be dead. It seemed useless to shake them, to cry into their ears; "Jean-Claude! Catherine? Jérome!" There came no reply. Gaspard Lefèvre, seeing his mother and Louise immovable, with clinched teeth, told Marc, that if they did not return to life, he would blow out his brains with his gun. Marc replied that each man must do as he liked; but for his part he should not do likewise on Hexe-Baizel's account. At length old Colon, having laid his burden down on a stone, Kasper Materne opened his eyes, and seeing the provisions, his teeth began to chatter like those of a fox pursued by the hounds.

They immediately understood the meaning of this symptom; and Marc Divès, going from one to the other, passed his gourd under their noses, which sufficed to bring them to. They wanted to drink its contents all up at once; but Doctor Lorquin, notwithstanding his condition, had still enough sense to warn Marc not to allow them to do so, and the slightest action of choking would be fatal to them. Each one, therefore, only received a morsel of bread, an egg, and a glass of wine, which wonderfully revived their spirits; then Catherine, Louise, and the others, were laid on sledges and were brought down to the village.

It is impossible to describe the enthusiasm and joy of their friends when they saw them return, leaner than Lazarus when he rose from his grave. They gazed at one another, and embraced, and the process was repeated on the arrival of every newcomer from Abreschwiller, Dagsburg, St. Quirin, or elsewhere.

Marc Divès was obliged to relate more than twenty times the story of his journey to Phalsbourg. The brave smuggler had had no luck. After having miraculously escaped from the balls of the *kaiserlichs*, he got into the valley of Spartzprod, and fell into the midst of a band of Cossacks, who ransacked him from top to toe. He had been compelled to wander for two weeks around the Russian posts which surrounded the town, exposed to the continual fire of their sentries, and running endless risks of being taken as a spy, before being able to get into the town.

Then the commandant, Meunier, at first refused to give any succour, assigning the weakness of his garrison as an excuse, and only at the pressing petitions of the towns-folk at length consented to detach two companies. Listening to his recital, the mountaineers gave vent to their admiration of Marc's courage and perseverance in the midst of danger.

"Well," replied the tall smuggler good-humouredly to those who thus congratulated him, "I have only done my duty; could I have allowed my comrades to perish? I well knew it would not be easy; those rascally Cossacks are sharper than the customs' folks; they sent you a league off like crows; but all the same, we have outwitted them."

Five or six days later everybody was on the alert; Captain Vidal, from Phalsbourg, had left twenty-five men to guard the powder; Gaspard Lefèvre was of the number, and the sturdy fellow went down every morning to the village. The allies had all passed into Lorraine, and were no longer seen in Alsace, except around the fortresses. Soon after came the news of the victories of Champ-Aubert and Montmirail; but a great misfortune was at hand; for the allies, notwithstanding the heroism of our army and the genius of the Emperor, entered Paris.

It was a terrible shock to Jean-Claude and Catherine, Materne, Jérome and all the mountaineers; but the history of these events does not belong to this tale. It has already been related by others.

Peace having been made, the farm of Bois-de Chênes was rebuilt in the spring; the woodcutters, the shoemakers, masons, wood-floaters, and all the workmen of the district, lent a hand in the work.

Toward the same time, the army having been disbanded, Gaspard cut off his moustaches and his marriage with Louise took place.

On the day of the wedding all the combatants of the Falkenstein and Donon came to the farm, where they were received with open doors and windows. Each brought his present to the newly married pair; Jérome, small shoes for Louise; Materne and his sons, a black cock, the most loving of birds, as all know; and Divès, packets of smuggled tobacco for Gaspard; and Doctor Lorquin a fine set of baby-linen. Tables were spread out, even in the granaries and sheds.

How much wine, bread, meat, and tarts was consumed I cannot say; but what I am sure of is, that Jean-Claude, who had been low-spirited ever since the entry of the allies into Paris, revived on that day, and sang the old song of his youth as cheerfully as when he shouldered his gun and set out for Valmy, Jemmapes, and Fleurus. The echoes of the Falkenstein repeated in the distance that old patriotic song; the grandest and noblest that has ever been heard by man. Catherine Lefèvre kept time on the table with the handle of her knife; and if it be true, as many say, that the dead come to listen when they are spoken of, our departed friends must have been happy, and "The King of Diamonds" have fumed in his red beard.

Toward midnight, Hullin arose, and addressing the newly married pair, said: "You will have fine children; I will jump them on my knees, I will teach them my old song, and then I shall go to rejoin my old comrades!"

So saying he embraced Louise, and arm in arm with Marc Divès and Jérome, descended to his cottage, followed by the rest, who sang together the fine old song. A more beautiful night was never seen: numberless stars shone out in the dark blue sky; the shrubs on the hillside, where so many brave fellows had found a grave, quivered slightly in the breeze. Everyone felt happy and softened; they shook hands on the threshold of the small house, and wished each other "goodnight," and departed, to the right and to the left, to their different villages.

"Goodnight, Materne, Jérome, Divès, Piorette—goodnight!" cried Jean-Claude.

His old friends turned back, waving their hats, and said to themselves: "There are some days when one is very happy on the earth. Ah, if there were never any plagues, or wars, or famines; if men would but agree to love and help each other; if they would but live in peace together, what a paradise this world would be!"